I0607195

Texas Blaze

by

Brenda Huber

This is a work of fiction. Names, characters, places, and incidents either are the product of the author's imagination or are used fictitiously, and any resemblance to actual persons living or dead, business establishments, events, or locales, is entirely coincidental.

Texas Blaze

Contact Information: info@thewildrosepress.com

Cover Art by *Nicola Martinez*

The Wild Rose Press
PO Box 708
Adams Basin, NY 14410-0706
Visit us at www.thewildrosepress.com

Publishing History
First Cactus Rose Edition, 2010
Print ISBN 1-60154-785-4

Published in the United States of America

She jumped, strangling off a startled shriek as she bumped against his chest. How did he manage to keep sneaking up on her like that?

Spinning to face him—irritated that he'd listened in on a private conversation, even if it had been with no one else but herself—she planted her fists on her hips again, glaring up at him.

"There's nothing wrong with the 'standards' of the men in Maryland." Her chin rose defensively. He was so close that every time she took a deep breath, the lace on her bodice brushed against his shirt, but she refused to step back. He wouldn't intimidate her with his size...or the wicked look in his eyes.

His lips curled, and her heart fluttered. "There must be something wrong with 'em if they prefer holding scrawny women."

Her scowl deepened and she sucked in an outraged breath at the word scrawny. Lifting her chin another notch in defiance, she did her best to ignore the twin points of fury heating her cheeks. "I wouldn't know about their preferences." Her tone slipped beyond the borders of haughty, straight into the land of ice princess. "It wasn't as though I went about hugging a bunch of men...much less asking their opinion on the matter."

"You didn't seem the type." Ethan's smile widened, turning decidedly provocative. "Of course, I didn't say huggin', I said holdin'. There's a difference, sweetheart."

Her brow wrinkled, and she gritted her teeth in consternation. "What are you talking about? There's no difference."

"Oh, yes, Hope. There most definitely is," he whispered as he leaned toward her...leaned into her. His unsettling gaze, vivid with temptation, traced her lips. When he lifted his smoldering gaze to hers, she felt herself falling into bottomless cobalt fire.

Dedication

This one is for my brothers,
Phillip, Kevin, and Tyler...

To the outside world, we all grow old.
But not to brothers and sisters.
We know each other as we always were.
We know each other's hearts.
We share private family jokes.
We remember family feuds and secrets,
family grief and joys.
We live outside the touch of time.

~Clara Ortega

Acknowledgements

Deepest appreciation to Patricia Tanner
for seeing the potential and polishing
my diamond in the rough.

Chapter 1

Johnston, Texas
Fall of 1884

Hope drew a bracing breath and stepped down onto the platform. The bustling mass at the small, dusty train station immediately enveloped her. Gripping her valise in a white-knuckled fist, she squared her shoulders, pushing toward the outer edge of the crowd, scanning faces as she went. Not that it did her much good. Wide-brimmed cowboy hats and impersonal shoulders thwarted her at every turn. The likelihood of finding one specific face in this crush was a long shot. She didn't have much to go on—a likeness in a tiny, tarnished daguerreotype—but she searched nonetheless.

A rude elbow caught her in the ribs. Careless feet trampled her toes. Stagnant dust and stale sweat pressed in on her as shifting bodies bumped against her. Hope struggled to remain calm. Just as her composure approached the breaking point, she managed to push free of the crowd, dragging in a deep gulp of fresh air.

Chewing the edge of her lip, she glanced around. Her gaze passed over, then settled on a long wooden bench running the length of the teeming depot. With a resigned groan, she gathered the bulk of her skirts and clambered up to stand on the weathered plank seat. Smoothing the wrinkles from her skirts with one hand, she scanned the milling swarm from a safe distance. Her startled gaze snagged on a tall man at the opposite edge of the crowd.

And tall he was, over a head taller than most in the crowd. His wind-swept hair, tawny gold in the late-afternoon sunlight, defied convention with its wild length. His skin was deep bronze, attesting to a lifetime of exposure to the harsh Texas sun. His shoulders were broad, his profile the epitome of masculinity...near Grecian in perfection. He was a golden, untamed Adonis. The man's narrowed eyes moved over the faces near the train with steady concentration. Hope sighed, frowning when his beautiful hair disappeared beneath a dusty cowboy hat. Despite the fact she should be looking for her uncle, she couldn't force her mesmerized stare away. The edge of wildness about the attractive stranger was unusually compelling.

"Hope?" A deep, gravelly voice addressing her from somewhere to her right drew her attention. "Is that you, darlin'?"

A broad-shouldered, mountain of a man strode toward her with purpose in his long-legged gait. With every step, his clothes billowed trail dust. His stained, broad-brimmed hat had seen better days. The man carried himself with the innate grace and confidence of a man who bowed to none.

His face had aged, carrying lines of worry and wear the portrait didn't. But the features were the same...strong, distinctive. Familiar. The shape and the color of his eyes were identical to hers. Portrait aside, Hope would've recognized him anywhere, for he bore a striking resemblance to her late guardian, James...and to her father, Jacob, brothers all three. A sentimental smile curved her lips. Standing on the bench as she was, she didn't have to tilt her head down even the tiniest bit to look him full in the face.

"You have to be Hope. I'd recognize that face anywhere. You look so much like your mother." His voice boomed deep and rich and, as he said the last, a little sad.

Hope reached to gather her skirts, but before she could step down from her lookout, strong, calloused hands circled her waist. Without warning, the station and the crowd spun before her eyes as he crushed her against a solid wall of muscle, swirling her in a wide circle. Just as she began to fight for air, the ground met her feet with a solid thump.

Hope may have gained her feet, but it took her a moment more to regain her voice. They'd exchanged frequent letters through the years, and he'd sent her a present every year at Christmastime and one again on her birthday, but, for all that, it was like meeting a stranger. A great hulking bear of a stranger. Nevertheless, looking at him—a walking, living, if somewhat older replica of James—brought a swift rush of loss, tying her insides in grief-stricken knots. Several awkward moments passed in silence while she stared up at him.

It took a moment for her to force words passed the lump of tears wedged in her throat. "Hello, Uncle Matt. It's so nice to meet you in person at last."

Matt blinked at her. The lines around his eyes tightened a bit, but his smile never slipped.

Hope reached up, pushing an errant lock of hair behind her ear. "I'm sorry if my being here is an inconvenience for you. Before he...well, James insisted I come to stay with you, at least for a while, but I can always return to Boulder if—"

"Nonsense," Matt rumbled, waving her worries aside. He took firm possession of the satchel in her hands. "I won't hear anymore talk of you leavin'. Now, where're the rest of your things?"

Hope indicated a man in uniform standing near the train, a huge steamer trunk on either side of him. Matt turned to a small man with dark skin and hair a few paces behind him and spoke in a language she'd never heard before. Turning back to her, he claimed her elbow, steering her toward rough planks lining the side of a nearby street. They walked some fifty yards before he spoke again.

"It's a long ride back to the ranch, too late to head back now. Figured you'd be tired, so I got a couple rooms at the hotel. We'll head out to the Bar M at first light."

Nodding, she gave him a small, relieved smile. After that last long stretch on the train, she'd prayed for a respite, however short it might be. An entire night without motion sounded divine. Some of the tension drained from her shoulders.

Matt led her around a corner, down another boardwalk, and into the hotel. "Ethan and I've got some business to tend to before supper. Will you be all right at the hotel alone?"

Hope opened her mouth to remind him she'd traveled across half the country alone, but then changed her mind and simply nodded. She was tired and irritable. It was unfair of her to take it out on him.

Following him up the stairs, Hope stopped outside a room at the end of the hall where he opened the door before turning to face her.

His green eyes were warm and sincere when he addressed her. "I'm so glad you're here. We'll be back around seven. Welcome to Texas, darlin'." He gave her shoulder an awkward pat. His eyes suddenly seemed a bit...glassy.

Hope blinked up at him. Surely, it must be a trick of the light. Perhaps it was exhaustion catching up to her, but for a moment there, she actually thought he'd had tears in his eyes. Before she could question him, Matt spun on his heel and strode back down the hall without another word.

Stifling a yawn, Hope closed the door behind her and surveyed the stark room. A soft breeze blew in through the open window, lifting the aging lace curtains. The comforting scents of lemon and beeswax surrounded her. Beneath her feet, the scuffed wooden floor was spotless. The linens on the bed were crisp and bright as sunshine. A deep, tired breath seeped out as she sank onto the edge of the mattress.

The bed was soft—a bit lumpy—but it was a bed, nonetheless. Hope lay back and stretched out, groaning aloud with relief. Pulling the patchwork coverlet over her, she curled into a tight ball and soon drifted into a deep and dreamless sleep, for once too weary for the nightmares to follow her.

****

Ethan leaned against the bar, resting his weight on his forearms as he toyed with his shot glass, lifting it in the cloudy, smoke-clogged light, watching the amber liquid slosh and swirl.

"I swear, Ethan, she looks just like her mother. For a minute there, I thought I was lookin' at Serena's ghost." Matt tossed his shot of rotgut back, grimacing.

"She's not Serena," Ethan reminded him, staring hard at Matt over the rim his own glass. Matt still wore the dazed expression that had been on his face when he'd come back to the train station to inform Ethan he'd found Hope and already settled her in at the hotel.

Unease sank into him, all the way to his bones. He'd never seen Matt so unsettled before. Discordant notes clanked from the saloon's off-key piano, competing with the surging noise of the local watering hole at the height of business on a Saturday evening.

Matt poured three fingers into his glass and pushed the bottle toward Ethan. "Hell and damnation, I still can't wrap my mind around it all. If I'd known James was sick…" Matt shook his head, banging a mutinous fist on the bar. "He had no right…" The fist eased, and he lifted his shaking hand to rake through his hair. His words tumbled out, rambling and disjointed. "Now he's gone and I can't… And Hope! My God, I mean, sure, at the time I had my suspicions. Who wouldn't? Serena swore to me Hope was Jacob's child. Hell and damnation." Matt dropped an angry fist to the bar again. The glasses jumped, and whiskey sloshed onto the scarred wood. "How could James keep somethin' like this from me for all these years?" He let out a long, miserable breath. "Maybe I knew… Deep down, maybe I knew and just didn't want to face it."

Ethan leaned forward, his brow furrowing. Seeing Matt like this was killing him. "You were young. It was a bad situation."

As Matt reached for the bottle again, Ethan gritted his teeth, in no way ready to watch Matt go down this path again, the same unpleasant path he'd traveled the day he'd received James's fateful missive. Matt had shown up on Ethan's doorstep, drunk as a cowhand on payday, shaking the crumpled letter in an angry fist. It'd taken Ethan several pots of thick, black coffee and most of the day—well into the night, in fact—before he'd managed to piece together what had happened.

In a way, James' letter had shed light on a hell of a lot more than Ethan ever thought to question. Now he understood why Matt had never married, never looked twice at any women, and, more important, had never—not once—gone back to Maryland to see his family. Not even for the funerals of his brother and sister-in-law. Matt's family, Hope aside, had been the one thing Matt never spoke of, and the one thing Ethan never pushed.

"She didn't have much to say when I met her at the station." Matt held his shot glass up, studying the amber liquid with rapt absorption, as though it held all the answers he couldn't find on his own.

"I'm sure she's still grievin' for James, and she's had a long, grueling trip. More'n likely, she's plain exhausted. Give her a bit to rest before you jump to any conclusions."

"Since when did you become the authority on women?" The liquor disappeared behind a grimace, and Matt smiled fondly, reaching for the bottle again.

"I doubt any such thing exists. But I do know," Ethan responded, pulling the bottle out of Matt's reach, "she won't appreciate you showin' up for supper, three sheets to the wind."

"You know it takes a hell of a lot more'n a few shots to put me under the table, but you're right." Matt pushed himself back from the bar with a resigned sigh. "I'm gonna need my head tonight. Good Lord, Ethan, she's lost so much. How do I tell her the man she thought was her father wasn't? How do I take that part of Jacob away from her, too?"

"You don't have to take Jacob away from her, Matt. From all you've told me, Jacob was as good a father as anyone could ask for. Don't try to replace him. Just be there for her now," Ethan advised. "This is eating you up inside, Matt. Give her the letter and get it over with."

Matt groaned, scrubbing his hands over the thick stubble on his chin. "I'll wait. I'll wait until we get back to the ranch. She's had enough upheaval. I ought to give her a couple weeks to settle in, then maybe I'll—"

"Well shit, Matt. Why bother tellin' her at all? I mean hell, she's been lied to all her life, why tell her the truth now?" Ethan scowled at Matt, more than a hint of sarcastic irritation colored his voice. At this rate, he'd need a damned shovel and a shit-wagon just to haul Matt's sorry ass out the swinging doors. "Let her go on thinkin' she's a damned orphan. What difference does it make?"

"What the hell's that supposed to mean? Not tell her?" Matt glowered, looking mean as a stomped on rattler. "I sure as hell ain't gonna lie to her."

"Then quit sittin' here wallowin' in self pity. This ain't you, Matt. You never hide behind booze and excuses. Damn it, buck up and bite the bullet. How old is she now?"

"She's…hell, Ethan, she's twenty-two!" Matt slung his head back on his shoulders and closed his eyes. When he looked at Ethan and spoke again, his voice was quiet, his eyes thoughtful. "She turned twenty-two this past June."

"She's not a child anymore. Is she dim-witted, slow?" Matt's fierce glare drilled holes in Ethan's hide. Undaunted, Ethan pushed on. "Are her sensibilities so tender she'll faint?"

Matt growled, "She's smart as a whip. You can see the steel in her eyes. She nursed both Serena and Jacob when they came down with the fever while James was in Virginia and no one else would go near 'em. She was little more'n a child at the time. She spent the better half of this last year nursin' him, too, by the sounds of that cursed letter. Refused to pawn it off on hired nurses or servants, you know that, you read James's letter, too. Weak sensibilities, my ass…she's got steel all right."

"I know you don't want to hear it, Matt, but she's a woman, full grown. Tell her the truth before you both end up with too many regrets to consider." Ethan's tone softened. "You both deserve the truth."

Reaching into his pocket, Ethan tossed a shiny eagle onto the bar for the bottle of whiskey. The barkeep nodded, beaming his appreciation as he continued polishing the shot glass in his hands.

"I'll tell her, but I'll wait." Matt held up his hand before Ethan could interrupt. "I don't want to do it now, not at a damned hotel. It'll keep till we get back to the Bar M."

"Are you sure you want me taggin' along tonight?" Ethan shifted, leaned an elbow on the scarred bar. "You two have a lot to catch up on."

"I got a feelin' if I go it alone tonight, I'm gonna end up chewin' on my own damned boot. I'd just as soon have you along."

Nodding, Ethan tossed back the remnants of his drink. He squared his shoulders, changing the subject. "Let's go talk to Sanchez and see what he dug up. If we're lucky, maybe we'll get a leg up on Vega." Unable to resist, Ethan wiggled his eyebrows and grinned with wolfish glee. "Then we can head back to the hotel so you can introduce me to your daughter."

Chuckling, Matt slapped a hand on Ethan's back as they exited the saloon. "You keep your hands to yourself, son, and we'll all get along just fine."

Ethan laughed aloud as they stepped out onto the boardwalk. There was the old Matt he knew and loved.

Chapter 2

Ethan beat his hat against his thigh in hard, agitated slaps. His hands itched to throttle someone. No matter how close they got to that vicious bastard, Vega always managed to slip away. He'd been so sure they'd get him this time. If they'd been a slim few minutes earlier, they'd have caught the thieving, murdering son of a bitch with his pants down…literally.

Well, at least they'd gotten some of what they'd come for. They knew Vega's next target. They'd have to settle with posting someone to eagle eye the brothel in case the renegade came back.

Disgusted, Ethan rammed his hat back on his head and growled, "Come on, she ain't gonna talk."

Matt stared hard at the life-hardened, naked woman, sprawled with casual disregard on a bed of stained, reeking sheets. "It's not over, not by a long shot. We'll find him."

"*No comprendo, señor.*" Though she claimed she didn't understand, her eyes told another story as she smiled with sticky-sweet venom. "*Vete al infierno!*"

Refusing to play her game, Ethan leveled cold eyes on the defiant female. "I'll see *him* in hell first. When Vega comes back, you tell him he faces men this time—not helpless women and injured men. He'll pay for every moment of pain he caused them. You tell Vega, I'm comin' for him, and God himself won't be able to save his sorry hide. Vega will get the same mercy he gave—none."

The whore's eyes widened with each chilling

prediction. With a trembling hand, she clutched the dirty sheet at her side and pulled it up to cover her amble breasts. Ethan turned away, repulsed.

Stepping out onto the boardwalk, Ethan drew deep gulps of air, as much to calm the anger boiling inside him as to rid his lungs of the cloying scent of bawdy perfume and cheap sex lingering like a heavy fog inside the rundown brothel. He paced beside Matt through the lengthening shadows in the dusty back alley.

Matt's voice broke the heavy silence. "She knows where he is."

"Yeah, but unless you're thinkin' on torturin' answers from women now, we hit a dead end there." Ethan fisted his hands at his sides. The muscle in his jaw jerked in fury. "She won't give him up. Not until he's finished with her...and, provided there's anything left of her, maybe not even then."

Matt shoved his hat back on his head with a knuckle. "I'm sick to death of these dead ends. When I get my hands on that bastard..."

"Get in line, old man." Ethan's voice was deadly soft, his comment nowhere near a joke. A dark, slow breath hissed out between his teeth as he glanced to the orange and crimson streaks trailing over the sky. "Damn, it's getting late. We'd better get a move on. You go on ahead, Hope's probably wonderin' where you are. I'll fill Masters in on Vega's plans. Much as I'd like to see the greasy weasel eat a bullet, the town's people are the ones that'll lose their money. I'll catch up."

****

Rejuvenated after her nap, hungry for the first time in she couldn't remember how long, Hope tossed her brush on the bed and rose to answer the knock on her door. She smiled a warm welcome as she opened the door to Matt. He stood in the hallway, hat in hand. His jaw was smooth now, his hair damp.

Hope caught Matt's thoughtful frown as his gaze flickered down to the cheerful apple-green dress she'd changed into after Matt's men delivered her trunks. She read the question in his eyes. Sadness tugged at her heart. "Uncle James forbade me to wear mourning garb."

Matt cleared his throat, offered her an understanding smile, and held out his arm. "Shall we?"

Hope placed her hand on the crook of his elbow. "Did you mention earlier Ethan was going to join us this evening?"

"He'll meet us downstairs."

"I must admit to a certain amount of curiosity. You've written of him in almost every letter you sent." She'd formed an image in her mind of Matt's friend and was curious how close to the mark she'd come. She pictured Matt's "*old pal, Ethan*" as a stately gentleman with a bit of a wild streak. A mature man close to Matt's age, with salt and pepper hair, laugh-lines, and a kind smile.

An "*old soul*" with the vibrant energy of misspent youth.

They entered the hotel dining room beneath a sign that read, *Mirabella's Place*. The first thing she noticed was the cheerful red and white checkered cloth covering the tables, with matching curtains adorning the windows. The floor was hard wood, clean and shiny. The walls were pristine white. Wall sconces, an elaborate chandelier, and a huge stone fireplace gave the room a cozy, golden glow. Grilled beef, fire roasted onions and potatoes, and fresh baked bread scented the air. Her mouth watered in eager anticipation.

As Matt led her across the room, more than one set of curious eyes turned their way. Matt nodded to several people, but he didn't stop to speak to anyone in particular. Hope was more than a little relieved. She might be feeling more refreshed, but she didn't think she was up to meeting half the town just yet.

A large landscape painting hung above the massive fireplace, drawing Hope's attention. The artist's adept brush depicted the mountains with dramatic life in vibrant colors and bold strokes. In the background just beyond the mountain's crest, a violent storm had built, seeming to roll ever closer. Gazing at the painting, one could almost catch the crisp scent of pine and the clean, heavy wash of approaching rain.

The wooden scrape of chair legs swung her focus around, and surprise widened her eyes when Matt stopped in front of the man at the train station…her golden Adonis.

Tilting her head back—way back—she offered a calm smile despite the butterflies taking nervous flight in the pit of her stomach. The top of her head fell several inches short of his wide shoulders. Hope felt utterly puny standing next to him. His profile was strong and chiseled, his jaw firm and stubborn. An easy smile spread across his lips as he greeted Matt, and her pulse jumped.

An alluring little indentation nestled in the middle of his chin, and slight creases lined the edges of his mouth. His deep blue shirt matched his eyes. Worn denim hugged his narrow hips and long, long legs. A gun belt slung low on his lean hips, and his brown leather boots were scuffed and dusty. Tiny golden spikes bristled along his jaw, but he smelled of soap, leather, and horses. The heady scent made her knees weak.

What was wrong with her? Why couldn't she look away? She fought to draw breath as his penetrating, cobalt gaze settled on her at last. Those creases formed at the corners of his mouth again, his eyes sparkled, and she lost the breath she'd worked so hard to attain. Her heart gave a weird little stutter-jerk.

The golden Adonis took her hand in his large one, folding long, nimble fingers over hers as he placed a light kiss on her knuckles. A tingle raced up her arm. His gaze lifted to hers, his mouth lingering on her flesh, as if he, too, sensed the jolt. Surprise flickered in the fathomless depths of his eyes, and corresponding warmth flooded her cheeks.

Matt beamed, his hand resting on her shoulder. "Ethan, this is Hope. Hope, Ethan Kincaid."

As soon as Matt identified the Adonis as Ethan, her startled gaze flew to Matt's face.

"But..." Her stunned gaze slid back to Ethan. "I'm sorry for my surprise, Mr. Kincaid. I've heard so much about you from Matt's letters. I guess I'd pictured someone much...well, older."

Ethan flashed even, white teeth. His voice slid around her like dark, rich velvet, with just a touch of grit. "I guess that makes us about even. I was expectin' someone much...*younger*."

She bit the inside of her cheek, offering him a tiny smile, and disengaged her hand from his unnerving grasp. The loss of his skin against hers left an odd, hollow feeling in the pit of her stomach.

Ethan stepped back and pulled a chair from the table, glancing at Hope. She slid onto the proffered seat, and the soft scent of jasmine caught him by surprise. Lustrous, jet-black hair swept all the way to her waist. The silken locks brushed against the backs of his hands, whisper soft and tempting. His fingers itched to sink in deep and grab a fistful. Her scent, subtle and warm, shot need straight to his loins.

As soon as Hope settled into her chair, Ethan retreated a safe distance, taking the seat opposite Matt. Nevertheless, he couldn't tear his eyes from her face. The flawless, ivory curve of her cheek tempted him to touch, to see for himself if it felt as soft as it looked. The beguiling blush riding her cheeks gave her a strawberries and cream complexion. Would she taste as delicious?

Bemused, he leaned back in his seat as a small man came from the rear of the room to take their orders, giving him a much needed opportunity to redirect his thoughts to something more appropriate than how delectable Matt's daughter had turned out to be. He'd revised his opinion of the pinafore and ringlets when he'd learned she was twenty-two, but he sure as certain hadn't been expecting this refined, delicate beauty.

By the time the waiter moved away again, Ethan had laid rein to his stampeding wits, even if his blood still jittered in his veins. "So, Miss Lewis, how was your trip west?"

"It was very...interesting, thank you. And please, call me Hope."

When that innocent, jewel-green gaze settled with full force upon him, Ethan momentarily forgot how to breathe. With an iron will, he kicked his mind back into motion, grasping at the first thing that came to mind. "Do you ride much, Hope?"

"No, I don't. Not anymore." She offered a half-smile, fidgeting with her napkin. "The last time I did, well, let's just say it wasn't a smashing success."

"We'll have to work on that," Matt insisted, drawing her gaze, giving Ethan a much needed reprieve. "You're going to be livin' on a ranch, after all. We can't have you afraid of horses."

Ethan used the excuse of food to try to center his focus on something other than the woman at his side. Mirabella's normally appetizing fare tasted like saddle leather each time those sparkling eyes turned his way, which was, it seemed to him, quite often.

Between hearty, flavorless bites, Ethan commented, "Matt tells me you enjoy reading."

"Oh, yes, I do." Her smile lit up the room. "Uncle James used to call me his little bluestocking."

It took a long moment for Ethan to find his voice. "Matt's got a decent selection of books back at the Bar M, but you're more than welcome to enjoy my modest collection."

"Modest?" From across the table, Matt let out a dramatic snort. He angled in his seat to meet Hope's curious stare. "It'd take somebody years upon years to work their way through his 'modest' collection."

She devastated Ethan with another delighted smile…a smile that connected like a sucker-punch to his gut. Hope leaned forward in her seat, tormenting him with the intoxicating scent of jasmine. "Oh, that's wonderful! Matt never told us you enjoyed reading. His letters always painted you as more of an adventurous, outdoorsy type."

"Is that so?" Ethan lifted a sardonic brow at Matt. "And what else did he tell you?"

"Oh, enough…" Hope turned mischievous eyes to Matt for a moment, caught the uncomfortable, apologetic look he shot Ethan, and laughed aloud.

The sound of her pleasure—like gentle raindrops tinkling against delicate crystal—washed over Ethan in a soft caress. Something stirred in his chest, something warm and more than agreeable.

Something he'd given up on long ago.

Nonplussed, he pushed the odd spasm aside with ruthless determination, and shot a mock-aggrieved glare at Matt. "I hope you won't think too poorly of me, Hope."

She grinned with unabashed, impish delight. "How could I ever do that when you've offered me the use of your library? As far as I'm concerned, you're a knight in shining armor."

That odd flutter in his chest intensified, refusing to be ignored, and he leaned back in his chair, unable to tear his gaze from her face. Her grin faded a little beneath his scrutiny and she dropped her gaze to her plate, toying with her silverware.

The rest of the meal proceeded in companionable conversation. Ethan caught her glancing his way a time or two. Each time their eyes connected, the color in her cheeks deepened. The shocking urge to lean over and taste her lips was almost uncontrollable.

Later, as the conversation wound down, the trio wandered into the hall connecting the dining room to the hotel. Sconces threaded feeble light throughout the hallway, casting the ends of the corridor in flickering shadows.

Hope lifted a hand to stifle a yawn. "I can't imagine how I could be so tired. I fell asleep right after you left and must have slept at least a solid two hours. But I still feel like I could sleep for a week."

"You had a long trip," Matt remarked, nodding acknowledgement at Ethan. "You should turn in early tonight. We'll be leaving at first light."

Hope glanced sideways at Ethan as they neared the bottom step. "Will you be going to the ranch with us?"

He had to make a conscious effort not to trip up the stairs beneath the full impact of those sleepy green eyes. His body reacted with violent need as his mind began to wander to places best left unvisited.

"Ah, yeah," he mumbled clearing his throat. "I'll be taggin' along. My place, the Circle K, is about five miles north of Matt's Bar M."

Matt opened the door to her room. "We'll see you in the mornin', darlin'. Sleep well."

"Good night, Uncle Matt." She reached up on tiptoe to kiss his cheek.

Ethan choked back his laughter as Matt's face turned beet red. But when Hope turned back to Ethan, laughter dancing in her eyes, he froze.

She hesitated for a moment, sobering. “It was a pleasure to meet you, Ethan.”

“The pleasure was all mine, Hope.” Ethan reached out and drew her hand to his lips, feathered a soft kiss against her silky skin. Her scent sank into him. The same elusive tingling took hold of his senses. He stood beside Matt as she stepped inside her room and closed the door. The click of her lock snapped him out of his trance. Good Lord Almighty, what was wrong with him?

Less than an hour later, on the other side of town, Ethan stared up at the sliver of moon hanging low in the dark sky, cursing his luck. So many things had caught him off guard tonight, made him edgy, vulnerable.

They'd gotten close to catching Vega today, closer than they'd been in a long time. To have Vega slip through their fingers was beyond frustrating. Then there'd been Christina's painting hanging over the fireplace at the hotel, Christina's gift to her friend, Mirabella. The sight of it was akin to pouring salt in an open wound. He'd made it a habit to avoid the restaurant—and that painting—at all cost. But Ethan had assured Matt he'd be there, and he wouldn't let Matt down for anything.

And last, but certainly not least, there was Matt's daughter. He'd heard all about her over the years from Matt, of course, watched her grow up through their letters. Seeing her face-to-face had been a revelation. Touching her had sent an unanticipated, violent shockwave of sensation through him. One he'd not even experienced with Christina. He shook his head and strode down the darkened alley, swearing beneath his breath with a vengeance.

Ethan prayed he'd at least been able to mask his reactions enough to fool Matt. Staying at the Bar M tomorrow night might not be such a great idea. Hell, if he had any damned sense, he'd saddle up and ride out into the foothills instead...keep right on riding until he had his damned head screwed on straight again. Too bad he couldn't very well do that, not without Matt asking a lot of questions. Questions Ethan didn't want to answer. He flexed his fists at his sides, his eyes scanned the shadows looking for trouble...*hoping* for it.

She's Matt's daughter, Matt's goddamned daughter*, for the love of God.*

The words revolved in his head, but the silent rebuke didn't much help. Instead, those words sliced at him, shredding him with guilt. He didn't have any business feeling this way, not about her. He had too damned much to deal with already without worrying about emotional entanglements. He stopped in his tracks and pivoted, slamming his fist against the rough plank wall of the livery, welcoming the sharp stab of pain radiating through his knuckles. The only thing that mattered was catching Vega, making him pay for what he'd done to Christina. How could he have forgotten that, even for a moment?

Chapter 3

The next morning, Hope sat in the hotel dining room sipping her coffee, lost deep in thought. Ethan's unsettling cobalt eyes and electrifying touch weighed heavily on her mind. She'd never reacted to anyone like that before, and was, even now, doing her best to chalk it up to nothing more than exhaustion, plain and simple.

"Pard' me, ma'am—"

"Oh..." She started. Her heart bumped against her ribs. Hope glanced up—and up—as she dabbed at the coffee splatters on the tabletop. Good heavens, were all the men out here veritable giants? She forced a polite smile and did her best to ignore her unsettled nerves.

"Good mornin', ma'am," he drawled. "I hope you don't mind, but I saw you sittin' here all alone, and I couldn't resist the urge to introduce myself—Daniel Masters, at your service."

The stranger bowed with consummate flair. His hair was deep brown, trimmed short. His dark eyes were oh-so-smooth. He sported a handlebar mustache over wide, sensual lips. His suit was dark blue, tailored, and, by her best estimate, very expensive.

Masters hurried behind Hope, assisting with her chair as she gained her feet. He wasn't quite as tall as Ethan was, and not quite as muscular either. He was attractive in a sophisticated, polished sort of way...the sort of way that put any woman with an ounce of sense in her head instantly on her guard.

She offered her hand. "It's a pleasure to meet you, Mr. Masters. I'm Hope, Hope Lewis."

Towering over her, not close enough to crowd her, but near enough to make her feel his interest, he took her hand in his, lifting it to his lips. His skin was smooth against hers, quite a distinctive contrast to Ethan's work-roughened calluses. Masters brushed a drawn out kiss over the backs of her knuckles, then, contrary to etiquette, maintained his hold on her hand as he spoke.

Lifting a brow, he clarified, "As in Matt Lewis of the Bar M?"

"Yes, Matt's my uncle."

Something flickered in his gaze, but he blinked and it was gone, leaving her to wonder if she'd imagined it. "You're not from around here, though. I would have remembered that face." He smiled again, oozing charm.

"I'm from Maryland." His familiarity made her uncomfortable. She tugged at her hand, to no avail.

Hope ground her teeth together in frustration. She didn't want to cause a scene, but she couldn't allow him to continue the inappropriate contact. She tugged her hand again, harder this time. He let go at last, but his eyes conveyed his reluctance.

"We'll have to see what we can do to make you consider staying on." Flashing a smile that wasn't quite benign, he opened his mouth to say more, but Matt joined them, interrupting him.

"We're all set." Matt addressed her before turning to her companion, his voice beyond frigid. "Masters..."

The two men nodded at each other with stiff formality. Masters turned back to her, dismissing Matt. "I believe that's my mark to excuse myself. It was a pleasure to meet you, Miss Lewis. I look forward to seeing you again."

Hope responded with a courteous nod. Puzzled,

her gaze settled on Matt's face. She tilted her head to the side, considering the deep grooves his scowl etched into his handsome features as he glared at the younger man's back.

"What was that all about?"

"Huh?" Matt blinked at her, distracted. "Oh, ah, nothin'..." He cleared his throat. "If you're finished here, we should get a move on. Ethan's waitin' on us outside."

Hope followed Matt from the hotel, stopping on the boardwalk. The sun peeked over the rim of the horizon and soft colors streaked the sky. Her gaze locked on the sunrise, and she stood motionless, utterly captivated, drinking in the majestic view for several long moments. When she turned to follow Matt, he was nowhere in sight. Scanning the dusty street, her eyes settled on Ethan, standing near three saddled horses. A bemused frown dug grooves between his eyebrows as he studied her. She paused mid-step, conscious once again of the odd flutter low in the pit of her stomach.

Ethan happened to glance at the hotel entrance when Hope stepped through the doorway and hadn't been able to tear his eyes away. Her face held such awe, such wonder, that his chest tightened. At that very moment, he, too, was looking at something just as wonderful, just as awe-inspiring as that perfect sunrise. The warmth of her gaze on his face snapped him out of his stupor. He tipped his hat in greeting and turned away before she could read the fascination in his eyes.

"Good morning, Ethan." Her voice broke over him like a warm ray of sunshine.

Gritting his teeth against the urge to sweep her off her feet and straight into his arms, he tightened the cinch on the saddle of a small dappled mare, tossing a bland smile over his shoulder. His knees went weak just looking at her. He could do nothing to disguise the husky hunger in his voice.

"Mornin', Hope."

"Matt said you were waiting. I hope I didn't keep you waiting too long."

Ethan shook his head, doing his level best to keep his eyes anywhere but on her. He failed, miserably. Resigned to conversation whether he could handle it or not, he offered, "Had a few things to take care of."

Hope glanced around, frowning. "Is Matt bringing the wagon around?"

"Wagon'll be around later for your trunks." Ethan grinned, patting the flank of the horse at his side, dashing her obvious hopes. "We'll ride."

She gaped at him, wide-eyed, as though he'd sprouted a second head. The color drained from her face, and Ethan tensed, preparing to spring forward should she swoon. Hope turned fearful eyes to the horses. Panic squeaked in her voice, lacing him with guilt. "But, I told you, I can't ride."

Firming his resolve, he replied, "You're gonna have to get comfortable ridin' sooner or later, might as well start now."

The shifting animals distracted Hope for a moment, allowing Ethan to slip behind her, settling his hands on her waist without warning. For a split second he paused, surprised at how tiny she was. He could almost span her waist between his hands. The gentle slope of her hips beckoned his hands, but he gritted his teeth and resisted.

Startled, she squawked, batting at his hands, "What do you think you're doing?"

Her eyes flew over the boardwalk, transparently frantic to find anyone that might stop him from putting her atop a horse.

"I'm helpin' you mount up, darlin'. Just relax now," he drawled, leaning in so close his chest brushed her back. Her hair was smooth as silk against his cheek. Ethan took a deep breath to get a grip on his control, and inadvertently drew her scent deeper. His blood raced in response, and he bit back a groan.

"Now just you hold on a minute!" She flailed her arms, struggling to squirm away. "You c-can't...I don't..." Hope stuttered, wiggling, clutching his wrists, pushing at his clinging hands. "I can't..." Her bottom banged against his groin. His loud groan startled her into stillness for a second. "Look, Ethan, I don't *want* to—"

Before she'd gotten her panicked thoughts marshaled into complete sentences, he tossed her up astride the horse where she landed with a firm thud. She caught the reins he tossed into her lap. Hope peered down at the ground, pale-faced. Her eyes swerved to the shifting horse beneath her. The oncoming panic attack was clear from a mile away. He had to do something...now.

Taking advantage of her distraction, he slid a hand up her calf—beneath her skirts. Her mouth fell open in surprise, her eyes rounded as she stared down at him, but her voice apparently failed her.

Ethan hid an amused grin and slid his hand down her warm flesh until he found her ankle. Placing her foot in the stirrup, he brushed her skirts aside to adjust the leather strap for length. His fingers lingered a bit longer than necessary on her ankle, and color flooded her cheeks. Biting back a chuckle, Ethan ambled around the horse.

Just as Hope began to sputter, he reached up beneath her skirts again, a little higher this time, and her voice choked off on a strangled gasp. Her skin was like satin beneath his fingertips, tempting him with unspoken pleasure. He clamped down hard on that thought, reminding himself not to go there.

All the same, he stared up into her glittering eyes as his hand slid along her leg in bold, possessive strokes. Oh, yeah, she looked good and mad now, mad enough to spit. Ethan smiled, slow and easy. Giving himself a mental pat on the back, he turned away, leaping up onto his own mount. That would give her something else to think about besides the fact she was riding a horse.

His grin slipped a little. His diversionary tactic had given him something to think about as well.

Matt came back then and swung up onto his horse. "All set?"

"We're ready. Course, if you're not comfortable, Hope, you can always ride with me." He winked, patting his lap, earning a confused stare from Matt and an offended scowl from Hope.

A fresh wave of indignant color rode high in her cheeks, belying the prim ice crystals in her eyes. "I'm fine right where I am."

"I kinda thought you might say that." He shot her a shameless, mischievous grin, wheeling his mount around.

****

Hope's eyes burned smoking holes in Ethan's back as she nudged her mount forward. They rode the better part of the day in silence, and by the time it occurred to her that she was riding a horse, her heart no longer pounded in her ears. She was wary, yes—wary and cautious—but not afraid.

She frowned, chewing at her lower lip. A considerable amount of time passed before she shook her head and rolled her eyes. Ethan's actions had nothing to do with interest in her person. He'd been trying—successfully, if she were honest—to divert her focus from her fear of being on the horse. Hope muffled a self-deprecating snort. He was Matt's friend, for Heaven's sake. What was she thinking? His method may have been questionable, but, she was nearly certain, his intentions were honorable.

They arrived at the ranch around midday. Hope

absorbed the details of Matt's home, delighted. The house was large, its massive outer walls made of a claylike substance. The roof was flat with no overhang in the front. The house had step levels with deep-set window and door openings. A rounded parapet stood sentinel on one end of the structure, and small round spouts shot through the adobe to channel rainwater from the roof.

A long porch ran the length of the house. Eight sizable, earthenware pots sat in a row along the front of the house, each held late-blooming flowers. Smaller pots filled with cacti and other native plants decorated the windowsills.

The bunkhouse, similar to Matt's home in its building materials, but smaller, and shaped in a simple rectangular design, sat just beyond the main house. Situated to the north of the bunkhouse was a long, wide wooden structure with an attached paddock on either side. An inviting, clear creek meandered near the house, stretching off into the distance. A sparkling pale blue ribbon threading its way toward the mountains.

Awed by Matt's home, Hope silently fell in line behind Ethan as Matt led the way to the stables. As they drew alongside the building, Matt dismounted and led his horse inside, seemingly oblivious to Hope's predicament. How was she to get down off this wretched horse? Ethan dismounted as well, but instead of following Matt, he let his reins fall slack and strode to Hope's side to assist her from the saddle. As unsettling as the thought was that he'd soon put his hands on her again, she was grateful for the help all the same. Hope smiled down at him, and his step faltered, his expression turned bemused. Ethan reached up to grasp her waist.

His touch was beyond unsettling. It moved through her like lightning, making breathing difficult as the fluttering sensation in her chest swelled.

Resting her hands on his powerful, broad shoulders, Hope leaned forward into his outstretched hands. Ethan lifted her from the saddle with ease. His intense stare scorched her as he held her, suspended motionless inches from the ground for a breathless moment. His hands flexed on her waist, lingering even after her feet touched solid ground.

Heat stole into her cheeks, and she had trouble holding his gaze. "Thank you for what you did back in town...for distracting me. I don't think I could have managed that ride if I'd been thinking about it the whole time."

Ethan blinked. His lips parted. Then his grin turned wolfish. "Anytime you need a distraction, darlin', I'm your man."

She was sure he'd meant his comment as nothing more than a joke but those last three words—and the glint in his eyes—raced shocking heat through her veins. Her smile faded, and she stepped back, uncomfortable with the way his hungry stare slid to her lips. His hands dropped to his sides, fisted. They stood like that for a long moment, staring at each other, motionless. Then he stepped back, gathered the reins of both mounts, and retreated inside the stables without a backward glance, leaving her to stare after him, hopelessly lost.

Chapter 4

Hope started as Matt stepped out from the dim interior of the stables, alone, and walked toward the house, motioning her forward to walk at his side.

"My housekeeper's name's Natalia Sanchez." He thrust his hands deep in his back pockets, his tone distracted. "She's been at the ranch for years. Manuel's been helping with your trunks. He works in the stables, does odd jobs around the place. He doesn't speak much English. My foreman's Antonio Diaz. He's young, but he knows his business. He's out with the other men right now, but I'm sure you'll meet him later tonight."

Hope nodded, filing the names away as they crossed into the shaded inner recesses of the house. A handsome, middle-aged woman with long, dark hair and velvety, doe-brown eyes greeted them. But for the faint laugh lines crinkling the edges of her eyes and deep dimples creasing her cheeks, her olive skin was radiant and smooth.

"*Bienvenida,*" she called as she bustled forward to clasp Hope's hands between hers in warm welcome. Drawing Hope forward, she pulled Hope's arms out and away from her body. "*Muy delgada…*"

She clucked her tongue. Shaking her head, she tugged Hope into a fierce embrace, pecking a kiss on both of her cheeks, then took her by the hand and led her down a hallway towards the back of the house, mumbling beneath her breath in Spanish. Incredulous, Hope's eyes rounded as she looked over her shoulder to Matt for help. Matt's laughter boomed through the room.

"Let her catch her breath, Natalia. I'll show her around first, then you can fatten her up."

Natalia hesitated, eyeing him as though she didn't believe him. Nevertheless, she released Hope's hand, patted her on the cheek, and rattled off a long, heated string of Spanish at Matt before she left them alone. Bemused, Hope stood in the tall archway, watching the older woman stride away with a graceful, rolling gait.

Hope turned back to Matt, catching him unaware. He'd been standing with his hands thrust deep in his back pockets again, watching her with the strangest of expressions on his face. Clearing his throat, he pivoted, motioning over his shoulder for her to follow.

Matt gave Hope a thorough tour of his home. Each room was comfortable, decorated with inviting, southwestern appeal. The house carried a well-balanced, tasteful design…not what she'd expected of a confirmed bachelor. The loving hands of a woman had shaped this home. Natalia, Hope surmised.

Matt led her to his sanctuary, a modest library with a large mahogany desk situated in one corner. Smiling her pleasure, she moved farther into the room, turning in a complete circle. Floor to ceiling bookshelves lined two full walls. A wide set of windows nestled in the middle of one wall of bookshelves, a padded bench seat rested below it, inviting a booklover to settle in.

On the far wall, opposite Matt's desk, two leather wing-backed chairs flanked a large, stone fireplace. Above the mantle hung a breathtaking landscape—one that put the landscape hanging in Mirabella's Place to shame. Hope stepped closer and tilted her head, peering at the artistic blend of color and shape. Her eyes drifted to the bottom corner where she found the dainty letters. C. Sanchez.

Curious, Hope glanced to Matt. He tugged at the collar of his shirt and hurried her along before she could lend voice to the question on her lips.

"I won't take you back to the kitchen, yet. She was serious about you being too skinny, you know. Better be prepared to have food shoved at you every time you turn around." Matt grinned when Hope sent him a startled look. Motioning toward the end of the hall, he drawled, "Stairs are back here."

On the second floor, Matt led her down a hallway with two doors on either side. Guiding her past the first set, he indicated the door on the left. "That's Ethan's room."

"He stay's here often enough to have his own room?"

As soon as the words tumbled out of her mouth, she could have bitten off her tongue. However, Matt didn't seem to find anything amiss, answering over his shoulder in bland tones. "Yeah, I guess so."

Matt stopped at the next set of doors and opened the one to his left—the one right next to Ethan's—and stepped aside for her. As soon as she walked into the room, Hope grinned, ear to ear.

The room was large. The furniture consisted of heavy, mahogany pieces, the colors and textures of the fabrics reflecting the rest of the house. On the far wall, doublewide windows stood open, allowing a gentle breeze to circulate inside the room.

A Sheraton secretaire sat in the corner, and a small earthenware vase overflowing with fresh flowers sat on the nightstand. The openness, the fresh breeze with undercurrents of lemon and beeswax, gave her a sense of renewal, a sense of vitality. This room was magnificent, and the view kept getting better the closer she got to the window.

Hope crossed the room in silent wonder and stood, gazing out at the mountains in the distance.

Sparse vegetation speckled the dry, sandy soil. Mesquite shrubs and prickly pear, yucca, cholla, and clumps of odd-looking grasses beckoned the eye. The majestic mountains rose up into the western sky forming the backdrop of this feast for the eyes. Matt approached on silent feet, stopping a pace away, standing in silent reverence for a moment as he, too, stared out the window.

"I came to Texas to visit Ethan's father. I never intended to stay. What you're seeing right there caught me. A body can roam for days and days and not meet another soul. The sunsets, the sunrises, everything in between, it all caught me. It's harsh and wild, unspoiled. I guess I needed this." Matt's voice was soft, hushed as though the words gave away more than he wanted to reveal.

"Where did you meet Ethan's father?"

The question roused Matt from his muse. He turned, regarding her for a long moment without a word. She wasn't altogether certain he'd even heard the question at first, or, if he had, that he intended to answer. His face was a study of deep sadness, filled with infinite regret and loss.

"I met Andrew Kincaid during the war."

When she was young, James had told her Matt had fought in the War Between the States. All three of the brothers had. Though they'd not all been under the same command, they'd all championed the North.

James had been a commissioned officer with an engineering detail, and Jacob had commanded an artillery unit. Matt had ridden scout for a small cavalry troop infiltrating enemy lines. Her father never spoke of the war, and James never volunteered any further details, but she knew Jacob, her father, lost his arm at Antietam...back before she'd even been born. She'd always been curious about that particular time in their lives, but, sensing their pain, she'd never broached the subject.

Matt cleared his throat and focused his eyes on her. "But that's a story best left for another day. I see Manuel and Pablo have arrived with your trunks. I'm sure you'd like to settle in. They'll bring 'em up soon." He started for the door. "I have to check on a few things this afternoon, but I'll be back in time for supper. We'll talk then."

"Uncle Matt." Hope called out to him just as he cleared the door. She crossed to him, reaching up on tiptoe to kiss his cheek. "Thank you, Uncle Matt. Thank you for taking me in when Uncle James..." Forced to clear her throat and blink away the tears, Hope forged on, "Thank you. The room is wonderful."

Matt smiled, though his voice was tight. "I want you to consider this your home now, darlin'."

He hesitated a moment, looking as if he'd like to say more. Sighing deeply, he turned and walked away.

A little over two hours later, Hope leaned against the window frame, lost in the vision of splendor before her. Warm rays of sunlight washed over her, relaxing away the tension she'd been carrying for the better part of the past year.

Manuel and Pablo delivered her trunks soon after Matt left. True to Matt's word, Natalia had followed close on their heels, delivering a tray groaning with food. Hope ate as much as she could stomach—admittedly not much—before setting to work unpacking. Now that she'd finished, she gave in to the irresistible urge to steal another peek at the breathtaking view before heading back downstairs.

"Sure is a pretty sight, isn't it?" Warm breath caressed the side of her neck. Ethan's husky voice slid over her senses, wrapping around her, sending her pulse skittering.

Hope whirled to face him, her hand pressed to her chest to keep her heart inside her ribcage where it belonged. "You startled me. I didn't hear you come in."

He was so close to her, had she taken one single step, she could have pressed full-length against him. That realization, as much as the look in his eyes, stole what little breath she'd managed to recover. The gears in her head ground to a screeching halt. Ethan smiled down at her, as though he were privy to some joke she was not. Then again, perhaps he was somehow aware of her sudden inability to think and found it amusing.

His gaze flickered over her head to the panoramic vista behind her, allowing her a much-needed moment to gather her wits. Then his unsettling stare rested once more on her face. His voice poured through her like warm, smooth honey. "All settled in?"

"Ah..." She blinked, disconcerted to realize it took great effort to answer his question with any semblance of intelligence. "Yes. Yes, I am."

Ethan grinned again, nothing more than a curling at the corners of his sensual lips. She started to sink into his eyes once more. He stepped back, and she could breathe again. More important, she could think again. She chewed her lip as he crossed to the table and scanned the contents of the tray, shaking his head mournfully.

"Natalia's not gonna like that," he predicted, pointing to the tray. "You realize she expected you to finish it all, don't you?"

"There was enough food for three people. She couldn't expect me to eat all that, not alone." Hope shook her head in denial. Her eyes rounded as Ethan's grin widened, refuting her claim.

"Most people wouldn't have had any trouble." He shot her a look of exasperation as he picked up a cold tortilla and tore off a chunk, waving it at her before popping it into his mouth. "She didn't know you eat like a bird."

Temper burbled up from nowhere, and she planted her fists on her slim hips. Her chest swelled with indignation. "I do not eat like a bird."

"You do," he disagreed in mild tones, adding as an afterthought, "Probably why you got bones stickin' out all over."

Her mouth dropped open, her eyes rounded…then narrowed. Her temper exploded, like lightning arcing between them. How dare he make such a personal observation? Civilized people didn't go around commenting on someone else's person. No one had ever spoken to her this way before. She didn't know how to respond.

Angered beyond reasoning, she sputtered, "I-I do *not*."

Undaunted, he settled into her seat, helping himself to the food she'd left. Between hearty mouthfuls, Ethan lifted a taunting brow, running his gaze down the length of her body. He serenely contradicted her. "You do."

Hope snapped her mouth shut, the angry click of her teeth echoed in the room like a shotgun blast. Heat flamed to life in her cheeks. She scowled as he took another enthusiastic bite and, despite years of proper training, she couldn't seem to stop the rude words from slipping between her lips. "Not everyone eats like a horse."

Grinning, Ethan leaned back in the chair, chewed, and swallowed. Ignoring her comment, he tilted his head. His discerning gaze swept over her petite frame once more. By the time his insolent gaze traveled back to her face, she glowed with anger, flushed with something else…something baffling and unfamiliar.

"Natalia will do you good. You could use a few pounds." He shoveled in another mouthful and waggled a torn piece of tortilla shell in her direction.

“Some rest wouldn’t hurt anything either. You look like you haven’t seen a decent night sleep this side of six months.”

“There’s nothing wrong with the way I look—”

“I didn’t say there was anything wrong with the way you look.” Ethan cut her tirade short. His steady, assessing gaze sparked an odd fluttering deep in the pit of her stomach. The intense heat in his eye burned her where she stood. “I said you could use a few pounds and some rest. There’s a difference. A man likes to have something soft to hold in his arms. He doesn’t want to be poked and jabbed when he’s tryin’ to get close to his woman.”

“Thanks for the tip. I’ll take that into consideration for the next time I find a man I’m interested in getting close to.” Hope folded her arms over her chest in a patent gesture of defiance. “Maybe you should move on now, I’d hate to accidently…poke you with my…boniness.”

She returned to the window to glower at an old fence post in the distance. A length of rusty barbed wire coiled over a nail protruding from the side of the splintered wood. Her breath seethed in and out. How dare he judge her? How dare he presume to tell her what she needed? How had he managed to goad her? Again? As a rule, it took a great deal to rouse her temper. He hadn’t seemed to make any effort at all, but he’d achieved outstanding results.

She took a deep breath, determined to steady her nerves. She was above such petty arguments. So what if he thought she was too skinny. She hadn’t asked him for his opinion anyhow. It wasn’t as if she was expecting him to hold her—whatever *that* was supposed to mean.

Hope muttered beneath her breath, “No one ever complained about me being too skinny until I came here…”

“The men in Maryland must have lower

standards," he whispered, his breath tickling her ear.

She jumped, strangling off a startled shriek as she bumped against his chest. How did he manage to keep sneaking up on her like that? Spinning to face him—irritated that he'd listened in on a private conversation, even if it had been with no one else but herself—she planted her fists on her hips again, glaring up at him.

"There's nothing wrong with the 'standards' of the men in Maryland." Her chin rose defensively. He was so close that every time she took a deep breath, the lace on her bodice brushed against his shirt, but she refused to step back. He wouldn't intimidate her with his size…or the wicked look in his eyes.

His lips curled, and her heart fluttered. "There must be something wrong with 'em if they prefer holding scrawny women."

Her scowl deepened, and she sucked in an outraged breath at the word scrawny. Lifting her chin another notch in defiance, she did her best to ignore the twin points of fury heating her cheeks. "I wouldn't know about their preferences." Her tone slipped beyond the borders of haughty, straight into the land of ice princess. "It wasn't as though I went about hugging a bunch of men…much less asking their opinion on the matter."

"You didn't seem the type." Ethan's smile widened, turning decidedly provocative. "Of course, I didn't say huggin', I said *holdin'*. There's a difference, sweetheart."

Her brow wrinkled, and she gritted her teeth in consternation. "What are you talking about? There's no difference."

"Oh, yes, Hope. There most *definitely* is," he whispered as he leaned toward her…leaned into her. His cobalt gaze, vivid with temptation, traced the lines of her lips. When he lifted his smoldering gaze to hers, she felt herself falling into bottomless cobalt fire.

Hope's blood began to warm, surging in response to the heat in his gaze. Instinct took over. Her eyelids drooped to half-mast. Her lips parted when he settled his large, hard hands on her hips, edging a little closer, until air had trouble passing between them. She braced her palms against his chest, but lacked the strength—lacked the desire—to push him away.

Heat built between them like a storm cloud churning and growing, waiting to discharge its bolt of hot lightning. She told herself she wouldn't let him kiss her. Hope called herself a liar even as he began to lower his head. His long fingers tightened on her hips, pulling her closer still. Her body brushed against his, tentative and testing. He tugged her closer, molding her against him in a perfect fit. Something primitive and hungry broke loose deep inside her.

Need, pure and raw, sparked between them, raging to near incendiary levels. Hope couldn't fight against it, couldn't steady herself. Her vision softened, hazed, and her eyes closed in expectation. The heat of his breath caressed her lips. Her own breath snagged in the back of her throat. The hard thump of his heart beat like an erratic drum against her palms, sending tingling anticipation streaking through her.

A cold rush of air slapped her in the face, and Hope's eyes flew open. Ethan's head snapped up, angling sideways, and his eyes focused with brutal concentration on some point in the distance. His hands tightened on her hips, his entire body went rigid.

His voice exploded, "Son of a bitch!"

Then he bolted from the room.

She stared after him, dazed and bereft. His

boots pounded along the hall, then down the stairs. Hope swung around, peering out the window as Ethan sprinted across the yard and inside the stables. The sound of his raised voice shattered the quiet. Then he was riding out of the stables, crouched low over his horse's neck at a full out gallop with two men trailing close behind.

The glint of steel flashed as Ethan drew his gun. Hope leaned out the window, squinting against the late afternoon sunlight. She searched until she spotted the faint puffs of gun-smoke and dust Ethan was, even now, angling for. Tiny figures moved in the distance, but it was impossible to tell who any of them were. Then Ethan joined the melee, and he, too, was lost to distinction.

Hope clutched the window ledge until her fingers went numb. She couldn't tear her eyes from the tiny dots on the horizon. Trepidation squeezed her chest in a mighty fist. Minutes passed, stretching into an eternity as she waited.

At last, a group of riders returned to the Bar M. Her heart lurched. She swayed on her feet, grasping the window frame for support. Something was terribly wrong. She counted six horses returning. Only four had riders sitting upright. The other two men hung face down in the saddle. Her breath caught. Her heart stopped. The blood froze in her veins. Then she found Ethan.

Blood soaked his shirt.

Oh, dear God, so much blood...

Chapter 5

The riders drew closer. Fear roiled through her veins like a noxious poison. Dark, crimson stains saturated Ethan's shirt, matting the material against his shoulder and chest. One full sleeve was drenched with blood. His jaw was set, his expression grim as he guided his horse toward the house. He led Matt's horse behind him.

Matt's limp body hung face down over his saddle.

Strangling back a sob, Hope tore down the stairs, fumbling her way through the house, and out onto the rear veranda. Natalia was already there. Her silent lips moved as she clutched her rosary in trembling hands. When Hope stepped onto the veranda, Natalia swung around, her face pale.

"Come with me," she ordered.

Hope darted a quick, apprehensive glance at the grim riders and hurried after Natalia. Together they hurriedly swiped dishes and food from the table. Natalia placed a large kettle of water on top of the cast iron cook stove, directing Hope to a small room off the kitchen.

A few moments later, Hope rushed back inside the kitchen with an armload of linens. She spread one of the pristine sheets over the table mere seconds before the men crashed through the doorway. Hope leaped back into the corner to get out of their way, forcing her eyes anywhere but the blood-soaked man hanging like a lifeless ragdoll between Ethan and Manuel.

Matt was white as the sheet she'd tossed over the scarred wooden surface. His head lolled, chin to chest, feet dragging behind him. Ethan and Manuel carried him to the table and laid him down on top of it, handling him with the care one would give a newborn babe. Manuel stepped back and hurried from the room as Natalia came bustling up, but Ethan didn't budge, forcing the older woman to push him aside.

Just then, a tall, broad-shouldered man came limping into the kitchen, drawing Hope's attention. His left pant leg was soaked with blood. Ethan looked over as the newcomer came in, hurried forward, pushing the wounded man onto a chair before returning to Matt's side.

"See to them," Natalia snapped, prodding Hope from the realm of shock into a flurry of motion.

Jolting forward, she snatched up a towel and a bowl of water. Hope hurried to Ethan first. He stood beside the table, unblinking, while Natalia work over Matt. When she took his arm to draw him to a chair, he waved her away.

"Help Antonio," he ordered. All his focus seemed centered upon the shallow rise and fall of Matt's chest.

Hope worried her lower lip in indecision, staring with wide, concerned eyes at Ethan's blood-soaked shirt. However, as he was the only one still standing on his own two feet, she gave up for the moment and turned her attention to the man in the chair. He was a handsome devil with dark chocolate-brown eyes and silky stick-straight hair the color of soft midnight falling well below his shoulders. The partial-day's growth of whiskers covering his jaw gave him a dangerous appeal, making him appear, at first glance, older than he was.

He was tall and lean, but a long way from gawky. The deep V where his shirt gapped open over his throat and chest gave her an impressive display of smooth bronze skin stretching taut over rippling muscle. He brought to mind a lithe, dangerous panther...albeit an injured one. Perched sideways on the straight-backed kitchen chair, he clutched his thigh with a crimson-slicked hand just below a blood-crusted, knotted bandana. His expression was drawn tight, stoic, his face pale beneath his tan as he, too, stared at Matt.

Hope sank to her knees beside him, offering him a tentative, if wan smile. While blood didn't make her swoon, her stomach still careened madly. She laid a gentle hand over his, moving it out of her way. Velvety brown eyes settled on her, following her every movement with a healthy dose of interest. Blood soaked the leg of his buckskin pants. She pulled at the material on his thigh, but it wouldn't budge. She gave up, turning to Ethan.

"Give me your knife." Still on her knees, she held her hand out to him, palm up, waiting.

Ethan glanced down at her, a puzzled frown wrinkling his brow as though he'd forgotten she was there, as though he couldn't understand why she was kneeling on the floor with blood on her hands. After a long moment, he blinked and shook his head. Stepping closer, Ethan unsheathed a large hunting knife. Instead of handing it to her, however, he knelt at Antonio's side, cutting the pant leg away himself.

Without a word to Ethan, she turned her focus back to her charge and began cleansing the blood away with cautious hands, rinsing the towel out in the bowl on the floor by her knees. Every time she extracted a piece of shattered rock from his wound, Hope cringed. Her patient didn't bat an eyelash.

It was a ragged flesh wound, but the bullet had passed through. The gash was close to four inches long, torn very deep, and would require stitches. Lots of them. However, sewing up human flesh was something she'd never done before, never had cause to even consider. The very thought pushed bile up the back of her throat.

The bleeding was sluggish now, but she pressed a clean towel against it nonetheless. Hope peered over her shoulder at Natalia, flat out refusing to lower her gaze to Matt's motionless form covered in all that blood.

If she lost him, too…

No, that kind of thinking would get her nowhere. She'd turn into a useless pile of mush if she allowed those thoughts to fill her head.

Natalia was absorbed in her task. She'd be of no use. Hope's considering gaze darted to Ethan as he stood vigil at Matt's side. She chewed on her lip again when she noticed the blood running unheeded from his wrist to his fingertips. From there, it splattered with ruthless precision onto the floor. Gritting her teeth, a flash of steely resolve slipping up her spine, Hope took hold of Antonio's hand, pressing it to the towel.

She did her best to ignore the flicker of pain in his eyes, and ordered, "Hold this…just like that. I'll be right back."

Ethan's face was ashen, the muscle in his jaw leaped and clenched. Blood crusted, unheeded, on the ridge of his cheekbone. Her eyes skimmed across the cut with concern.

"Ethan…"

No response.

She touched his forearm, and he jolted.

"Help Antonio—"

"I need you," she interrupted. Then, when his narrow-eyed stare swerved to her face, she forced a swallow and hurried on, "I think Antonio needs stitches, and I don't have any idea how to…I'm not sure what to do. You're hurt, too. Your arm needs tending."

"My arm?" Blank confusion dug deep grooves between his brows as he lowered his stare to the arm in question. He shrugged, unconcerned. "It's a nick, I'll be fine."

Fear and anxiety snapped the leash on her temper. "You won't be any use to him if you pass out from loss of blood, you stubborn fool." She had his full attention at last, and she barked, "Sit down."

When it looked as if he would argue, she braced her hands against his chest and, unrelenting, pushed Ethan away from the table. She'd spent the last year lifting and maneuvering James and she was stronger than she looked, but still it was a strain just to budge him. He raised his eyebrows at her, but sat in the chair opposite Antonio's all the same.

Hope stood in front of him, right between his knees. His head tipped to the side, but she moved into his way again, determined to get his attention, one way or another. His irritated gaze flickered to her face, and he opened his mouth to speak. She leaned over him then, chewing her lower lip with concentration as she began unbuttoning his shirt. Whatever he'd been about to say died as nothing more than a shocked gurgle in the back of his throat as his hands shot up to cuff her wrists.

Hope's startled gaze flew to his in alarm.

"What are you doing?" He hissed between his teeth, shooting a glance over her shoulder at Natalia and Matt, as though he were afraid to draw attention to her actions.

"Well, I can lop the sleeve off, but I figured I'd save the extra thread for his leg." She gave a sharp jerk of her chin in Antonio's direction, glowering down at Ethan, exasperated. "I can't very well clean your wound like this, now can I?"

Ethan blinked in surprise at her tart reply. He'd been drowning in the fear. Fear of losing Matt. Fear of reliving that day over again, the day he'd lost Christina. Brutal memories had been bombarding him from the minute he'd seen Matt slumped against the crumbled limestone wall of the Old Mission, drenched with blood and unconscious. Even now, the fear choked him as his partner and mentor—his friend—hovered at death's door.

Yet, somehow, Hope managed to slip beneath the fear, drawing him back from the edge.

He released her wrists, and she finished unbuttoning his shirt. The innocent brush of her fingers against his skin heated his blood, despite his worry. He leaned forward so she could ease the shirt over his injured shoulder and down his back. Her hair swept over his bare skin, tormenting him. His nose brushed her smooth, bare collarbone, turned into the tempting curve of her neck. Only by sheer dint of will did he control the impulse to press his lips there.

Her scent enveloped him, bringing a swift, all-too-physical reminder of the near kiss they'd almost shared. Dangerous as that line of thought was, he clung to it like a lifeline. Anything to keep him from going back to the night he'd held his fiancée's broken, lifeless body in his arms. Focus on Hope's smell. Absorb Hope's heat. At the same time, he kept his hands fisted at his sides to keep from reaching for her. Look but don't touch. Breathe but don't kiss. Want but don't take.

He was only human.

His lips feathered over her floral scented skin. He grazed his cheek along the curve of her neck. White-hot need raged through his system like greedy wildfire through a mesquite thicket. Ethan leaned back in his seat when she pulled his shirt free, and he couldn't help but feel a bit smug at the dazed, disconcerted expression on her lovely face. She shifted uneasily beneath the weight of his deep stare, blushing clear to the roots of her hair.

The bullet had skimmed a long, thin groove through his flesh. Hope knelt between his knees, balancing bandages on one of his thighs. It took a considerable amount of self-control not to yank her onto his lap and let his hands wander at will. While she worked, she chewed on her lower lip, eyes narrowed in acute concentration. His gaze had locked on her perfect, pearly teeth, and on her swollen, pink lip, and hunger of a primal sort gnawed low in his belly.

As she gently wiped the blood from his chest and arm, checking for further injuries, her hands trembled. Her blatantly nervous stare skidded across his naked flesh and flickered to his face. The knowledge that he affected her so strongly only served to heighten his awareness.

Once she'd finished with his shoulder, she turned her attention to the dried blood on his cheek. She refused to meet his eyes. With infinite care, she sponged at his cheek until his wound was clean. It stung like hell, but her gentle touch made him forget the pain. She opened a small tin and smoothed the thick ointment along the cut, then wiped her hands on a clean towel. As Hope set the towel aside, her lips—swollen and bright pink from her incessant chewing—curved into a small, relieved smile. Her eyes connected with his, and she froze.

Ethan leaned forward, drawn to her lips like a moth to a flame. He had to kiss her, had to taste her. He'd surely die if he didn't. Right this very second.

The chair in the corner creaked, and Antonio muffled a groan.

Her attention snapped to Antonio, breaking the spell. Leaping to her feet, she hurried to Antonio. Obsessed with the unexpected need to be near Hope, Ethan followed close on her heels, glancing worriedly over his shoulder at the still unconscious Matt. No change there.

Turning his attention back to Hope and Antonio, he leaned close as she peeled the makeshift bandage away from Antonio's leg to reveal the gruesome wound. Worry shadowed her eyes as Hope stared up at him.

"He's going to need stitches, isn't he?"

Ethan studied the gash, and nodded reluctant affirmation. Then he, too, glanced over to Natalia. Damn it. She was still busy with Matt.

And Matt had yet to open his eyes.

Worry over Matt surged again, and so he centered his focus on Hope and Antonio. Ethan had to help where he could, and right now he'd only get in Natalia's way. He went to one of the cabinets and returned a moment later carrying a bottle of whiskey. Hope eyed him with a curious frown until he shoved it under Antonio's nose.

"Drink," Ethan ordered. "Drink, Antonio."

Antonio obliged with a grim smile.

A short while—and almost a third of the bottle—later, Ethan took the liquor from Antonio. Glancing from the ragged wound on Antonio's thigh and back to Hope, Ethan took a long draw off the bottle himself, savoring the hot sting before pouring a healthy splash over Antonio's wound.

Antonio let out an explosive string of Spanish. Hope had retrieved a needle and thread, scissors, and some fresh bandages while Antonio had been drinking. She was pale as death itself, but she looked as ready as she was ever going to be. After threading the needle, Hope held it up so he could pour the amber liquid over it. His brow wrinkled as he lowered his gaze to the trembling hand holding the needle and thread. He poured, but before she could begin, he placed a restraining hand on her shoulder and held the bottle out to her.

She crinkled the side of her nose, shaking her

head. "No thanks."

"Drink." Resolute, he thrust the bottle into her hands.

Hope glared at him, her eyes mutinous, but she accepted the bottle with an ungracious huff. She lifted the bottle to her lips, wrinkled her nose and flinched.

He was determined, his tone unwavering. "Drink!"

Heaving another sigh, she sucked in a deep breath, tipped the bottle and filled her mouth, forcing a swallow. Tears sprang into her eyes, and she gasped for air, wheezing. Ethan took the bottle from her with one hand, clapping her on the back with the other. In spite of himself, he couldn't stop the corner of his lips lifting the tiniest bit in admiration. He passed the bottle back to Antonio.

Ethan watched as Hope braced herself, blinking the moisture from her eyes. She laid needle to flesh, and he cringed inside as her face turned a shade paler. Antonio's muscles twitched, but he uttered not a sound. Praise God for that small favor. He didn't think Hope would be able to finish otherwise. She wouldn't look at either of them; instead, she focused on her task with ruthless determination. He was impressed.

Hell, he was in awe.

She had steel all right.

Little more than halfway through, however, she faltered. Her hands began to shake as fresh blood oozed. The flesh she stitched looked slippery. Sweat beaded on her forehead and upper lip. She looked ready to pass out. Ethan glanced to Natalia again, but she still hovered over Matt, extracting a slug from his shoulder.

His guts twisted. How he wished he could spare Hope from having to go through this.

Ethan reached out, settling both hands on

Hope's shoulders, squeezing gentle encouragement, willing her extra strength. Even through her clothing, she felt cold to the touch. Her hands steadied a bit, her breathing leveled out. Her fingers flew, the needle flashed, and she tied off the last knot. The stitches wouldn't win any blue ribbons, but they were small and tight. They'd hold, and that was all that counted.

Her lips compressed into a tight line as she applied the fresh bandage and wrapped strips of linen around Antonio's thigh, tying it off. Her task complete, green around the gills, Hope sucked in a ragged breath. Jumping up—startling him—she ran from the room.

He stared at the doorway, glanced out the window. It was full dark out. Hope might need air, but Vega was out there somewhere, and she wasn't safe. Shaking his head at the crooked, woozy grin on his friend's face, he told Antonio to stay put. Antonio saluted him, sloshing whiskey onto his chest.

Ethan glanced over to Natalia and Matt. She'd finished removing the bullets, tied off the last stitch, and now sat, sponging his chest clean. She met Ethan's worried look. Matt's eyes remained closed, but Natalia smiled with tired resolve in her eyes. Matt wouldn't be dying tonight, not if she had anything to say about it.

Relieved, Ethan turned on his heel and made for the back door. It took him a moment or two of scanning the shadows, but he found Hope kneeling beside the creek. She'd washed the blood from her hands, and her face glistened with crystal droplets. She rocked back on her heels, gulping deep breaths of cool, fresh air as if trying to cleanse the scent of blood from her memory.

Ethan stood beside her while she regained her composure, a protective sentry in the night. His eyes scanned the surrounding area, delving into the shadows. His palm rested on the butt of his gun. There was a storm brewing over the mountains, scenting the air. He'd have to post an extra man or two to keep an eye on the herd. The last thing they needed right now was a stampede. Through it all—with all his responsibilities running circles through his mind—her presence was there, undeniable and tempting. And, oddly enough, soothing.

She stood at last. He silently took her by the elbow and led her back inside the house. When he steered her towards the kitchen, she wrenched her arm free.

Ethan frowned. "Matt needs us."

"No, I…I can't…" Hope backed away, shaking her head.

Anger, confusion, and lingering memories of another time and place swelled again. He lashed out, "Matt needs us, Hope. He's lying in there hurt… He needs us, and you choose *now* to get squeamish? Sweet Christ, you haven't even looked at him once since we laid him on that table. How can you be so emotionless, so uncaring? What the hell's wrong with you, woman? He's your goddamned—"

Ethan broke off, one angry word shy of revealing Matt's secret. He wouldn't break Matt's confidence, no matter how upset he might be. Drawing a deep, steadying breath, he took a good, long look at her. Fear and grief shadowed her eyes. Remorse stabbed him in the heart.

Oh hell…were those tears?

She stared at him. Her eyes were enormous and glassy, her face pale. Blood stained her dress—his blood, Antonio's blood—he didn't know which, but it didn't really matter. The memory of what she'd done—sewn a man's flesh back together—swam up before his eyes. She'd drawn on an inner strength most people didn't possess in order to help a stranger, and he'd blasted her for being emotionless and uncaring.

He was an ass, a monster.

She blinked. Without warning, with the unerring speed and accuracy of a bolt of lightning, her arm snaked out, and she slapped him hard enough to make his ears ring. Before he could react, she bolted down the hall and up the stairs. The slamming of a door somewhere overhead reverberated throughout the house.

Ethan's shoulders slumped. He closed his eyes and hung his head. His cheek throbbed, hot and pulsing. He deserved it. If there'd been a hole handy, he'd have gladly crawled right on in and buried himself. What a miserable, God-awful mess.

Bone-weary, he returned to the kitchen. Antonio hung half off the chair now, waving an empty bottle as he warbled his way through a little ditty about a Mexican senorita that was free with her charms. His tongue didn't seem to be cooperating. Ethan glanced over to Natalia. She hadn't moved from Matt's side.

"Take him to the bunkhouse," she addressed Ethan in Spanish. "Bring Pablo and Manuel back with you. We'll move Matt to his bed."

"Carlos is dead." Ethan's hollow words echoed in the room between them.

Natalia's sharp gaze shot up, and, once again, he prayed for that hole…and maybe a spade to make it a little deeper.

Her hands stilled. Her eyes clouded in grief before she closed them tight. When they opened, they were dark, the shimmer of tears held at bay with fierce determination. She nodded, turning her determined stare to Matt. Her hands resumed their work, steady and competent.

Ethan didn't say anything more, just nodded. It seemed wise at this point to keep his mouth shut. He'd inflicted enough pain for one evening. He hefted Antonio to his feet. Staggering, they weaved an unsteady path to the door. Before they cleared it, though, Natalia called Ethan's name. Glancing over his shoulder, he held Antonio tight against his side.

For the first time since they'd returned from the ambush, the flicker of a grin edged the older woman's lips upward. "When you get back, you can tell me what you said to make little Hope slap you."

Ethan stared at her in disbelief. "How do you know she slapped me?"

"Even if I had not heard it, her handprint is still on your cheek." She smiled at him, the wide, fond smile of a mother who'd caught her little boy in trouble and in need of an understanding ear. "She has a good swing, eh?"

Ethan harrumphed, both grim and baffled, as he turned back to his task.

****

Hope sank to the floor in her room, the back of her head resting against the door. The tears came at last, tears for James, tears for Matt.

Tears for herself.

They soaked her cheeks in a torrential downpour. Great, heaving sobs racked her shoulders. She wrapped her arms around her knees and rocked back and forth. Seeing Matt like that had been a nightmare brought to life, like losing James all over again. She could rail against death, claw at it and fight it with every breath she had, but in the end, she was helpless to stop it. Just like with her parents. Just like with Uncle James.

Matt was the last of her family. If he died, she would be alone, again.

She curled up in a tight ball, there on the floor in the dark, and cried until the tears dried up. She prayed until she was hoarse with it, sobbed until her head ached. When moonlight filled the room, she uncurled, and sat up, stretching the kinks from her limp muscles, drained. Stars twinkled in the night sky, visible through the open window. A gentle breeze filtered through the lacy curtains. She sniffled, hiccupped, and bunched the edge of her skirts in her fists as she made to rise. There on the colorful material, brought into strong relief by the light of the silvery moon, the crimson stains mocked her.

Dried blood splotched her dress and smeared her sleeves. *So much blood.* Hope leaped to her feet, tearing at her dress. Frantic fingers tugged and tore at the material. Buttons popped and flew, seams ripped. She didn't stop with the dress. Hope stripped until she stood naked, shivering in the dark.

She stumbled into the shadows, found the pitcher of water, and poured some into the basin, sloshing a little over the edge onto the table and floor. Snatching a towel off the peg, she grabbed up the bar of soap and scrubbed until her skin was red, too numb to feel the sting. Then she turned her attention to her arms, her chest and face, her legs. She scrubbed until she was exhausted.

Then she scrubbed some more.

The cool air nipping at her skin brought her some sense of sanity. She stepped back and peered at herself in the ornate mirror suspended above the delicate washbowl. Shadows and darkness were all she could see. Then again, there wasn't much more than that inside of her either.

Hope crossed the room, her shoulders sagging in defeat, and picked up a towel. She dried herself and dressed in a simple cotton nightdress. Picking the towel up, she padded across the room, barefoot. After mopping up the water she'd spilled, Hope hung the towel on a peg to dry. The motions were automatic, wooden. She lit the oil lamp on her nightstand and climbed into bed.

As she reached to pull the cool sheet up over her, an irrational thought—a panicked thought—

entered her mind. What if this was all her fault? She'd been with her parents when they'd died. She'd gone to live with Uncle James, and he'd died, too. She'd come to live with Uncle Matt, and look what happened. It had to be her. Everyone she loved died.

No. She shook her head. Her breath raced. Irrational determination roared in her ears. She wouldn't let it happen to Matt. Tomorrow she'd pack up her things and go back to Maryland. She was old enough. He couldn't stop her. She'd leave, and Matt would be safe.

No one else would have to die because of her.

She'd live alone.

Alone…

Terror choked her, twisting her in knots, but she fought it down. She refused to give in to the fear. Hope burrowed into her pillow, forcing her eyes closed. To save Matt, she'd manage…somehow.

A small clock on the mantel ticked innocuously in the silent room. Exhaustion won out, and she drifted to sleep, pursued by images of those she loved—Serena and Jacob, James and Matt—all gray as death, cold with it. They clutched at her, pulling at her hair and clothes, stinging her skin with their icy breath. They called to her, their voices piercing like howling February winds.

It's your fault, Hope, they accused. *Now you're all alone…*

Chapter 6

Ethan leaned against the doorframe, silently watching Natalia smooth blankets around Matt. Her hands twisted as she settled into the chair at Matt's bedside, staring anxiously at the deathly pale man on the bed. "What happened?"

"I was...Hope...and I...talking. We were talking." He shifted from one foot to the other, uneasy over the slight distortion in truth. His gaze flickered over her face before sliding away. Guilt washed through him. "I saw the ambush from her window. By the time I got there..."

Natalia turned an indulgent, maternal smile in Ethan's direction. "No, what did you do to make her slap you?"

"Oh." Ethan crossed the room and sank onto the side of Matt's bed. Explanations rolled through his mind like tumbleweeds in a duster. Any way he looked at it, there was only one answer. "I was an ass."

Her smile held as she let the silence stretch on. When Natalia spoke at last, her voice was soft, her eyes understanding. "She is very beautiful isn't she?"

"What the hell," Ethan yelped in surprise, shooting off the bed as if *she'd* slapped him, too. Then he glanced towards Matt's sleeping form. His guilt near to crushed him. "What's that got to do with me bein' an ass?"

"Sometimes it is not always easy—the attraction a man feels for a woman. A man doesn't always handle the things he feels very well."

"I don't—it isn't..." Ethan choked over the denial, uncomfortable heat climbing into his cheeks. All that sage understanding in her eyes made him want to squirm, want to slink from the room with tail tucked between legs like the yellow-bellied coward he was. "It's not like that," he mumbled toward his boots.

"I saw the way the two of you stared at each other in the kitchen. I may be getting older, but I am not blind." Her matter-of-fact logic pierced his hide as no paltry bullet could do. "Ethan, my daughter has been gone two long years. You must let go. She would not want you to go on the way you have been, only half-alive. She would want you to live, Ethan—a full life. Christina would be happy to know you feel passion again. Do not be ashamed of it, embrace it."

Ethan said nothing, just gawked at the woman who'd almost become his mother-in-law. Deep down, Natalia's words held a ring of truth, but it still felt like betrayal on some level. He'd loved Christina. What he'd had with her had been fresh and innocent.

The feelings Hope stirred inside him with a simple look, with an innocent touch, baffled him...left him reeling and off kilter, consuming him—whole. They were anything but innocent. Feelings like that left a man vulnerable. Weak. But if the things going on inside his body were any indication, he had little choice in the matter. He drew a deep breath and lowered a culpable gaze to Matt. When it came to Hope, the better part of rational argument grappled with possessive instinct.

To his utter dismay, rational argument was fast losing ground.

Suddenly, unaccountably determined not to be the only one twistin' in the wind, he stared pointedly at Natalia. "How long before you take your own advice?"

Natalia's eyes widened. Her shocked gaze flew from Ethan's grin to Matt's sleeping face and back again. She opened her mouth, but for the first time in Ethan's recollection, Natalia had no ready response. Ethan pushed to his feet, his grin spread, and swaggered from the room, whistling a tuneless song.

Ethan made a circuit of the house, checking the locks on the doors, securing the ground floor windows before making his way up to his bedroom. He didn't use a lamp, didn't need one. He'd traveled this path too many times to count, knew this house as well as his own. He'd all but grown up here as a kid. All but lived here after Christina…

As he walked, he raked a hand through his hair, cursing beneath his breath.

Had he been so obvious with Hope?

He paused in front of his bedroom, his hand on the doorknob, and glanced over. Dim light spilled from beneath Hope's door. He dragged in a deep breath. If she was awake, he should speak to her, apologize. He owed her at least that much. He had been an ass.

A royal, boot-chewing jerk.

Ethan covered the distance to her door in a few long-legged strides and, squaring his shoulders, he rapped his knuckles against wood.

There was no response. He rapped again.

Nothing…

He hesitated, his brow furrowed.

Should he check on her? Her light was on, after all. Hell, she was probably just ignoring him. He didn't blame her.

No, he should leave her alone. After the way they'd parted, he was certain she'd prefer he stay the hell away from her, but that didn't sit with him. Regardless of her attitude where Matt was concerned, he'd had no right to come down on her that way. Her relationship with Matt was none of his business. He was going to have a difficult time sleeping as it was, he didn't need that particular helping of guilt on his plate as well.

Natalia's words circled in his mind like a swarm of vultures waiting to strip away his defenses. Hope's face drifted into his thoughts. Not so long ago another face would've been there before any other. True, over time he'd had to try a little harder to call Christina's face to mind.

The whole situation gave him pause.

The muscle jumped in Ethan's jaw. He was here to apologize, nothing more. It had nothing to do with any attraction he may feel for her. Not that he felt any. Ah, hell... Who was he trying to fool? His conscience refused to let him take the coward's way out, forcing him to acknowledge the truth. He wanted her. He'd be a liar if he said or thought otherwise.

It wasn't as if he intended to do anything about it though. He shook his head. He was here to apologize to Hope. He was *not* here to seduce her. The one had nothing to do with the other. Nothing at all.

Gritting his teeth, Ethan twisted the doorknob like a condemned man walking to the gallows. He pushed the door inward and dipped his head through the opening, ready to leap back should some unexpected projectile come hurdling at him from across the room. "Hope? Hope, are you awake?"

There was no response. He should have given her more credit than throwing things. She was a lady, through and through. On the other hand, after the way she'd slapped him earlier, he wouldn't be underestimating her again. His ears were still ringing, his cheek still faintly warm. His gaze skimmed the washstand, the tangled heap of her blood-stained dress and underclothes in the corner, and the open window with its fanciful curtains blowing in the breeze. He found her, huddled in a tight ball in the center of the bed. She looked so small there, her dark hair tossed on the pillow behind her in wild disarray.

Hope lay facing the door. The soft light from the lamp kissed her delicate features. Her porcelain brow wrinkled in a deep frown, her eyes scrunched closed. One small fist clutched at a corner of the sheet, pressing it tight to her chest. Her breathing was deep, ragged. She moaned, soft and low, in her sleep. He hesitated.

Should he wake her?

He knew all about nightmares, more than he'd ever imagined possible, and a part of him ached a little for her. Then he fingered his cheek, remembering the sting she'd given him earlier. Natalia had been right. Hope had one hell of a swing. She sure as certain wouldn't appreciate him being in her room, not after what he'd said to her earlier. She'd end up slapping him again for his efforts anyway. God knew she'd have every right. No, tomorrow would be soon enough to face her. He slipped from the room, closing the door softly behind him.

Inside his own room, he stripped down and washed in the dark. When he was finished, he sat on the edge of his bed, naked, letting the frigid night air wash over him, hoping to cool his blood even as the image of her lying there on the bed crept back into his thoughts. Ethan ran his hand through his damp hair, then slid back and lay down on the cool, crisp sheets.

Sleep never came without a fight for him, not since the night of the raid. However, tonight it was images of Matt's daughter, fire flashing in her eyes, troubling him. She was a puzzle to him. He'd expected her to show some emotion over Matt's injuries. Fear. Anger. Shock...something. He'd expected her to insist on taking care of Matt herself, the way she'd done for James. Then again, he wouldn't have been surprised if she'd simply fallen apart. Some women could get a might squeamish about blood, after all.

Instead, there'd been nothing. She'd given no hint of fear or concern for Matt. In fact, she hadn't glanced once at Matt the entire time she'd been in the kitchen. It was just—odd.

Ethan tensed. Was that a—

Wait, there it was again. A thump followed by a muffled whimper. He was out of bed in a shot, his mind raced. The window in her room had been open. Had one of Vega's men managed to scale the wall and get inside somehow? He yanked on his buckskin trousers, not bothering with the buttons, and snatched his gun from the holster hanging off the back of a chair.

Ethan raced into the hallway. He shoved Hope's door open, ready to do battle. His eyes probed the shadows, searching for an intruder. All he found was Hope. She was sitting up in bed, her back pressed hard against the headboard. She clutched the sheet to her heaving chest as she stared, wild-eyed, at visions he couldn't see. Tears welled and rolled unheeded down her luminous cheeks.

Ethan peered around the room to make sure he hadn't missed something, but no one else was there. The tension drained from his body. Without conscious thought, he hurried to her side, sinking down on the bed, unmindful of his state of semi-undress. The gun slid to the floor. With careful hands, he took her by the shoulders as she shook her head from side to side, her eyes locked on some point beyond him.

Her tormented whisper wrenched his heart. "No...Please...Please don't leave me. No—come back, daddy…" Her voice caught on a hiccup. "Uncle James, don't leave me alone…"

"Hope…" Ethan reached up and stroked her face, fearful of frightening her further. "Hope, you're dreaming, sweetheart. Wake up now."

"Uncle Matt…No, it's my fault, I'm so sorry—Matt, please…Please don't die." Her anguished entreaty broke on a sob.

Ethan shook her again. Guilt over his unjust accusations pierced his conscience. "Hope! Snap out of it!" His voice was harsh.

Hope blinked, glancing around the room with red-rimmed eyes. Peering at Ethan, she frowned. She was so cold, goose bumps raced up his arms just sitting this close to her. She lifted her hand to the square patch of white bandaging on his bicep. Without warning, she dissolved into a fresh storm of tears. These were no feminine sniffles, no dainty weeping—not for Hope. No, she went the full mile with tear-soaked, gut-wrenching sobs.

Ethan sat motionless, staring goggle-eyed at her. Oh, shit. What the hell had he gotten himself into?

Instinct pulled her flush against his bare chest. He tucked her head into the crook of his neck and patted her back. It was like hugging a weeping block of ice, the hands that crept around his waist were pure frost against his skin. He ran his hands up and down her back and arms, trying to chafe some warmth into her. She burrowed into his heat in response.

Through tears and incoherent sentences, he got a rare and unexpected insight, at least to some extent, of the toll her losses had taken on her, both physical and emotional. He thought of the things he'd said to her earlier, and a sharp wave of self-loathing crashed through him. Then something caught his attention.

Her muffled voice tickled his chest. "I'll go. I'll hurry, before anything else happens."

His heart lurched. "What?"

Hope pushed away from him a little, though not all the way, as he'd yet to relinquish his hold on her. She used the corner of the sheet wedged between them to dry her face before she looked into his eyes.

"I'm leaving...tomorrow." Her voice was a little steadier, but a sniffle slipped out.

Ethan snarled, "The hell you are!"

"You don't understand. I don't have any choice." He had to strain to hear her now. "I have to go, for Matt's sake." Then her eyes lit on his bandage once more, and she softly added, "For your sake."

"You're not making any sense. Matt needs you. You can't just walk away."

He gripped her shoulders, keeping her caged, unable to move away. Her hands fluttered in the slight space between them, settled on his chest. Ethan forced himself to focus on her words, even as the silk of her hands seared his bare flesh.

"Do you think I want to go? Do you think I want to be alone?"

"Then why go?" His fingers dug into her upper arms. He had to be hurting her, but he couldn't make himself let go.

"If I don't go, Matt will die! Just like daddy, just like..." She bit the words off, but it was too late. He knew exactly where she'd been heading.

"Just like James?" He stared at her for a long moment, until she couldn't stand it any longer and turned her head away. Shame stained her cheeks bright pink. He gentled his hold on her and sucked in a deep breath through flared nostrils. She tried to hide behind the thick curtain of her hair, but Ethan refused to yield. He pressed the tip of his finger beneath her chin until their eyes met once more.

He deliberately kept his voice calm and

reassuring, his stare earnest. "You didn't kill them, Hope. It wasn't your fault. The fever...the illness took them."

"But I wasn't strong enough to stop it," she whispered, her hushed voice filled with torment. "I should've been able to...I don't know, I should have... I wasn't enough."

"How could you have stopped the bullets that wounded Matt?" Ethan reasoned. His heart wrenched at the abject pain etched on her beautiful face. He knew, too well, what it felt like not to be enough.

"If I'd...I should have..." Hope stumbled over the explanation, her hands fisting fitfully against him. "I could tell Matt wanted to talk to me about something, I should have asked him to stay. He wouldn't have been out there if I'd only—"

"The man who shot Matt would've tried again later. Another time. A different day. Nothing you might have done would've changed that." He prayed she wouldn't ask about that man, or the reason he'd had Matt shot. He wasn't ready to have that conversation. Not yet. Maybe never. "I'm sorry, for earlier. I shouldn't have said those things. I know you care." He moved his face closer to hers, peered harder into her eyes. "I won't let you leave, not now. I'm sorry, sweetheart, but I can't do that."

What troubled him was he didn't know *who* he was keeping her here for. Matt? Or himself?

She stared at him, silent and thoughtful. Her beautiful eyes were still bright with unshed tears.

"I'm sorry, too—for slapping you." Hope smiled tremulously, taking a deep, steadying breath. Her fingers traced the contours of his cheek, sending shivers of awareness coursing through his body. Her breath was sweet upon his lips. "You've been so kind and helpful, with the horse and—"

"Stop it!" Ethan's fingers dug into her shoulders

once more. “Don’t look at me like that. I’m not another one of your damned uncles. Kind to you, my ass—” He gave her a rough little shake. “If you’re not careful, you might find out how much I—”

Her eyes widened in surprised wonder. That was his first mistake...looking into her eyes instead of standing up and walking out the door. A yawning chasm opened up in front of him. His second blunder was letting his gaze slide to her lips. Want gave him a vicious shove, and he tumbled into that yawning hole. Ethan crashed headfirst into a churning, implacable sea of desire.

Ethan gave up without a fight, letting the current drag him under.

His mouth lowered to hers. Lips caressed, teeth nipped. By slow degrees, Ethan deepened the kiss, surrendering to the spell that was Hope. He slid his tongue inside her mouth, tightened his arm around her waist, pulling her hard against him. His tongue mated with hers, tangling over and over, growing more insistent, more demanding by the second.

Hope’s hands tightened on his shoulders. Instead of pushing him away as he half-wished—half-feared—she would, she drew him closer. His muscles flexed and rippled beneath her tentative exploration. Her skin was a powerful aphrodisiac, and he imbibed without restraint. Her hands explored his flesh, burning him, enflaming him. They slid up over his flexed biceps, across the tense muscles of his back, down to his waist. Everywhere she touched, she left a trail of scorching need in her wake. Her guileless, innocent kisses were driving him delirious.

Ethan’s own hands were by no means idle. With steady determination, he worked loose the tiny row of mother-of-pearl buttons cascading down the front of her thin nightdress. Cool night air whispered between them for a fleeting moment before his hand covered her breast, possessive and hungry. Restraint snapped. Ethan angled his head, deepening the kiss, giving himself over to ferocious need. His free hand fisted in the material at her back, dragged her nightdress over her shoulders, down and out of his way.

Tugging her arms free, she reached for him again. She gasped aloud as his lips blazed a trail down the side of her throat, nipped at her collarbone, then branded their way back up the other side of her neck. She tasted so sweet; he couldn't get enough. The sound of her ragged breath was music in his ears. By the time his lips settled on hers again, his own breathing became a thing of the past, inconsequential in the face of desire.

Her pulses thrummed beneath his tongue, driving him crazy with the knowledge that he affected her the same way she did him. His mouth turned voracious, passions he'd held tightly reined broke free—raged free—eager to incinerate them both.

Ethan eased her down onto the mattress, settling over her as spears of pleasure raced through his blood. His mouth plundered hers as his hand caressed her silky flesh. His fingers skimmed over her delicate skin, plucked at puckered nipples, and traced the contours of her flat stomach. She arched up against him, silently begging for his next touch, his next caress. Her lips were soft, and oh-so-responsive beneath his.

Ethan's good intentions fell by the wayside. The waking had turned to comforting. The comforting to unbridled passion. Now, her skin was his world, her lips his soul. Her passions were the volcano into which he joyfully leaped. Burying his throbbing shaft deep inside her was more important than breathing.

Claiming her for his own became Ethan's sole

reason for being.

Her hands slid up over his chest, and he forgot he had no right to be holding her like this. She purred deep in her throat as he flicked her pebbled nipple with the pad of his thumb, and he could no longer remember she was vulnerable. She tunneled her fingers in his hair, her tongue parrying and thrusting right along with his, and he forgot she was Matt's daughter. He lost all touch with reality as he stretched out on her bed, half covering her, ravishing her mouth, exploring, memorizing, savoring the feel of her body writhing beneath his.

Hope's hand worked between them, her inquisitive fingers tangled in the light trail of hair that disappeared into his sagging trousers. The sensitive skin below his navel tightened beneath her gentle touch as her explorations grew increasingly bolder. His lips slanted again, devouring hers as he surged his hips against her in greedy demand.

Ethan worked the hem of her nightdress up until his palm rested on her bare hip. The gauzy material pooled around her waist. His eager fingers smoothed over her supple skin, angling for the silky triangle of curls at the apex of her thighs. She writhed beneath him, whimpering low in her throat.

A bright flash of lightning illuminated the room. The resounding crash of thunder shook the house, rattling the windowpanes. Sheets of rain swept down, pouring into her open windows, splattering on the tiles of her floor in fat, heavy drops. The wind picked up speed, swirling through her room, extinguishing the lamp, plunging them into darkness.

Ethan tore his mouth from hers. His hands stilled, but they didn't lift from her flesh. Not yet. He blinked down at her through the shadows, his ragged breath sawing in and out. Laying rein to his desire was almost more than he could manage. The brilliant flash of another lightning strike illuminated her face. She looked as disoriented and lost as he felt. Reality exploded, like the roar of thunder following the lightning. Hope closed her eyes and sucked in a sharp breath. She tried to cover herself with shaking hands, a task not easily accomplished as his hands were still upon her—as was he.

Ethan took his lead from her, removed his hands from her body. Reluctance and regret knifed at his gut. He turned away and sat on the edge of her bed. His mind was sluggish, bogged down with unappeased desire. He scrubbed his hands over his face. Her scent clung to his skin, the taste of her lingered on his lips. With a stifled groan, he gained his feet, strode to the window, and closed it. Pressing his forehead to the chilled pane, Ethan willed his blood to cool, waited for his racing heart to slow.

He turned at the slight rustle behind him and found her sitting up once more, clutching the sheet to her breasts. Her hair fell about her in wanton abandon, dark as ink against her milky-white shoulders. She was wide-awake now, he had no reason to linger. And yet he couldn't force his feet to carry him to her door.

Her eyes were wide and luminous. Her lips were swollen from his kisses. His blood—still simmering—roared to life once more. He took an involuntary step forward, then gritted his teeth in frustration and forced himself to stop. He was speechless. What was he supposed to say? Sorry seemed a bit lame, and she'd see right through him anyway. He wasn't sorry. Confused, maybe. Shocked by the intensity of his need for her...definitely. Hard as granite inside his buckskins for want of her...desperately so, yes.

But he was *not* sorry.

"Don't...don't say anything, just please...please go."

Ethan stared at her for several long moments. Although it went against what he wanted—went against everything inside him screaming for him to stay—he nodded, retrieving his gun from the floor, and did as she asked.

Cursing himself every step of the way.

Chapter 7

Ethan avoided Matt's room all morning. He couldn't continue to do so for much longer, not without drawing some serious questions. He'd ducked from Natalia's questioning frowns several times as it was. She'd finally cornered him in the stable, informing him Matt was awake and asking after him. Her smile was a bit too knowing for his peace of mind when he'd given her one excuse after another as to why he couldn't go to Matt right away.

Now here he stood, staring at the door to Matt's bedroom, bracing himself. Praying Matt wouldn't be able to read the guilt all over his face. Squaring his shoulders, he pushed the door open and sauntered in with what he hoped was a bright smile plastered on his face and a glib comment on his tongue. Matt would expect nothing less, after all.

Matt reclined against a small mountain of pillows, pale as a ghost against the white sheets. Heavy bandages covered his chest and shoulder. Dark circles smudged his eyes. He offered a lackluster smile as Ethan ambled into the room and strode to his bedside.

The pit of Ethan's stomach felt oddly hollow, but he forced a teasing glower. "When we agreed to combine the herds, I thought we'd be sharing the workload. I didn't realize I'd be stuck doin' all the damned work. What the hell do you think you're doin', lollygaggin' in bed at this hour?"

He finally noticed Hope seated in the far corner by the window. An open book lay on her lap, and a healthy blush tinged her cheeks. His confident banter faltered. She wore a vibrant green morning gown the same shade as her beautiful eyes. Her hair was loose and flowing down her back, reminding him of how she'd looked last night, sitting on her bed with nothing but the sheet to shield her from his hungry stare.

Their eyes connected, and the color in her cheeks deepened before her gaze slid to the intricate floral pattern on her coffee cup.

He cleared his throat, shuffled feet. It took him a long, uncomfortable moment to find his voice. "Mornin', Hope."

She lifted her wary gaze to his. Faint shadows lingered beneath her eyes. Her face was pale beneath her blush, but she looked damned good to him—too damned good. Desire balled in his gut, hot and hard, making it difficult to breathe.

"Good morning, Ethan," she replied, subdued.

"It's about time you got here." Matt sounded like he'd sprinted through the South Pass. He drew a labored breath and croaked, "I need to talk to you. Hope, would you mind givin' us a minute."

Ethan's stomach dropped to his knees. How the hell had Matt found out? Was the guilt written on his face for the world to see?

Hope shot to her feet, startling him. She'd startled Matt, too, judging by the sudden frown he shot at her retreating back. "I'll go and check on your broth, Uncle Matt." Her eyes were riveted to the floor as she hurried from the room.

Ethan shifted from one foot to the other, turning his hat round and round in his hands. Nerves jumbled inside him, worse than the time the old priest caught him kissing Mary Elizabeth Sanders out back of the church. He jumped when Matt broke the silence.

"Hell and damnation," Matt growled.

"Look, Matt, I know what you're thinkin', but I can—"

His words crashed with Matt's grumbled complaint. "Damned broth…I got shot, for the love of God. There ain't a blasted thing wrong with my stomach."

The uneasy explanation died in Ethan's throat, and he frowned.

Matt motioned him forward with a flick of his wrist, his expression preoccupied. "I need you to do something for me."

Moving closer, he sank down onto the chair Natalia had pulled close to the bed last night, relaxing a little at Matt's tone, and nodding.

"I need your help with Hope. I don't know how long I'm gonna be laid up like this," Matt rasped, grimacing as he shifted his weight. "I need someone to look after her till I'm back on my feet."

Ethan's initial response was to shake his head and tell Matt that it was a bad, *ba-a-a-ad* idea, but he couldn't do that without explaining why. The reasons were numerous—and damning. Hope's soulful eyes and quiet confidence. Her temper and her alluring lips. Her strength and her luscious breasts. Those reasons and more were too much temptation for him to resist for long.

Instead of denying the request, however, he found himself sitting still as a statue while Matt went on speaking.

"It's not fair to let her take care of me, not the way she did James, not the way she had to do with Jacob and Serena…" Matt's voice trailed off, his pensive gaze centered on the highboy on the far wall.

"For Christ sake, Matt, you're not dyin'—"

"Well, of course I ain't dyin', don't be ridiculous." Even though his exhaustion was obvious, Matt's tone rang with sudden irritation. "It'll take a hell of a lot more'n a couple lousy bullets to put me down. I just don't want her cooped up in the house while I'm laid up."

"Nobody's safe with Vega still out there," Ethan reminded Matt.

He ran his hands down the thighs of his trousers, his palms gone damp at the prospect of hours and hours, day in and day out thrown together with Hope. Unchaperoned. He needed to get his mind off that subject—pronto—so he launched a diversion.

"I've been thinking it's high time we took this war to Vega. The tracks washed away in the rain last night, but I have a pretty good idea where they're holed up. My bet's on the canyon west of the Old Mission. I know it sure as I'm standin' here, Matt. That place is riddle with caves. He could slink off into one or another at any given moment, and no one would be the wiser. Hell, some of those caves interconnect. I could go out with some men and we could smoke 'em out..."

"No, Ethan." Matt shook his head, exhaustion thinning his voice. His face seemed paler than when Ethan had first come inside the room. "No. He'll be expecting you. They know they got me. Maybe Vega thinks I'm finished this time. He's a sneakin' rat, but the bastard's smart. He'll guess that's what you'd do...go tearin' off lookin' for revenge. Vega'd use your anger to his advantage. He'll have another ambush waitin', and you'd ride headfirst into it."

"I can't sit here and do nothing—"

"I need you here," Matt cut in. "Hope need's to know she's safe. I can't protect her, not like this. I know I'm asking a lot, but you have to stay at the Bar M. I don't want her to feel like a prisoner. Give her ridin' lessons. Take her out and show her your place. I don't know...just keep her interested. I need you to stay close to her, keep her safe for me."

Matt paused, seemed to choose his next words

with care. Ethan had been scrambling to come up with a plausible excuse—any excuse—why he couldn't be in constant contact with Hope, but one glance at Matt's pale face and Ethan's excuses flew right out the window. Her words, her plans last night to leave came back to haunt him. Matt needed this time with his daughter. What kind of friend would Ethan be if he didn't do everything within his power to see that Matt got that time?

"Ethan, I need you to make her see this is a good place to be—not just a place to visit once in a while—but a good place to live. I don't want her to be afraid to stay after last night. I don't want her goin' back to Maryland. I've lost so much time with her already.

"I know she's old enough to decide for herself if she wants to stay or go. Lord knows, she can afford to do either. James and Jacob left her everything: the house, the farm—hell, Ethan. Accordin' to the figures James's lawyer sent, she's as well off as you or I. Hell, maybe more so." Matt shifted on the bed, sweat beading his brow.

"If Vega finds out about her, how much she's worth...or that she's my daughter..." Matt gasped, touching a shaking hand to the thick bandage on his chest. Ethan cringed. Surely it wasn't good for Matt to be getting worked up like this. "Lord, I can't even bring myself to think about what he'd do. It's almost enough for me to send her away again. God help me, I'm startin' to sound like James, but I don't want to lose her. Not when I finally have her."

"And when are you gonna get around to tellin' *her* the truth?" The minute the words left his mouth, Ethan could have kicked himself. The last thing Matt needed right now was a lecture.

"I planned to last night after supper. Let me get a little stronger, and I swear I'll tell her. Please, do this for me. Give her a reason to stay."

With the events of last night in Hope's room still fresh in his mind, Ethan found it difficult to agree to something that should've been so easy he wouldn't have given it a second thought. All Matt had done was ask his friend to watch after his daughter while he was laid up. Show her a good time. It was a reasonable enough request.

However, what Matt essentially had done was give the wolf a key to the henhouse. More to the point, what was eating at Ethan was the fact that, either way he went...whether he refused Matt's request and confessed to Matt about last night, or whether he held his tongue and did as Matt asked...he was damned.

When Ethan hesitated, Matt's brow began to wrinkle. "I realize you'll need to go check on things at your place now and again. Antonio's young, but he's capable. I'll ask him to—"

"All right," Ethan barked, holding up his hand. "Okay."

Matt settled back into the pillows, relief smoothed the lines on his brow. "Thanks, Ethan, I owe you..."

"No." Ethan shifted, gritting his teeth as the weight of the days to come—and what could happen between them during that time—settled upon him, heavy and burdensome. "No, you don't owe me a damned thing."

"You saved my butt out there last night. I owe you for that, at least," Matt argued.

"Let's call it even and leave it alone." Ethan toyed with the brim of his hat, unable to meet Matt's eyes.

"Not yet," Matt hedged. "There's one more thing."

Ethan tensed, waiting for the deathblow.

"Last night made one thing clear to me. If something happens to me, Hope would be on her own. I trust you more than I trust anyone. You know that. I need to ask you, as my friend, Ethan, if something happens to me, I'd rest easier knowing you'll be there to look after her. That you'll take care of her…at least until she finds a husband."

A feather would have knocked Ethan from his the chair. Dear God, this was too much. How was he supposed to respond to a request like that? Unable to form a coherent word, he stared at Matt as though he'd lost his mind. Then Matt's last comment hit him—right between the eyes—and he wanted to howl a furious denial. How in the hell was he supposed to sit back and watch her with another man? His mind reeled, and one predominate thought outweighed all else.

Over his dead body.

Before he could respond—not that he had any idea *how* to respond—the woman under discussion gave the door a sharp knock and pushed the door open. She carried in a large tray, filled to overflowing with food and set it down on Matt's bedside table, careful to sidestep Ethan as she went.

Matt eyed the pile of food with a mixture of alarm and hungry interest. "I swear! That woman's answer for everything is to shove food down your gullet! Honestly, where does she expect me to put all that? Well, hell…" He struggled against his pillows, gritting his teeth. "I guess it's better than that damned broth."

Hope smiled at Matt's gruff words. "When I told Natalia that Ethan was with you, she said he skipped breakfast this morning. Sorry, Matt, all you get is broth. I believe the rest is for Ethan." She bustled to the bed and helped Matt lean forward while she stuffed more pillows behind him.

"Where the hell am *I* supposed to put all that?" Ethan echoed Matt, wide-eyed. Then he got a better peek at the tray. "Oh, no, you don't. I see *three* cups here, Hope. She intended for you to eat as well."

Hope shook her head, avoiding his eyes. "I already had my breakfast hours ago."

"What'd you eat?"

Hope fisted rebellious hands on her hips, her chin elevated. "Coffee and toast."

Ethan snorted and grumbled, "Bird food."

Twin points of crimson burned high on her cheeks. "It's what I always have for breakfast. And it's *not* bird food!"

"It is," Ethan argued. He eyed her, determined. "Sit down and eat."

"I will not. I told you, I've already eaten."

"Sit down and eat something—or I'll feed you." Ethan lifted a brow when she wheeled around to gape at him, silently challenging her to push the issue.

Annoyance bubbled in her eyes. Ethan was vaguely aware of a strangled gurgle coming from the back of Matt's throat—he felt the weight of Matt's confused stare upon him—but his determination would not be swayed. Hope needed to take better care of herself.

Just as Ethan was about to rise, she stomped to the tray and picked up Matt's broth, holding it between them like a shield. "Matt needs to eat first."

She lifted the mug to Matt's lips, cradling the back of his head in her hand. Carefully avoiding Matt's eyes, Ethan followed her movements, noting the ease with which she aided Matt. Yes, she'd done that before. A twinge of sympathy tickled his breastbone, but he was careful to harden his expression when she returned the mug to the tray.

"Your turn," Ethan reminded her.

Hope shot him a quelling look as she sat down with a harrumph and began nibbling at a large pile of eggs on one of the plates. Ethan rolled his eyes, but, under the circumstances, he didn't push his luck. She was following orders. It was a start.

Hope remained quiet and watchful, while Ethan discussed relocating the herd with Matt. Having picked up on Matt's deliberate avoidance of mentioning Vega's name, Ethan followed Matt's lead and carefully phrased his comments accordingly.

"Why don't you set your own trap for this person whose name you're trying so hard to keep quiet? I'm assuming he's the one who had Matt shot?" She looked first to Matt, then to Ethan. "You know, you might be able to come up with a solution if you weren't so busy trying to talk over my head."

Matt let out a troubled sigh. Ethan turned a disgruntled frown her way.

"She was going to find out sooner or later, Matt. She might as well hear it from us."

Hope frowned, waiting for someone to speak. "Well?"

Ethan looked to Matt, who seemed to be weighing his options. When Matt continued to hold his tongue, Ethan pressed, "Vega's dangerous. Forewarned is forearmed."

Matt shifted, grimaced again, and nodded. "We started havin' serious problems with rustlin' about four or five years ago," he began. "We've learned the renegade's name is Vega—Juan Carlos Vega y Montoya. From what we've been able to piece together, he came up from the Val Verde area. He's been right busy...burnin' buildings, rustlin' cattle, startin' stampedes. In recent years, he's grown bolder...added kidnappin' and murder to his resume."

Ethan caught Matt's troubled gaze flicker his way before sliding back to Hope's face. "Rumor has it he feels Texas should still be part of Mexico, and he picked this area, for some reason, to lay siege to white interlopers. He left several messages to the effect that his mission is to 'cleanse the land of all gringo's.'"

"But...you and Ethan—Ethan's family—you've all been here for years and years. It doesn't make any sense." Hope turned a puzzled stare to Ethan. "Does he even know you?" She turned back to Matt. "Does he know either of you?"

"Not to our knowledge." Ethan shifted in his seat, turned his weary gaze toward the open window. "He's hit a few of the other cattlemen, but in the past couple of years, he's been targeting the Bar M and the Circle K almost exclusively." He didn't add one crucial fact, didn't want to give her anything else to haunt her nightmares. Vega knew enough about him and Matt to hit where the damage would hurt the worst.

If Vega found out about Hope, found out what she meant to Matt...what she'd come to mean to him... Ethan's blood ran cold in his veins.

"Can't the authorities do anything?"

"In this territory, men are a law unto themselves." Matt scowled, gently touching the bandage over his shoulder. "There are the Rangers, of course, but they've been focusin' on rustlin' around the border. The U.S. Marshals have bigger fish to fry, and the local sheriff's as worthless as tits on a boar."

"Has he made direct attacks before? Has he...has he hurt anyone else?"

Tension hung heavy in the room as Matt's eyes darted to Ethan once more. Ethan leaned back in his chair, gritting his teeth against the rush of memories. He stared at a point on the wall, just above Matt's head. He couldn't look at her, not with those images of that long ago day burning in his heart. Matt cleared his throat.

After an interminable moment of silence, Ethan snapped, "Yes."

As if sensing the strain in the room, Hope stood

up and laid a hand to Matt's brow. "Are you in any pain, Uncle Matt? You look pale, perhaps you should rest now."

Matt's relief was written clear as day all over his face. Ethan felt like he'd run gut-first into a longhorn stampede. Hope leaned over Matt and plumped his pillows, pulled the sheet and blanket a little higher, and tucked them at his sides. Ethan's gaze followed her movements, and he was struck once again by her efficiency in a sick room.

Not bothering to look his way, she addressed Ethan from over her shoulder. "Matt needs his rest. You'll have to come back later."

His eyes lingered on her even as he told himself to turn away. The feminine scent that was so uniquely Hope lingered in the air. Ethan caught himself drawing it in deep, savoring it. Cursing beneath his breath, Ethan stood and stalked to the door. With eyes glued to the floor, Hope reclaimed her perch by the window.

Matt's voice stopped him on the threshold. "Ethan, about earlier..."

Ethan's gaze slid to Hope again. She stared with rapt absorption at her book, blatantly ignoring the tension in the air around her. Despite himself, he couldn't fight back the grin. She hadn't noticed that her book was upside down. Ethan turned his eyes back to Matt. He stared long and hard, then nodded reluctant acceptance.

Before he could give his motives a second thought, Ethan hurried from the house. He didn't stop until he was inside the stables. Distracted, Ethan nodded to Manuel as he passed on his way to the back of the building. Apollo twisted his head around to see who was interrupting his lunch. Snorting a soft welcome, the animal went back to chomping. Ethan slipped a brush from a nail on the wall. The horse glanced around again as he chewed, as though to ask what he'd done to warrant the extra attention.

With each stroke, the tension in Ethan ebbed a little. When Apollo's coat glistened, he led the horse from the stall and began mucking it out. Once he'd finished with Apollo's stall, he turned to another and another, seeking refuge from his attack of conscience in hard, physical labor. As the day wore on—and he ran out of work in the stable—Ethan wiped the sweat from his brow with his forearm and made his way back to the main house. He passed a horse tied to the hitching post. His eyes narrowed. His pace quickened.

Damn…how long had *he* been here?

The sound of tinkling laughter greeted his ears as he entered through the door off the kitchen. He followed the sound down the cool hall and into a little-used parlor at the front of the house, the muscles in his stomach clutched tight.

Hope sat at one end of the small sofa, cup in hand. Daniel Masters sat beside her, his arm draped along the back of the sofa behind Hope with casual nonchalance. She was smiling over something Masters had remarked on, residual laughter gurgled from her lips. Ethan's vision blurred, he saw green first.

Then he saw red.

Blood red…

Unmindful of the fact he'd spent the better part of the day mucking out stalls—and smelled unpleasantly of his chores—Ethan sauntered into the room as though he owned it and everything in it…including the woman on the sofa.

"Masters," he snapped. His greeting was cold, his posture hostile.

"Kincaid," Masters bit out, matching him look for look, tone for tone.

Ethan stared at Masters as if he were something

undesirable stuck to the bottom of his boot. "What brings you out here?"

The cool smile on Masters's face turned predatory. "I met Miss Lewis at the hotel yesterday, and I couldn't wait to get better acquainted."

"Is that so?" Ethan's voice was whisper soft, very smooth. Deadly.

"I'm sorry to hear about Matt's...unfortunate mishap." The sticky sympathy Masters poured on for Hope's benefit made Ethan's stomach churn.

"I'll just bet you are, you sorry son of a—"

"Mr. Masters has been entertaining me with stories of his travels abroad," Hope interjected with smooth finesse. She lifted a delicate eyebrow at Ethan's filthy clothes. "Matt is resting right now. You should have plenty of time to clean up before you go in to see him."

"I'm sure Matt would want me to see to our guest's comfort." He gave Masters a brittle smile. "How soon will you be leaving?"

It was all Hope could do not to gasp in shock at Ethan's rude behavior. Though her words were for their guest, she pushed to her feet and glared at Ethan. "I'm sorry, Mr. Masters. If you would excuse us for a moment, I need to have a word with Ethan...*in private*."

Masters smiled, oozing charm so thick it was small wonder the man didn't float out the door on the tide of it. "By all means, and please, since I hope we can be...*good* friends, I do wish you'd call me Daniel."

If Ethan hadn't been present, she'd have politely ignored the request. As it was, she simply offered their guest a perfunctory smile and acquiesced. "Daniel."

Ethan snorted. He stood, waiting for Hope to move ahead of him to the door. He followed her out into the hall, but he stalled her when she was about to speak by taking her arm and leading her farther down the corridor toward the stairs. Once they reached the foot of the stairs—well out of earshot of the parlor—he released her arm and leaned a careless elbow on the banister.

"Why are you being so...so boorish?" So much for her legendary composure.

"He's no good, Hope."

Cocking her head to the side, Hope pressed, "How is that, exactly?"

Ethan rolled his eyes and heaved a put-upon sigh. "He's a snake. He runs that damned bank of his on a lick and a promise because he knows the people in town don't have any other options. He's so crooked he'd steal a bone from a blind dog. Look, if you don't want to believe me, fine, but ask Matt...hell, ask Natalia. Just steer clear of him."

Hope pursed her lips, eyeing him with growing frustration. While it was true she'd spent most of her life tucked away from self-centered rogues such as Masters, she wasn't a complete simpleton. Yes, she'd invited Masters in for a cup of coffee. Yes, she'd laughed at a few of his jokes. She was being a gracious hostess, nothing more. She was not a rube. She'd read the look in her guest's eyes, read his body language well enough. She knew where his intentions lay.

His intentions held no sway...or say...with her.

She didn't need Ethan—or anyone else for that matter—pointing them out to her as though she were a naïve child fresh from the schoolroom. The fact that Ethan felt the need to enlighten her rubbed her the wrong way. It made her...oh, what was the word she'd heard that man at the train station shout at his mule? Ornery, that was it.

Yes, she was definitely feeling ornery.

"Hmm..." She tapped her lip with one finger. "I'll keep that in mind. But, so far he's been *very* kind." Hope cocked her head sideways and added with suggestive innocence, "Perhaps I should ask him what his preferences are as far as—holding skinny women, was it? Do you suppose he'd be accommodating?"

As she turned away, the corner of her mouth curved in a sarcastic smirk. Ethan's hand snaked out and grabbed her arm, yanking her roughly back to face him. The cord in his jaw ticked with rapid-fire fury, every muscle in his body was rigid. His narrowed eyes flashed with dangerous fire. "What the hell is that supposed to mean?"

She gave her arm a vicious tug. "It means that you're an even bigger idiot than I thought. I'm not stupid, Ethan...believe it or not. I've dealt with men like him before and still managed to walk away with my virtue intact. Give me *some* credit."

The thought crossed her mind then that the only man to hold any real threat against said virtue now stood glaring at her as though he'd like to turn her over his knee.

"Then why are you even talking to him?"

"I was being polite, you...you bonehead. I don't know what the business relations are between Matt and him, and I didn't have time to ask anyone before he showed up unannounced. I didn't want to offend someone who may be important to Matt." She tugged in vain at her arm again. "But I'm seriously beginning to rethink that policy."

Hope glared at him, giving her arm one last good jerk, yanking it from his slackening grip before she turned away.

Then she stopped in her tracks, glancing over her shoulder with regal disdain.

"Oh, and, Ethan, you really should go dunk yourself in the stream." She wrinkled her nose, aiming it high in the air. "You stink."

With that parting shot, she glided away.

His harsh bark of laughter caught her by surprise. She paused for half a heartbeat, gritting her teeth, but she refused to glance back at him, unable to determine who'd won that particular round.

Chapter 8

Despite the yawns she'd played up for Daniel's benefit, she wasn't anywhere near ready to retire for the evening. It was still early, and sleep held no appeal. That didn't mean she was ready to face Ethan though. No, she needed time before she dealt with him again.

The walls were closing in on her, so she wandered out the back door and across the yard to the bunkhouse. Matt's foreman had been in rough shape the last time she'd seen him, it wouldn't hurt to check on him. The fact it was well on to dark now—and she was about to knock on the door of a bunkhouse that could be filled with strange men—didn't hit her until her knuckles were inches from the wood.

At that moment, as her hand hovered in sudden hesitation, the decision was no longer hers. The door swung open and a tall, half-naked shadow stepped through the opening. She gasped, scrambling to leap out of the way.

"What the hell..." The shadow's strong hands shot to Hope's shoulders, steadying her, then jerked away.

She gasped, heat rushed up her neck, clear to the roots of her hair. This was all Ethan's fault. If he hadn't pushed her temper beyond reason, she'd have thought this through a little better, would've realized what a bad idea this was *before* she'd come out here.

Determined to make the best of a bad situation,

she forced a disgruntled smile and chirped brightly, "Ah, hello!"

Matt's foreman's lips twitched, but he stepped back to a polite distance. Light poured out through the door, bathing them in a golden glow. His silky, dark hair hung in a straight sweep down his bare back. His naked chest was lean and smooth, yet corded with defined muscles. A second wave of heat burst in her cheeks. Sheltered as she'd been, naked male flesh was the stuff of imagination and girlish whispers. Now that she'd come to Texas, encountering it face-to-face seemed to be a regular occurrence.

She didn't know whether to giggle, or swoon.

Velvety, dark eyes scanned her face. Sensual, sculpted lips twitched again. "Hello."

"I didn't get the chance to properly introduce myself last night, and I wanted to check on your wound, make sure you're doing all right. I don't have any experience stitching up—well, you know—and I wanted to make sure I didn't do more harm than good. How do you feel by the way?" She was babbling, so she snapped her mouth shut. Then, realizing she hadn't even given him her name, she thrust her hand at him. "I'm Hope, by the way."

Enveloping her hand in his, he brushed his lips across her knuckles before releasing her. "I am Antonio. It's nice to meet you…again."

Her eyes closed for a moment in mortification at her own forwardness. Drawing a deep, fortifying breath, she blurted, "How are you feeling?"

"The leg throbs a little, but you did a good job sewing me up. I was actually going to come to see you in the morning." He braced himself against the doorframe. The line of his jaw tightened. "I wanted to thank you, though to be honest, I don't remember all that much. Did I, ah…did I do singing by any chance?"

Antonio's easy candor and shamefaced expression soothed the tension in her shoulders. A hint of a mischievous grin toyed at the corners of her mouth. Hope solemnly nodded her head, confirming his fears, and couldn't stop herself from giggling as he closed his eyes and slapped his palm to his forehead.

"*Madre de Dios*," Antonio muttered.

He rubbed at the back of his neck, slid his eyes to hers with a sheepish half-grin. "And, did I, ah…did I say anything else?"

Something about the way he blushed tickled her. She couldn't resist teasing him…just a little more. Grinning with mock innocence, she bantered, "Don't you remember?"

If his eyes rolled any harder, she feared they might well pop from his head and land at her feet. He groaned, loud and long. She couldn't help it. Laughter boiled over.

Crossing his arms over his chest, Antonio suddenly chuckled. "You're teasing me."

"Actually," she drew out, making his chuckle short-lived. "You did quite a lot of talking. It was all in Spanish, though, and I don't speak the language, I'm afraid. I'm sure you could ask Ethan though, if you want to know what you said. Or Natalia…"

Antonio groaned when she mentioned Ethan, groaned louder when she added Natalia's name to the list of those who'd witnessed his shame. The sound was so miserable, so harassed, that Hope had to fight not to laugh aloud again.

She failed.

Antonio shifted against the doorframe, easing some of the weight from his leg. She noticed the motion, caught the glimpse of the pain flicker over his brow, and sobered. "You need to get off that leg."

"I will in a spell." He shrugged, obviously playing it down.

"Now," she argued.

She took him by the elbow, steering him back inside like a feeble invalid. With as much dignity as possible, given the circumstances, he hobbled across the room and settled on his bunk, his frown disgruntled. Hope picked a pillow up, plumped it, and leaned toward him, intent on stuffing it behind his head.

His expression changed so abruptly, Hope nearly giggled again. The man was truly priceless. He was handsome…almost as handsome as Ethan, in fact. But she hadn't giggled this much since she was a young girl. His eyes swerved to the door. Suddenly, he couldn't seem to get her out of there quick enough. He jumped off the bed as though shot into the air by springs and bundled her toward the door so fast she could do little more than stutter in surprise.

"Thank you for all your help last night, but you shouldn't be here." He hobbled behind her, knocking his knee on the foot of one of the bunks. A heated string of foreign words ripped from his mouth, but he propelled her forward without breaking stride. "The others will be back soon. It wouldn't do for them to…they might think that…"

It took a moment, but his cobbled sentences finally clicked. Nevertheless, his fluster was so comical, Hope burst out laughing again. As she cleared the threshold, she turned back to say goodnight. Before she could open her mouth, the door closed in her face. She stared, slack-jawed, at the weathered wood mere inches from her nose. Hope blinked. She must be losing her mind, for the sight of the door, so close to her face, wrung a fresh peel of laughter from her.

It seemed a book in her room was the only safe bet this evening. Hope meandered back inside the house and up the stairs, still smiling to herself. She stepped inside her room and lit the lamps. Humming to herself, she crossed to the chest to retrieve a soft nightdress. Hope's mind began to drift while her fingers fumbled with the tiny buttons lining the bodice of her dress.

She'd seen more excitement in the short time she'd been at the Bar M, than she'd had the entire time she'd lived with James. It was like living in the middle of a dime-store novel. Gunfights and renegades. Rustlers and ambushes. She shook her head, astounded by it all. Awestruck. Then Matt and Antonio's injuries—and Ethan's—came flooding back to her. Any one of their injuries could have been lethal. Her smile died, replaced by an uncertain, worried frown.

After changing, she opened the window. A gust of fresh air swept inside, and she filled her lungs, savoring the crisp scents. She closed her eyes on a blissful smile. Humming again, a haunting melody remembered from childhood, Hope opened the lid of her trunk and leaned in to retrieve a dog-eared book.

Her gaze fell of the corner of the thick packet of letters Matt had sent to James.

She chewed on her lower lip as she withdrew the packet. She'd intended to return these letters to Matt. Drawing a deep breath, she set the book aside and let curiosity get the better of her. Clutching the packet of letters, Hope crossed to the chair near the window.

With infinite care, Hope untied the faded ribbon and lifted the first letter from the stack. The envelope was worn and mud-stained. The writing on the outside was barely discernable. Anticipation built as she slid the ragged piece of paper from the envelope, fascinated. She frowned then, confused, as she stared at a torn section of old wallpaper roughly the size of a piece of stationary. Peering closer, she noted the light, sideways scrawl on the faded floral design.

The letter, addressed to Matt, was from Martha Lewis, Hope's grandmother. The spidery lettering sent an odd pang of longing through her. Martha had died well before Hope had been born. This letter was a sad reminder of the family she'd never had a chance to be a part of. She swallowed the painful lump in her throat, strained her eyes.

"All is well at the farm and Jacob is home for a few days. There's been no word from James yet, but we've heard there's trouble near him. Jacob and Serena are getting married..." Hope's heart skipped a beat as she strained to read the scrawl at the end, but the words trailed away into a smear of grime, and she could read no more.

She leaned back in the chair and stared at the piece of paper, her lips twisting in disappointment. The mention of her parents tugged sentiment from her heart. She missed them so much. As she lifted the paper, she turned it over in her hands, hoping for something more on the back.

She was delighted to see her hopes had not been in vain. There was writing, but not the spidery scrawl of her grandmother's hand. No, these were the bold, slashing strokes of Matt's flamboyant penmanship. He'd pressed much harder on the paper, and his words were still legible. This letter was to James, dated Christmas of '61. He'd used the back of his mother's letter to write to James. She remembered James explaining this had been common practice during the war when there was a shortage of paper.

Her eyes skimmed Matt's letter. He'd made vague mention of a skirmish near the border, and he'd commented that his regiment was sure to see more action before the campaign was finished. There was a very brief, almost terse, sentence requesting James convey his regards to the newlyweds.

And that was it—nothing more.

Hope's brow wrinkled as she tucked the letter back inside the envelope and set it aside. One would think Matt would've been a little more enthusiastic about his brother's impending nuptials.

She reached for another envelope. Matt referenced the tensions heating up around the border, although he didn't specify where he was. He stated the fighting he'd predicted had begun, preventing him from coming home as he'd earlier assumed he'd do. He wrote of some of the horror's he'd seen, the details were gruesome and unfiltered, the confidences of one soldier to another—one brother to another.

The next several letters were the same, filled with fighting and bloodshed, and very little about his family. Hope set the letters aside, her expression troubled. Her heart went out to the man who'd written them, he'd sounded so disheartened, so lost. She shuddered at the missions he'd described, so cold and violent.

So dangerous.

What must brutality like that do to a man? It was no small wonder Matt had survived any of them. She hesitated to read more, but then she noticed an envelope dated just after her birth. She couldn't resist.

The letter was succinct, the tone more than a little stilted. Matt gave the name of his new post, inquired as to Serena's health, and that of the babe. Was it a boy or girl? Had mother and child come through without any difficulties? How was Jacob's health?

The letter ended there—no offer of congratulations for his brother on the birth of his first—and only—child. He offered no regards for Serena, nothing more. Hope frowned. Uneasy now, Hope set the letter aside. She couldn't quite put her thumb on it, but something had changed in the timbre of Matt's letters. He'd withdrawn from his family right there on the pages before her eyes.

Hope sifted through the next several missives, noticing the dates were spaced farther and farther apart with each successive note. The contents were limited to general inquiries of health and made mention of some of the action he'd seen, Burkittsville and Crampton's Gap. Then Chancellorsville, where Matt had sustained a serious wound. There was no further mention of his family after Chancellorsville, no inquires, no acknowledgements. Sequentially, Matt's letters tapered to non-existent until after the war ended.

There was a large gap in time, and she almost chose that intermission to call it a night. However, the date at the top of the page on the next letter leapt out at her. Her hands shook as lifted it from the stack.

Some of the words were blotched, as though droplets of water had splattered the page. The letter was crumpled and dog-eared.

James,

I received your telegram in St. Louis. Know that my heart is there with you, and with little Hope. I am a coward, brother. I cannot turn my footsteps home. You have to understand. You, of all people know how I feel…how I felt.

I can't bear to see them in the ground. I can't bear to think them gone. I guess if I don't see the graves, if I don't see the tears in little Hope's eyes, then maybe I can go on believing they're still alive and well and living happily on the farm Jacob loved so much. Please don't think ill of me. I can't help the way I am. I know I've let you down. I know I've left you to shoulder my burdens as your own, and for that, I'm truly sorry.

I understand the farm is struggling right now. I'll send what money I can to help on that score. I know it's not nearly enough, but it's the best I can do. Look after Hope, God knows she's better off there with you than with me, wherever I end up. I'm heading out to Texas, to the Kincaid ranch outside of Johnston. You can send any correspondence for me there for the time being. I'm sorry, James. Know that my heart is with you and Hope, even if I can't be.

Matt

Hope let the letter flutter to her lap. Memories, clear and sharp, flickered through her mind, a poorly written tragedy reenacted. The shadowy scene of a cemetery under the haze of drizzling rain swam before her eyes. The scent of damp, freshly turned soil and the pungent aroma of autumn leaves clung to the air. A chill, so bitter it took root in her very bones, came back to her along with the memory, making her shiver once again.

The scene sharpened. A warm palm rested on her shoulder...James's palm, supporting her, giving her the strength to stand, dry-eyed and stoic, near the side-by-side gaping holes as rain turned the mounds of fresh dirt into mud. From that point on, it had been the two of them. The two of them, as the mourners arrived. The two of them as the mourners straggled away.

Just the two of them...

A flash of anger bubbled inside Hope. How could Matt abandon James like that? He'd left James to face burying his brother and sister-in-law, left him to deal with a failing farm. On top of that, James had shouldered the burden of raising a young girl, alone. Matt had left James all alone at one of the most difficult times in his life. How could Matt have been so irresponsible, so selfish?

Her hands fisted at the injustice. Then they

eased. She'd never once heard James utter a single harsh word against his brother. Quite to the contrary, every time James had mentioned Matt, it had been with a note of pride in his voice. Pride and unmitigated love. He'd never held Matt's absence against him.

Drawing a deep, cleansing breath, she set the letter aside. She stifled a wide yawn. Shivering, she stood and rubbed her arms. She paused for a moment, staring out the window at the mountains in the distance. Could she blame Matt for running away? She'd wanted to do the same thing so many times herself. If James could let it go, she'd no business dragging it back out and picking up a grudge for it. She could let it go, too.

Hope closed the window and stepped back. She extinguished the flame of one lamp, turned the other down low, crawled onto the bed, and burrowed beneath the blankets. The tone of Matt's letters weighed heavy on her mind as she lay there, considering the moonlight seeping through the curtains. The man who'd written those letters was so unlike the warm and welcoming Matt she'd come to know.

What had happened to him? Why had he been so distant and impersonal with a family that clearly needed him? Sleep flitted just beyond her reach for a long while as doubts and questions filled her mind.

****

Ethan returned to the main house on silent feet, treading straight to his room. He stripped down and washed before dragging on a worn, comfortable pair of buckskins, not bothering with the buttons. He prowled the confines of his room like a lethal predator scenting blood on the air…waiting impatiently for the kill. The plans he and Antonio devised to lure Vega rolled through his mind. Anticipation held him alert and tense, denying him sleep he knew he needed. He wanted to catch Vega so much he could almost feel his hands around the man's throat.

As always, when the need for vengeance snapped at him, memories of Christina—and her death—were never far behind. Unbidden, scenes flashed through his mind, so vivid his pulses raced. The fire at his ranch haunted him as if he were standing right in the middle of it all over again.

Acrid smoke rose up around him, choking him. The scent of charred flesh filled his nostrils, making him gag. His eyes burned, his lungs begged for air. The dying screams of horses pierced his ears as white-hot flames raced out of control. The stables had gone up like dry kindling before the rampant flames of a wildfire. But the stables had been a diversion designed to keep them busy while Vega launched his lethal campaign. Nothing more than a clever opening act.

A cruel precursor of the horrors to come.

After they'd failed to save Ethan's stables—the horses never stood a chance—the men returned to the scene of utter devastation at the Bar M. Matt's own stables had been torched, the corral destroyed. Bodies littered the ground like broken playthings.

The destruction at the ranch hadn't held a candle to the horrors they'd found in the mountains. The gruesome carnage waiting for them there made full-grown, seasoned men retch in stunned shock.

That cold mountain pass flashed before Ethan's eyes. A thin wisp of smoke from the cooling embers of the bonfire curled grasping fingers into the night sky. Smoke rolled from the corpses even as his men stumbled from their horses, sick with grief.

The abducted women lay prone...broken and mutilated beyond recognition. Stifling the urge to gag, his nose buried in the crook of his elbow, Ethan turned the charred bodies over, one after another, searching for Christina, his heart lodged in his throat, his mind trapped in some strange limbo, torn between horror and hope. Once they'd identified the last body and she'd not been among them, he prayed as he'd never prayed before. Prayed she'd somehow managed to escape.

Prayed she still lived.

Matt's startled, horrified curse had shattered his soul.

Ethan sprinted across the clearing on legs that had gone strangely numb. Even as he fought Matt and Antonio to get to her, he knew. He wrestled free, falling to his knees at her side, terror and disbelief, grief and hatred all swelled inside him…killing everything else.

Ethan gasped for air, bracing his hands on either side of the window. Chilly night air washed over his body, drying the cold sheen of sweat the memories provoked. He fought against remembering, but the memories were stronger than he was, sucking him back, dragging him deeper.

Vega had staked her fragile wrists and ankles to the ground, her clothing lay about her in bloody shreds, the bone handle of a huge hunting knife protruded from the middle of her chest. Blood pooled in the dirt beneath her, soaking the ground in a congealing black puddle. Cruel letters bloodied the tender flesh of her bare stomach.

'Gringo whore.'

Sobbing, Ethan cut her free. Hot tears streamed down his soot-soaked cheeks. He gathered her close, cradling her in his arms as he rocked back and forth. Her head fell back against his shoulder. The straight, dark brown hair disappeared and a lustrous cloud of ebony spilled over his arm. Ivory cheeks held not a hint of color, and glazed gem-green eyes stared lifelessly back at him.

Ethan jolted, cursing.

This was not Christina's face but Hope's haunting his vision, and he reeled in shock.

Ethan gasped for air. He ducked his head through the window into the cool night, fighting back the waves of nausea. On weak knees, he stumbled across the room. Dropping onto a chair, he braced his elbows on his knees, and braced his forehead on his palms. Drawing a ragged breath, Ethan ran his splayed, shaking fingers through his hair. His hammering heart threatened to crack his ribs.

Ethan hadn't fully regained his equilibrium when a familiar cry pierced the night. He was on his feet and running to her before he could even draw breath. He skidded to a stop inside Hope's doorway, his eyes locked on the huddled form on the bed. He couldn't turn away, couldn't stop himself from sitting down next to her. With shaking hands, he reached for her.

She'd twisted and thrashed in her sleep, tormented by the images in her mind. The sheets lay tangled at the foot of the bed. Her thin nightdress had worked its way up above her knees, and the buttons at her throat were loose. Her tousled hair lay all around her.

Ethan's hands fisted as desire rose up inside him, unbidden...unwanted. He paused for a moment, forcing himself to draw back. He'd almost convinced himself to get up and leave, when she flipped over on her side. She must have sensed his presence, felt his heat, because she wiggled closer, curling herself around him, seeking comfort.

Ethan stiffened.

She whimpered.

He froze.

Hope's brow was troubled. She murmured in her sleep, tossing her head from side to side. Then the words began to escape her lips. Tremulous and whisper soft. Terrified and burgeoning with grief. He couldn't have been more stunned had a brutal fist reached inside him and ripped his still pumping heart clean out of his chest.

"Ethan! No, please…don't go…don't leave me…"

His eye swerved to her face. She was still asleep—and apparently dreaming about him. An odd tenderness flared in his chest. Protective instinct spurted throughout his body with every spasm of his yearning heart. He pushed her hair back from her face, smoothed his thumb over the grooves between her brows. Maybe he could ease her out of the dream without waking her. Then he'd slip from the room, and she wouldn't even have to know he'd been there.

"Shh, sweetheart, shh," Ethan crooned softly.

Hope's eyes popped open. Her disorientated gaze darted around the room, frightened.

So much for slipping out undetected.

"Hope?" He touched her shoulder. "Are you all right?"

"Ethan?" She peered up at him. "You…You're not…oh, thank God, you're not dead."

He blinked at the absurdity of her comment.

She bolted upright, almost knocking him from the bed. Her small, cold hands flew to his chest, gliding up over his neck and shoulders, patted down his ribs, smoothed across his stomach.

"Hope—" Ethan's strangled groan choked off the rest of his words as her fingers brushed the open waistband of his buckskins. The feel of her hands running over his body—in his already aroused state—was more than he could bear.

"Thank God, you're okay," she cried, collapsing against his chest. "I thought you'd been shot, I thought you'd—"

"I'm okay." He captured her hands, laid them flat on his chest so she could feel the strong, if albeit unsteady beat of his heart.

He sat on the edge of her bed, clad only in unbuttoned pants. She lay across his lap with nothing but the flimsy barrier of her nightgown separating him from her soft flesh. Her bare thighs pressed to his side. Skin on skin. Ethan gritted his teeth in torment.

"I'm sorry," she mumbled, dropping her forehead against his chest, leaning into him. Her hands trembled on his bare skin. "Give me a minute."

"Sure, no problem," he croaked.

Ethan squeezed his eyes closed—tight—and willed his hands to stay motionless on her back. He tried to force his mind onto something other than her sweet curves pressing against him, encased in the thinnest barrier of soft cotton.

He failed.

She took a deep, calming breath. Leather, soap, and warm male. The unique combination of Ethan's scent enveloped Hope, slipping through her senses. His heat surrounded her. The raw strength of his work-roughened hands gliding over her back melted her muscles, draining away the last of her night terrors. She relaxed into him, her body softening in his arms, and she was helpless to resist. His lips brushed the top of her head, and the unexpected caress warmed her from the inside out.

She leaned back in the circle of his arms, her hands lingering on the smooth muscles encasing his ribcage. Tipping her head back so she could look into his eyes, she murmured, "I'm sorry." Ethan's cobalt stare was intense, and she couldn't maintain eye contact for long. She closed her eyes, dropping her chin in mortification. "Maybe I should move to another room so I don't keep waking you up like this."

He pressed the side of his crooked knuckle beneath her chin, regarding her with a shrewd stare. "Do you have these dreams often?"

Her embarrassed gaze slid sideways, but she nodded, a tiny, almost imperceptible motion. "Often enough..."

"You will *not* move to another room." His tone left no room for argument.

Startled, she met his eyes once more, her lips parted at the fierceness of his expression. Swallowing, she nodded.

Ethan released a long sigh and shifted away from her without another word. She assumed he would leave now. Deep down, she dreaded the thought. Instead, he turned the lamp off and nudged her over, crawling onto the bed beside her.

She squawked, squirming away. "What do you think you're doing?"

"Getting comfortable," he muttered as he rolled to his side, reaching for her.

Hope batted at his hands, her breath trapped deliciously in her throat. He ignored her gasps of protest, ignored her flailing hands, and slid his arm around her waist, pulling her snug against him.

"Ethan, you shouldn't—"

"Go to sleep, Hope," he whispered against her ear. Slipping an arm beneath her head, Ethan curled his warm body against her stiff back.

She may have been an innocent, but the hard line of his arousal pressing against her backside was unmistakable. Every long, rigid inch of it branded her, and her head swam. Craning her neck, she twisted her head around to look at him as best she could. Her voice went an octave higher than normal. "What do you think you're doing?"

The grin he shot her reeked wicked intent, rattling what little composure she'd managed to scrape together. "You already asked that question."

"Then give me a real answer." She wiggled, trying in vain to turn in his arms so that she could glare at him more effectively. So that the intimate press of him didn't rattle her quite so much.

"Hold still, damn it." Ethan groaned aloud, pressing her tighter against his body, subduing her movements. He hissed between his teeth, his words sounded strangled and forced. "Did the nightmare come back after I left last night?"

Unable to squirm away, Hope stilled in the steel cage of his embrace, startled by his astute question. His eyes met hers, penetrating in the dim light, and she couldn't lie. Somehow, he'd know.

"Yes, they did. But—"

"Exactly," he countered in a serious, matter-of-fact tone. "So I'll stay with you tonight. That way, if the nightmares come back, I can chase them away again."

Her heart melted. Her mouth fell open in surprise, but words were beyond her.

"Go to sleep. I'll behave if that's what you want—even if it kills me," he promised, solemn and steady, though his eyes held a mysterious, alluring promise of their own. His burning gaze fell to her lips. A wolfish grin spread across his lips, sparking those funny flutterings she couldn't seem to shake whenever he looked at her that way. "Unless, of course, you'd like me *not* to keep my hands to myself, because I'd be very happy to..."

"No, no! This is fine. We'll sleep, just sleep." She shifted her face away from his and wrapped her arms tightly around the arm he'd slipped around her middle. After a grin like that, she didn't trust him not to change his mind.

As if her feeble efforts were enough to hold him at bay should he chose to misbehave.

A deep sigh whispered over her skin as he nuzzled his nose into the curve of her neck. "Then I guess we'll sleep."

The softest of kisses feathered along the side of her neck, just below her earlobe, sending her pulses skipping. His head settled on the pillow behind her. Long minutes passed, and she began to let her guard down, relaxed into him. Her eyelids drooped, her breathing started to slow down, even out, and she began to float into oblivion.

Warm breath tickled her ear. His husky voice rumbled, "Hope?"

It was so dark, so comfortable. She was safe at last, cocooned in his arms. Sleep was so close, had never come with so little effort before.

"Hmm?" she murmured, oblivion hovered only a few flutters of her eyelids away.

His warm hand brushed the bottom curve of her breast. Something hot and hard rubbed against her bottom once, twice. "Feel free to change your mind—anytime."

It took a long moment for reality to bring her to the surface, but when it did, her eyes snapped open, and she stiffened like an oak plank in his arms. His chuckle was dark, tormented. He tightened his arms, holding her in place when she would have squirmed away. She didn't relax again until his steady, deep breathing announced his slumber.

Sleep snuck up on her quickly then, cradling her in soft dreams.

****

Sunlight streamed across the bed, warming Ethan's eyelids. Soft curves warmed his side. A very pleasant way to wake up indeed, he thought as he stretched languidly. He opened his eyes and squinted, yawning. With that yawn came instant understanding of where he'd spent the night.

In Hope's bed.

He turned his head, peering down at the top of her head where it nestled comfortably in the crook of his shoulder. Her slim arm draped across his naked chest. Her nightdress had worked itself high on her thigh, and she straddled his leg. One of her bare knees wedged between his thighs.

Stifling a moan, Ethan rose to the occasion accordingly. He'd intended to wake hours ago and slip from her room, well before Natalia woke. He eyed the angle of the sun and wryly decided there was no chance of that anymore. He couldn't remember the last time he'd slept so late, or so peacefully. He stretched, and Hope snuggled closer.

He smiled.

Might as well make the most of the morning. One little kiss—or two—and the sight of her blushes would be one hell of a way to start the day.

Ethan gently nudged her until she rolled onto her back. He really shouldn't be doing this, but she was more temptation than he could resist so early in the morning. Hell, she was more temptation than he could resist regardless of the time. He moved cautiously, easing himself atop her. Slowly, teasing, he nipped at her lower lip, nuzzled his way along the fine arch of her neck, intent on waking her with pleasant kisses.

She purred soft and low, deep in the back of her throat, stretching cat-like, pressing her breasts against his chest. Encouraged, goaded by his inner demons, he slid his hand up over her curves, working free the last three buttons on her nightdress before slipping his hand inside to caress her warm flesh. Ethan set his lips to the pulse fluttering at the base of her throat and suckled, laving her flesh with his tongue. He felt more than heard the breath catch in her throat, and Ethan grinned, radiating male satisfaction.

Ethan lifted hungry lips to hers, and she responded with wild abandon. Their breath mingled, tongues danced. Her inhibitions had completely deserted her in this state of semi-slumber, stealing his breath, wreaking havoc on his control. Her breast filled his hand, her nipple hardened against his palm. Ethan burned with need.

Suddenly that limited contact wasn't enough. His hand slid down to her knee, sliding slowly up to her hip, pushing the thin material higher. His fingers encountered the silken curls covering her womanhood, and his insides clenched tight. She was hot and wet, and he shuddered.

Only a few more inches, a lascivious voice somewhere in the back of his mind taunted. It'd be such a simple matter to lower his buckskins a few inches—they were already unbuttoned and riding low as it was. It would be so easy to slip inside her tight heat and ease the excruciating ache in his loins, to hell with honor and self-restraint.

She lifted her knee, braced her foot on the bed, and rubbed her thigh against his. Her hips moved in suggestive invitation. Conversely, it was that motion that snapped him back to his senses. Ethan tore his mouth from hers. He drew a ragged breath, tormented by the murmurs of protest slipping from her lips. It hit him then, exactly what he'd done. Gazing down at those sleepy, passion-drugged eyes, he ground his teeth at his own stupidity.

He'd gone too far...pushed her too far to stop now.

She probably wouldn't be too happy with him for this later, but she'd be a whole lot angrier if he left her like this, writhing in unquenched need.

Ethan shifted slightly to the side, muffling her incoherent, mumbled protests with his lips. Hope wrapped her arms around his neck, and Ethan deepened the kiss, stroking his tongue against hers as his hand skimmed her thigh. He reached higher, higher until his nimble fingers found the small nest of silky curls once more. There he set his fingers to play, deftly fanning the flames.

Her hips began to rock against him. Her breath came in shallow gasps and ragged pants. The delighted sounds escaping her lips tormented him. He was ravenous. Her responses were driving him out of his mind. It took a will of iron not to take her then and there.

Ethan angled his head, deepened the kiss, savoring her passions, drawing out her pleasure. Each approving purr and every delectable sigh echoed in his painful, throbbing manhood. He slid down her body, kissing and licking as he went until he set his mouth against her, wringing a startled, strangled groan from her lips. Her hips bucked up against him in surprise…in supplication. He was all too happy to oblige. And when she was there, balancing precariously on the precipice, he hurled her over the edge and into oblivion. Her cries of ecstasy filled the room until he settled back at her side to quiet them with his own mouth.

Ethan soothed her body with his hands and lips, settling her back into a blissful haze of satiated sleep. He leaned back and gazed at her peaceful features. The tenderness in his heart, for all the smoldering heat, warmed him through and through.

Ethan leaned down and placed a gentle kiss, lighter than the brush of butterfly wings, on her lips. Reluctant, he slid from her bed and slipped from the room, cursing himself as the pain of unquenched desire ripped into him with cruel precision.

Despite that gnawing need, a smug grin curved his lips and his steps were light.

One hell of a way to start the day, indeed.

Chapter 9

Hope stood in the open doorway, squinting with narrow-eyed fury into the dim shadows inside the stables. There she spied her quarry. He moved with efficient, masculine grace through the wide aisle and into a large stall at the far end of the building, a bucket in one hand and a grooming brush in the other. Murmured voices drifted through the dust motes in the cool interior, warning her he was not alone. She didn't care. Fury outweighed common sense.

She trembled from head to toe as she stomped through the aisle, tiny fists clenched at her sides. Fresh hay crunched beneath each purposeful step. Several horses poked their massive heads over stall doors. Inquisitive equine eyes followed her progress as Hope neared her destination. The stall's door was propped wide open. Ethan's unmistakable, deep voice—murmuring Spanish words with such effortless grace—grated on her last nerve even as it sent a shiver of intimate recognition through her.

After what he'd done, how *dare* he sound so calm, so…so unaffected.

She stopped in her tracks just outside the stall. Manuel and the horse both turned her way. Ethan didn't acknowledge her at all. Instead, he continued to brush the animal's sweat-slicked coat with steady focus, addressing Manuel in quiet, unperturbed tones.

The bastard.

She was dimly aware of Manuel's tentative

smile. His tone was polite, if subdued. "*Buenos días, señorita.*"

She slashed a narrow-eyed glance his way. Though she knew her expression bordered on lethal, she struggled to maintain at least some semblance of civility, and worked to level her tone. "Ah, I'm sorry. I don't speak Spanish."

"He said good morning," Ethan supplied, deadpan, his eyes riveted to the horses hide.

She glanced back to Manuel, gave him a tight smile. "Good morning."

Then, in the snap of a finger, she turned wrathful eyes on Ethan. Her toe tapped a steady, impatient pulse on the hay-strewn, hard-packed ground. "I'd like a word with you." The blade-sharp spear of anger sliced through her voice.

Seething, she waited for Ethan to put the brush down and face her. He didn't move. She'd worked herself into a fine snit as she'd dressed a short while ago, methodically constructing a scathing set-down in response to his audacious impudence. Now she was ready to let it loose. How dare he do those...those...things to her when she'd been unable to defend against them, against him?

Just as soon as he damned well turned around to look at her she was going to let him have it.

However, to her utter frustration, the blackguard continued to groom the damned horse, and he ignored her. She gritted her teeth, ready to explode. She couldn't, wouldn't tolerate a second more. Stepping into the stall, she reached around him and yanked the brush from his hand. Manuel's eyes widened. He took a hasty step back, presumably to watch from a safe distance.

"Turn around and look at me, damn you," she snarled.

Ethan faced her with insolent calm. The corners of his mouth curled with grim amusement. His eloquent, scorching gaze started at a point on her skirt at knee level, and rose in languid approval, lingering on her hips and her breasts.

Hope clenched her teeth and watched his lascivious stare rove intimately over her body. Her fury knew no bounds. She pushed aside those odd flutterings his stare awakened within her with ruthless determination. The sudden weakness in her knees, the nervous flutter in her stomach, the unexpected breathlessness. None of that mattered. The speech she'd rehearsed on the way to the stables filled her mind and helped refocus her anger.

Then the full brunt of his smoldering and decidedly unrepentant stare locked with hers. The burning desire in those bottomless cobalt depths swept through her like a fevered, physical stroke of his hungry hands on her bare flesh. The half-formed words lodged in her throat. To her mortification, all she could do was sputter for the glimpse of a moment, which, of course, poured fuel on her already raging fury.

Without thinking, without warning, her hand shot out and she slapped him, catching them both by surprise. The crack of her hand on his cheek echoed in the building, stunning her. Ethan didn't flinch, didn't as much as blink. The pink outline of her hand glowed on his cheek. Moreover, to her chagrin, the heat in his gaze intensified.

Hope's eyes widened. Shocked as she was by her own actions, when he reached for her, she was ready. She dodged his outstretched hands and scurried back several steps, scowling dire warning at him. He continued his determined advance, and she panicked. Hope threw the brush at him, aiming for his chest. Whether because of the adrenaline pumping through her, or because she was not of the habit of throwing things, the projectile missed its mark, and, instead, almost smacked him in the forehead. He ducked, and the grooming brush skimmed the top of his head, mussing his already tousled hair.

His eyes narrowed on her with a predatory glow, and he took another step forward. Again she retreated. Manuel's surprised chuckle brought her enough sense to beat a hasty retreat. She pivoted on her heel, snatched up her skirts, and ran. Nothing but harsh silence followed.

Hope rushed inside the house, refusing to glance over her shoulder for fear he pursued her. Her pulse pounded, her head spun. Forcing deep, even breaths, she marched down the hall, and, unthinking, straight to Matt's room. She remained silent and refused to meet his curious stare as she bundled about the room, struggling to regain her composure. Heat burned her cheeks as she selected a book from Matt's shelf and settled into the chair at his bedside to read to him aloud. A sound at the door drew her attention.

A long relieved breath seeped from her as Antonio strode inside the room, smiling. "Up for visitors?"

Hope set the book aside. She smiled as Matt motioned Antonio forward. Antonio presented a welcome distraction. He startled her though when he pulled a generous fistful of wildflowers from behind his back.

"I wanted to thank you for sewing me up."

Remembering their disastrous meeting last night at the bunkhouse, her lips twitched. "You're welcome."

Antonio sat down in the chair beside Hope, stretching his long legs in front of him, careful not to crowd her. His gaze lingered on her face, an odd, curious light in his eyes, and he cleared his throat and turned to Matt. "Did Ethan talk to you about his plans for the herd?"

Matt's health was improving. It showed. So did his worry. "Grazin' close to the ranch won't last long like this, but until we can decide what to do with Vega, it's the best we can do. Still, it poses a lot of risk. Ya'll are gonna have to be careful. I wish you'd wait till I was up and about."

"Ethan says now's the time to move. He's right." Antonio leaned forward in his chair and propped his elbows on his knees. "We've posted watch on the Old Mission, but nothing's panned out yet."

"Keep your eyes open."

Antonio nodded, turning to Hope. "I was wondering if you'd go for a ride with me later. Natalia mentioned you haven't left the house, and I thought you might like to get out and about for a while."

"Oh, well…actually, I don't really ride." Hope fidgeted with her skirt. Her fingers fumbled with the stems of Antonio's bouquet as she considered her history with equestrian success. The last time she'd ridden had been uneventful, unless you took into account Ethan's method of distraction. Regardless, the thought of riding made her skittish. Then again, maybe it was the memory of Ethan's calloused, hard hand gliding over her legs that turned her knees to mush.

What he'd done with those hands this morning…

Her blind-eyed stare shot to the flowers in her hand, heat burned her cheeks, and Hope popped up, catching both men off guard. She scurried from the room, mumbling beneath her breath, "Let me find something to put these in, I'll be right back…"

She took the flowers to the kitchen, cursing herself with every step for letting Ethan get to her again. She took a few moments to compose herself before returning to Matt's room.

Antonio's tone was cautious. "If you'd rather not

ride, Matt's suggested using Natalia's curricle."

Determined not to let Ethan—or his shocking behavior—ruin her day, she smiled sunny enthusiasm. "I'd love to go for a ride with you…in the curricle."

Antonio leaned back in his chair, grinning. "We should go now before it gets too late. We could take a picnic with us, if you'd like?"

Hope glanced at Matt, scrutinizing the peculiar expression on his face. He wasn't fooling her. He had the same look on his face James always got when he was up to something.

She turned back to Antonio. "Of course, let me grab my shawl."

Hope looked to Matt, lifted a shrewd brow as if to say, 'I'm on to you,' and left to fetch her shawl. She was back in a few moments, and bent to kiss Matt on the cheek. "Do you need anything before we leave?"

"No, no. You go on and have fun. I'm going to settle in for a nap." His grin was much too innocent for her piece of mind.

****

Ethan stomped into Matt's bedroom and demanded, "You see Antonio? We need to get a move on if we're going to get the rest of cattle in by sundown."

Matt lowered the book to his lap and smiled like a pup who'd just discovered his tail. "He took Hope for a ride and a picnic."

"It's the middle of the goddamned afternoon. There's work to be done and—what the hell? Hope doesn't like riding," Ethan snapped, eyes narrowing with his suspicion.

"They're taking Natalia's curricle." Matt marked his page with studied care and closed the book, tossing it aside with a devilish grin. "I gave him the afternoon off."

Ethan barked, "What the hell for?"

"Antonio was kind enough to offer to show Hope around. And since you haven't made any effort, I didn't see the harm." He prodded, all innocence, then he added in a sly tone. "He brought her flowers."

Ethan scowled. What was Matt talking about, flowers and picnics?

Stomping to the foot of Matt's bed, he gripped the footboard in white-knuckled fists. "It's not exactly safe to be gallivanting around out there with Vega still on the loose, you know. What the hell were you thinking, letting her out of the house?"

"I was thinkin' since you ain't gonna show her around, she'd be safe enough with Antonio. He was more than happy to keep her busy. I gotta say it. Ethan, I'm disappointed. I've never known you to go back on your word. But, since you ain't interested in helpin' me, I had to rely on *someone*." Matt's gaze turned thoughtful. "Then again, all things considered, maybe I shoulda sent Natalia along to chaperone."

Ethan pinned Matt with a hard stare. His reply was sharp and swift. "Why the hell would they need a damned chaperone? I thought you said he was just showin' her around?"

"Yeah, and takin' her on a picnic. Antonio and I had a little visit when Hope took the flowers he brought for her to the kitchen. He's requested permission to court Hope—"

"*Court* her? That's ridiculous. He doesn't even know her." Ethan bristled, tetchy as a long-tailed cat in a room full of rockers.

Ethan stomped around the room, grinding his teeth. He liked Antonio, he really did. But if his friend thought for one second he had a shot at Hope, then he damned well better get that thought right the hell back out of his head. She'd just got here, for the love of God. She was Matt's damned daughter—

not that Antonio or anyone else knew, of course. Hell, she was still in mourning, for Christ sake. She was...

She was...

She was *his,* goddamnit.

Matt's somber voice broke into his possessive train of thought. "I'm not used to havin' a girl to look after. You know, now that I think about it, I sure as certain should have sent a chaperone. That boy could charm the knickers off a nun. And the way he was looking at her when they left..."

Ethan stopped dead in his tracks, leveling an alarmed stare at Matt's face. Visions of Hope in Antonio's arms ate at him. Antonio kissing her. Antonio touching her...

He thrust those images aside and narrowed a suspicious stare at Matt. He was up to something, sure as Ethan was standing there. While it was true Antonio had more than his share of luck with the ladies, Ethan had never known Antonio to be anything less than a gentleman where any woman was concerned. Ever. Something was definitely going on here, and it stunk to the Pecos and back of a set up.

"What are you up to, old man?" Ethan glowered. Matt's gaze wavered for a split second, and Ethan pounced. "Matt, what are you up to?"

"I want her to stay in Texas, Ethan," Matt growled, cornered.

"And you'd do anything to get your way?" Ethan couldn't believe what he was hearing. "You'd push her on the first guy who comes along and shows the slightest interest?"

Matt crossed his arms over his chest, thrust his jaw out, and turned stubborn eyes to the wall.

The muscle in Ethan jaw leaped to life. He couldn't force a single word around the livid fist of fury clutching his throat closed. He exploded, slamming his palms hard against the footboard of Matt's bed, letting out a nasty string of inventive expletives.

"You know, none of this would've been necessary if you'd kept your word and shown her around, Ethan." The arrow of guilt missed the target, but, in a roundabout way, told Ethan all he needed to know.

It was a good thing Matt was already out of commission, or Ethan might very well have knocked him on his ass. "Oh, no, you don't, you sneaky son of a bitch! You're not putting this at my door."

"I'm just statin' the obvious. You know, I've been doin' a lot of thinkin'. Maybe Hope's not enough to draw the right prospects by herself. If I make it known she's my heir..."

Ethan's head was going to explode any second now...surely the next time Matt opened his cursed mouth. His nostrils flared. Knock him on his ass hell...Ethan was ready to strangle him with his bare hands.

Fearful of doing just that, he resumed pacing a rut in Matt's floor with a vengeance, ranting, "Are you insane? She's more than any man can handle, more than any man deserves. If word gets round you're putting the ranch up for—Hell, I can't even say it." Ethan snorted in disgust. "Every gold-digging mother's son this side of the Rio Grande will be chasing her skirts, and then some. Do you realize the position you'd put her in?"

Matt gave a casual shrug, but his gaze was too speculative, too knowing. "I guess it doesn't matter anyway. You obviously didn't want to get involved, so don't worry about it. If she stays because she falls in love with the ranch and the mountains, or she stays to marry Antonio—or someone else—what difference does it make? The end result is the same. She'll stay in Texas. Either way Hope ain't your problem anymore."

Ethan stopped pacing to glare at Matt, the muscle in his jaw working overtime. He exploded. "You want me to take her riding? Fine, goddamnit. You want her to fall in love with the goddamned mountains? You got it." He started pacing again, pointing a long finger in Matt's direction like a gun…loaded, cocked, and aimed with lethal intent. "You want her to stay? All right, damn you. But you keep the ranch out of it!" He stopped again, raked a rough hand through his hair. "And stop pushing Antonio or some other goddamned asshole down her blasted throat. Damn you to hell and back, Matt Lewis!" Ethan railed, shaking his finger again. "Just you remember—you asked for it!"

He stomped to the door with tunnel vision, too furious to see straight. Then, turning back once to glare at Matt's smiling face, he slammed the door hard enough a picture fell from a nail on the wall in the hallway. With a vicious snarl, Ethan stepped right over it and kept on walking. He wouldn't have been at all surprised had he walked by a mirror and saw steam rolling from his ears.

Chapter 10

Ethan stood in the doorway as the compact, two-wheeled conveyance pulled alongside the main house. Drawing back into the shadows, he waited, grinding his teeth. Hope leaned back against the seat of the curricle as her companion steered the horses into the yard, a warm smile curving her beautiful lips. Her shawl draped about her elbows, and her hair tumbled down her back, glistening blue-black in the late afternoon sunshine. He groaned, remembering how soft and seductive her hair had been against his bare chest.

The sound of her laughter floated to him, tinkling and light. Taunting him. Ethan ground his teeth again and, catching himself at it, forced his jaw to relax. It was a nasty habit he'd picked up with great gusto, it seemed, since Hope had arrived in Johnston. He snorted with a healthy dose of self-disgust. At this rate, he'd be gumming his steak and beans like old man Thornton down at Mirabella's Place.

"Thank you for taking me out, Antonio. The canyon was beautiful." Hope reached up and snagged a tendril of hair snaking across her face, tucked it behind her ear. "The picnic was perfect, just what I needed. I can't remember the last time I enjoyed myself so much."

Her words cut Ethan off at the knees.

"I'm glad you had a good time. I'd like to take you out again—soon." Antonio grinned, catching the errant lock that refused to be contained. Ethan stiffened as Antonio smoothed the strand between his fingers before tucking it back behind her ear.

Turning away from her, Antonio looped the reins around the brake and climbed down from the seat. Hope leaned forward into Antonio's outstretched hands. Once her feet touched solid ground, his hands fell to his sides but he didn't step back. Ethan couldn't see Hope now, hidden as she was by Antonio's broad back, but the tilt of Antonio's head was unmistakable.

Ethan almost came off the veranda, fists first. The kiss was over before it began and Antonio stepped back, but Ethan's body still vibrated with barely leashed violence. The kiss could have been nothing more than a friendly gesture, yet the thought of Antonio's lips on Hope's pushed Ethan straight onto dangerous territory. Territory he'd been precariously skirting since his little visit with Matt. Ethan's nostrils flared as he sucked in great, slow breaths with murder in his heart.

****

Hope's lips parted in surprise as she stared up at Antonio. She hadn't seen that one coming. She didn't know what to say.

Before she could react, Antonio took hold of the horse's halter and shot a smile over his shoulder at her as he walked away. "I'll look forward to the next time."

Hope stared after him, bemused, as he led the animals to the stables. Ashamed of herself for assuming the worst, she chalked the kiss up to nothing more than a friendly gesture. It sure as certain hadn't been as soul rending as Ethan's kisses were, after all.

Her brow wrinkled. Antonio was a very attractive man. He'd been so thoughtful and attentive today. She couldn't quite explain why, but being around him was easy, comforting. He'd make some woman very, very happy someday…some *other* woman, some *other* day. She gave a troubled sigh and turned to go inside.

She nearly tripped in surprise.

Ethan lounged in the doorway, arms folded forebodingly across his chest. She couldn't see his face clearly for the shadows, but the vague line of a frown marred his handsome brow.

How long had he been there? Oh, dear heavens, had he seen…

She clenched her teeth, determined not to let him upset her. She'd done nothing wrong. She'd spent an enjoyable afternoon with a pleasant man, nothing more. Besides, it was none of Ethan's business what she did, or who she spent her time with. Her gaze flickered over the yard in annoyance. The only other way into the house was to walk all the way around to the front door. There was no help for it, not without looking like a coward. She'd have to walk by him to get inside.

Straightening her spine, squaring her shoulders, she marched up the steps, back stiff as an iron poker, her eyes riveted on the doorframe at his side. Unfortunately, Ethan was taking up too much space, and she couldn't slip around him. He apparently wasn't of a mind to be accommodating.

"Excuse me," she snipped.

He didn't move an inch. "That looked cozy."

She glared at him but stood her ground. "*That* was none of your business. Please, step aside."

"I didn't realize you made a habit of kissing every man you come in contact with," he sneered, not bothering to conceal the dark growl in his tone.

"I don't!" Flustered, she planted outraged fists on her hips. "*You* kissed *me*. *He* kissed me. I *didn't* kiss him back. Kissing anyone wasn't a problem until I came here!"

He looked somewhat placated when she'd denied

kissing Antonio back. The sudden smile curving his sensual mouth sounded alarm bells in her head.

"Oh, but darlin', you did kiss *me* back. Don't you remember?" His eyes burned her as he slowly pushed away from the doorframe. "Because I do. I remember how you press against me every time I take you in my arms, I remember how you melt when I—"

"Stop it!" Her cheeks flamed. It was a wonder the main house didn't go up in flames for the heat rolling from her cheeks. "Just stop—"

"If you need a reminder, sweetheart, I'd be very happy to refresh your memory." Ethan stalked her, seductive intent boiled in the mesmerizing depths of his deep blue gaze.

"Ethan, don't—"

She threw her hands up between them and gasped, back peddling across the veranda until she teetered on the edge of the top step. Hope drew up, but not quickly enough. Her heel slipped off the edge, her arms wheeled. Ethan's strong hands shot out to catch her shoulders, steadying her. The fleeting contact sent shockwaves through her system. He pulled her forward, steadied her until she regained her footing, and dropped his hands to his sides. His eyes held her captive, trapping her right where he obviously wanted her.

Enthralled.

Damn him.

One stutter of her heart shuddered by…two stutters…then he lowered his head. His lips hovered a whisper from hers, stealing what little breath she had left, making her shake and yearn with a force she couldn't deny. He waited, his mesmerizing eyes half concealed beneath the thick sweep of his lashes, his hands loose at his sides.

In the end, it wasn't his lips lowering, but hers lifting that closed the distance. She gripped his shoulders. For balance, she lied to herself. Her body slid close, brushed against his. She had no ready excuse for that impulse. Her tongue slipped tentatively inside his mouth, mimicking the motions he'd taught her. She gave up trying to analyze—or justify—her actions.

This time, Hope steered the kiss, and left him physically trembling beneath her hands. Encouraged, she deepened the kiss, setting a wanton pace. She pressed herself against his arousal and rubbed, wringing a moan from him. His hands claimed her hips at last, holding her still, but he followed where she led, making certain she was keenly aware that *she* was the one in control.

Feeling deliciously wicked, Hope reveled in her power over him, savored the feel of his bunched muscles as they rippled beneath her inexperienced touch. Then, by infinitesimal degrees, he took hold of the kiss, bringing it to the surface until she hovered on the edge of reality. He drew his lips from hers, trailing kisses to a point below her ear.

Ethan's warm lips nuzzled the side of her neck, slipping beneath her defenses. "Promise to go riding with me tomorrow?"

"I promise," Hope mumbled, breathless, lost in the intoxicating warmth rushing through her veins. At that moment, she'd have gladly given a king's ransom—anything he asked, anything at all—if he'd just kiss her again.

His lips nibbled on her earlobe. "Hope?"

She melted a little at his tone, leaned into him, working to force sound through her parted lips. "Hmm?"

His tongue traced the contour of her ear. He drew her earlobe into his mouth, suckling gently. She shivered.

"*You* definitely did the kissing this time, sweetheart."

Ethan's grin was a mile wide as he stepped back and winked at her. He bounced down the steps, and swaggered to the stables—over six feet of smug, muscle-packed temptation—leaving her to stand on the top step, gaping like a half-wit at his backside.

Then again, what a backside it was...

Frowning, she gnawed on her lip and gave a tiny, bemused sigh.

****

The next morning, after taking her breakfast with Matt, Hope retreated to her own room for the morning. She'd spent the better part of the night eluding Ethan, hiding either in Matt's room or in the kitchen with Natalia. However, the way Matt and Natalia were acting was so bizarre, just being around them was beginning to give her a raging headache.

One minute they were polite, housekeeper to employer. The next, they were barely on speaking terms, though she knew not why. And, more puzzling yet, Natalia had begun sending her sympathetic glances. Then, just as baffling, the two of them were fawning, starry-eyed over each other.

It made no sense at all.

When you factored in Antonio's unexpected kiss—and Ethan's shocking behavior—she'd begun to think everyone on this blasted ranch had lost their bloody mind. Throw in a rotten night of tossing and turning, fighting off the nightmares, and it all factored for a sour mood, to say the very least. She'd half expected to wake up in Ethan's arms at some point in the night, but then she remembered he'd gone out late after supper with Antonio to check on the herd and didn't expect to be back before dawn.

Just as she picked up a worn page from the stack of letters, a sharp knock at her door broke her concentration. She glanced up in irritation and shuffled the letters below a heavy book. Swinging the door open, Hope came face-to-face with the very man who seemed to occupy so much of her thoughts lately. Her heart lurched. Her palms went damp. He looked so handsome standing there beating his hat against his thigh. His hair was windblown, spun gold. His quick grin floored her.

Ethan's sparkling eyes swept down over her dress, and he lifted a brow. "You're not wearing that are you?"

She frowned down at her dress, then up at him, confused. What was wrong with her dress?

Heaving a sigh, he shrugged. "All right…lets go."

Hope shook her head, baffled. "Go where?"

"Don't tell me you forgot." He crossed his arms over his chest. His lips curled. "You promised you'd go riding with me today."

"I did no such thing. I wouldn't—"

"Oh, yes, you did. Right after *you* kissed *me* yesterday," he enunciated.

"I, ah…I…" Hope sputtered, finally recalling the promise he'd slyly extracted while she'd been…otherwise preoccupied.

"Don't tell me you're going to try to back out now?"

"I never go back on my word." She glared, offended, stepping neatly into his trap.

"Well, then, is that what you planned to wear ridin'?"

"No, I have a riding habit, but—"

"Then you put it on, because we're leaving soon. That is, unless you need help getting' out of that dress," he suggested, wiggling his brow. His grin turned lascivious.

Hope's mouth fell open in shock. "I do *not* need your help."

He compressed his lips, looking more than a little disappointed, but his sinister grin took over once more. "I suggest you get to it then. I'll expect you out back in fifteen minutes."

Ethan turned to walk away, but suddenly stopped and glanced over his shoulder as she stood in the doorway wondering how he'd maneuvered her with such ease.

"And sweetheart," he murmured, his stare heating as it skimmed down to her toes and back to her face. "If you're not down in fifteen minutes, I'll assume you've changed your mind about wantin' help."

The slamming of the door was all the reply she gave him. His laughter echoed in the hallway as his boots pounded down the steps. How dare he?

Fifteen minutes later, almost to the second, Hope marched from the house and out into the bright, late-morning sunlight. A soft breeze stirred the tendrils of hair hanging loose at the nape of her neck. She adjusted the wide-brimmed hat she'd worn to shield her face from the glare of the sun.

Ethan stood between two saddled horses, holding their bridles, a grin flirting at his lips. Hope stepped down onto the hard-packed ground, and Ethan moved forward, looping the reins over the nearby hitching post.

She pointed at the familiar woven basket hanging from the side of Ethan's saddle and frowned. "What's that for?"

"Natalia figured we might not make it back for lunch, so she sent a picnic." Ethan took hold of her resistant hand. He firmed his grip, pulling her along.

"This is Daisy." He drew her in front of the small mare. "Hold your hand out so she can scent you."

Poised to spring back should the mare show the slightest interest in taking a bite out of her, Hope reluctantly offered her hand.

"She's gentle as a lamb. Matt kept her around the ranch for Natalia and—"Ethan broke off abruptly, cleared his throat. "She hasn't been ridden in some time, so I'm sure she'll appreciate the exercise."

Stroking the horse's muzzle with a cautious hand, Hope asked, "You're sure she's gentle?"

"Positive," he answered with a small smile, apparently aware she'd latch on to the slightest excuse to bolt.

Then, because she wasn't moving, he stepped behind her, placing his hands on her waist, pushing her ahead of him. Ethan kept his hands on her waist, guiding her until she was stable astride the mare. He smoothed his hand down her leg, adjusted the stirrup for length, before moving to the other side of the horse, repeating the process. When he was finished, he slid his hand back up her calf, over her knee to rest intimately high on her thigh, fingers splayed.

"We'll be riding into the foothills today. Some places are a little steep. Trust Daisy, she's been through the foothills thousands of times. She'll follow Apollo. You won't have to fight her." Ethan stared up at her, giving her thigh a gentle squeeze.

"Hold the reins firm, but don't yank 'em or you'll hurt her. She responds to pressure commands. If you want her to turn left, press with your knee, like this..." Ethan slowly slid his hand down her thigh until his palm rested on the side of her knee and pressed it to the mare's side. "Do the same on the other side to turn right."

"I feel like I'm going to fall off." Hope eyed the ground—so very far away.

"You won't fall off," Ethan assured her, his gaze intense, piercing. "Just keep your legs wrapped tight and enjoy the ride. I think you'll find you're a natural."

His lips twitched suddenly, and he turned away.

Ethan vaulted up onto his own saddle with a

confident grace she envied. He checked his rifle, and restored it to its sheath. Urging Apollo to a pace she could easily follow, he rode in silence. By slow degrees, Hope grew more confident that the horse beneath her wouldn't toss her into the dust and bolt for home at the slightest provocation. After a while, the tension eased from her shoulders as the beauty of the surrounding landscape filled her with wonder.

"These foothills are in the Guadalupe Mountain range. West Texas was once primarily inhabited by Apache, Comanche, and Kiowa, at least until after the war." Ethan's eyes scanned the land around them as he gave her a brief rundown of the area's history.

"A lot of ranches sprang up in the last decade or so. Until the last few years, we drove the cattle north to the markets. The Comanche, in particular, used to pose a very large problem. They hit the cattle trails pretty hard every year. All the ranchers took heavy losses. They stirred up enough trouble the government took notice. Back in '75, the army sent Shafter to clear out the Indians. Now we've begun to rely on the railroad to transport the herds. Did you know Matt rode with Shafter for a time?"

"I remember Uncle James talking about Matt doing some Indian fighting, but he never went into detail."

Hope glanced curiously at Ethan, wondering at how much more he knew about her uncle than she did.

Chapter 11

Hope's gaze lingered on Ethan as he nudged the brim of his hat back with a knuckle. He was a handsome man. There was no doubt about it. Just watching him set that odd little flutter loose beneath her breastbone. The tenor of his voice reached out and grabbed hold of her, drawing her into the story of Matt's life, so much more than those cryptic letters ever could.

"Back in '77, the army asked Matt to join the hunt for the infamous renegade, El Victorio. But by then he had the ranch going and too much on his plate to take off again." Ethan glanced at the sun's angle, and he nudged Apollo with his left knee. The horses began the gentle ascent up a dry, rocky slope dotted with prickly pear and clumps of long grasses. Daisy followed Apollo without any direction.

Hope frowned, searching her memory, mumbling, "El Victorio?"

She'd never heard the name before, and Matt hadn't mentioned him in any of the letters thus far. Then again, she'd come to learn that particular fact didn't mean all that much. It had become more than apparent James had elected to filter much of what he'd read to her about his brother's wanderings. For that matter, Matt's own letters themselves proved enigmatic more often than not.

"Victorio was one mean hombre," Ethan drawled, cutting into her musings. "He was a Mescalero Apache leader, chief of a renegade band of Chiricahua. He had a long and illustrious career, including raids up and down the Guadalupe Range and into Mexico. Victorio broke out of the San Carlos reservation in '77 and then, later, fueled an uprising on the Mescalero Reservation near Fort Stanton. The U.S. Cavalry and the Texas Rangers pursued him for two years. Mexican forces joined the fight below the Rio Grande. There's a canyon in the Sierra Diablo that carries his name."

The renegade sounded larger than life. But then, she'd come to view Matt that way as well. If not for the ranch, perhaps they'd have made formidable adversaries.

By the time they reached the plateau, the sun was high in the cloudless, cerulean sky. Ethan reined the horses in and dismounted, then helped Hope down. His hands lingered on her waist for one tense moment before he released her to hobble the horses.

Handing her the picnic basket, he reached for the blanket behind his saddle. As he spread the blanket on the ground, Hope wandered to the edge of the clearing, gazing down to the valley below. The Bar M was a small dot in the distance. Tiny men on miniscule horses herded miniature cattle, pushing them into an area near the small stables.

Her gaze drifted north to Ethan's ranch, and she smiled in pleasant surprise. The main house was a long, two story, sprawling adobe residence, with a large enclosed courtyard at one end. Ethan's spread was larger than Matt's, dotted with numerous outbuildings and two separate corrals. The smaller of the two was currently in use.

In the valley below, a group of men straddled the split beam railing, waving their arms in the billowing dust cloud. Though their voices couldn't reach her, it was quite clear they were offering encouragement to the man inside the corral...the one who'd just gone sailing through the air to land on his rump in the dust, hard. Hope stood motionless, fascinated, as the vaquero climbed to his feet, picked his hat up, and beat it against his leg. He rammed the mangled hat back on his head and advanced on the beautiful white horse with slow, easy steps. The animal danced away.

Without warning, Ethan's warm breath tickled the side of her neck. "Julio's saddle breaking the stallion today."

Hope jumped, bumping against him. Before she could move away, his hands spanned her waist, anchoring her in place. He didn't say anything else for the moment, just stood there, holding her against him. She stiffened, but when he made no further move, she relaxed, her attention centered on the struggle for dominance unfolding in the distance.

Hope watched as the vaquero approached the horse a little more cautiously now, holding his hand out to the jittery animal. The horse sidestepped, his attention affixed on every motion the vaquero made...the same way Hope was aware of the powerful man behind her. Aware of every breath he drew, conscious of his hands sliding over her stomach, shifting until he held her caged in the warm, steel band of his arms.

The basket dangled from her hands, nearly forgotten.

Her gaze followed the cowpoke as he made contact with the stallion. His hands began soothing, smoothing down the stallion's neck, running over its massive shoulder and flank. Always touching, always maintaining contact. The horse stilled.

Hope let out the pent up breath she hadn't realized she'd been holding. Ethan's arms tightened infinitesimally. The rough scrape of his stubbled cheek nuzzled her ear, and she leaned into him, unable to stop herself.

She bit her lip as the cowboy drew the horse's

head down, his face close to the animal's eye. He stood motionless for uncounted minutes, then he let go of the animal and walked away. Baffled, Hope waited while the vaquero strode with a slight limp to the opposite end of the corral, his back to the horse. The crowd around the corral went motionless. The breeze even seemed to still in anticipation.

Hope held her breath.

Ethan's cheek skimmed the side of Hope's neck, his day's growth of whiskers felt like sandpaper against her skin. A shudder of pleasure rippled through her. Where had her hat gone? Funny, she couldn't remember having taken it off. His hot, moist lips nipped at the delicate rim of her ear, and she forgot all about the hat. The scene in the valley below blurred before her eyes. It took no small effort to keep the low moan of pleasure locked away.

"Julio's foreman at the Circle K, been with us since before Pa died. He's the best man I have for green-breakin' horses." The soft brush of Ethan's breath against her ear tugged at something low in her belly. "He can tame a horse—any horse—without breaking its spirit."

Hope struggled to focus on the corral below, on the man and horse locked in a battle of wills. She couldn't force herself to move out of the enchanted circle of Ethan's arms. Tingling sensations raced through her system as his breath feathered down the side of her neck. Distracted, she fought to keep her gaze on the cowboy and the horse, worked to ignore the impulse to strain closer to Ethan's warm lips.

She succeeded at the former, failed—miserably—at the latter.

"He sounds very...talented." Hope swallowed, breathless.

"He is." Ethan's mouth hovered over her skin, brushing light kisses against the sensitive curve where her neck met her shoulder. "He taught me everything I know."

Hope blinked as far below, the horse took a tentative step. Julio remained motionless.

Hope tilted her head to the side, allowing Ethan more access to her sensitized skin. He didn't hesitate, and she breathed a sigh of relief. He nibbled his way up her throat, feasted on the susceptible spot where her pulse throbbed below her ear. Liquid heat pooled low and deep within her.

"He's gaining the horses trust," Ethan murmured, nipping at her skin with his lips. "He's piquing the stallion's curiosity." Ethan licked at her tender flesh. "He's making the horse come to him on his terms." Ethan nuzzled the side of her neck.

His teeth scraped her skin, and though Hope trembled, she didn't shy away. Her eyelids sank half closed as she absently followed the progress in the valley below. The stallion closed the distance, nudging Julio's shoulder with its muzzle, pleading for his attention. Hope waited with baited breath until Julio turned and caressed the horse's neck. The stallion snorted, bowing its majestic head, willing to concede to Julio's demands. Julio moved to the animal's side and tucked his boot in the stirrup. Great muscles twitched beneath the snowy hide. Hope expected the horse to bolt at any moment, but the proud beast stood still, suspiciously accepting his weight in the saddle.

"Apollo's the first horse I ever worked with. I'm the only one he'll allow in the saddle." Ethan fanned butterfly kisses over the side of her neck. She couldn't help it, her eyelids sagged closed, and she savored the delicious sensations his lips generated.

When she opened her eyes again, Julio was nudging the animal into motion. The stallion pranced sideways, tossing its proud head in defiant cooperation. Then the stallion began pacing within the confines of the corral under the vaquero's adept guidance. The men lounging on the railing threw their hats in the air and slapped each other on the back, as if they'd done all the work themselves.

"All it takes is a bit of patience," Ethan trailed hot, wet, open mouthed kisses back to her ear, along her jaw, adding, "and a whole lot of finesse." His teeth grazed the skin below her chin, and his hands splayed over her ribs, supporting the bottom curve of her breasts. "You have to make the horse want to be tamed." Heat enveloped her breasts, kneading them. "Make her need it more than anything else." His thumbs flicked over her pebbled, aching nipples.

She gasped for air. Her heart hammered in her chest. She knew he could feel it, but she couldn't find it in her to care just now, not with his intoxicating hands molded against her body. Not with his lips on her skin. A moan gurgled to her lips.

His hard body pressed against her. His words slid over her skin, husky and sensual. "You have to give her exactly what she needs." The hard ridge of his erection thrust against her bottom, ground against her, once, twice. "Make her crave only you."

Hope's mouth watered for a taste of him. The tip of her tongue snaked out to moisten her lower lip.

Ethan's possessive hands tightened slightly. His breath was ragged in her ears. His thumbs massaged slow circles over her nipples. "Only then can you make her bend to your will."

His words sank through her, and Hope's pleasure died a swift, cold death. Her eyes snapped open, and she pushed forward out of his arms, beguiled but furious nonetheless. He hadn't been talking about taming horses, he'd been talking about taming women...taming *her*.

He let her go with a soft sigh. She whirled around to face him, eyes flashing indignant fire. He grinned, unabashed, and she hoisted the picnic basket between them. A shoddy defense, to be sure, but it was all she had. It was on the tip of her tongue to snip at him that she wasn't some damn horse in need of taming, but he took the basket from her hands, pulling the edge of the checkered towel aside, poking his nose inside.

"Something smells delicious." Though his head angled down, he lifted piercing eyes to lock with hers. "I've been tempted this whole ride to steal a nibble." His soul-branding gaze dipped to her neck. His grin spread like warm honey over hotcakes.

From the look in his eyes, the nibbling was far from over, and the contents of the basket had nothing to do with his appetites. However, rather than reaching for her as she'd expected—as she'd suddenly and fervently wished he'd do—his hand disappeared inside the basket as he turned toward the blanket. Hope sighed, unable to determine whether she was relieved or disappointment.

He dropped to his knees at the corner of the blanket and began unpacking the food while she stood motionless, rooted to the spot. When the basket was empty, Ethan set it aside, stretched out on his side, crossed his ankles, and held up a shiny red apple. The corner of his mouth lifted to a sensuous angle. His eyes poured blue flames, burning her with a glimpse of the passion within.

"Now, let's see if we can tempt *your* appetite, sweetheart."

Her lips parted. Her wide-eyed gaze darted from Ethan's eyes to the apple and back again. Her breath stuttered in, tripped out. Without conscious effort, her feet shuffled forward. Suddenly she stood beside him, staring down into the very eyes of temptation incarnate. She extended her hand. The jolt of lightning passing between them when their fingers brushed helped to break her trance.

Turning away from his enticing gaze, she sank

onto the farthest corner of the blanket. She forced herself to take in their surroundings, to look at the food, at the mountainside, anything except Ethan sitting there, looking more delectable than anything Natalia had packed. Hope scrambled for something to say to break the tension.

"I know so much, yet so little about you—and Matt, of course," she quickly added. "I know Matt originally came to Texas to visit your father, but I don't know where or how they met."

Ethan was silent long enough that she began to worry she'd bumbled into a taboo subject. As she scrambled for a different topic, Ethan's voice filled the void. "Matt met my father during the war, in the field hospital after Chancellorsville. They ended up spending a fair bit of time together there. Then, at a skirmish several months after their release, they ran into each other, quite by chance. Matt's unit stopped at a small farm for provisions and ended up pinned down under enemy fire. Pa's cavalry detail came charging to the rescue, as it were. When the war was over, Matt came to visit." He gave a careless shrug. "He never left. He bought the spread to the south of ours, and he and Pa were inseparable after that—much to my mother's everlasting annoyance." Ethan smiled.

"Matt never made mention of your father in his letters, or your mother for that matter, though he spoke often enough of you. I guess I don't know anything about your family." As soon as the words were out, she could have bitten off her tongue. Ethan's gaze turned troubled. "I'm sorry. I hadn't meant to—"

"No, it's okay." He smiled at her, but the lines around his mouth were tight, strained. "My mother died three years after Matt came to Texas. It was good Matt was here, Pa took the loss hard. Matt pulled him through the worst of it, but Pa never really recovered. Matt was there for me, too. I think I would've turned out much differently if Matt hadn't stepped in when he had."

Hope bit her lip and waited, curious.

"I was hurt and confused—and big for my age. I took up brawlin' and drinkin', a bad combination for a kid. Bad combination for anyone," he noted with a faraway look in his eyes. "My Pa was tied up with the ranch and grievin', and I was more than he could handle. Matt took me in hand, gave me direction and purpose...understanding. Matt tried to help Pa, too. But after a while, Pa pushed him away. He pushed everyone away..."

Hope's heart ached for the anguish on Ethan's face. He continued speaking, subdued, lost somewhere in his past. "Matt warned Pa not to move the herd that day...reminded him there was a storm coming. The herd was in a good place to keep them contained in case of a stampede. Pa and Matt fought over it anyway, I remember. Matt said Pa should have had more sense than to even suggest such a fool idea and wasn't it Pa himself who'd taught Matt better. Pa stomped off to the house in a huff, and we'd thought that was the end of it.

"I rode into town with Matt for supplies then. By that time, I'd have followed him into hell and back." Ethan blushed suddenly and glanced away. He looked so endearing, her heart melted...again. "As we were on our way back that night, Julio met us. It was pourin' rain, cold as a hell, lightenin' rippin' at the sky. He said Pa went out to McClain Pass roundin' up strays when a stampede broke out. Julio saw Pa go down somewhere near the middle of the herd but no one could get to him in time."

Hope tensed, knowing what was to come, wishing to high heaven she'd never brought the subject up.

"We found him the next morning," Ethan stated,

deadpan, the look in his eyes said the rest, speaking eloquently of the horror…and the loss.

"Ethan, I'm so sorry! I had no idea." She fumbled for the appropriate words, regretting the pain she'd caused.

His gaze met hers, and she found no blame, no judgment there. He drew a deep breath and pushed on. "Matt stepped in, took over both ranches until I came of age. Then he turned the Circle K over to me…lock, stock, and steer. I already knew the workin' end of the ranch, but he taught me the business end of things. The spreads are technically two separate entities, but it's a partnership, equal down the line. Matt and I got into a few scrapes along the way, but it's been a hell of a ride."

"So Matt's letters said," Hope grinned, trying to lighten the mood.

Ethan lifted a taunting eyebrow. "You know, James's letters to Matt were just as informative."

Apprehension creased Hope's brow. What had James told them?

"I hope you're not going to pretend innocence." Ethan teased. "Or weren't you the one that got kicked out of not one but *two* hoity-toity etiquette schools?"

Hope nearly groaned aloud. She'd never imagined Ethan would know about either of those dreadful incidents. Her face burned, but she managed not to fan herself. Maybe he'd think she was just getting too much exposure to the sun.

"I did not get 'kicked out'," she primly informed him, nose in the air. "Uncle James determined those particular establishments were not conducive to my betterment."

He chuckled, toying with the fringed edge of their makeshift table. "Why'd you dump tea on the headmistress anyway?"

"I most certainly did not '*dump*' tea on *her*." The

heat in her cheeks intensified. "She accused me of having the grace of a bull in a china shop, and the manners of a goat. I asked her if she preferred one lump or two, then I *poured* the entire contents of the teapot onto her Persian Rug. I informed the old...woman...that she was a pompous windbag. Then I politely excused myself to go upstairs to pack."

Ethan gasped between hearty gales of laughter, "How old were you?"

"Thirteen." Her lips twitched, giving her away.

"And what about that other finishing school? Didn't you have problems with tea there too?"

She primly adjusted her skirts. "Well, that really wasn't my fault."

"Sure it wasn't." Ethan pressed, "Come on, fess up."

"Mary Beth Martin put a burr in my saddle."

"I'm sure she did," he placated, grinning.

"No, you don't understand." Hope leaned forward in her earnestness. "She put a real burr under my saddle, just before morning ride. I've always been a bit tentative on a horse. That incident put me off riding altogether. My mount threw me when we went over that first jump." Then she glanced away, guilty. "Sure, we weren't supposed to be jumping that day, and I should never have taken that dare, but really! What a childish prank to play. I hobbled for nearly two months waiting for the pain in my ankle to go away."

"That wasn't a childish prank." Ethan's eyes turned serious. He pushed himself up, leaning toward her with an odd, fierce light in his eyes. "You could have been—"

"I got her back," Hope interjected, glancing at Ethan from beneath lowered lashes. "As soon as I was able to get up and about, I poured ink in her teapot." Then Hope grimaced, chagrined. "I wish I'd known she was having breakfast with Miss Throgmorton, the school dame, though. I might have waited for a better time. Imagine my horror when the woman smiled to bid me a Merry Christmas." A reluctant chuckled escaped her. "Her teeth were black as pitch."

Ethan blinked at her, then he fell back, arms around his middle, shaking with laughter. His mirth was infectious, and she soon joined in.

Between hoots of laughter, Ethan proclaimed, "I think you'd best stick with coffee. Tea seems to be your Achilles Heel."

She was helpless to do more than nod in agreement, holding her sides as she, too, laughed. Tears welled and rolled down her cheeks, and it felt good. Sure, she'd laughed with Antonio—quite a bit actually—but she hadn't really let go. It was something she'd not done since before James had fallen ill.

Finally, when the laughter subsided and the remains of the picnic had been packed away, Hope perched beside Ethan on a large boulder overlooking the valley. The corral at the Circle K stood empty in the late afternoon sunshine, the men scattered, going about their chores.

Hope considered asking about Vega. She was curious about the man who'd plagued Ethan and Matt, but she didn't want to ruin the afternoon. Without warning, Ethan put his arm around her shoulders, drawing her snug against his side. The weight of his arm around her—his warmth sinking through her—felt so right, it never occurred to her to protest. They sat in companionable silence for a long while, until the wind picked up, biting to the bone. She shivered against him.

"We better head back, its cooling off early today. The nights up here get down-right frigid this time of year." When she placed her hands in his so he could help her down, Ethan hissed out a sharp breath and chaffed her hands between his. "Why didn't you tell me you were so cold?"

"I guess I didn't notice."

"Come on. Let's get you back to the ranch and in front of a fire before you catch your death," he chided.

Hope walked beside Ethan back to the horses, her hands clasped firmly in his. Once they reached the horses, he squeezed her hands and released her to stow their gear on Apollo's saddle. She reached up to gather Daisy's reins. The animal let out a wild-eyed shriek and danced sideways into Hope, knocking her to the ground. The mare reared up on its hind legs for a breath-stealing heartbeat. The horse's hooves came down, missing her by a handful of skinny inches.

Hope scrambled sideways to avoid injury when the mare took flight. But the peril was far from over. As she twisted sideways, she came face-to-face with a very angry, coiled rattlesnake. Larger than life and so very deadly. Hope froze, paralyzed with terror as the snake gave her a horrifying view of lethal fangs. Its warning rattle rang like a death knell in her ears.

Hope lay there in the settling dust, unable to move, waiting for those razor-sharp fangs to pierce her flesh. The snake pulled its head back in preparation of the strike. She braced herself for the pain, cringed in fear of the venom. Then, right before horrified her eyes, the rattlesnake's head exploded with an ear-popping bang. She screamed, scrabbling backwards on palms and heels. Her feet tangled in her skirts, her eyes riveted on the twitching, headless body.

Suddenly, the unyielding wall of Ethan's chest blocked her view. She threw her arms around his neck, sobbing, vaguely aware of the furious pounding of his heart beneath her cheek. An eon passed before she was certain her legs would support her again. By then, she'd managed to stop bawling like a baby, and mopped her tears away with her sleeve. He stood then, pulling Hope up with him, his hands trembled beneath her own. She offered him a tremulous smile, one he didn't seem able to return.

Hope cleared her throat. Her voice was as wobbly as her knees. "I don't know about you, but I think I've had about all the excitement I can handle for one day."

Ethan stared at her for a full minute, his expression grim. Without warning, he swept her into a bone-crushing embrace, sealing his lips to hers in a short, bruising kiss that left her head swimming and her pulses racing.

Had she just said she'd had enough excitement? Surely not. She could take excitement of this kind all day long. The world began to tilt beneath her feet. All she could do—all she *wanted* to do—was cling to Ethan, the only solid thing in her crazy universe. He cut the kiss short, far shorter than she liked, and set her back on her feet. He gathered up Apollo's reins as she fingered her lips in bemusement, staring at his back, willing her senses to return to normal. His movements seemed stiff, jerky. Maybe he was as lost as she was about this odd attraction between them, she mused.

"Here," he directed, sounding a little unsteady himself. "Climb up onto the rock we were sittin' on and give me your arm. That's right," he encouraged. "Now, hop on."

She settled behind him and wrapped her arms tight around his waist. She'd thought Daisy was tall. Apollo was colossal in comparison. Ethan nudged Apollo forward. The air held a distinct bite by the time they reached the valley. Her teeth chattered as she burrowed against his back, shivering against the cold. He reined the horse in when the land leveled out, and retrieved the blanket they'd used for their picnic, twisting in the saddle to tug it around her shoulders.

"Here, keep this around you, tuck it in." He waited until she did as instructed, then ordered, "Now, wrap your arms around me and hold on tight."

He didn't have to tell her twice. No way was she falling off this horse. She'd break something for sure.

Ethan quickened Apollo's pace and the ground flew beneath them. Hope smiled, warm at last, and rested her cheek against Ethan's broad, strong back. For the first time in memory, she actually began to enjoy riding a horse.

Chapter 12

A vague sense of unease crept through Hope as they neared the ruins of the Old Mission. Ethan reined Apollo in. A coppery tang hung heavy in the air. She'd come to recognize that scent—recognize it, and hate it. Blood. The agitated horse pranced beneath them. Unnerved, Hope tightened her arms around Ethan's waist. Patting Apollo's neck, murmuring soothing words, he urged the horse closer to the steps. His muscles tensed beneath her cheek, and a vicious curse slipped beneath his breath, but he dropped his hand to cover hers, squeezing gentle reassurance. She peered over his shoulder, straining to see what his broad back blocked from her view.

Ethan guided his horse alongside the mound on the steps, and Hope gasped, horrified. A steer, or rather what was left of a steer, lay on its side, its stomach ripped wide open, its entrails spilled down the steps. Dark crimson trickled over each rise to form a puddle on the landing below. Had it not been for the bloody letters carved on the animal's pale hide, one would've assumed the steer gutted by wild animals.

Ethan glanced at the message and swore again, loud and clear. Urging Apollo around, he pushed the horse into a dead gallop back to the main house, forcing Hope to hold on for dear life. Once there, he threw a long leg over the animal's neck and leaped to the ground. Reaching up, he unceremoniously pulled Hope down, and gave her a push towards the house.

"Go inside," he barked.

Still reeling from the shock, her footsteps lagged. "What did those words mean, Ethan? I couldn't understand the Spanish writing. Why would someone—"

"I don't have time for questions right now, Hope, go inside." His tone held no margin for flexibility. When she didn't follow his order, he roared, "Now."

Startled, Hope hurried up the steps. She turned in the doorway as Ethan disappeared into the bunkhouse. Not knowing what else to do, she made her way to the kitchen. Natalia wasn't there, but an inviting pot of coffee bubbled on the iron cook-stove. She moved to the shelving and took down a mug.

Her hands shook, but she managed to keep from pouring the steaming liquid all over herself. Hope set the pot back on the iron grate and wrapped her hands around the mug to warm them. Lifting the cup to her lips, Hope tried to force the memory of the carcass from her mind. The bitter liquid raced heat to her insides, snapping her out of her fog.

A flurry of boots tramping down the hall drew her to attention. She set the mug down and hurried after the sound. Had Ethan come back?

"Son of a bitch," she heard Matt roar as she scurried down the hallway and darted inside the room. "He goddamned well should *know* better."

"I tried to stop him, but you know Ethan. I sent Pablo and two others out after him," Antonio offered, looking every bit as angry as Matt sounded.

"Well, at least he has some back up." Matt raked his fingers through his hair in frustration. "Send him in as soon as he gets back. Better yet, send a couple more men out, tell 'em to keep their heads down so they don't get 'em blown off by accident."

"Matt, most of the men are still out with the cattle. I'm hesitant to send anymore away. I don't want to leave the main house with nothing more than a couple of lame men." Antonio glanced pointedly from his leg to Matt's chest to Hope.

Matt's face lost all color, and Hope feared a relapse. Before she could interrupt, he muttered, "Yeah…yeah, just…let me know when he gets back."

Antonio nodded. Limping, he crossed to Hope, nudging her out into the hall.

"Ethan said you were with him when he found the carcass." Antonio's eyes scanned her face. Concern etched deep lines in his frown. He chafed a hand up and down her arm, squeezed her shoulder. "Are you all right?"

"I'm fine. You're limping is worse…"

"I twisted something." He scoffed. "It's a nuisance, nothing more."

"Did Ethan go back out there? Is that what you were talking to Matt about?"

Something flickered in Antonio's eyes, something she couldn't quite decipher. "He went back to the Old Mission to try to find tracks."

"Surely he wouldn't go after the men who did that, not alone?" She frowned at him, incredulous.

Antonio shrugged, but his eyes were troubled.

Ethan's bullheaded one-track mind nearly crossed her eyes with frustration. "It was Vega's men, wasn't it?"

Antonio stared long and hard at her before he nodded curtly. "*¡Si!*"

Hope glanced through the doorway. Natalia hovered over Matt, urging him to lie back on the bed, insisting he rest. Hope's shoulders drooped. Worry lines creased her forehead, and she snagged her lower lip between her teeth. Antonio placed his hands on her shoulders, steering her to the foot of the stairs.

"It's been a long day. You should go to your room and rest for a while. I'll have Natalia bring a tray up for you later," Antonio insisted.

His touch was gentle, his eyes kind, but his manner was insistent. Moreover, he was right. It had been a very long day. She smiled, grateful to have found such a good friend in such an unexpected place. Reaching up, she smoothed a palm over his cheek. Why couldn't Ethan have been as concerned about her well-being?

"Thank you." Hope offered Antonio a weary smile, then trudged upstairs without any argument.

Two long hours passed in which Hope paced a trench across the floor from her door to her window, unable to rest. Unable to touch the food Natalia had delivered. She'd used the water on the washstand to scrub her hair and skin clean, splashing more water to rinse. Then she resumed her pacing. Her worry over Ethan kept her wound tight as a watch-spring.

She jolted when very loud, very angry shouting shook the floor beneath her feet.

Fear raced through her. Hope ran toward the door, only remembered to snatch up a robe to cover her thin nightdress as she rushed around the bed. She pushed the damp tangle of her hair over her shoulder as she shook the robe out.

She was still thrusting her arm into the sleeve as she flung herself into Matt's room, skidding to a halt less than a foot from Ethan. With her entrance, the room fell silent. Her frantic gaze skimmed over him. She found no blood, no wounds. A relieved breath hissed from her lungs. Hope finished pulling the robe on, cinched the belt tight at her waist with trembling fingers, and eyed the room's occupants each in turn.

Matt leaned against the headboard, propped up by a mound of pillows. His scowl was fierce, his face mottled. Fire crackled in his green eyes. Natalia hovered close, fussing with the pillows and the blankets, murmuring in soothing tones. For the first time since Hope arrived at the ranch, Natalia's years showed in the concerned lines on her face. Antonio perched on the edge of the chair beside Matt's bed. Temper sparkled in his dark, velvety brown eyes. His expression was grim.

Beside her, Ethan stood silent and motionless, staring at her as if she'd sprouted a second head.

****

Ethan had been about to tell Matt to calm down when Hope burst in. His heart tripped inside his chest at the sight of her. His tongue ceased to function. Her dark hair was stark against the snowy white nightdress and robe. Her bottom lip was swollen and bright pink, her eyes wide with concern. Bare toes peeped out from beneath the hem of her nightdress, reminding him of how her feet felt, curled around his calf at night, seeking warmth while she slept. God, she was beautiful. Ethan couldn't look away. Jasmine engulfed his senses. His body reacted—violently.

It was all he could do not to reach for her.

"What's going on in here? I could hear the yelling all the way upstairs," Hope demanded, her eyes floated over each of them, waiting for a response.

As if on cue, chaos descended. Matt, Natalia, and Antonio vied for control of the argument. Amidst it all, Ethan stood there, unable to look away from her, unable to utter a sound. He must be going deaf, too, for the heated debate raging around him died to a muffled hum. More than anything, he wanted to scoop her up, toss her over his shoulder, and carry her off.

And once he had her alone…

She stuck her fingers in her mouth and let out one long, shrill whistle, and he blinked, yanked back to the here and now. Once more, silence reigned.

"Well, now. I think we've all had more than

enough shouting for one night." Hope turned to face him. "Did you find anything?"

It took him a moment to realize she'd addressed him. It took a moment longer to find his voice. "No."

"Then I don't see as how any of this can't wait till morning." Now she frowned at Matt. "Until after we've *all* had a chance to calm down and rest."

Antonio opened his mouth to speak, but Hope glared him silent. She pointed at the door, shooting him a meaningful look. "Out!"

Antonio's eyes widened. The set look on her face apparently deterred him from making any further comment. He snapped his mouth closed and left the room without another sound. Ethan waited until Antonio departed, then he turned to Matt.

Drawing herself up with the starch of a tiny army general, Hope glared daggers at him, enunciating each letter with a painful jab of her finger against his chest. "O. U. T!"

"Hell and damnation—"

Hope swung her condemning finger toward the bed. "And you," she accused Matt. "What are you thinking? If you don't calm down, they may as well hall you out and dump your sorry butt next to that cow—"

"Steer," Ethan corrected quietly.

"Steer," Hope repeated, barreling on, "because you'll be just as dead. What good are you to any of us if you have a relapse?"

Matt's mouth opened and closed, looking for all the world like a landed trout. Hope waved her palm at him in unmistakable dismissal. "Oh, be quiet."

Matt's eyes bulged, his mouth dropped open, and he sputtered. Natalia sat down on the side of the bed, grinning from ear to ear, her eyes twinkled.

Ethan couldn't help but chuckle.

Turning to Ethan, Hope snapped, "Didn't you hear me? Matt needs his rest. Shoo!"

Shoo? Did she actually just shoo him?

Ethan, who was as surprised as anyone by Hope's behavior, found himself in the hall before he could draw breath to argue. Starring at Matt's closed door, he dragged his hand over the back of his neck and grinned, shaking his head. She'd singlehandedly swept into the room and assumed control with one little purse of her lips. She'd been a veritable tyrant.

He hadn't realized she had it in her.

He damned well should have.

She fired his blood when she was bossy like this.

He made his way to his room, gathered up a towel, a bar of soap, and a change of pants. On silent feet, he descended the stairs, pausing outside Matt's still-closed door. All was silent within. A smile snaked across his lips.

Ethan picked his way to the stream, hoping it was cold tonight. The image of Hope in that thin nightgown flashed in his mind and he shivered. On second thought, that water better be downright frigid. As he stepped into the icy stream, he bit back a hiss and moved deeper. He'd need every goose bump he could get to cool his overheated blood.

He couldn't figure out why his reaction to her tonight had been so intense. It wasn't as though he hadn't seen her in a nightdress before. Nevertheless, as she'd stood in Matt's bedroom—with her hair unbound and fire in her eyes—ordering them all around, Ethan could see the steel of which Matt had spoken. Damned if he couldn't get the sight of her out of his head. Of course, it didn't help matters that the nightdress she'd worn had been thin as gossamer, provoking the imagination.

And that robe had been a useless defense against his overactive imagination.

He shook his head with a sigh. If he didn't start thinking about something else, he'd need another dousing in the stream before he made it back inside the house. Ethan sauntered across the yard in the dark. Dim light from Hope's room pooled on the ground beneath her window. He let out another heart-felt sigh and entered the house, turning his feet to the stairs.

He wandered to his room to put his things away. He didn't bother to light a lamp as he crossed the room to stare out the window. Then, just as pensive, Ethan leveled a wry glance over his shoulder, distastefully contemplating his own all-too-empty bed.

****

Hope punched her pillow. Why couldn't she get him out of her head? Why did she continue to let him affect her? He hadn't once asked how she was, hadn't taken the time to check on her, not the way Antonio had. He hadn't apologized for being so harsh with her when they'd gotten back to the ranch. He'd just stood there. And stared. What was *wrong* with him? She hadn't grown an extra head since he'd dumped her on Matt's doorstep.

Unfortunately, she was so relieved he hadn't been hurt, that none of the rest mattered. If she had any sense in her head at all, she'd be falling head over heels for Antonio, rather than lying here, wide-awake, thinking about a stubborn, insensitive pain in the neck.

The sound of wood scraping wood drifted to her through the wall adjoining their rooms. Then silence. With a small, disgusted groan, she told herself to go to sleep. It didn't work. She remained wide awake. The clock on her mantel ticked away the minutes, mocking her.

The doorknob turned, and relief washed over her. Her door edged open, revealing Ethan's silhouette. Hope lifted her head from the pillow, leaned up on her elbow, regarding him in silence.

He paused on the threshold as if uncertain of his

welcome, wearing nothing but a pale pair of buckskin trousers with the top few buttons undone. The soft glow of lamplight cast a glistening, golden hue over his muscular chest and taut stomach. Her gaze caught the flecks of moisture falling from his damp, tousled hair. The lamplight turned them to glittering diamonds on his bronzed skin. His smoldering gaze burned her from across the room.

How could she turn *that* away?

She angled her head to the side, considering him. Her pride wouldn't let her make this easy for him, even if it was what she wanted. Stepping inside her room, he closed the door behind him. With slow, purposeful strides, he crossed the room, towering over her bed, staring down at her in wordless entreaty.

Her heart fluttered a little beneath her breastbone at the heat in his stare. Without a word, she slid over to make room for him on the bed, lifting the bedclothes in unspoken invitation. He let out a deep sigh, extinguished the lamp, and slid in beside her. As Ethan lay back, she dropped the sheet over him. He lifted his left arm, curling it around her back. Hope settled herself against his side, nestling her head onto his bare shoulder. And she sighed.

Ethan's heat surrounded her. His scent sank through her. His smooth skin was warm beneath her cheek. The sound of his heartbeat thudded in her ear, soothing her as nothing else could. She slipped her arm across his stomach, resting her palm in the middle of his wide chest, and draped her thigh over his.

Snuggling closer, she slipped her cold feet against his warm calf. Ethan's cheek bunched against her forehead, and a chuckle rumbled low in his chest. His large hand settled over her hand, holding it tight to his chest, and she sighed, closing her eyes, lulled into soft, warm dreams.

Chapter 13

Hope woke to an empty bed. As with before, Ethan's scent still lingered on her pillow. She pulled it to her and breathed deep, resting her cheek on it as her thoughts circled around him. Ethan was such an enigma. He could spark her anger with terrifying ease, then douse it with a simple touch. He could open up and let her in, then shut down and push her away with little to no warning at all.

Those times he pushed her away hurt far more than she'd believed possible.

Ethan could make her feel things, overwhelming all-consuming things, things that were equal parts frightening and thrilling. The way he'd come to her room last night, the way he'd held her as though he needed—more than anything else—just to be near her, had made her feel safe and important to him.

Needed.

She hadn't intended letting him stay last night, but she hadn't been able to turn him away either. Still, one unfortunate fact was certain. She couldn't keep allowing him to come to her room at night. She *shouldn't* allow it. It wasn't proper. Yet somehow, when he was with her—when he touched her—what was proper didn't seem to matter all that much.

If she were honest with herself, she'd admit part of allowing him to stay had been purely selfish on her own behalf. When Ethan held her, she could sleep. The nightmares held no substance. There was no reasonable explanation for it.

It was just so.

Hope groaned, rolling over to stare at the ceiling in consternation. She couldn't keep swinging back and forth like this. She needed to draw the line. Now before things got any farther out of hand. Ethan was Matt's friend. It was all too complicated. She had no business kissing him, letting him in her bed at night…regardless how comforting his presence was.

Hope rose with a determined sigh and dressed, resolved to set the matter straight as soon as possible. She'd tell Ethan that while she appreciated his intentions to help her with her nightmares, she couldn't allow him to continue to come to her room anymore.

And there'd be no more kissing.

Romance was the last thing she wanted right now. She'd had too much upheaval, too many changes in her life. Now all she wanted was calm.

She'd be firm, but she'd be careful with his feelings. After all, as determined as she was to keep him at arm's length, she still wanted to maintain a friendship with him. For Matt's sake, she told herself.

She grimaced into the mirror for a moment at her thick, unruly hair. She'd never had to deal with it much, other than to tie it back. On the few occasions she'd required elaborate hairstyles, her maid had always taken care of it. She took a deep breath, raised one eyebrow, and considered her own head in the mirror from several different angles. It couldn't be all that difficult.

It took some doing, and more than a bit of inventive cursing, but she managed to get her hair twisted up into what she hoped was a becoming style. A few tendrils had escaped her, but they curled down her neck in demure ringlets, so she left them. She gave one last glance in the mirror and, satisfied with her appearance, squared her shoulders and left the room in search of Ethan.

She didn't have far to go. She'd no more than stepped into the hallway outside her bedroom, when Ethan's door swung open. As soon as he saw her, he seemed to hesitate, almost as if he wanted to go back inside his room and shut the door in her face. He visibly ground his teeth. The fine muscles along his jawline ticked as he joined her in the hallway.

May as well start on a pleasant foot, she decided. "Good morning."

"Mornin'," he mumbled, rushing toward the steps.

"I was hoping I'd get a chance to speak to you this morning." *Why did you sneak out?*

He hesitated on the top step but didn't face her. "Oh?"

Hope stared at his rigid back, at a loss for how to proceed. She got the distinct impression he didn't want to talk to her, didn't want to be anywhere near her, and she couldn't understand this sudden change in attitude considering he'd been the one to come to her last night.

Baffled, she floundered, "I, ah, I…I thought we should talk. I thought perhaps we might go for another ride today?"

She grimaced. That sounded like an inadequate excuse to draw him into some kind of conversation. Desperate—stupid even—considering her aversion to riding. But he was acting so strange, it was difficult not to flounder.

"I don't think so." He lobbed the shot over his shoulder, taking the first step down.

Blinking at his surly tone, Hope stepped closer, stopping just shy of reaching for his arm. Why was he being so difficult? So…*cold*?

"Why?"

Still, he refused to look at her. He studied the pattern of the sunlight pouring in through the open window onto the worn flagstone landing below. His gaze wandered to the intricate Spanish mosaic on the wall at the bottom of the stairs. He contemplated the curve of the wrought iron banister with an inordinate amount of concentration. He looked at anything—at everything—but he would not look at her. Hope bit her lip, determined not to let his confusing attitude get the best of her self-control.

"In case it slipped your notice, there is a killer on the loose. You might as well paint a target on your back," he growled.

His tone was just scathing enough to get a rise out of her.

"He was out there yesterday, too, but that didn't stop you from dragging me out then. What's so different about today?"

"I should never have taken you out yesterday. It was a stupid thing to do, a waste of time. I have a ranch to run—two until Matt's back on his feet. I don't have the time or the inclination to be your personal tour guide." His gaze lifted to hers, but his stare strayed to her lips, and he glanced away again, scowling.

Hope stiffened, frowning. His words sliced her more deeply than they should have. "I realize you have responsibilities, and I certainly didn't expect you to be my personal guide. I thought after last night we should discuss—"

"Yeah, well, I'm not a nursemaid, and I'm not interested in scaring away your childish ghosts anymore."

Hope sucked in a sharp breath at his snide, cruel tone. Despite her resolve to set appropriate boundaries between them, she took his response—his tone—personally, as he'd obviously intended. She held herself rigid, lifting her chin a notch. Clutching her hands in tight fists at her side, she battled the fierce desire to feel the sharp sting of her palm against his cheek again. Her teeth clenched tight.

She refused to give him the satisfaction of so much as a glimpse of emotion. But furious tears welled in her eyes, refusing to wait until she was safely away from him. She blinked, unable to defend against the callous words. How could she have been so stupid as to trust him?

Tour guide? Nursemaid? Here she'd been trying to keep things amicable. Try as she might to feel he was making things easier for her, she couldn't quite pull it off. A lone tear escaped her.

The lines around his mouth tightened, his expression instantly turned contrite, and he reached for her. "Hope—"

"I understand perfectly. I apologize if I've inconvenienced you," she spat, the tight rein she held on her control strained to the limit. "I won't bother you again."

Before he could catch hold of her, she swept her skirts aside and rushed past him down the staircase. She blinked back tears with every step. She'd trusted him, she'd let him in—something she didn't do lightly—and he'd stomped on her trust with deliberate malice. She was a complete idiot.

"Hope, wait." His boots pounded down the steps after her.

She told herself not to look, told herself to just go inside the room, shut the door, and forget all about Ethan Kincaid. Hope turned her head and glared at him through a blur of unshed tears. Before he could reach her, she slipped inside Matt's room and closed the door firmly behind her.

Hope stood just inside the door for a moment with her eyes closed and her mind racing, her heart lodged in her throat. What happened? She was dumbfounded. What had she done to make him so angry, so spiteful? She wanted to yell. She wanted to scream. She wanted to kick and throw things.

She wanted to curl up like a small child and cry.

Fortunately, her temper kicked in again, saving her the indignity.

If he didn't want to be alone at night, well then...he could go sleep with his damned horse. She stomped across the room and jerked a book off the shelf without looking at the title. She couldn't stand his spiteful, unfeeling disdain. She'd done nothing to warrant it. He'd come to her last night, not the other way around, damn it.

And they say women were contrary creatures.

Hope stalked over to the chair, kicking it back a couple inches before she spun around and sat down with a loud harrumph. Bursting with furious energy, she ignored Matt's puzzled stare and shot to her feet. Crossing to the window, she scowled at the stables. She'd figure out how to get a lock on that damned door.

Her face fell, and she felt a painful twinge somewhere in the vicinity of her heart.

Given what Ethan had said in the hall, that didn't sound like it would be a problem anymore... his coming to her room anymore. He wasn't interested in '*playing nursemaid*,' as he'd so bluntly phrased it. A profound sense of loss settled in the pit of her stomach. Torn, she shook her head at her own foolishness.

She'd gotten what she'd set out for, hadn't she?

Too bad she'd been the one to come away bruised and bloodied.

"Is something wrong, Hope?" Matt broke into her thoughts. "You seem a little—out of sorts."

Reconciling herself to putting on a brave face, Hope took a deep, steadying breath. "I'm fine."

"If you need to talk..."

"Thank you, but I'm fine," Hope assured him again as she glanced out the window, unable to lie to his face. She stared hard at Ethan as he crossed the yard from the stables to the bunkhouse, disappearing inside. She cursed his hide with each step of his long legs.

"Actually, there is something I'd like to talk to you about." She pinned Matt with a shrewd gaze as she settled into the chair at his bedside.

Matt shifted, edging upward in bed. "What would that be?"

"I want you to tell me about Vega. Tell me what the message said, the one carved on that steer."

Matt frowned, looking as though he'd rather face a firing squad. This time she wouldn't relent.

He let a long moment pass before clearing his throat. Matt leaned back against the stack of pillows. "We learned the renegade's identity a few days ago. Until then, he was an elusive phantom, rustlin' and raidin' along this stretch of the Guadalupe's." Matt frowned, pleating the edge of his blanket. "He's brutal, a vicious monster without a conscience. I don't want to scare you, but you have to understand how dangerous he is. It's important you stay close to the ranch—don't ever go riding off alone."

Hope smiled. "I don't think you have to worry about that."

"I meant what I said before. We're going to get you comfortable on a horse. You live on a ranch now. It's only practical. But, riding aside, when you do go out, you need to stay close to Ethan or Antonio, at least until I'm up and about again."

"Agreed," she conceded, then tossed out the attached string, "But you need to tell me the rest."

"Hope…" His eyes held both warning, and plea.

"Matt, I'm not stupid. Everyone's been dancing around something. What aren't you telling me?" She narrowed her eyes at him, refusing to be swayed. "The message on that steer was in Spanish. I know Ethan told you what it said. Tell me."

Matt stared at the ceiling, as if pleading divine

intervention. When none seemed imminent, he heaved a deep sigh. "Time's up, Gringo."

"What? I don't understand."

"The message said 'Time's up, Gringo.' Vega's plagued us on and off for years. Until a few years past, he was little more than a nuisance. Then, a couple years ago..." Matt clenched his jaw. Anguish dug deep grooves in his face. "Vega attacked the ranch in a brutal, all-out raid. We were out gatherin' up the cattle. Old Grease broke his leg just as we were setting out, so Natalia agreed to fill in for me on short notice. If she hadn't, she would've been here when..." He shook his head and swallowed hard, closing his eyes.

Hope waited until Matt spoke again. Anxious worry gnawed at her.

"The Bar M was largely unprotected. He'd started a fire in one of Ethan's stables to draw any able-bodied men out of the way. Only a few men and women were here. He couldn't have planned it better. He and his gang rode in, bold as brass, and torched the barn and a couple small houses the married hands lived in with their wives, destroyed the corrals, chased off the livestock. He left the main house and the bunkhouse intact. Evidently, he wants those for his own.

"At any rate, he rounded up everyone who'd been left behind, herdin' 'em up like cattle. They slaughtered the men outright. They were the lucky ones. The women he took up into the mountains. Vega and his men showed no mercy. The message carved into the steer, that's Vega's signature move, and he hasn't limited himself to carvin' on animals..." Matt closed his eyes.

Hope reached out and squeezed his hand. "It's all right. You don't have to say anymore."

"Give Ethan a chance, Hope. The raid... I don't think he ever really recovered," Matt added enigmatically, his face pale and drawn.

Rather than pushing for answers, as she wanted to do, she let it go…for now. "All right," she promised, patting his hand. "Lay back and rest now."

Hope fluffed his pillow and tucked him in. She pulled the door closed behind her and paused in the hallway. Worrying her bottom lip, she set out for the front door, needing some fresh air to clear her mind.

****

Ethan sat in the saddle, as lifeless as a corpse. The gelding he rode picked its way down the well-worn path on his own, seemingly unmindful of his contemplative rider. In the distance, a couple of vaqueros led in a handful of strays from the dried riverbed bisecting the spreads. In a few places along the riverbed, water had begun to form small standing puddles. There hadn't been standing water in this riverbed for as long as Ethan could remember. If these puddles were any indication, they might see resurgence in this river. That might prove a logistical problem when moving the herd, but the additional watering source would be welcome. He'd have to speak with Matt about it.

Ethan passed a clump of prickly pear, the top fruits were gone. The base of the plant was brilliant green, a pure vivid emerald the same shade as Hope's eyes. That was all the reminder Ethan needed for his turbulent thoughts to circle back to Hope. He groaned, swiping a hand over his gritty eyes.

That morning, he'd told Matt he'd been away from his own place for too long, said he needed to check on things. He'd warned Matt he might be gone a couple days. An outright lie, and even now, he cringed at the telling of it. After more than three decades, the Circle K ran like a well-oiled machine. No, the bottom line was, Ethan just needed to get away, needed to find his bearings.

Just when he'd talked himself into letting go of the past—letting go of Christina—the past had jumped back to bite him. Sunk its teeth in deep, it had. The message carved on that steer had made damned certain of that. Then he'd gone on the wild ride of swirling emotion, up and down, back and forth. He had needed to track the monster down while he had a viable trail.

When he'd failed to find a single track, he'd felt like such a failure...again.

He should never have gone to her last night. In the dark of night, haunted by ghosts—taunted by memories of the solace he could find only in her arms—her presence had called to him, beckoning him like the lure of a siren's call. He hadn't been able to resist it. He hated the way he'd given in to the weakness without even putting up a token fight.

He'd gone to her, taken what comfort he could in holding her, because he wouldn't allow himself to do more than that, no matter how badly he'd wanted to...*still* wanted to. Nevertheless, he'd reached his limit last night. Holding her wasn't enough now. He wanted much, much more. Seeing her this morning on the stairs had reinforced that. He'd faced the truth in the bright light of day, and it rankled.

He hadn't wanted to see her this morning. Then fate had stepped in, with a vicious left hook. She'd looked so beautiful, so innocent. He'd come so close to the sudden, unreasonable urge to yank her into his arms and kiss her senseless, to carry her back to her room so that he could make love to her, that it had terrified him.

And so he'd deliberately been an ass, pushing her away the only way he knew how. She'd been so vulnerable—and so mortified—that his heart ripped right down the middle. Damn it, she deserved better, but he couldn't risk that kind of pain. Not ever again. He'd taken his confusion and disgruntlement out on her, with cruel words and malicious intent. He'd broken the fragile bonds he'd painstakingly forged on their picnic.

He hated himself for that, too.

Congratulations jackass, you got what you wanted. So why then did he feel so miserable? His gaze wandered out across the foothills. No, let it go, he thought. Let *her* go. It was best for everyone involved, he told himself. After all, look what happened the last time he'd fallen in…

His brain screeched to a grinding halt.

No.

No way. *That* word had nothing to do with him and Hope. Nothing whatsoever. But her wounded eyes came back to haunt him. She hadn't been able to hide the pain his betrayal caused, and the sight damn near brought him to his knees. He told himself once again it was for the best, but the words rang hollow. Like a mirage conjured from the heat of his desire, a vision of her in the filmy nightgown she'd worn last night swam before his eyes. His body reacted, and he shifted in the saddle, cursing violently enough to startle his unshakable Apollo.

Several times, he'd almost turned the horse around so he could beg forgiveness, only to set his jaw and push onward. He needed to think, and roundin' up strays in the foothills obviously wasn't going to get his mind off this startling obsession he had for his best friend's daughter. No, he needed to go home to think and brood.

He needed to go home to face his demons, alone.

****

Late that afternoon, Hope strolled beside the stream. Sunlight sparkled on the crystalline surface, dazzling the eyes. Warm rays of light caressed her face, and she turned into them, savoring them. She sighed at the pleasure of the simple act and lifted her gaze to the imposing mountain peaks in the distance, so beautiful and burgeoning with life despite their forbidding façade.

Danger lurked there, too, she reminded herself. She'd seen some of it firsthand. Snakes and bandits waited to pounce on the innocent and unsuspecting. Ethan's warning about cougars yesterday drifted through her mind, and she added one more threat to her list. Grimacing, she kicked at a small rock with the toe of her kid boot as she eyed the slumbering giants to the west. Appearances—and all too frequently actions—were sometimes deceptive. This trip west was proving to be more than she'd bargained for.

She'd wanted to meet Matt, wanted to get to know him. Now she wasn't all together certain if her choice had been worth the pain. The restrictions of an isolated ranch and living under the constant threat of a murderous renegade were enough to give anyone pause. Not to mention dealing day in and day out with a neighbor who lived under the same roof and couldn't make up his mind whether he wanted to treat her as if she were something precious or something to be toyed with and ridiculed.

To her dismay, Ethan and his irascible moods seemed to take disproportionate priority. His callousness this morning had cut her, deeply. She'd almost convinced herself he was mean and contradictory. Then a little voice in the back of her mind taunted her that when Ethan decided to be nice…he could be so very, *very* nice.

She grimaced and kicked at a pebble, pushing that line of thought to the side. If she had half the sense she'd been born with—half the sense James had been so proud of—she'd march herself down to the train station and buy herself a ticket straight back to Boulder.

She had the means to go back and live quite comfortably, all alone if she so chose, for the rest of her life. Being of age, there was little Matt could say about it. She knew he wanted her to stay, sensed it every time they spoke, but she chalked it up to sentimentality, having recently received news that his brother had died, and she was, after all, his only remaining living relative. That was not to say he didn't care for her as a person, because he did, it showed in his eyes.

But she didn't want to go. In the short time she'd been here, she'd had more excitement—more *living*—than she'd had all those years in Maryland.

James had been good to her, good *for* her. He'd provided stability, a home, and a sense of family. He'd given her traditions and roots. Nevertheless, James had preferred the uneventful, the dull. He'd made it his purpose in life to protect her, to cushion her from whatever pain and unpleasantness he could. The Bar M, with its mountainous backdrop and its seductive, tempting neighbor, had given her a freedom and a sense of adventure she'd never before had. A sense of conquering the untamable. A feeling that there was more out there waiting for her, calling to her.

She understood, somewhere in the depths of her soul, it was what Matt had referred to on her first day here, as he'd stood at her side, staring out her window at the mountains. That indelible, indescribable thing—such an elemental part of this place—gave her wings. She wasn't ready to relinquish them. Not just yet. Ethan and his mercurial moods be damned. She gave her head a sharp nod to punctuate her decision.

For the first time in her life, she resolved to live for no one but herself. Her life was her own. She wouldn't allow anyone else to dictate it—not anymore. That resolution left her with a self-satisfied sense of purpose.

Hope turned her eyes back to the main house,

farther away now than she'd intended, and Matt's request for caution came back to her. Apprehensive, she glanced at the foothills and hurried her footsteps home. Unexpectedly, her step faltered. She'd accepted Matt's declaration that this was her home, taken it at face value. Just now, here by the stream, she'd claimed the ranch for herself.

Home…

A small smile tugged at the corners of her mouth, and she resumed her pace with renewed vigor. Newfound determination lifted her chin.

Chapter 14

Ethan perched on the split rail, grinding his teeth on a piece of straw as Julio worked with the new mare. She was a gorgeous chestnut, small and lightning fast, with a temper to match. Ethan's slow grin spread despite his sour mood as his foreman sailed through the air for the umpteenth time today. Julio had met his match. He was really working for it with this one.

Beating dust from the seat of his pants, Julio limped to the gate and motioned for one of the younger hands to bring him some water. While he waited, he wiped the sweat from his brow on his sleeve. For the first time in Ethan's recollection, Julio's years were beginning to show.

"Losing your touch, old man?"

"This one," Julio grumbled, spitting the dust from his mouth as he thumbed at the mare behind him, "she's different. I ain't seen one like her since that nag a' yours come stompin' through my gate."

The mare tossed her head and pranced around the corral, eyeing the top rail as if biding her time before she made good her escape.

Impulsively, Ethan threw a leg over the rail and dropped to the ground inside the corral. "Let me have a go at her."

Julio's brows lifted, but he stepped out of the way. His smirk suggesting he was more than content to sit back and watch his young boss eat a big helping of his pride. Shifting from one foot to the other, Julio rubbed at the thin, gray bristles on his weathered chin, propping a shoulder against the gate as Ethan square off with the skittish mare.

Julio's words of long ago echoed in Ethan's memory. It'd been a while since he'd done this, but it all came back as if it had been only yesterday. Before, with the other horses he'd tamed, it'd been a simple matter of gaining trust and establishing dominance…the exception, of course, being Apollo.

He began as he had that long ago day with his own beloved horse. They sized each other up, the horse and he…and then the dance began. Ethan stepped in, the mare shied away. He retreated, and she held her ground. Each time he got a little closer, but he could feel he wasn't gaining the particular ground he needed.

After one particularly nasty spill, Julio taunted from the gate, "It's you what's lost yer touch, boy."

Scowling, Ethan threw his hands in the air as he hobbled to the railing. "That horse should be shot."

"You ain't focused on what you want, boy, from that mare…or from yourself. Whatever gripe you got goin' on in your head, you'd best leave it at the gate."

"It's no use, she can't be tamed." Ethan glared at the mare. She gave him back a bit of sass with a toss of her head, flaunting his failure with smug glee.

"You can't give up now, boy. I stepped aside for you. You give up, we may as well set her loose 'cuz she ain't never gonna give her trust again. I'd have ta break her spirit to put her under a saddle, and you know damned well I don't work that way."

Visions of Hope flashed through Ethan's mind. How she'd looked the night of the ambush, when he'd accused her of not caring about Matt. He could see her, clear as if she stood before him right now, as she'd been that very morning when he'd stomped the fragile trust she'd given straight into the dirt. Her eyes haunted him, whether filled with fire and desire, or drenched in vulnerability and the pain of betrayal.

Julio shifted a piece of straw from one corner of his mouth to the other. "You want I should set 'er loose?"

Ethan faced the chestnut mare, narrowed his eyes in determination. He took a moment to respond, but when he did, his voice filled with steel. "No. She's not going anywhere."

With a renewed sense of purpose, he strode back into the center of the corral, more the man he used to be before the raid. Centered, sure of himself, sure of what he wanted and unafraid to claim it for his own. The horse sensed the change as well. She sidestepped, snorting and pawing at the packed ground. He squared his shoulders. He would grant no quarter. She was as good as his.

The mare put up a valiant fight, but in the end, Ethan's determination won out. As he crossed the yard to the hacienda that evening, Julio at his side, he grinned. He was heading back to the Bar M in short order. Indeed, he'd begun planning the rest of his night in thorough, unwavering detail. Oh, yes. The mare was his.

And soon, so would the woman be.

"Keep workin' with the chestnut while I'm gone."

Julio grunted.

Ethan stopped, turning to stare at the mare. She pranced inside the corral, defiant and beautiful. Spinning on his heel, he continued walking. "Pull her from the string. Take extra good care of her. She's gonna be a gift."

Julio's eyebrows shot up at that, and Ethan caught his sidelong glance.

"Come, old friend, let's go eat. Then I'm headin' back to the Bar M. Got something to do…something I shoulda done long before now." Ethan's grin stretched, wide and wicked.

****

Hope tiptoed by Matt's bedroom. She'd seen Natalia go in and close the door a little while ago, and she didn't want to interrupt. Once she'd gotten beyond the initial confusion, she thought it rather sweet, the way the two of them mooned over each other. Regardless of how jaded her feelings were about the softer emotions between men and women—excluding her parents of course—she was pleased for them. Matt had been alone a long time. He deserved someone who could make him as happy as her mother had made her father.

Between reading to Matt, helping Natalia in the kitchen, and visiting the stables, she'd been successful, at least to a certain degree, in pushing Ethan from her thoughts for the lion's share of the day. She'd taken Matt at face value when he'd spoken of her getting comfortable around the horses, and Manuel had been helpful…even if she did have difficulty understanding his instructions.

Hope's footsteps faltered just outside Ethan's room. A strange mix of emotions bubbled inside her. Gritting her teeth, she forced herself to keep walking. With any luck, he'd stay gone. Right now, all she wanted was the bath Natalia had sent up to her room and a good night's sleep. Hope pictured a tiny wooden barrel she'd be lucky if she had room to sit down in…never mind soaking. Ah, well, a bath was a bath… and it was far better than the stream.

Hope opened the door to her room, and her mouth fell open in surprise. There, in the corner of her room, sat a large copper tub, filled to the brim with water. Steam rolled from the smooth surface, beckoning her closer. She smiled with pure joy as she crossed to her trunks, blessing Natalia with every breath she took. She pulled a large jar filled with jasmine scented bath oils from one of her trunks and poured a liberal amount in the tub, then rolled up her sleeve and swirled the water with her hand.

The steam didn't lie. It was hot enough to turn her skin red as she slipped beneath the fragrant surface. For a long while, she closed her eyes and leaned against the raised lip of the tub, letting the water soak away the ache in her muscles. After an eternity, she picked up the dwindling stack of Matt's letters.

There were a few mundane letters describing Matt's travels. Then she came across one that made her sit a little straighter in the tub. This one had no date, held no names to denote about whom Matt had been writing. The scrawl was wild, blotchy—not the usual bold and certain strokes of Matt's pen. The note was short and to the point. The anguished words were painful to read, but it was the countless spots, where dried tears blurred the ink, that tore at her heart.

James,

My God, how am I to go on? I thought running away was the answer. Even over the miles I put between us, her memory haunted me day and night. Now her ghost does. Will I ever be free? I wonder if I would've been able to save her. If I had spoken up and made my feeling known, would she somehow still be alive? If I'd been there, could I have prevented this...somehow? How do I survive knowing that she is no longer of this world? I feel so empty! My heart is dead but I still breathe, how is that possible?

Matt

She set the letter down, hesitant to pick up another. Her brow furrowed. James had never mentioned a woman in Matt's life. Of course, if she'd died, perhaps James hadn't mentioned her out of deference to Matt's feelings. She'd started reading these letters to gain answers; instead, all she'd found were more questions. Puzzled, she gingerly laid the stack of letters aside and reached for her scented soap. Her brow furrowed as she lathered and rinsed.

Hope stepped from the tub and toweled herself dry in the cool night air, grateful for the roaring fire burning in the grate across the room. She blotted at her hair, wrapped the damp towel around her body, and reached for her brush.

Crossing to stand at her window, she held the edge of the curtain aside with one hand. Hope gazed at the silhouette of the mountains against the starry sky while she dragged the brush through her wet locks, stroke after slow stroke. The sight of those mountains, blanketed with pale moonlight, was soothing, a balm for the soul.

A slight flicker caught her eye—not outside in the darkness, but in the light reflected on the windowpane, the light coming from inside her room. She whirled on a gasp, her brush clattered to the floor. How had he come in without her hearing? Oh, dear heavens, how long had he been standing there?

Ethan leaned against the closed door, thumbs hooked in his pockets, watching her with smoldering eyes. His expression was all too serious for her peace of mind. She couldn't find her voice, could barely breath. His unwavering gaze locked on hers, holding her captive.

He didn't blink.

Finally, as Hope feared she'd pass out from lack of air, his gaze left hers at last. But the breath she'd managed to steal snagged in her throat as the heat in his gaze slid over her, like one long stroke of his hands down the length of her body. The corner of his mouth curled up, very slowly. Light from the fire danced shadows across his masculine features, but the blaze in his eyes was unmistakable.

When his grin reached maximum potency, he

deliberately pushed away from the door, his nimble fingers working the buckle of his gun belt loose. Drawing the belt from his waist, he let it trail to the floor as he sauntered forward, a predator tracking a decadent bit of prey. Hope gasped. Her heart stopped in her chest when his long fingers freed the buttons of his shirt.

No, she reminded herself, this wasn't going to happen. She was furious with him. Wasn't she? Just now she wasn't certain of anything but the weight in her chest and the delicious, fluttering warmth pooling deep in the pit of her stomach.

Hope did her level best to glare at him despite her hammering pulses. That glare felt pitifully ineffective. "You shouldn't be here. You're not sleeping here tonight."

His grin was a bit lopsided now, but his voice slid around her like smooth, dark silk. "Oh, I doubt there'll be any sleeping goin' on in here tonight."

Eyes narrowed, he stalked Hope as he slipped the last button free and tossed his shirt aside. For a fleeting moment, all conscious thought flew from her mind as Hope watched the shirt sail through the air. His boots hit the floor, one after another, and she jumped, staring in wide-eyed fascination at the muscular expanse of his chest. She couldn't look away.

His illicit stare traveled down the length of her once more. By the time his steady gaze returned to her face, his eyes were hot enough to set her on fire, scorching her with their sensual intent.

Hope's eyes widened and her mouth went dry. Panic rose up, choking her. "Whaa..." She forced a swallow. "What do you think you're doing?"

His fiery gaze roamed over her face before sweeping down the length of her neck and over her bare shoulders, stopping on the spot where she'd tucked the bunched edge of the towel just over her breasts. Blatant desire strained the lines of his face. His feral, hungry gaze lit on her lips then rose to her eyes. Locked.

"I'm gonna make love to you, sweetheart." Fact, not question. His voice—the very words themselves—shot spears of excitement coursing through her body.

Her knees shook. Her mouth fell open in stunned disbelief. At last, when her lungs burned in protest of the lack of air, she dragged in another ragged supply.

Ethan's fingers made short work of the buttons on his pants, and the waist of his denims sank dangerously low on his narrow hips, enticing her unwilling gaze to follow the smattering of fine golden hair downward over the defined muscles of his taut stomach. The rock hard muscles of his chest and abdomen rippled and flexed as he drew closer, closing in on her with a carnal gleam in his eyes.

By the time he stood before her, the fierce flutter low in her belly had eaten away a sizeable chunk of her resistance. Her gaze flew to his, and she was trapped, unable to look away from the sizzling blue flames.

She shook her head in denial, but her voice was a weak whisper. "No, Ethan…"

He took one last, deliberate step and reached for her, caging her hips in a firm grip before she could make good an escape. Belatedly, she pushed at his chest, but her hands stilled as the heat of his skin seared her palms.

"I've made up my mind, sweetheart. If you can look into my eyes—if you can kiss me and make me believe you don't want me, I'll go. I'll walk out that door and ride back to my ranch tonight." Ethan waited. His lips twitched, and he added, "Though I can't promise I won't be back."

She couldn't form the denial to send him away,

though somehow she still managed to keep the pressure on his chest, managed to keep a modicum of distance between them. His impassioned stare wore her resistance down.

Her strength wavered as he continued to speak, his voice velvety seduction—raw unadulterated temptation annihilating her defenses. "But you won't do that, you won't tell me to go…"

"Won't I?" Brave words, but her hands trembled against him, giving her away.

"No, you won't." His thumbs caressed slow circles near her navel, and the flutter inside her turned into a primal clawing need. The towel irritated her sensitive flesh, an intrusive barrier where none was truly wanted.

Hope searched in vain one last time for resistance, for common sense. Anything to stop this madness. "How do you know I won't?"

Ethan's heart pounded an accelerated cadence against her palm, communicating his need and his desire every bit as much as his eyes and voice were. His muscles bunched beneath her greedy fingertips.

"You don't want me to go, Hope." He drew her closer. "You respond to me every time you're in my arms. That knowledge haunts me, day and night. I remember the feel of your skin against mine, the taste of you. It's all I've been able to think about," he murmured, lifting a hand to trail it over her shoulder and down her arm. "Holding you at night—holding you and not tearing your clothing off and ravishing you—has been next to killing me." His hand slid to the small of her back.

Sweet heavens, what those words did to her.

Swallowing hard, she scraped up the last dregs of her resistance, shoving at his chest, shaking her head. He didn't budge an inch. "No, Ethan. I can't face your cruelty and your disdain in the morning when you decide you don't like me again. You don't know what you want, Ethan. Just leave me alone."

Ethan tilted his head down until his face was inches from hers. His direct, sensual gaze bore into hers, burning in its ferocity, striking a chord of longing deep inside her. "I *do* know what I want, Hope."

His lips feathered over hers, the hint of a butterfly kiss.

"I. Want. You."

She blinked at him, dazed, speechless.

"Don't ask me to leave you, sweetheart, because I can't. Somehow, you got under my skin." Certainty rippled in his voice, swam in his eyes. "You're in my blood, Hope. I swear, from here on out you'll never have anything but pure heat and passion from me. I can't run from this anymore. Forgive me..." He nibbled at her jaw. "Hate me..." He suckled at her earlobe. "But just don't ask me to leave you tonight, because *that* I cannot do."

Her hands no longer had the strength to hold him at bay as the heat from his supple, golden skin tempted her to touch more, to feel more. He tightened his hold on her hips, pulling her to him, pressing his rigid arousal against her. There was no escape.

His voice grew hard, implacable. "Show me you don't crave this..."

With that, Ethan lowered his head and sealed his lips to hers. His mouth slanted, ravaging her senses. Nothing could have prepared her for the shock wave of desire rippling through her.

Before the fires could burn out of control, he released her lips, leaning back to look into her eyes. "Now, tell me to go."

She stared up at him, her gaze searching his. Lucidity, cold and clear pushed through the haze of desire. She'd chosen the Bar M as her home. She'd chosen to make her life her own. Now, she faced another choice. *This* was her choice.

She chose Ethan.

Sinking her fingers deep in his hair, she tugged his lips back to hers, granting him what they both so desperately needed.

He froze for half a heartbeat, then his lips seized hers with feral possessiveness. Her hands dropped to his shoulders, her fingers dug into hard muscle, grasping for something solid to cling to while her world careened madly. Ethan's mouth claimed hers, again and again. His tongue thrust, laving against hers, tangling, demanding her surrender.

His hands swept upward to cup her breast through the towel. A low growl rumbled deep in his throat. The sound both frightened and excited her. He kept her head spinning with his heady kisses, as his deft fingers found the corner of the towel. The damp material fluttered to the floor at her ankles.

Ethan lifted his head and gazed down at her. His expression was so fierce, so intense, she took an involuntary step back. He followed, snaking his arms around her again, crushing her to him as his mouth devoured hers once more. He swept her up into his powerful arms and turned toward the bed, closing the distance in three, long-legged strides. His mouth still on hers, he lowered her to the bed and came down on top of her.

His weight, his heat was delicious. Hope wrapped her arms around his neck, eager for more. The sensation of his naked skin sliding against hers was intoxicating. She tunneled her fingers deep into his hair, trembling as he drew her tongue into his mouth and sucked. Her skin flamed to life as questing, calloused fingertips trailed down her neck, feathered across her collarbone, lingering at her breast as if memorizing the texture of her skin.

His hand slipped down between them, and his fingers caressed the heated flesh between her thighs.

She gasped at the shocking pleasure of his hands on her. Then the ache swelled, growing uncontrollably. Her hips rocked in a wordless plea, and he shuddered in her arms.

Ethan shifted to finish removing his pants, but Hope refused to let go of him, fearful the moment would slip away...or worse yet, that one—or both of them—would regain sanity. Her hands slid over his muscled back, reveling in the play of thick, corded muscles beneath her fingertips. His chest rasped over hers, caressing her sensitive breasts, tormenting her as he shifted once again to cover her with his heat. She bit back a whimper. Her hands pulled at him, tugging him closer, urging him on.

Ethan ravaged her mouth, sinking one hand deep into the thick, wet mass of her hair, cupping her head in his palm. She felt so good against him he could hardly think straight. He settled a hand on her hip, anchoring her beneath him. She was wildfire in his arms. Greedy. Ready to consume. He reveled in her responsiveness...in her passion. The scent of her midnight locks, the flavor of her skin enveloped him, making him ravenous and impatient.

He'd meant to coax her, to prepare her small body with a languid, sensual assault. But as she writhed beneath him, Ethan fought a losing battle to control the tidal waves of lust crashing relentlessly over him. She whimpered into his mouth, pushing her hips up against him.

Ethan surrendered.

The broad head of his manhood press into her core. Her heat burned him, made him tremble with need. She raised her knees on either side of his hips, moaning against his lips. She arched into him as his thickness ruthlessly filled her, stretching her. God, she was so tight. So unbelievably hot. Then he butted against the thin membrane of her innocence.

Euphoric possessiveness, primal hunger roared

through him.

She was his. She had never—would never—belong to another.

Unable to harness even a ghost of gentleness, he pulled back slightly, and thrust hard, burying himself inside her...so deep he swore their souls touched.

He captured her startled scream with his mouth. The sting of her nails scoring his back brought him some tattered vestiges of control. Ethan stilled, allowing her precious moments to adjust. She turned her head away, tears slipping down her cheeks to soak his wrist.

His heart twisted with a new tenderness. Ethan captured her reluctant lips, pouring all the boiling emotion seething inside him into the kiss. Determined, he brought her hesitant body back into the throes of passion with his lips, his hands, and his body.

When she once again responded to his kisses with eager abandon, when her body began rocking against his, matching the rhythm he set, he surrendered what little control he had left. Her moans and gasps of pleasure drove him on, drove all thoughts of restraint from his mind. His mouth branded the pulse at the base of her throat. He guided her legs around his waist and surged inside her, slamming into her over and over, pushing them both straight over the edge of carnal delirium into a sea of euphoric satisfaction. As she pulsed around him, crying out his name, Ethan poured out his seed deep inside her, positive he'd found heaven right here on earth.

At last, when Ethan came to his senses, he trailed tender kisses across her damp cheek, wrapped his arms around her, and rolled onto his back taking her with him. She went boneless and loose-limbed. Her head settled on his chest, tucked beneath his chin, his heart pounding furiously against his rib cage. His hands smoothed over her shoulders and down her back, until her breathing evened out, and she drifted to sleep. Ethan followed her into slumber a short while later, contentment like he'd never known filled his chest to the point of aching.

****

Sometime later, as the moon rode high in the night sky, Hope woke to feather-light kisses on her neck. Darkness held the room in shadows. The lamps were cold, and glowing embers winked in the grate, but tonight the shadows didn't bother her, not with Ethan's hands on her body. Not with his lips finding all her sensitive spots.

He covered her with his heat again, nibbling the susceptible skin below her ear, until she moaned with pleasure.

His lips hovered at her ear, as his thick shaft slid, deep and sure, inside her. "I believe I promised you heat..."

This time, the heat he gave her was a long, slow burn that expanded, slow and steady, into an explosion so fierce, so complete she clung to him, whimpering his name.

Chapter 15

Hope woke, replete and languorous, as dawn crept over the horizon. It took quite a few moments to marshal the strength to open her eyes. When she did, it was to find she was alone...again. However, this time, as she rolled to her side she discovered a single wildflower lying on Ethan's pillow.

Smiling, she lifted the blossom, inhaling its sweet, innocent fragrance. Rolling to her back, she stretched, cat-like, and giggled. She couldn't wait to see Ethan again, couldn't wait to see that wonderful smile of his. Bounding from the bed with a spurt of happy energy, she hurried to dress. Leaving the wild mass of her hair unbound, she picked Ethan's flower up and made her way down the stairs on light feet.

Her happy footsteps faltered outside of Matt's room as Ethan's angry voice surged through the crack in the doorway.

"You're well enough now, Matt, get it over with," Ethan demanded. "Tell her the truth, for Christ sake. She has a right to know. Give her the letter James wrote if she needs proof, but you have to tell Hope you're her father! You don't have any logical reason to wait any longer."

Hope froze, her mind raced, tripping over itself. What was Ethan talking about? Matt thought he was her father? Impossible. What letter?

Matt's rough voice broke through the haze, and she crept closer to the door.

"How am I supposed to tell her?" Matt's tone took on a mocking timbre. "Hope, my dear, could you please pour me a cup of coffee. Oh, and by the way, I fell in love with your mother before she ever married your father and one night, when we thought Jacob had died, we made love in a fit of grief. According to James, you're the result."

The flower fell from her numb fingers, landing on the floor outside the doorway without a sound. Agony and shock slapped at her, and she stumbled back a step. Words and phrases from some of the letters Matt had written to James tumbled through her mind in a chaotic rush. Hope pressed a fist to her chest and one to her mouth in a vain attempt to quell pain surging in unbearable proportions. Whatever else they said was lost to her. A wave of nausea rolled through her until she almost doubled over with the force of it. She placed a palm on the cool wall to brace herself for a moment.

Hope stumbled down the hallway on wooden legs, her eyes locked on the door ahead of her. The rest of the hall dimmed. The walls pressed in on her. Air was nonexistent. She passed the kitchen and kept right on walking. The clank and clang of pots and pans echoed in her head, hollow and tinny. The cheerful sunshine on the veranda couldn't warm her. Her chest felt tight, as if a steel band squeezed her lungs, crushed her heart. She couldn't breathe.

Matt was her father? It wasn't possible. Her mother loved her father...Jacob...with all her heart. She'd never have betrayed Jacob. No, this all had to be a horrible mistake. Matt had to be mistaken. Ethan was mistaken.

Ethan...

Ethan knew about something like this—mistake or not—and hadn't said anything to her about it? After last night, how could he keep something like this from her?

She had to escape. She had to get away from the ranch, away from Matt, and away from Ethan. Away from words that shook the very foundation of her existence. Everything seemed to be closing in on her at once. Her world wobbled and spun.

Then she found herself in the stables, standing eye-to-equine-eye with the gentle Daisy.

****

Natalia barged into Matt's room without knocking, the stable boy in tow. "Ethan, you have to come—hurry."

Struggling to sit up, Matt demanded, "What's wrong?"

"It's Hope. She told Roberto to saddle Daisy for her, and she rode off alone."

Ethan turned to the boy, unease growing inside him. "What happened?"

"Si, señor, the lady—Miss Hope—very upset when she come into the stables. She tell me to saddle the little mare, then she ride west, to the mountain." The boy eyed Ethan, shamefaced, shifting from one foot to the other, fidgeting with the tail of his shirt.

A flash of white in Natalia's hand drew Ethan's gaze. An apprehensive fist constricted his heart. He pointed to the familiar flower. "Where'd you get that?"

"It was lying on the floor outside Matt's door."

Ethan's gaze swung to Matt, and he watched the color drain from his friend's face. Was his own face as pale?

"Go," Matt urged Ethan, frantic. "You have to find her..."

Ethan was already running from the room, his heart in his throat. That morning, his men had confirmed Vega's renegades were keeping a constant vigil on the ranch from the foothills west of the Old Mission. Pablo and some of the others had stumbled across one of their outposts, cold but well used. They'd found tracks to a point beyond the Old Mission where Vega's men had been meeting someone.

Someone who'd returned to the Circle K.

If Vega's spies saw her riding from the ranch alone, it would be so easy for them to... He couldn't even finish that thought. He'd seen firsthand what those brutal monsters were capable of doing to an innocent woman. Fear rose up to choke him. His delicate little Hope wouldn't stand a chance.

Ethan raced across the yard, legs pumping, stomach churning, eyes scanning the western horizon, but she'd already disappeared into the foothills. Swearing, he darted into the stables and saddled Apollo in record time. He tore away from the ranch a short while later, praying to God he'd find her before they did.

****

Hope's thoughts were too tangled to divide her attentions. She gave Daisy free rein, letting the mare race where she would. Ethan's words kept circling in her mind. Then there were Matt's astonishing comments to deal with. And this letter James was supposed to have written...she didn't even know what to make of that.

James...

She shook her head, battling tears. James had been her rock. If he had known about this—this absurd assumption—he'd never have kept it from her. He'd have told her. But a small voice in her head whispered with niggling doubt.

Wouldn't he have?

The suspicions came. What would he have done to protect her? What would he have done to protect his brothers? She couldn't accept that her mother had been involved with Matt...but if the situation was as she'd overheard, why hadn't Matt mentioned something sooner?

She couldn't even begin to deal with Ethan's part in all this. He'd withheld the information and slept with her anyway. He'd made love to her, knowing this *lie* hung above her head, waiting to cut her down with no way to defend against it. Raw betrayal knifed through her chest, tearing at her insides. Tears pooled in her eyes and overflowed. She dropped her head and squeezed her eyes closed tight, damning herself for her weakness as hot tears scalded her cheeks.

A dark shadow fell over her as she passed near a large boulder. She glanced up in time to see a large streak of filthy tan sailing through the air. The impact cut her scream short. Before she knew what was happening, she found herself lying flat on her back in the dust with a terrifying predator straddling her chest, pinning her to the ground.

Saliva dripped from the corner of his gaping mouth. Jagged, yellowed teeth flashed, and the stench of his breath made her gag. The violent gleam in those feral, amber eyes promised a very slow, very painful death. Terror coursed through her.

Hope's assailant leaned back on his haunches as soon as his partner came out from behind the boulder. They were as night and day. The man pinning her to the ground was brawny and heavy-featured, his partner lean, bordering on gangly, with a remarkably handsome face. A real Pretty-Boy—if not for the evil glint in his eyes and the well-used gun strapped to his thigh.

The two men argued in rapid Spanish. Although she couldn't understand a word, it was obvious whatever they'd agreed upon didn't bode well for her. The Brute leered down at her, swiped the back of his hand across his gaping mouth, and reached down to squeeze her breast in a punishing grip.

Her arms were pinned at her sides. She couldn't fight him, couldn't scratch his eyes out. Hope battled the urge to vomit, gave in to the need to scream. Pretty-Boy barked at the Brute, his palm resting on the butt of his gun with ominous, unmistakable threat.

The Brute glared at Pretty-Boy, but he dragged her up by a handful of her hair all the same, laughing when she let out an involuntary cry of pain. He shoved her toward Pretty-Boy, laughing again when she stumbled. He stalked toward Daisy.

Hope forced a swallow and faced her captor, preparing to plead for her release.

She'd underestimated Pretty-Boy, taken him as the lesser of the two evils, perhaps because he'd prevented the first from mauling her. Maybe because he at least looked as if he'd seen the right side of a bath within the last month. His expression was bland, almost bored, his grasp lax.

Hope learned the error in her judgment.

As the Brute came back with the skittish mare, Pretty-Boy drew a huge, wicked-looking knife from a soft leather sheath strapped to his leg. His grip on her wrist tightened like a steel vise. Hope gasped first in shock, then at the searing pain, as he drew the honed edge of the blade across her palm, taking obvious pleasure in her pain. Blood welled. Before she could guess at his intentions, he laid her wounded hand flat on the horse's neck, smearing her gruesome handprint down the animal's glossy coat. With a cruel laugh, he slapped the horse's rump, sending the mare flying back down the slope.

Pretty-Boy turned on his heel, dragging her resistant form behind him. The Brute set out in the opposite direction. God only knew where they'd take her if they managed to get her on horseback. She had no one to rely on but herself. If she wanted to survive, she had to keep her wits about her.

Her desperate gaze dropped to the ground. A rock lay in their path. As soon as they reached it, she fell to her knees—careful to make sure her skirts covered her hand—and grasped her fist-sized weapon. As she went down, she wrenched her wrist free from her abductor's grip. Her fingers sank into loose gravel and curled. She ignored the bite of gravel in her open wound.

She waited.

Her timing would be crucial. Pretty-Boy let out an irritated curse and came back, bending to reach for her. As he did so, she pelted the sand into his eyes. Covering his face with both hands, he snarled viciously.

Springing into action, Hope leaped to her feet, swinging the rock with every ounce of desperation roiling in her veins. The rock connected with the side of his face. He went down, hard. She didn't wait around to see whether he moved or not, whether he breathed or not. Yanking up her skirts, Hope ran for all she was worth.

Her kid boots skidded on the loose rocks as she stumbled headlong down the incline. Pebbles and sand skittered down the side of the slope ahead of her in minuscule landslides. She snatched at the sparse vegetation, trying to maintain her balance without slowing herself down. Once she was on the level ground—in the wide open, the Brute would easily ride her down, but she couldn't stop. She'd deal with that particular difficulty when she got there. Right now, she needed to focus on getting down this slope without breaking her neck.

Brute's irate shout drifted to her on the wind, and she cursed, wishing she could have had more of a head start. She didn't spare a glance over her shoulder, kept clawing her way down the incline. Her skirts snagged on prickly pear, and she yanked them free. The long cut on the inside of her palm stung from sand and sweat, but that pain was inconsequential when compared with what they would do to her if they caught her again. Her breath raged in her ears, her lungs burned.

Then she was falling, rolling, tumbling. Sky and earth blurred. Jagged rocks gouged and bruised her tender flesh, shredding her dress. Her hair whipped into her eyes, blinding her. Pain seared the inside of her cheek, and the coppery tang of blood burst in her mouth. Her head swam and darkness loomed, waiting to snare her. She fought to stay lucid.

If she passed out, she was dead.

When she finally stopped rolling, Hope scrabbled to her knees. The earth wobbled and tilted beneath her feet, but the approaching thud of hooves pushed her onward. She used the slope of the land more than actual eyesight to determine which way to run. Something massive rushed past her. The ground rose up to smack at her face. The pain grew distant. The thudding returned. Cruel laughter brought tears of frustration to her eyes. Even so, she struggled to regain her feet. She wouldn't willingly lie down and die.

Throwing the hair back out of her eyes, Hope forced herself not to flinch at the thundering hooves aimed in her direction. Glancing out the corner of her eye, she gritted her teeth. Could she throw herself out of the way in time? She trained her unblinking gaze at the Brute, poised to leap at the last possible minute.

A bright burst of crimson exploded in the middle of the Brute's filthy shirt. His yellowed eyes rolled back in his head, and he toppled from the saddle. His boot tangled in the stirrup, and the charging horse veered to the side at the awkward drag. Then he fell free, rolling to a stop not fifty feet from her. Dust swirled around his motionless body. Half expecting to see the second of the two abductors bearing down upon her, Hope glanced up.

A grateful sob ripped from her throat. Relief brought her to her knees. Ethan drove Apollo right to her side. He vaulted from the saddle and dropped to his knees beside her. With a gun still in hand, Ethan jerked her against him, caging her to his chest, angling his body between her and the foothills.

"Are there any more?" His heart slammed at her ear.

She managed to subdue the violent, wracking sobs, but she couldn't restrain the tears. Ethan's hand tightened on her shoulder as she buried her face against his neck and began weeping, clinging to him.

"Hope…is there anyone else out there?" His voice was urgent, his body tense.

She gave a brief nod. His muscles turned to rock beneath her cheek. "One for sure—but I, I hit him with a rock. I think…I knocked him out…"

Ethan hesitated.

"Damn it," he swore under his breath.

He leaned back, peering down to her eyes. The blood drained from his face. His hands flew over her body, probing, searching. His fingers trembled as he tilted her face up to his. "You're bleeding." He gathered her close, his free hand still searching her arms and legs as he mumbled, "Oh, God…you're covered in blood."

She tried to talk, tried to tell him she was all right, but her words only came out in a helpless whimper.

"I need to get you back to the ranch. Can you ride?"

She nodded, clinging to him, fighting to stem the tears gushing down her cheeks. Ethan stood, his eyes riveted on the hillside. He scooped her into his arms, whistling for his horse. Apollo pranced to his master's side.

Rather than getting up onto the saddle himself, he lifted Hope up and set her across the seat. Apollo tossed his head, but he stood his ground. Ethan put his boot in the stirrup and pulled himself up behind her, wrapping his body around her like a shield, then he urged Apollo back to the ranch. She shook violently in the warm cocoon of his body. Closing her eyes, she struggled for control, all too aware there was precious little to spare.

Even as they drew alongside the main house, she remained silent, subdued. She buried her face against his neck, refusing to look at any of the faces lined up along the veranda as Ethan lifted her down. She remained silent as he cradled her against his chest and carried her all the way to her room. Hope let it all float by her, retreating to another time, another place...distancing herself from the horrors she'd faced...and the betrayal she'd discovered.

Ethan shouldered the door to her room open, carried her inside, and bent to lay her on the bed. His concerned gaze searched her face, skimming over her blood-soaked, torn clothing. Before he could speak to her, Natalia and Manuel came bursting into the room. Natalia took one look at Hope, and ordered Ethan from the room. He stiffened, his eyes locked on Hope's face, pleading.

She was, even now, so very aware of his presence, yet Hope refused to acknowledge him. Anger and betrayal held her in their unrelenting grip, just beneath the surface of icy shock. Despite his having saved her, she couldn't get passed the duplicity. How had he kept such a horrendous secret from her? Come what may, the trauma she'd just lived through seemed to magnify her anger. Worry and anguish brimmed in his beautiful blue eyes, but she focused on a point beyond his shoulder. He could go ease his guilty conscience somewhere else as far as she was concerned.

****

Frustration and dismay coursed through him as Ethan tried to get her to look *at* him, instead of *through* him. He had to talk to her, needed to know how much she'd heard. He wanted to ask her about Vega's men.

God help them if…

He wanted to kiss her, wanted to hold her. More than anything else, he needed to make that wounded look in her eyes go away. She was so battered, so helpless.

"Hope—"

"Go, Ethan." Natalia cut him off, pushing him to the door. "I need to see to her."

Ethan wouldn't leave her. He had to help her. Somehow, he had to make this right.

But Natalia wouldn't be denied. She shoved at his chest, her lips pressed in a flat line. "Not now, Ethan. Let me clean her up first, see how badly she's hurt."

"I'll be back, sweetheart," he called over Natalia's head, trying one last time to draw her attention, unsuccessfully. Frustrated, Ethan backed out into the hallway, and Natalia closed the door in his face. Responsibilities weighed heavily upon him. He had men to wrangle, a herd to check, horses to tame, and bandits to track.

None of that mattered now.

He wouldn't leave this spot until he'd seen with his own eyes his Hope was all right.

Please, God, let her be all right…

Chapter 16

The click of the doorknob snapped Ethan's tormented gaze from the floor. He strained to peer around Natalia—his worried stare seeking the center of his world—but the door closed before he could catch more than a fleeting glimpse of the battered woman on the bed. Ethan shoved away from the wall, tense and impatient.

"Is she all right? Did they..." He glared at the door behind Natalia, fists clenched at his sides. "How badly is she... Has she spoken yet?"

Natalia's sympathetic eyes roamed his face as she laid a gentle hand on his forearm. "She's bruised and battered, scrapped up a bit, but she'll be fine. The wound on her hand was not deep enough for stitches, but it took a while to clean out all the gravel."

"Did they..." He couldn't force another word passed the lump in his throat. Visions of Christina's misused body swam before his eyes.

"I'm certain they did not touch her in that way, Ethan," she assured him with far too much understanding in her sad, dark eyes. She laid a comforting hand on his cheek. "She's going to be fine, *mijo*."

Dragging his hands over his face, Ethan sagged against the wall. The breath he'd been holding expelled in a loud whoosh. His shoulders slumped.

Natalia's voice cut through his relief. "You should give her some time..."

Her words trailed away, as he was already

reaching for the doorknob. Shaking her head, Natalia descended the steps muttering beneath her breath in Spanish.

Ethan stepped inside the room and closed the door behind him. Hope sat on the edge of the bed, clad in her dressing robe. Damp tendrils of silky ebony spilled down her back. The beginnings of a nasty bruise rode high on her left cheek. Tiny cuts and scrapes peppered her pale skin. She stared, expressionless, at the bulky bandage wrapped around her left palm.

Ethan leaned back against the door, hands braced flat against the wood at his sides, much as he had last night. His intentions couldn't have been more different. She was so bedraggled and bruised…vulnerable…and so very beautiful. His heart ached.

"I'm not leaving until you talk to me," he vowed, searching her face for a hint of reaction, a flicker of emotion…anything.

An eternity passed before Hope drew a deep, labored breath and lifted a vacant stare. Her eyes were empty. No anger. No tears. No emotion at all. His heart froze in his chest. He was across the room in a heartbeat, reaching for her.

Hope bolted. Tucking her hands behind her back, she edged around the side of the bed and backed several steps away, and croaked, "Don't touch me."

His frozen heart shattered. Ethan stopped in his tracks. His hands fell to his sides, empty. Loss ate a hole in his chest a mile wide. Hope's lower lip trembled, tears welled in her eyes, and Ethan dredged deep for patience. He didn't advance, but, likewise, he refused to retreat.

"Sweetheart, we have to talk. I know what you must have heard this morning. It may have sounded bad, but—"

"Bad? Bad!" Her sudden fury lashed at him. Her eyes flashed churning green fire. "How could you ever think that particular conversation could have sounded bad?"

"Hope, you have to give Matt a chance to explain." He moved forward, but she scampered away once more.

"The hell I do," Hope snarled, backing herself up against the far wall. Hysteria crept into her eyes.

"You owe it to yourself to hear the truth," he persisted.

"I know the truth," Hope barked, glaring at him. Her hands fisted at her sides. "My father was Jacob Lewis."

"Sweetheart, go to Matt. He can—"

"Don't you *dare* call me sweetheart! You knew all along Matt had this"—her unbandaged hand waved wildly in the air, punctuating her words—"this *ridiculous* notion, and you never said anything to me. Even after I let you—" Hope pressed her fist against her lips for a moment, her flaming eyes accusatory, raking at his conscience. "How could you be so cruel? I'll never forgive you for this, Ethan. I won't forgive you for—"

Ethan took hold of her shoulders before she could sidle sideways, cutting her off mid-sentence with a little shake. Hope braced her hands on his chest, shoving against him. Her beautiful lips pulled back on a snarl. He didn't budge. He didn't let go. But his heart bled.

"Damn you. Let go of me, you..."

Ethan's fingers bit into her shoulders. He was losing her, right before his eyes, and terror consumed him. "Look at me, Hope."

"No." She stared at his chest. "Let go—"

"Look at me, damn it." He gave her another sharp little shake. Control slipped like water through his fingers. "Hope, sweetheart, please..."

Her furious emerald stare snapped to his face. Her lips parted, but he moved in before she could argue, filling her mouth with his tongue, wrapping his arms around her, crushing her against his chest.

Desperation clawed through him. Her fists fluttered against his shoulders. She arched her back, straining to evade the heat of his kiss. Her breath sobbed out against his lips. Hope twisted her head to the side, but he wouldn't yield.

His hand skimmed up her back beneath her hair and locked around the nape of her neck, forcing her to accept the full brunt of his invasion. Gripping her bottom, he wedged his knee between her thighs, grinding himself against her. Sanity fled in the face of his overwhelming need to hold her closer, kiss her deeper, and unleash the passion she fought so hard to deny.

She stilled in his arms, no longer fighting him.

Then Hope was kissing him back and a grateful sob burned the back of his throat.

Hope's fingers tangled in Ethan's hair, and she strained to pull him closer, returning his kiss with unrestrained ardor. Truth and secrets be damned. She'd survived. She was alive. She wanted to *feel* alive. Her hands tore at Ethan's shirt, but no matter how much she touched, she couldn't slake the desire to feel more still. His hot, moist lips branded the side of her neck, and his hands released her to shed the remainder of his clothes. When the last sock hit the floor, his hard, rough hands found their way to the belt at her waist.

Hope tugged her arms from her robe and wrapped them around his neck. Ethan lifted her by the waist, pinning her to the wall with his large frame. His splayed, demanding hands gripped her thighs, guiding her legs around his waist. Hope accommodated him, locking her ankles, tilting her hips in impatient demand. His hands shifted, clutching her hips in a bruising hold as his mouth slanted over hers, again and again, devouring, ravaging her senses.

"Tell me, Hope," he rasped against her mouth. The tip of his hard, pulsing manhood poised to invade. His breathing was ragged against her skin. "Tell me you want me. Tell me you need this, too."

Unable to put words to her turbulent thoughts, Hope dug her fingers into his hair and yanked his head to hers, sinking her tongue inside his mouth. Ethan groaned, deep in his throat. His straining sex surged inside her, slamming her back against the wall in fierce possession, and Hope cried out at the thrilling sensation. He thrust deep, rocking his hips against her. Again and again. She moaned, urging him deeper. The scent of him engulfed her, enflamed her need. His skin was hot against her, thawing the icy shock encasing her brain, caressing her heart. She couldn't get enough of the way he tasted, the way he felt...the way he moaned her name.

She was *alive.*

Every powerful flex and thrust of Ethan's hips was affirmation of life, and she savored every second.

The world fell away for Hope. The only thing that existed—the only thing that mattered—was the man in her arms. She dove headlong into emotions and sensations only he could make her feel, surrendering everything to him in that moment.

Everything.

Hope's wild surrender sank through Ethan, all the way to his bones, overwhelming him. What little restraint he'd held over his baser passions crumbled like the walls of the Old Mission. He drove into her with feral abandon, his ragged breath fluttering her hair. His teeth scraped the side of her neck, and he lapped at her with his tongue. Pain seared across his shoulders and down his back where her fingernails scored his skin.

Hope tensed in his arms, panting harder and harder with every thrust. He gasped against the side of her neck as her body convulsed in his arms, milking his shaft. Ethan sealed his mouth over hers, gulping down her screams as he exploded inside her, fusing them together. Body and soul.

For a long while afterwards, ragged panting echoed in the otherwise silent room. His heart banged against his ribs. Ethan trailed his hands down her ribs, and she flinched. Her injuries...how could he have forgotten? Cautiously, he edged his upper body back until he could see her face, his lower body still locked in place. Had he hurt her? His heaving heart wrenched inside his chest.

"Sweetheart, are you all right?" Tears dampened her anguished face. Tenderness like he'd never known poured through him. He'd do anything to make the pain go away.

"Please, just go," she whispered brokenly, turning her head aside.

He stiffened. Anything but that, he silently amended. "Sweetheart, I can't leave you—"

"Go away, Ethan." Hope's voice shook. Her bottom lip quivered.

Determined, he clenched his jaw, wrapped his arms around her waist to support her weight, and leaned back from the wall, taking her with him, his rigid manhood still embedded deep within her.

Hope gasped. Her arms and legs locked around him. Her eyes widened. "What are you doing?"

"I *won't* leave you like this," he enunciated.

Ethan cradled her close as he leaned over the bed, lowering them both to its softness. Buried inside her as he was, he was still hard...and getting painfully harder by the second. Before she could voice the protest building in her beautiful eyes, his lips covered hers in a kiss so filled with tenderness it shattered her resistance every bit as much as his raging passions had moments ago. Hips undulating, he began rocking inside her, slow and deep. He caressed her with reverent hands. His lips worshipped her skin.

Ethan poured his heart and soul into every touch, every kiss, desperate to prolong their lovemaking. She moaned, writhing against him. Her eager cries drove him on. When he couldn't hold that final moment of completion off any longer—when the dam burst and swept them up and away—Ethan slowed and deepened his thrusts even more. Hope sobbed his name when she climaxed, sending him over the edge. He spilled his seed deep inside her womb, collapsing against her shoulder, spent and unable to move.

Long moments passed before Ethan rolled to his side, gathering her sleeping form up in his arms. He held her as the sun shifted in the sky, casting shadows over her lithe body. She sighed against his shoulder, murmuring his name in her sleep. The painful, uncomfortable thudding in his chest had nothing to do with his physical exertions. Shaken to the core, Ethan disentangled their limbs and scooted from the bed. He pulled on his clothing and sat on the edge of the bed to tug on his boots.

Hope murmured again, as if protesting the loss of his heat, and rolled onto her side, curling into a small ball. His horrified gaze locked on the vicious bruises and abrasions marring her tender back. Ethan gritted his teeth, battling to contain his fury. He'd find them, he vowed. He'd take pleasure in killing every last one of those bastards for doing this to her.

He also blamed himself for her condition. If he'd shut Matt's damn door… If he'd told her the truth… If he hadn't insisted she get comfortable riding… If he'd only…

Ethan stopped himself. It was no use going down this road. Guilt had changed nothing the last time. It would change nothing now. He had recriminations aplenty, but in the end, it all boiled down to one thing.

It was his fault.

Again.

Ethan shook out the blanket on the foot of Hope's bed and covered her, tucking the sides close. Bending over her, he placed a whisper soft kiss on her lips before he slipped from her room.

Turning his feet toward the stables, he forced his mind to the responsibilities at hand. He needed to get the hell out of here for a while. If he couldn't see her, then maybe he wouldn't want her so damned much.

Her scent clung to his skin, mocking him with the fact that out of sight didn't always mean out of mind.

****

Hope woke with a start. Her gaze darted around the room, but Ethan was gone. Heaving a mixed sigh of regret and relief, she considered rolling over and going back to sleep, but her stomach growled and her throat was parched. With a groan, she dragged herself up, crawled out of bed, and got dressed. Dear Lord, she hurt.

She didn't want to see anyone yet, not Matt, and particularly not Ethan. She tiptoed past Matt's silent room and down the hall into the empty kitchen where she found a bowl with some odd looking fruits. With a little further scrounging, she uncovered a loaf of crusty bread and a hunk of cheese.

Hope located a knife and set to work, sawing on the bread. A muffled thump from the doorway startled her. She fumbled the blade, missing her fingers by a slim inch. Whirling around, knife at the ready, Hope came face-to-face with Antonio. He raised his hands in mock surrender, but his velvety brown eyes were dark with concern. Exhaling an unsteady breath, she turned back to resume her task without a word.

"Are you all right? I got back a few minutes ago and heard—"

"I'm fine," she replied over a stiff shoulder, but her hands shook, forcing her to lay the knife aside for a moment lest she lop off a finger. That'd be just about her luck today, and a fitting end to a horrible day.

Broad, warm hands settled on her shoulders. Hope bowed her head in defeat. She didn't resist as Antonio turned her, drawing her into his arms. He was solid and undemanding, offering only comfort and understanding. She fisted her hands in his shirtfront, laid her forehead against his chest, and let the tears fall.

But for the slow caress of his hands as they soothed up and down her back, Antonio didn't move a muscle. She poured out the terror of the abduction and, even when she revealed what had driven her into such a reckless act as racing away from the ranch alone, he held his tongue.

Eventually her tears subsided. She pulled herself from his embrace, offering him a crooked, wet smile of gratitude. Turning back to the counter, she mopped at her face with a dishcloth, sniffled, and cleared her throat.

Antonio moved to stand at her side. As if sensing she no longer wished to be touched, he laid his hands flat on the work surface in front of him and waited.

"Thank you, I guess I needed that." Hope resumed awkwardly hacking her way through the bread.

Grimacing, Antonio took the knife from her. "I

must admit, I don't completely understand the situation with Matt—"

Hope interrupted with a jaded snort. "That makes two of us."

Antonio tilted his head, regarded her with steady eyes. "It seems to me the only way to understand would be to talk to Matt."

Hope shook her head. "I don't want to see him right now. I don't want to hear anything he has to say. I should've stayed in Boulder."

"Hope, Matt's a good man. I've never known him to be anything but honest. If he's convinced you're his daughter, there must be a reason." Then he grinned at her. "And I, for one, am very happy you came to Texas."

Hope glanced up, surprised by his tone, suddenly uncomfortable with the odd light in his eyes. He pressed on, however, before she could over-analyze his comment, or his strange expression.

"Many years ago, when I was a boy, I stole from Matt. I'm not proud of it, but it was probably the best thing I've ever done, for it brought me to where I am today." Antonio picked up a hunk of bread and offered her a portion. "I was alone, eleven years old, living hand to mouth on the streets of a tiny town just this side of the border. Matt caught me with his pocket watch and money clip. He chewed me out, cleaned me up, and brought me here. I've worked hard to get where I am, but I wouldn't be the man I am without Matt. He gave me a chance when no one else would have looked at me twice."

Touched by his confidences, Hope stared into Antonio's dark, velvety eyes and a smile tugged at her lips. "I think you give Matt too much credit. You'd have found your way. You're a good man, too, Antonio."

Antonio reached out and covered her hand with his, squeezing. "I ask you to give Matt a chance. Let him explain."

Silent, Hope absorbed his words, taking comfort in the innocent touch of his hand.

After a long moment, she nodded. "All right, I'll talk to him. But first," she held up the mutilated hunk of bread and the wedge of cheese, "I'm going to eat. Want to join me?"

****

Their voices drifted away as Ethan stepped back from the doorway and wandered out into the golden glow of the evening sun. The lingering vision of Antonio holding Hope in his arms drove Ethan crazy. Why could she accept comfort from Antonio…but not from him?

Ethan's shoulders drooped as he crossed the yard. His steps faltered as the sound of Hope's soft laughter drifted through the window, taunting him with his own failures. She'd never forgive him for keeping Matt's secret from her.

He'd lost her.

Once in the stables, he saddled Apollo…again. As if sensing his master's misery, Apollo swung his massive head around and nudged Ethan's shoulder in a gesture of commiseration. Ethan couldn't even summon the ghost of a smile. He patted Apollo's neck and told himself it was just as well. Antonio was stable and compassionate, always a gentleman. He'd give Hope a solid future. A future without ghosts. Antonio could give her what Ethan couldn't. A whole heart, unscarred. Undamaged.

One thing was certain, however. As long as they were under the same roof, she was within easy reach. It was just a matter of time before he turned to her again, a matter of time before he gave in to the constant, overwhelming need she aroused in him. Sooner or later, she would come to hate him for it…if she didn't already. He had no choice. He had to go. Now, before it was too late. Before he lost his heart.

Ethan led Apollo from the stables. He stopped for a moment in the yard, glancing at the main house. Hope's laughter drifted from the kitchen window again, and he rubbed at the ache in his chest.

God help him, maybe it already was too late...

Chapter 17

At the muted shuffle outside his door, Matt marked his spot in the book with his finger and glanced up, eager for a diversion. This confinement to a sickbed had frayed his last nerve. Hope lingered on the threshold. Her hand gripped the doorframe. From the expression on her face, she'd already begun to regret her decision to come to see him.

"Hope," he blurted. The book fell to his side, forgotten. "Please, come in?"

She hesitated a moment, then, lifting her chin as if girding herself for war. Taking the chair at his bedside, Hope stared hard at him, frowning fiercely, fists clenched tight in her lap.

He pushed himself higher against the headboard, ignoring the twinges of pain in his chest and shoulder. He searched her battered face. The bruises and welts were vivid, and his hands shook with his anger. Nonetheless, he forced himself to remain calm. This encounter didn't need to be any more difficult than it already was.

"Will you let me explain?"

Hope caught her bottom lip between her teeth, gave a tiny, obviously reluctant nod.

Matt closed his eyes for a moment, and prayed for the right words. "I've gone through this a thousand times in my head, but it still don't seem to wanna come out right." He shook his head, gritting his teeth, determined to make the most of the opportunity she'd granted him. "Growin' up, not havin any kin but her own ma and pa, Serena tagged after us all the time. She wormed her way into my heart almost from the start. But she was so much younger than I, so I kept my feelings to myself."

Rubbing at a crease in the blanket on his lap, Matt sighed. "Then the war broke out and everything went crazy. Families divided. Friends were forced to take sides. I came back whenever I could at the start. The fightin' was so bad sometimes, I..." His words trailed away, and he ran a hand down the side of his face. "Well, I decided I was gonna lay it all on the line and let Serena decide. I'd finally worked up the gumption to tell her how I felt, but somewhere along the way, while I was draggin' my heels, Serena and Jacob fell in love. I couldn't face it, so I threw myself into the fighting, comin' home less and less."

He shifted again, grimacing at the spasms in his shoulder and chest. One more reminder of why he had to get the air between them cleared, sooner rather than later. Vega's ambush could have been fatal...the next one just might finish him off. Not that he was ready to die, not by a long shot, but he damned well didn't want to do it with a conscience full of regret and guilt.

"I got a letter from Ma. When I found out Serena was gonna marry Jake, I went straight out and asked for—no—I *demanded* the most dangerous missions my superiors could find. I was so reckless, so angry. Then, at Antietam..." Matt's voice trailed away as he shook his head, haunted by visions of carnage and brutality that still held the power to ravage the soul.

"It was one of the bloodiest battles of the war. The Rebs held Burnsides Bridge, protectin' it from a higher vantage point, shreddin' our forces as we tried to cross. The air was full of smoke and bullets, blood and screams. I'll never forget the sight...the water in the creek ran red with all the blood." He shook free of the violent images, recalling her presence and the purpose of their conversation.

"When the fightin' was done, I was assigned to round up deserters. It was a dangerous job, and after that bloodbath, there were more of 'em than you could shake a stick at. Even so, bein' that close, I had to make sure the farm was all right, that Serena was all right. I couldn't stay away. By then both my parents were gone, and our sister, Althea, too. Serena's parents had passed on the year before. She was all alone."

Hope leaned forward the tiniest bit, her face pale. Her bright green eyes were large and filled with reluctant curiosity.

"I was there with Serena when an officer came to the farm. He told us Jake had been killed in Miller's field during the worst of the battle, claimed he'd seen him fall with his own eyes." Matt swiped a shaking hand over his anguished face. Clearing his throat, he forced himself to continue. "Serena took the news hard." He tried to clear the lump from his throat again, but it wouldn't budge. "It all happened so fast. Losing Jacob. Not knowing where James was...or if he was alive. We were both so terribly lost. Serena was inconsolable. I guess, maybe I was in shock. Neither of us was thinkin' straight. It just...happened.

"A few days later we got word Jacob was hurt. Hurt but alive. He suffered a ragin' fever from lying among the dead for hours before anyone noticed he was still breathing. The injuries he'd sustained to his arm were too extensive and gangrene set in. The doctors amputated. He was weak, near comatose. We weren't given much hope he'd survive."

Matt shifted against the pillows, grimaced. "As soon as we heard he was alive, we went to the field hospital and brought him home. We never told him what happened. To my knowledge, he never learned the truth. Later, when Serena discovered she was pregnant, I went to her. I asked her if the baby—if you—if you were mine. She swore you were Jacob's."

He stared at the ceiling before forcing his gaze back to Hope's. "I was such a damned coward. I think deep down I knew the truth, but I let it go. I let her convince me. Until Jacob found out about you, he'd been ready to give up. I could tell it as sure as I'm sittin' here. There was no reaching him. When Serena told him she was pregnant, he came back to us, truly alive and full of hope."

He pleaded for her understanding. "The farm was strugglin', they were fightin' to stay afloat, but I couldn't stay. Not knowing what I knew, not loving her as I do…as I did, and knowing in my heart you were my child. A child I couldn't claim. The truth would've killed Jacob, and very likely Serena, too; she was so in love with him. So, even though they needed me…I left."

In a hushed voice, Hope reasoned, "If what you say is true…then Mama lied. She lied to everybody."

"Not everybody," he informed her, unable to keep the resentment from his voice. Anger still lingered as he pulled a battered envelope from his nightstand. "James knew the truth. He knew all along."

Hope's hands shook as she accepted the tattered envelope. Holding the stained paper in her lap, she stared at it with dread.

It seemed an eternity passed before she drew a deep breath and pulled the crumpled parchment from within. Smoothing the folds open, she glanced to Matt, then back to the letter.

He didn't need to see the words written therein. He'd read the missive so many times—searching for answers between the lines—that he'd memorized the entire thing.

Matt,

I write to you with the heaviest of hearts. I pray someday you'll find it in your heart to forgive me for what I've done. My intentions were to protect you and Jacob from the pain I knew the truth would surely cause. I know that is no excuse. Even less comfort to you, I'm sure, is the fact that I've lived with guilt all these years. In all honesty, were the choice given to me to do it all again, I would do the same.

I think, deep down, you always knew the truth. Hope is your *daughter. Serena confided in me about that night and the truth of Hope's paternity. Please, don't blame Serena for lying to you, or for lying to Jacob. Passing Hope as Jacob's child was solely my idea.*

I knew you loved Serena, probably before you did, for the signs were so easy to see. I still wonder sometimes that Jacob never saw. Then again, perhaps he did and played along with our little charade. In any event, I knew if Serena told Jacob the truth of Hope's conception, it would put the final nail in his coffin, and I couldn't face that. Not after all we'd lost already.

I should've told you the truth when Serena and Jacob died. Hope was so young, too young to understand. I guess, in my own way, I, too, loved Serena, and Hope was all I had left of her, and of you and Jacob. I didn't want to cloud Hope's memories of her mother and father. They were such a happy family, if only for a short time, and I didn't want to take that from her. I admit I was selfish. For when she came to live with me, she filled a huge hole in my life. She became the daughter I was never fortunate enough to have. Hope was my light.

I am ill, Matt. Alas, another secret I have kept from you. My health has been failing for some time now. The doctors have told me it is consumption. It is only now, near the end, that I could force myself to write this letter, and only for Hope's sake. She's lost so much, and still she faces my impending death stoically. She's like you, stubborn and independent...with a fierce sense of right and wrong. But she needs someone to rely on, someone to take care of her for a change. She needs you, Matt. She needs her father, and so I send her to you.

I know what I've done was unforgivable. I forsook one brother to protect the other, but I could see no other way. I am sorry for the pain I've caused you...will cause Hope when she finds out. It is with a humble heart that I pray for forgiveness from both of you and ask—when she's ready—you'll give her the letter I've enclosed for her.

Take good care of her, for she is the daughter we all three shared. She was Jacob's hope, and my light. Let her be your peace.

James

Hope drew a long, ragged breath and closed her eyes. A long moment passed in silence before she stood, placed the letter on Matt's bed, and crossed the room to stare out the window. He should say something to comfort her, anything to ease her obvious pain. But words failed him, and so he remained silent, allowing her time to come to terms with the truth.

Hope stared out the window while her mind clung tenaciously to her memories. Memories of a laughing Jacob. Memories of her father, as he got down on the ground to play with her and her kittens in the barn. Flashes of the day he'd picked her up from the dust when she'd climbed the side of the chicken coop and fallen swirled through her mind. He'd held her tight, cradled in his one arm, and kissed the scrape on her forehead, all the while scolding her for being so reckless. One after another, snatches of other, bittersweet memories flooded her.

Warm, loving recollections with Jacob at center stage. The niggling doubts receded. Jacob was the only father she needed or wanted.

She faced Matt, her expression blank, her voice void of emotion. "May I have the letter James wrote of?"

Matt's troubled eyes searched her face as he reached inside the nightstand once more, drawing out a second, sealed envelope. His face was pale as he offered it to her.

"Thank you," she murmured. The crisp paper felt cold and impersonal in her hand.

Without another word, she walked to the door. Somewhere along the way, her knees had turned to jelly.

Matt's deep voice filled the room, stopping her on the threshold. "Hope, please. Stay on at the ranch, at least for a little longer."

She didn't look at him while he made his request. Her heart felt like a lead ball rattling around in her chest. Unable to respond, she left the room.

Dazed, Hope ascended the stairs. The anger built with each step from Matt's room to hers. The pressure in her chest threatened to explode. Furious, she crossed to the fireplace, made to toss the unopened letter into the cold grate. James's face flashed across her thoughts, and her hand faltered. She couldn't bring herself to do it, no matter how angry she was with him right now.

She sank down onto the chair by the window, miserable, staring at the envelope in her hands through a shimmer of unshed tears. Heaving a weary sigh, she rested her head against the back of the chair and closed her burning eyes.

A lone tear traced a wet path down her cold cheek.

Hope wasn't sure how long she sat there, but as

she turned her head to gaze out the window, she absently noted the light spilling from the bunkhouse windows. All was quiet in the twilight.

Setting the letter aside, she went to her dresser, pulled a nightgown from one of the drawers, and dressed for bed in the darkness, her movements mechanical and jerky. She lifted the blankets and climbed in bed, not bothering to light a lamp against the nightmares. Light would be no help anyway.

Hope huddled beneath the blankets, shivering with the cold sting of emotion. She lay there, staring at the door, and finally let Ethan slip into her thoughts. Although she wasn't exactly in the mood to be fair, she had to allow that he'd been arguing with Matt on her behalf, urging Matt to tell her the truth. A cold knot of regret settled in the pit of her stomach. She'd let her anger and pain spill over onto him.

He hadn't deserved the way she'd treated him. She owed him an apology for her behavior. When he came to her tonight—for surely he would, he had almost every other night—she'd tell him she was sorry, that she forgave him for keeping the truth from her. And she'd make him promise never to keep things from her again.

She'd come to rely on him, it frightened her how much. She missed the scent of him, his warmth, and his strength surrounding her. Hope missed the way he held her and made the nightmares disappear. He could make her tremble all over with a mere smile.

She missed *him.*

Hope willed her door to open. She wanted to see him there, sauntering boldly into her room, as though he'd every right.

She waited, and waited.

And finally, with disappointment as a cold companion, Hope closed her eyes and accepted he wouldn't come to her tonight. The tears came then, hot and bitter, scalding a wet path over her cheeks to soak the pillow where Ethan's head should have been resting.

****

Ethan went sailing through the air, landing hard on the packed earth in a cloud of dust. The mare snorted her antipathy at him before prancing away, tossing her head with regal disdain. Ethan struggled to his feet like a bruised old man, dusting the seat of his pants. His pride hadn't been the only thing to take a beating this day.

"If you don't get that temper of yours under control you'd best not go near the herd. You're liable to stampede 'em straight to Mexico," Julio warned,

Ethan erupted, "My goddamned temper's just fine."

"My ass it is," Julio retorted, loud and clear, eyeing Ethan with blatant disbelief. "You been tetchier'n a den full of stomped on rattlers since you got back from Matt's place. Somethin's stuck in yer craw, all right. Ya don't believe me," he thrust a chin toward the far corner of the corral, "take a good look at that mare."

Ethan glared at the older man, but kept his lips clamped shut. He wouldn't give Julio any more ammunition to shoot at his injured hide. Ethan stomped to the split rail with as much dignity as he could muster, knowing damned well he'd managed to ruin any trust he'd gained with the mare. He sure as hell didn't need Julio rubbing his nose in it. Right now, that was the only part of his body that didn't ache.

Ignoring the speculative looks his vaquero's shot him as he passed, Ethan stalked to the stables. Apollo snorted his welcome over the top of the gate. Ethan heaved a deep sigh and reached up to scratch between the animal's large dark eyes.

"Have I been all that bad?"

Apollo snorted affirmation, stamping his foot as he bobbed his head, and Ethan grimaced. He scrubbed his hands over the rough stubble on his chin and turned to stare out the stable doors toward the corral. In the distance, Julio soothed the mare. The sight grated on Ethan's nerves. He considered turning the mare loose after all. It'd be for the best, her spirit was too strong to tame.

Besides, Hope probably wouldn't appreciate his gift…not anymore.

Still, he couldn't bring himself to give the order. It felt too much like severing a vital tie. Heaving another sigh, he unhooked a brush from a nail on the side of Apollo's stall and began smoothing it over the horse's shiny coat in long, therapeutic strokes.

Ethan set his mind to spend the night—and many more to come—at the Circle K. Hope needed time to come to grips with what she'd learned. She'd be angry with Matt and her mother, with James—and with him. He couldn't blame her one bit. He wasn't sure how he'd react in her shoes.

He also knew if he went back, he'd go straight to her. He wouldn't be able to help himself. She wouldn't be ready for that. As it was, he shouldn't have made love to her that afternoon, and he condemned himself for his weakness. He should've backed off when she asked, should've given her the space she'd needed. But he hadn't been able to keep his hands off her, hadn't been able to stop from touching her, from tasting her, needing to reassure himself she was alive and whole. He'd complicated the hell out of everything.

Images of Hope, tormented and hurting, filled his mind. The nightmares she suffered would surely be worse tonight after all she'd endured. He'd dropped the brush and reached for the saddle before he caught himself. He clenched his fists at his sides. She wouldn't want to see him. No matter how much he wanted to hold her, right now, what she wanted was all that mattered. Bending, he picked up the brush and set to work again, feeling for all the world as if he'd left his heart with Hope, bleeding on the ground at her feet. He considered the cold night—nights, he corrected—ahead of him, and he groaned aloud. It might very well kill him, but he would respect her wishes. He'd leave her alone.

He'd get through this...somehow.

Chapter 18

The pleasant aromas of Natalia's kitchen wafted about Hope as the first rays of cheerful morning sunshine poured through the open window. She stood in the doorway, her gritty stare following Natalia as she hummed to herself, her hands a flurry of busy activity as she added to the pile of tortillas at her side.

Natalia's voice startled her. "Good morning, Hope."

"Good morning," she responded, distracted.

Natalia called over her shoulder, "Let me finish this last batch, and I will fix you a plate."

"I'm not hungry." Hope crossed the room and picked up a cup. "I'll just get some coffee."

Natalia sent her a scolding look. "Do not be foolish, *chica*. You will waste away to nothing. I will fill a plate for you, and you will eat."

Despite herself, Hope's lips twitched as she recalled Matt's warnings about Natalia pushing food at her at every turn. She gave up without a fight, taking a seat at the table, sipping at her coffee as Natalia finished her work.

"Did Ethan mention where he'd be today?" She'd been rehearsing her apology for Ethan this morning while she'd dressed. She was eager to get it over.

"He returned to the Circle K." Natalia's dark eyes flashed with irritation, unmistakable as the ring of righteous church bells. "He left late yesterday afternoon."

Hope frowned, apprehension knotting in her

belly. "Will he be back for supper?"

"I got the impression he won't be back for some time." The older woman set a plate on the table in front of Hope. Her lips were pursed, and her brow furrowed. "Eat."

Hope stared at the plate for long moments. Heaving a sigh, she picked the fork up and took a bite. She could have been chewing sawdust for all she tasted of Natalia's fine cooking. Hope forced a swallow, pushing the rest of her food around her plate.

Well, fine. He didn't deserve an apology if he could take off without so much as a backward glance. He was beyond her contempt. If he thought, for one minute she'd languish away pining for him, then he had another thing coming. Just wait until he came back. He'd get both sides of a good tongue-lashing...and at least one side of her hand, too. But nothing more, so help her God. Her teeth clenched and her brows scrunched together.

Had she been so lacking?

If she had, then why had he come to her the second time, she puzzled. Her eyes clouded as she thought about the promise he'd made. Nothing but heat and passion, ha. She'd never felt colder than she did right now.

To think she'd given him her innocence without a second thought. She'd been such a little fool. She'd given him her body. She'd given him her—*No!* She thrust that thought aside as she chewed another bite with vicious force. She'd most certainly *not* given him her heart, she denied. But the truth hit her right between the eyes. Hard.

Hope leaned back in her chair, suddenly sick to her stomach. Good heavens, who was she trying to fool? She *had* given him her heart. Her whole heart. She'd never have been able to give him her body otherwise. She closed her eyes and swallowed the bite of tortilla, swallowed again when it lodged in her throat, just above the lump of tears. What good had giving him her heart done her? She'd opened herself up for more pain. What did she have to show for it? Nothing but empty promises and a trampled heart.

What a fool she'd been.

"Matt told me you went to see him last night," Natalia murmured. "Hope, please..."

"You knew..." She leaned back in her chair, dropping her fork, narrowing her eyes. "Of course, you knew. I seem to be the only one left in the dark about that little secret."

"I know this must be confusing for you—"

"Oh, no, Natalia, it's not confusing at all. In fact, it's quite simple. Everyone who claimed to love me, Mother, James, Matt..." she trailed away, stopping just shy of including Ethan in the group. To be fair, he'd taken her innocence, but he'd never spoken that tender lie. "They all lied to me. Everything I've known has been nothing but a lie. I wish I'd never come to Texas. I wish..." Frustrated, she clutched her fists in her lap. "I would like to speak to Manuel as soon as possible. Is he in the stables?"

"Manuel? Why do you need to speak to him?"

"I would like to arrange transportation of my belongings back to the train station. I'm going home," she announced, determined.

"Oh, Hope, I know you've had a terrible shock, and I know things aren't going as we would like with Ethan"—Natalia pleaded, hurrying on when Hope shot her a suspicious scowl—"but leaving now would be the worst mistake you would ever make. I know you're angry with Ethan. You will regret not giving yourself a chance to spend time with Matt. I would give anything for one more day with Christina."

"Christina?"

Natalia bit her lip and nodded. "Christina was

my daughter. She was killed in Vega's raid."

Instantly contrite, Hope clasped the older woman's hand in sympathy. "I'm so sorry, Natalia. I didn't know."

"I do not wish for you to suffer regret once it becomes too late." Natalia smiled. "I know Matt has lived with too much of that all these years as it is."

Guilt nagged at Hope, and she lowered her gaze to their clasped hands.

Natalia pressed, "Will you stay?"

Feeling maneuvered, Hope withdrew her hand from Natalia's and fiddled with her fork. After a long moment, she nodded, but then qualified, "For a little while, at least."

Natalia beamed, then sobered. "I know things between you and Ethan are difficult." She lifted a hand, palm out, and pressed on. "Please...give him the chance to make things right. His scars run deep."

"I can't—no—I *won't* keep bouncing around like a ball on a string for his amusement."

"I can see I have upset you." Natalia rose and began gathering up dishes. She paused a moment and turned once more to Hope. "I will apologize now, because I fear I will over-step my bounds by what I am going to say to you. Even in the best of circumstances, love is a difficult thing to deal with. If you give it a chance, you will find it is worth the pain. Give Ethan a chance, Hope, and he will come to face the truth, as you should."

Her temper snapped, and Hope lashed out without weighing the cost. "I'm sick to death of truth and second chances. You want to talk about the truth? When are you and Matt going to get around to facing the truth? When are you going to admit the two of you love each other?"

As soon as the words left Hope's mouth, the color drained from Natalia's face. The dishes clattered to the counter. Natalia stared at her for a long moment, then turned and marched from the kitchen with a quiet dignity that brought shame to Hope's heart.

Hope closed her eyes and dropped her forehead on the table, banging it once more for good measure. Could things get any worse?

Avoiding Matt, she made her way to her room and picked up the envelope she'd been avoiding. Her hands shook, but she broke the seal. The parchment slipped from the envelope, smooth as a whisper. The familiar, flowing script brought tears to her eyes. She settled back in the chair, swiped the moisture from her eyes, and shook the letter open.

My Dearest Hope,

You must be very angry with me. You have every right, my dear, for I've deceived you. Please believe me, I love you as I would have loved my own child, and I never meant to cause you this pain. I'm so sorry. I know Matt will have shown you the letter I wrote to him by now. I'm hoping you've given him a chance to explain his role in this. Please don't be too harsh with him. He was a victim in this deception as well. I'm sure he's hurting every bit as much as you are, and if you trust in each other you'll both heal.

By now, you know the circumstances of your birth. That aside, I'm sure you have many questions. First, let me assure you, Serena loved Jacob with all her heart. The memories of the family you were a part of were all very real. When your mother told me what happened between her and Matt, she was devastated. It was my *idea that she should pass you off as Jacob's child, my idea and mine alone. I convinced her it was better for everyone that way. I take sole responsibility for the pain we caused both you and Matt.*

I honestly believe you were the sole reason Jacob

survived the war. He loved you, my dear, more than anything. I can't even begin to tell you what you meant to him. You were his reason to fight, his reason to survive. You were his hope for a happy future. When you look back, after you've had the chance to think things through, you'll see Jacob truly was your father. In every way that was important. You must not forget that. You must not forget him.

As for myself, I admit, I was selfish. At first, when your parents died, I withheld the truth from you because I didn't want to confuse you. You were so young, but already you were so bright, so spirited, and so strong. I was so very proud of you, even when we decided those horrid schools were not for you. I was afraid they'd crush your spirit. I was wrong. I didn't give you enough credit.

Later, when you were older, I knew you could handle the truth, but I couldn't. I couldn't face the pain I knew you'd feel. I was a coward, and part of me wanted to keep you with me for a little while longer. You were so good to me, and I had no right to you. I never deserved you. I pray, for your sake, you'll be able to come to terms with all you've learned. Give Matt the opportunity to get to know you, to love you, the way Jacob and I did. Don't let our mistakes tarnish your future. Find your own happiness, my dear. I love you.

Uncle James

Her shoulders shook with the force of her anguished sobs. Hope found herself kneeling before her trunk. Opening it, she dug inside until she found what she was after. Sinking down onto the floor, she laid the precious bundle in her lap and unfolded the linen handkerchief. Hope stared for long moments at the tiny treasure. Lifting the precious object free, she held it up to the light shining through the window, mesmerized by the prism of colors it cast.

A tiny crystal dove spun at the end of the thin gold chain dangling from her trembling fingertips. James had surprised her with the necklace at breakfast on her sixteenth birthday, instructing her to hold it to the light. He'd laughed at her when she'd giggled in delight as the sunshine caught and refracted, casting a kaleidoscope of color onto the pristine tablecloth. He'd helped her to put it on, and kissed her on the top of the head, instructing her that whenever she looked at the crystal bird, Hope was to remember she was his light.

She captured the tiny bird in the palm of her hand and clasped it to her chest. All the tears she'd kept locked inside since the day James died broke free at last.

****

Ethan swore a blue streak as he scowled down into the ravine. The drone of feasting insects filled the air. Vultures wheeled lazy circles in the sky, waiting for their go at the bloating carcasses. He turned his nose into the crook of his elbow for a moment, fighting down the bile the stench stirred up.

"How many?"

"Ten, maybe fifteen head, both brands," the vaquero confirmed.

His hands gripped the reins in a white knuckled fist. Damn it. How he wanted to break something right now—preferably Vega's neck. "How the hell did he get to the herd?"

The vaquero gave a helpless shrug. Ethan swore again and shifted in the saddle. "Tell Antonio to double the watch. I'm headed over to Matt's place." He pointed Apollo south and let him have his head.

He tracked Matt down in his den a short while later. Matt grumbled, "It's about damned time you dragged your sorry hide back here. How the hell could you leave me all alone with those two?"

Ethan ignored Matt's barb and cut to the chase. "Vega hit again. Ten to fifteen head left to rot in a ravine in the foothills."

Matt pushed a stack of papers aside and leaned his elbows on the desk. "How the hell did he manage that?"

"I don't know. A couple vaqueros found 'em this morning while they were out roundin' up strays. The bastard managed to cull both brands without anyone noticing."

"Now what the hell are we supposed to do?" Matt thumped an angry fist on the ornate mahogany desk. "How does he keep slipping by us?"

Ethan heaved a weary sigh. Frustrated tension caught up with him as he braced his palms on the back of the chair. "The herd was protected. I don't understand how it could have happened without anyone seeing something. Unless..." Shooting a furtive glance at the closed door, Ethan pulled the chair out and sat down.

Matt prompted, "Unless what?"

"Vega has to have someone working inside the outfit. It's the only way. Think about how convenient it'd be for him if he had someone to tell him when to strike, and where. Someone to look the other way when the time was right."

Matt scowled, but he didn't interrupt.

Leaning his elbows on the table, Ethan urged, "Think about it. Those beeves shouldn't have been such easy targets. He shouldn't be able to get to us so easy and then get away undetected, not without inside help, it's not possible."

Matt rubbed at his chin and growled, "Who?"

Leaning back in his chair, he shook his head, discouraged. "I don't know."

"How many men have we hired on since the raid, or just before it?"

Ethan chewed the inside of his cheek for a

moment as he ran count. "We took on a lot of extra help after the raid, most stayed on." He leaned forward again, staring at the top of the desk. Guilt gnawed a hole in his gut. "Why the hell didn't I think of this sooner? My God, Matt, all this time he's had someone here, day in and day out, privy to every move we make. No wonder he could strike whenever he liked. How could I have been so blind?"

"Now, Ethan. Don't go blamin' yourself for this. I'm just as much at fault. Right now, we need to focus on smokin' 'em out."

Shuffling footsteps echoed overhead, Ethan darted a quick glance at the door again. The tightness in his shoulders eased a few moments later when Natalia opened the door and poked her head inside.

"Oh, Ethan, I didn't hear you come in." Natalia shifted a huge bundle of bedding from one arm to the other, pushed a stray lock of hair behind her ear. "I put fresh sheets on your bed. I'll be making apple pies for desert."

Ethan muttered noncommittally, shifting uncomfortably in his seat.

Natalia's eyes narrowed, and she tilted her head, just the slightest. Her lips compressed, then she opened her mouth, only to snap it closed. She heaved a deep sigh, shook her head, then ordered, "Don't tire Matt out. He shouldn't even be out of bed yet. I'll be back in twenty minutes," she warned, turning her pointed stare in Matt's direction. "I expect you to be resting when I get back."

With a stern nod in Ethan's direction—a silent warning that she'd hold him personally responsible if Matt over-taxed himself—Natalia disappeared from view and closed the door behind her. Ethan's gaze flicked to Matt, guilt of a different kind lurked in his heart.

Pushing it aside, he focused on matters at hand.

"Where do we start?"

"First, we need to figure out who we can trust." Matt nodded his head as he began formulating a plan. "Then we need to work our way through the rest of the outfit." Matt drew a piece of paper out and began writing up a list of names. When he finished, he pushed the sheet across the desk for Ethan's perusal. He added a few more names and pushed the paper back.

"Okay," Matt drawled, drawing a line through several names, beginning with Antonio. "I'll vouch for these men."

Ethan took the paper back and crossed off several names himself, remarking, "Julio, Patch, Enrique, and these men also. What about the rest?"

Matt blinked at the remaining names, numbering fifteen. They spent the next half an hour discussing each man. At last, when they were finished, they'd whittled the list to six in question, two on Matt's payroll, four on Ethan's. The sound of movements in the adjoining room drew Ethan's attention again, and he fidgeted with the paper.

He couldn't quite hold Matt's puzzled stare. "I'll speak to a few of the men…the one's I trust to keep quiet about this. I'll assign a watch on those left on the list."

A loud crash came from the kitchen, and he nearly jumped from his chair. His guilty gaze swung back to Matt, and he caught the older man's exasperated, knowing smile.

"She ain't here."

"What? Who?" Feigning a look of disinterest, Ethan shifted in his seat, stared blindly at the paper in his hands.

"Hope," Matt replied. "She's out ridin' with Antonio."

His eyes narrowed. "Oh?"

"They've been spendin' quite a bit of time

together since you left."

Ethan's temper broke loose. "What's your point, Matt?"

"You've been jittery as a field mouse in a room full of tomcats since you walked in that door, boy," Matt smirked. "Don't take no scholar to figure out why."

"I don't know what the hell you're talking about, old man," Ethan snapped, pushing his chair back.

"Sure you don't," Matt poked at him. "Figured you for more backbone, Ethan."

"You must've hit your head harder'n we thought, 'cuz you ain't makin' a lick of sense." He glared, willing Matt to drop the subject.

"I got more under this hat than hair, boy." Matt thumped the wide brim of his hat and heaved a harassed sigh. "You wanna go through the rest of your life like me, a miserable old bachelor filled with regrets? Too afraid to fight for the woman you want?"

Ethan's eyes flared, and he tensed. How much did Matt suspect?

He leaned back into his chair. If Matt had any idea of how much Ethan wanted Hope—that he'd actually made love with her—Matt would've put a bullet between his eyes by now, friend or not. All the same, Matt managed to prick Ethan's temper, and his guilt.

"You're being a jackass," Matt griped. "You're pushing her straight into another man's arms, is what you're doin'. Same as I did to her mother. You do realize that, don't you? Is that what you're aimin' for?"

"It doesn't matter what I want."

Fire flashed, jewel-green, in his eyes...just like Hope's did when her temper got riled. "What about Hope, Ethan? Don't it matter what she wants?"

"She's better off with Antonio," Ethan snarled,

as much for Matt's benefit as for his.

A long, silent moment passed, then Matt knocked the floor out from under him, "Maybe she is, at that."

Ethan blinked. Matt couldn't have stunned him more had he shot him in the gut. Subdued, Ethan snapped, "I'll speak to the men."

Without another word, without another glance, he turned and stalked from the room, and from the house. Betrayal and self-disgust ate a hole in his stomach.

Chapter 19

Ethan rode away from the Bar M as though the hounds of hell were hot on his heels. He'd thought he'd succeeded in pushing Hope from his thoughts by throwing himself into his work. He couldn't have been more wrong. He hadn't been able to stop thinking about her from the minute he'd left the Bar M to the moment he'd returned. The mere possibility of catching a glimpse of her was enough to make his heart trip double-time.

It'd been a crushing blow when Matt confirmed she was out with Antonio, apparently a regular occurrence now. Shoulders slumping, he headed home, a whipped dog with his tail tucked firm between his legs. This was as it should be, the way he'd wanted it.

Wasn't it?

As he neared the ranch, Ethan spied Julio in the corral putting the mare through her paces. Riding straight to the split railing, he hailed his foreman. The older man had to dismount in order to go to him, as the mare refused to get anywhere near Ethan or his powerful stallion.

"I need you, Enrique, Xavier, Patch, and Santos at the main house within the hour."

Julio nodded, smearing a sleeve across the sweat dampened dust on his brow.

He stared at the mare, rubbed his damp palm down his denim-covered thigh. "How's she comin' along?"

"Well enough." Julio used the tip of his finger to

push the brim of his hat back on his head. "You change yer mind 'bout keepin' 'er?"

Ethan thought long and hard. Dug deep to find an answer, but it was illusive. "Don't know."

Julio lifted a speculative brow. "Gonna start on the new string today. Plannin' on stickin' round?"

"Could just as well, I suppose," Ethan allowed, his mind already elsewhere.

Julio rolled his eyes. "Don't bother lessen yer gonna change yer attitude, boy."

Ethan glowered, pointing a threatening finger in the aging foreman's direction. "I get called 'boy' one more time today, I'm liable to take exception."

Julio raised an unimpressed brow. "That mare won't even come near you. You think the others'll be any different?" Julio snorted in disgust and turned away, calling over his shoulder, "Go for a ride and figure out what you're gonna do 'bout that woman. You're shit worthless like this."

Ethan shifted in the saddle, pushing his own hat back on his brow. "What the hell makes you think there's a woman involved?"

Julio turned back and studied him for a moment. A slow, wide grin spread over his craggy face. "Only a woman can put that kind' a mad on a man."

Fuming, he glared holes in Julio's back as the mare came, docile and accepting, to the vaquero. Muttering a string of obscenities, Ethan wheeled Apollo around and raced off. He was back within the hour, his temper simmering, to collect the group of men he'd designated. They all headed to the Bar M.

As they drew rein in front of the Bar M's main house, Ethan singled Antonio out. He dismounted and strode to the corral, motioning Antonio to the side. Remembering where the young foreman had spent the afternoon—and with whom he'd spent it—Ethan thrust his fists deep in his back pockets for fear one would find its way to Antonio's nose.

"I talked to Matt a bit already," Antonio explained as soon as they were isolated. "I called in a few of the men we decided on. They're waitin' in the bunkhouse."

Ethan nodded and glanced over Antonio's shoulder, nodding Julio forward. "Let's get this over."

As Ethan turned to follow Antonio, a flicker of movement in the den window caught his attention. Even as his head swiveled, he told himself not to look. Hope stood motionless, book in hand, gazing out into the courtyard. His stare collided with hers, and a white-hot fist grabbed hold of his guts, twisting like a rusty blade. Forcing himself to turn away, Ethan stepped inside the bunkhouse.

The exchange hadn't lasted more than a second or two, but it left his knees weak and his hands shaking.

****

Hope watched Ethan disappear into the bunkhouse, without as much as a nod in her direction. A dozen or so men trailed in behind him. Disappointment jabbed at her, and she turned away, moving to the stairs and up to her room. Anger and pain cut deep. One thought kept racing around and around in her mind. After all this time, he'd come back to the ranch and hadn't bothered to come to her, hadn't shown the slightest interest. Out in the courtyard, he'd seen her—she knew he had. Yet he'd turned away without so much as a flicker of emotion in his expression.

She crossed the room and plopped down on the chair, determined to push him from her life, as he'd seemed to have done with her. She stared at the words in the book for several long moments, then gave up and set it aside with an angry harrumph.

The lone letter lying on the nightstand drew her

gaze. It was the last one left from the stack Matt had sent to James. Hope retrieved the page and settled herself in the chair once again. Her brow wrinkled at the date on the envelope. Wouldn't this date have been sometime around the raid on Matt's ranch?

Her stomach knotted.

Telling herself it couldn't be all that bad compared to some of the things Matt had written about the war, she lifted the flap and slid the parchment free. Shaking out the folds, she smoothed it onto her lap, oddly hesitant to begin reading.

Twice she'd come close to refolding the paper and replacing it inside the envelope. Twice, she willed herself to leave it as it lay—open and exposed. At last, calling herself a coward, she picked the page up and began to read.

She was unprepared for the shock and horror Matt's letter unleashed.

James,

Vega raided the ranch. Ethan and I—nearly all the men—were out with the herd. Those close by went to the Circle K to put out the fire Vega set in Ethan's new stable. The Bar M was largely unprotected, nothing but a few men and a couple women, were left here. Thank Heavens Natalia was with us, or she'd have been here, too. James, dear God in Heaven, I don't even want to write this on paper. Natalia's daughter, Christina, was here during the raid.

No one survived. It was so brutal! I can't even force myself to recount most of it. Vega killed the men here at the ranch. I know how this is going to sound, but they were lucky. Vega took Christina and the other women into the mountains. The horrors they faced were unspeakable. We were barely able to identify what was left of them. Christina was the worst. They'd staked her to the ground. Used and tortured her. She'd been such a sweet, beautiful girl.

They mutilated her precious face, James, and her body. The bastard carved 'Gringo whore' onto her stomach as a message for Ethan.

I tried to stop him, but he saw her. I'll never forget the look in his eyes as he cut her free, or the sight of him as he held her battered body. He loved her so much, and they'd just gotten engaged. Losing her like that, I don't know how he'll ever recover.

Hope dropped the letter to the floor with a startled sob. Her mind whirled. Her stomach lurched. Why hadn't anyone told her? Dear Lord, the things Ethan must have endured…

With shaking hands, she bent to pick the letter up. Her eyes scanned down the lines until she found the point where she'd left off.

…I don't know how he'll ever recover. My heart bleeds for him. Since we came back from the mountain, he's barely spoken a word. He hasn't shed a tear, and he won't speak of it at all. He goes through the motions of life, eating and sleeping and working, but there's no life inside him now. He's an empty shell.

I fear he might do something reckless and end up getting himself killed. To look at him right now, it's like seeing Jacob right after he lost his arm…when he was ready to give up. I don't know what to do for him. I know the pain he suffers at having the woman he loves taken from him, but I can never know the depth of the pain he feels, for at least when Serena passed, she was at peace.

The torture Christina suffered is eating away at his soul. He blames himself for not being here to protect her. His pain grows with each day that Vega goes unpunished. We've gone into the mountains time and again, but I swear, it's like chasing a ghost. Somehow, the bastard always seems to stay one step ahead of us. With each failure, Ethan becomes more obsessed.

I don't know what to do for him. I hope he'll find a way to come to terms with this. I know from experience life goes on, despite the pain, but that's cold comfort to him right now. I can only pray he'll find something to save him from himself. Keep us in your thoughts, brother.

Matt

Ethan's loss knifed through her. Tears coursed down her cheeks, yet she couldn't move to wipe them away, nor couldn't put the letter down. She rubbed at the ache in her chest.

Why had no one told her?

****

The traitor sat in the corner of the bunkhouse listening as Ethan outlined his suspicions about an informant in the outfit. Ethan identified six names suspected of the crime. Five of those names had been innocent. One was not. While useful, Rodrigo had now become a liability.

His own cover was still intact, or he wouldn't be here, privy to this conversation. He hid a smug smile.

If they only knew...

Next, Ethan began outlining their duties. They were to keep vigil over those six men, watching every move...who they spoke to, where they went, what they did. The men were to report to Antonio, Julio, or Ethan if they witnessed anything even remotely suspicious.

The traitor swore beneath his breath, hoping he could get to Rodrigo unnoticed before the watch began their duties. Ethan rose, signaling the end of the meeting. The ride back to the Circle K was tense, each man jumpy as an eggless hen come Sunday mornin'. As the group drew near the ranch, Julio motioned each man off to his assigned task.

The traitor rode directly to the Circle K stables. He glanced about, confirming no one had followed. As soon as he entered the stables, he began to whistle a tuneless song. His accomplice slid from the shadows, a whisper in the night.

"Tonight, soon as the sun sets, ride straight to El Jefe's camp. Tell him the Old Mission's bein' watched, and he's to use the fall back. Tell him—exactly as I say now—tell him 'a bird in the hand.' You understand me?"

Rodrigo nodded before melting back into the shadows. With cold, calculating eyes, the traitor turned away as his accomplice slipped from the stables. It was a shame, he thought. Rodrigo had proven not only useful, but also loyal to the cause as well. Tossing an indifferent shrug, the traitor turned back to his work, softly humming to himself. There were always other young men eager to step up and prove themselves.

Rodrigo wasn't his problem anymore.

****

Hope trudged to the kitchen on wooden legs, Matt's letter circled in her feverish mind. Pots clinked and plates clattered as Natalia set about preparing the evening meal.

"Natalia," she called from the doorway.

"Oh, Hope, I didn't hear you come in." Natalia turned to face her, her expression reserved. The moment Natalia got a good look at her, however, she bustled forward wiping her hands on a rag, her brow wrinkled with concern. Natalia urged her into a chair. "What is wrong? What has happened?"

Hope couldn't maintain a level tone. "Why didn't you tell me about Christina and Ethan?"

Natalia took a shocked step back. She cleared her throat, struggled to meet Hope's eyes. "I did not tell you because I felt it was Ethan's place to do so. I see now I was wrong. I shouldn't have expected so much of him."

Natalia reached for the coffeepot. She returned with two full cups and placed one on the table in front of Hope, then took the chair across from her. Her hand was unsteady as she sipped at the steaming brew. Natalia's cup rattled against the table as she blinked up at Hope.

"I came to work for Matt many, many years ago, soon after my husband died. Christina was just a little girl then. Being the only two children around, she and Ethan spent a lot of time together. Later, when Antonio came to live with us, he tagged along after Ethan and Christina, but a special bond had been formed between the two of them by then." Natalia's eyes pleaded for Hope's understanding.

"It came as no surprise when they decided to marry. We were all so happy then, everything seemed so perfect. Ethan was healing from the loss of his father. Matt seemed to finally be getting over whatever it was that had driven him to us. The ranches were prospering.

"There was no way of predicting what Vega would do. For all the pain that day brought to me, it shattered Ethan. He blamed himself for not keeping her safe." Lines of grief etched Natalia's face, aging her beyond her years. "I worried he would never heal. Then you came along and forced him to live again. You cannot know how happy that has made me—Matt, too. You both have suffered so much loss, more than anyone should have to face, but you have a chance at happiness again. Do not give it up without a fight."

Natalia swam in Hope's teary vision when she finally forced her gaze away from her coffee cup. "I don't think he's capable of loving anyone else."

"I think, if you look inside your own heart, you will find you are wrong."

"It doesn't matter what's in my heart, Natalia," Hope snapped, angry now. 'It's what's in Ethan's heart that's in question. There's no room for me. He pushes me away every time I get close. He doesn't want me. He proved that by leaving after he—" She cut herself off before she could reveal too much. She shook her head. Doubt echoed in her voice. "No, he doesn't want me, not anymore."

Hope pushed to her feet and stalked from the room, unable to face the truth. She'd fallen in love with a man who would never love her. Drawn to the stables, Hope meandered to Daisy's stall and stopped. She stretched over the half door, reaching out to pet the horse's silky muzzle. Hope tried to smile at the animal and failed, suddenly wishing she could saddle the horse and ride off, all the way back to Boulder. On second thought, why stop there? She'd ride until she ran out of land, then she'd board a ship to somewhere far away.

Then maybe she'd ride some more.

There had to be a place where the scent of Ethan couldn't haunt her. Someplace where the memory of his breath on her neck couldn't stir feelings best forgotten. Somewhere she couldn't feel the heat of him, as though he were standing right behind her, waiting for her to turn around and fall into his arms. She hadn't been able to escape that feeling the last few days, whether awake or asleep. Apparently, even hurt and angry as she was, right now was no exception.

Sweet heavens, that heat felt so *real.*

Her name feathered over her neck on a soft whisper of longing, and she nearly jumped out of her skin. She whirled around, and her feet tangled up. Strong, hard hands encircled her waist, drew her hard against the tempered steel of a rock-solid, familiar body. Her hands flew to Ethan's broad shoulders. His lips hovered over hers, so close, yet so far away. His hungry, heady gaze locked on hers, and she couldn't breathe. His lips descended with the force of a lightning strike. She felt the impact reverberate clear to her soul.

Hope's urgent hands slid over his shoulders, skimming up his neck, tangled in his hair. His arms closed around her, crushing her to him. She melted into his arms, melted against him. His lips slanted over hers. His tongue delved deep. The feel of his body pressed to hers brought back a rush of intimate sensations, recollections of skin on skin and illicit pleasures. Her knees shook with the fierceness of his need.

Ethan leaned into her, pushing her back, pinning her between the rough planking and his scalding desire. Using his hands and his mouth—his entire body—he overwhelmed her senses. She sank into greedy need like a drowning woman, pulled under without a fight, reveling in her own demise. Ethan tugged the hem of her skirts higher and higher, and the chilled air swirled around her calves. Lost in the realm of sensation, her swirling senses steeped in the pleasure of his kiss, of his touch. Hope moaned against his lips.

The soft whicker of a horse brought sanity crashing down on her. Harsh and unforgiving.

Heaven help her, she couldn't do this. Not again. She pushed at his shoulders, desperate to twist away from his kiss. She didn't know where she found the strength, grateful only that it was there. Regardless of how much she wanted him, wanted this, she refused to cave to temptation, not with so much confusion between them.

He nuzzled his face into her hair, inhaling deep. Several long moments passed before he released her. He stepped back, his eyes filled with harsh desire and regret, his breathing ragged. He thrust his hands deep into his pockets.

"Hope," he groaned. His voice dropped, miserable and low. "I'm sorry, I shouldn't have—"

"No, you shouldn't have." Tears of pain and frustrated desire tightened her throat. She pushed away from him, straightening her clothes with trembling fingers. "I thought you left. What do you want?"

He blinked at her. His brow wrinkled. Desire, unmistakable and smoldering, clouded his eyes. "I did leave, but I'm back now. I want—" Ethan choked off whatever he'd been about to say, blinked, and rocked back on his heels. His face leached of all color.

She fought the desperate urge to throw herself back into his arms. "You want what?"

"I had to…take care of some business," he trailed off, taking a step back.

"Well, don't let me stop you."

The muscle jerked in his jaw. His eyes raked down the length of her. The heat in his stare shook her resolve, cut off her air. Ethan took a step toward her, reached for her.

Panicked, she backed away, pressing against the stall door in her bid to keep from touching him. Ethan's hands fell to his sides as he drew a long, uneven breath. His eyes settled on Daisy.

"Have you been riding?"

Her brows drew together, thrown by the sudden change of subject. "Yes. Antonio's been taking me out. He's a good teacher."

"I have a feeling he'll be too busy to be spending much time with your riding lessons for a while." The corner of his mouth hitched up the tiniest bit.

"What's that supposed to mean?" She scowled at him.

Ethan's gaze turned thoughtful. "It means he's going to be busy. But I'd be more than happy to—"

"Don't bother," she hissed. Her heart still bled

from the last time they'd gone riding together. The more space she kept between them, the better. "I'll wait for him."

"It might be a long wait," he snapped, but his eyes were smoldering again.

"I'll wait," she insisted, unwilling to bend.

Ethan edged closer, crowding her. His voice went seductive and soft, and her heart trembled despite her resolve. "What's the matter, Hope? Are you afraid of spending a little time alone with me? You don't need to hide behind Antonio."

He trailed the back of his fingers down the side of her cheek, along her neck, and across her collarbone. The look in his eyes taunted her, as though he could see through her defenses and hungered to set loose the rampant desire within.

"I'm not hiding behind anyone." Oh, why couldn't she just turn away? Why did her voice betray her?

"Prove it," he challenged, whisper-soft, teasing her with another feather light caress.

The corner of his mouth hitched upward again. Ethan edged forward, towering over her. His chest rubbed against her, making her so very aware of the untamable desire throbbing between them like a living entity all on its own. The heat in his stare intensified, and she felt herself falling into the blue flames of his sultry gaze, reckless and impetuous. Her resolve to distance herself vanished. It would take a stronger woman than she to withstand this elemental, magnetic connection between them.

Who could blame her for giving in when temptation had wicked eyes like his?

"You and I have fire, Hope," Ethan boasted. "I guarantee you won't even come close to what we have with *him*."

He started to lower his lips to hers, but Hope blinked, the hazy softness in her brain dissipated.

She snapped her mouth shut and reared her head back, chagrined at how effortlessly she'd taken the bait. Fury burbled up inside her. Her fury may have been self-directed, but that didn't mean he could walk away unscathed. She slapped her palms against his chest and shoved, fighting to contain the tears forming a lump in her throat.

He wouldn't budge; instead, he gazed down into her eyes in an obvious display of masculine dominance. Ethan dipped his head again, blatantly intent on rendering her witless once more with his intoxicating kisses, but she turned her head to the side, denying them both what they craved more than air, more than life itself.

Hope allowed the pain and the anger to rise up in her. Her pride fed the flames, and she lashed out. How dare he throw Antonio in her face? He'd accused *her* of hiding. She wasn't the one hiding, and certainly not behind Antonio. Ethan was the only one guilty of cowardice...and *he* hid behind a ghost no less. Before she stopped to think, before she stopped to consider the pain she would inflict, she told him so.

"You used me—again. You kiss me and make me forget myself, then you touch me and I can't..." she trailed off, shocked that she'd almost admitted aloud this unconscionable hold he held over her. At last, the tears refused to be contained and welled in her eyes, spilling over, hot and damning. "You accused me of hiding behind Antonio. But I'm not the one guilty of hiding—you are."

She glared at him through the tears, daring him to push her, challenging him to ask.

His eyes narrowed. The muscle in his jaw leaped to life. "You think *I'm* hiding?"

Ethan shook his head. Stepping back, he turned away to kick at a bale of hay, thrusting his hands in his back pockets.

She ground her teeth together, fuming. "That's exactly what I'm saying. Where have you been these last few days? I thought you agreed to stay on until Matt was back on his feet." Fury exploded. "Why have you never told me about Christina?"

She immediately regretted her outburst. Ethan spun around and stared at her, his eyes emptied of any and all emotion. His body was rigid, strung tight as a bow, his fists clenched at his sides, the muscle in his jaw leaped to life.

"She has nothing to do with what's happening between us."

"Why didn't you mention her, or the fact that you were engaged? You had ample opportunity. Wasn't she important enough to you...or wasn't I?"

For one fleeting moment, pain, raw and agonized, flashed in his eyes. Ethan's whole demeanor became glacial. He stood, silent and remote, for so long she thought he wouldn't speak to her. Then his fury hit her like an icy fist, unexpected and sharp. "She's *dead*."

Without another word, Ethan spun on his heel and stalked away. She stood in the strewn hay, and stared in horror at his stiff, retreating back. Everything inside her iced up, frozen by the look in his eyes. Collapsing on the bale of hay he'd been kicking, she hung her head in shame. How could she have let things get so far out of hand? How could she have been so thoughtless and cruel as to use Christina to hurt him like that?

The sound of thundering hooves drew her attention to the rear doors of the stables, still thrown wide open from the activity of early evening. She caught a fleeting glimpse of Ethan, crouched low over Apollo's glossy neck. Horse and rider disappeared into the night in a dark streak, and she closed her eyes, letting the miserable tears burn her cheeks once more.

Chapter 20

Ethan came abreast of the Bar M as the sun broke the horizon. He rode straight to the bunkhouse and looped the reins over the hitching post. Pushing the door to the bunkhouse open, he strode inside without knocking. Pausing long enough to allow his eyes to adjust to the dim light, he made his way to an occupied bunk against the back wall. The mound on the bed mumbled and rolled over, a dark head lifted off the pillow to glare at the source of noise interrupting his sleep.

Antonio's voice was gruff, slurred by exhaustion. "Ethan?"

"I know you just got in off night hawkin', but I need to talk to you." Unapologetic, he sat on a neighboring bunk and leaned forward, propping his elbows on his knees.

Antonio shifted and ground the palms of his hands into his bloodshot eyes. The black curtain of his hair slid over his broad shoulders as he pushed himself up in the bed. The blankets fell away from his muscular chest.

Antonio gave a lusty yawn. "What's up?"

"Rodrigo Gomez disappeared last night…right after the meeting. Julio said no one's been able to find him."

Antonio frowned. "No one said anything last night about being short handed."

"Julio had Enrique fill in. I told him to keep quiet about Rodrigo," Ethan informed him, twirling his hat in his hands between his knees.

Both men stared at each other for long moments.

Antonio's eyes narrowed on Ethan's face, and he speculated, "You think *he's* the traitor."

"It's lookin' that way. Maybe he got jumpy and took off before we could point the finger in his direction."

Antonio shoved his hair back and leaned an elbow on his upraised knee. "What do you have in mind?"

"Keep your eyes open. If he turns up, I want him brought to me for questioning. It won't hurt to keep the other five in our sights."

Antonio nodded, yawning again, and he settled against his pillow. Ethan's next comment snapped his eyes wide open.

"I don't want Hope leavin' the ranch," Ethan ordered. "There'll be no more riding lessons, and no more picnics."

Antonio pushed up on an extended arm, glaring at Ethan. "What? Why the hell can't she…"

"She's an easy target. Hell, his men have already tried for her once. You think you could protect her out there all alone, you're full of shit." He raised a brow at Antonio, daring him to argue. Part of him—a larger part than he liked to admit even to himself—was really hoping Antonio would put up a stink. He couldn't think of a better way to burn off all this unsettling emotion than a good fistfight.

Antonio leaned back on his elbow, appraising him through speculative, deep brown eyes.

Guilt flashed through Ethan then, as fast as the urge to fight had. He wouldn't fight Antonio, wouldn't use his confusion and anguish over Hope to tear into his friend.

"Is her relationship with Matt the only reason she's in danger? She'd be as much a target if she were involved with you." Antonio drawled, assessing

Ethan with a knowing smile. “Then again, maybe this doesn’t have a damned thing to do with Vega.”

Ethan fisted his hands at his sides, gritted his teeth. He would not rise to the bait. He wouldn’t. He and Antonio had been friends for far too long. Having made his point, Antonio smirked, communicating his knowledge without words, as only a friend can do. Antonio wasn’t about to make things easy on him. Regardless, no matter how he wanted to throttle Antonio for stepping in where he had no right, Ethan forced himself to remain calm. When he failed to deny or confirm his connection to Hope, Antonio's brown eyes flared.

“Fish or cut bait, Ethan. Either claim her for your own, or set her loose, man. Stop yanking her around.” Antonio demanded. Then, in a softer voice, he warned, “Of course, you realize if you don’t intend to claim her…I will.”

Like hell...

Ethan tensed to spring, strained to hold himself in check as territorial male instinct kicked in.

Antonio wasn’t finished. “You know, on second thought, why don’t you keep on doing whatever it is you’ve been doing. It’s workin’ out real nice for me.”

The last word had barely cleared his lips, when Ethan flew at him. In the blink of an eye, he shoved Antonio back against the wall, one hand clamped tight about Antonio’s throat, and the other fist drawn back in anticipation of impact.

He wanted blood.

Tempting fate, Antonio grinned up at Ethan like a weasel in the hen house. Ethan’s telling reaction to Antonio’s barb had been all the answer Antonio had needed, even if it made the situation more difficult. Antonio’s grim smile brought sanity flooding through Ethan in a hot rush of embarrassment. He released Antonio and stepped back, clenching and unclenching his fists. His chest heaved, and he glared holes through Antonio's hide. Turning on his heels, Ethan stalked out the door, letting it bang in his wake. Antonio's bitter laughter followed him into the dawn.

He stomped across the yard and into the main house, not even pausing to stick his head in the kitchen, as was his custom. He went straight to Matt's room, his mind wrestling with Antonio's warning. He didn't pause, just reached out to fling the door open as he stomped.

He stopped dead in his tracks.

Matt and Natalia sprawled across Matt's bed, entwined in a lover's embrace. Ethan felt foolish, standing there gawking at them, bug-eyed and gulping like a fish out of water, but he couldn't seem to help it. Matt finally tore his mouth away from Natalia's, glowering up at Ethan.

Lifting a disgruntled eyebrow, he growled, "Boy, don't you know enough to knock on a closed door?"

"I, uh...you're, ah, well... Well, I...I didn't... Shit..." He sputtered, heat rising in his cheeks. Spinning on his heel, he made for the door before he made any more of a fool of himself.

Matt's voice stopped him, but Ethan didn't dare look back. "Well, now that you interrupted, you could at least offer congratulations."

Despite his resolve not to look, Ethan swiveled his head. "What for?"

Matt smiled down at the flustered woman trapped beneath him. "Natalia finally agreed to marry me."

Ethan raised both brows, offering a crooked grin. "It's about damned time."

"Now, if you'll excuse us." Matt glanced at the door, adding, "Come back later."

Grinning, Ethan closed the door behind him. He stood in the hall and considered the couple within. His grin widened, and he shook his head. About goddamned time indeed.

Just as he was about to take a step, light footsteps tapped their way down the hallway. He hesitated, Antonio's words haunting him. Following the sounds of movements to the kitchen, he paused in the doorway. Hope stood at the stove, pouring a cup of coffee, her back to him.

Ethan tensed to leave, but couldn't force himself to go. Too much had been left unsaid between them, and he'd be damned if he'd let her believe what had happened between them wasn't important to him—that *she* wasn't important.

"Christina painted that landscape hanging in Mirabella's...and the one in Matt's den." Emotion clogged his throat, making it a strain to get the words to come out right.

She whirled around, wide-eyed, clutching a cup in one hand and her throat with the other. Drawing a deep, uneasy breath, she set the cup down on the counter beside her with a shaking hand, but kept her eyes riveted on him, waiting for him to speak.

"She was forever painting," he went on in a hushed voice, drawn back in time through the memories. His eyes were on her, here and now, but he saw another woman in another time. "She would load Daisy down with paints and canvases and ride into the foothills to paint for hours on end. She'd forget to eat, forget to sleep. I'd have to go out after her; she'd lose all track of time."

Hope moved toward him, silent. She came to stand on the opposite side of the table, facing him, and rested her palms on the cool surface.

Ethan's gaze fixed on the foothills in the distance, visible through the window behind her. "She was shy unless you knew her really well. She didn't laugh, she giggled. She loved spicy food, the hotter the better...and daisies."

There was pain in the telling, pain in the

recollections. But there was a healing as well. A relief at finally allowing those memories to spill forth, like a boil lanced and drained. Somehow, that it was Hope listening made it both harder, and easier. He couldn't do this with anyone else but her—wouldn't do it *for* anyone else.

"I should have been here to stop Vega." His gaze returned to Hope's face, and he wondered why she looked so pale, so sad. "I left her here, unprotected. She didn't stand a chance. I should have done a better job keeping her safe. She was my responsibility, my fiancée. The things they did to her... I can still see her staked to the ground—broken and lifeless. Sometimes, late at night, I can still see her blood on my hands." His shoulders drooped in defeat. "I failed her. I didn't—"

"Ethan," Hope's voice, soothing and gentle, broke into his self-castigation. "There was no way for you to know what Vega planned. Her death was not your fault."

She'd leaned forward over the table, her weight on her hands, as she spoke. Her gaze was intense, pleading with him to believe her. It would be so easy to take what she offered, accept the forgiveness and the understanding. But he'd lived with the guilt far too long to just shrug it away. He couldn't let himself off the hook.

Emerald eyes narrowed on him. "Do you blame Matt for what happened?"

Ethan reared back as though she'd slapped him, scowling. His gaze snapped to hers, fierce and outraged. "Of course not."

"You are no more responsible for what happened to Christina than Matt...or Natalia, for that matter. You can't go on blaming yourself, Ethan. What Vega and his men did was horrific, but it was *not* your fault," she insisted.

The vehemence in her voice surprised him. Her

defense was a healing balm for his soul, easing some of the guilt he'd carried with him for years. Ethan's gaze roamed over her face. Her eyes softened, and his breath caught in his throat. Then he frowned, and the beginning edge of her smile fell from her lips. He stared at her, his eyes drilled into hers.

"Christina was important to me. *You* are important now," he growled, implacable. His words cut through the soft emotion hanging in the room between them.

Hope's mouth fell open. Guilt rippled in her eyes. Ethan stepped back through the doorway, and stalked from the house.

Chapter 21

Ethan kept himself occupied most of the day, going well out of his way to avoid Hope. Not an easy feat when, at every turn, Natalia or Matt came up with one errand or another for their impromptu engagement party that almost always tossed him directly in her path, or vice versa. While he didn't regret telling her about Christina, the telling had raked those wounds raw, and he needed time to let the pain settle.

Ethan stopped by the stream to wash the sticky dust from his face with a cool, dripping bandana. His rolled sleeves tightened around his biceps as he wrung the bandana one last time. His hair was damp, and rivulets sluiced down his neck to soak his collar and his chest. Stripping down and jumping in would feel damned good right now, but there was just too much to do right now for that indulgence. A dip in the stream would just have to wait.

The fine hairs on the back of his neck lifted, and half a heartbeat later, the scent of jasmine wafted to him on the breeze. Biting back a tormented groan, he didn't turn or acknowledge her in any way when she stopped at his side. He dipped his bandana in the cool water once more, swiped it across the back of his neck, wishing the cool water could chill the flames she'd set loose in his blood just by standing so close.

From the corner of his eye, he watched as she fidgeted with her skirts, chewing her lower lip. He wanted to touch her, wanted to draw her into his arms and forget about everything else. The good Lord knew he wanted in her bed, wanted to hold her as she slept.

Hell, he hadn't had a decent night sleep since the last time he'd shared her bed.

Pride was a damned cold companion.

Ethan pushed to his feet, but, rather than turning to face her, he gave her his back and reached for Apollo's reins.

"Ethan, please..." Her touch on his arm was light, hesitant.

He froze. A jolt of longing shot through him, crippling his resolve. Glancing down at her hand where it rested on his arm, he took a deep breath, closed his eyes, and let a heated string of curses fill his mind. Resigned, he pivoted to face her, his expression carefully impassive.

"Please, don't go," she beseeched him...so vulnerable, so contrite, his heart flipped over in his chest.

Folding his arms across his chest—a defensive move to keep from reaching for her, Ethan silently waited.

"I owe you an apology for my behavior last night in the stables." Hope wrung her hands. Her beautiful eyes were glassy with unshed tears and riddled with remorse. "I had no right to say the things I did, no right to bring Christina up in such a cruel, heartless way. I was angry, and I didn't think... I was wrong. I lashed out, and I'm sorry." Her gaze dropped to his chest, but she forced it back to his, gnawed at her swollen bottom lip once more.

Before she'd even finished delivering her apology, the tension rolled from his shoulders. He relaxed his stance, letting his arms drop to his sides. Her apology caught him off guard. He'd been prepared to begin the next round of their fight, had steeled himself for it. He hadn't expected the honest regret and the anxiety he saw in her now.

He nodded.

He still suffered the potent urge to draw her into his arms and offer comfort, but he kept seeing Antonio holding her as she confided in him. She'd allowed Antonio to offer solace, accepting his comfort—something she continued to resist with Ethan—and it chafed, leaving him resentful despite her apology…and his acceptance.

"You seem to be settlin' in pretty well." It was a statement, not a question. His eyes lingered on some indiscernible point beyond her left shoulder. He ought to just walk away now, but just couldn't seem to make his feet obey.

"It's easy to do here."

"Matt would like you to stay."

A thin line formed between her brows. "I haven't decided what I'm going to do. I love it here…but I have responsibilities in Boulder that I can't ignore."

It was her choice, her decision. He wasn't going to meddle. He wasn't going to… "Matt could help you, if you'll let him. He could take care of all of it. You wouldn't have to go—"

"No," she interrupted, shaking her head. Then, looking up at him, she softened her tone, but her eyes filled with familiar determination. "I've spent too much of my life letting other people—letting other things—dictate my course. I won't let anyone else decide what's best for me, not anymore."

A heavy silence stretched between them. Ethan weighed her comments. Was she referring to her life before she'd arrived at the ranch…or after? Whatever the case may be, the look in her eyes spoke volumes about how serious she was in her endeavor for self-reliance. A surge of uneasy admiration swelled in his chest.

Turning the topic to safer waters, he remarked, "You've been busy today."

“I’ve been trying to help with the party, but I think I’m in the way most of the time.” Hope’s hands fluttered at her sides. “Natalia’s given me lists upon lists of things she needs help with, but it just seems like busy work.”

Given where those lists had led her, he’d begun to have his own suspicions about Natalia’s all-important lists of errands. “You’re more help to Natalia than you realize. It’s good they’ve finally taken this step. It’s been a long time coming,” he confided. “I’m glad to see you approve. It would make things difficult for Matt if you weren’t happy with his decision.”

“Matt’s been alone for a long time, he deserves to be happy.”

He tilted his head, searching her eyes. “Have you accepted him, Hope?”

Her eyes darkened, and he thrust his hands into his back pockets to quell the urge to reach again, unwilling to feel the sting when she pushed him away as she was bound to do. The abject misery on her face poked holes in his control. Why hadn’t he just kept his damned mouth shut?

“I understand the truth of the situation. I guess I understand what happened between my mother and Matt. But…” Hope trailed away, drawing a shaky breath.

Her troubled gaze sought his, and anticipation leaped in his chest. Would she let him in at last?

“Jacob was my father. I can’t turn my back on that, or on him. I know Matt’s a good man. I know I’m lucky to have him. But daddy was a good man, too. He didn’t deserve to be deceived. He was honest and loving.” She shook her head. Vulnerability and confusion shadowed her eyes.

He caught a glimpse of her anguish before Hope turned away to stare at the mountains beyond the Mission. He couldn’t stop himself from reaching for her now, rejection be damned. She was opening up to him—and he wanted more. He wanted to be the one she confided in, the one she trusted with her fears.

He closed the distance between them, claimed her shoulders, drawing her unresisting form back until she leaned against him. His gaze was on the panoramic glory of fading colors as evening settled over the mountains, but all his focus was on her. He breathed a silent sigh of relief when she relaxed, leaning back against him.

He slid his arms around her waist and rested his chin on the top of her head. Her breath seeped out. He offered his strength. Hope covered his arms with her own, as if afraid he might withdraw them. Warmth surged in his heart, and he echoed her sigh. She was where she belonged at last...right here in his arms. And he was whole once more. He tipped his head, sliding his cheek along her silky hair.

Long moments passed before Hope spoke again. Her words were little more than a whisper. "I know Matt's not to blame for this situation. In a way, I understand some of what he must be feeling, I guess. But, I can't..." She paused, as if struggling to find the right words. "Thinking of Matt as my father feels...wrong."

When Hope fell silent, he tilted his head and murmured into her ear. "Matt doesn't want to replace Jacob. He just wants to be a part of your life, sweetheart. He's missed so much with you, missed so many years. He blames himself. He feels he let you down." Hope's breath shuddered in and out, and he tightened his arms around her. "You won't betray Jacob's memory if you acknowledge Matt. There's more than enough room in your heart for them both, Hope. You don't have to choose between them."

She stiffened, and he cursed himself for going too far, too fast. She suddenly dragged in a deep gulp of air, then another, and she began to shake. A wrenching sob ripped its way loose, and Ethan panicked. What had he done? What had he said? The hot splash of her tears on his forearms punched him in the gut. He loosened his hold, and she turned in his arms. Once she did, he tightened his arms again, cradling her against his chest. His hands stroked her back, gentle and soothing despite his galloping, mangled heart.

Her arms wrapped tight around his waist, and Hope buried her face against his chest. Her hot tears soaked his shirtfront. Her sobs tore at him. Ethan absorbed it all in silence. His heart twisted in his chest as he pressed soft kisses to the crown of her head. What he wouldn't give for the right words to sooth her, for the right words that would make her pain disappear.

"I'm sorry," she murmured at length. "Lord, I feel like all I've done since coming here is cry. Emma would be so disappointed."

"Emma?"

"Next to James, she was the closest friend I had," Hope explained, sniffling. "She was always so calm—nothing could throw her off-stride. Everyone must think I'm such a watering pot."

"No one thinks that, sweetheart." She'd lost so many of those she'd loved, and yet she'd held on to her compassion. She'd met each adversity with courage and grace. He couldn't even begin to express the depth of emotion he felt for her, and so he simply pressed his lips to her forehead and held her like the precious gift she was.

She lifted her hands and rested them against his chest, toying with a button at eye level. He was inordinately pleased she wasn't pushing him away, relieved she'd let down her guard at last. The soft play of her hands on his shirt sent awareness flooding through his system.

Her eyes were puffy, the tip of her nose pink.

Her lower lip was swollen and moist from her chewing, and he couldn't resist. His gaze fixated on her lips. Before she could deny his intentions, he lowered his head with unquestionable purpose, sealing his lips over hers, firm and slow. He smoothed his lips over hers.

At that moment, Ethan wanted her more than he'd ever wanted anything in his life. But she was vulnerable, and he wouldn't press. Not now. It took every ounce of his control to pull away from her. His breathing was as ragged as if he'd run up the side of the mountain, but he couldn't release her, not yet. He dropped his forehead to hers, the tips of their noses touched.

The deep, clear emerald of her eyes mesmerized him. She hadn't wanted the kiss to end, he could see it, and that knowledge eased the ache in his heart, even as it added to the ache in his loins. Lifting a hand, Hope cupped his cheek with such tenderness. Her thumb caressed the lines of tension at the corner of his mouth. He closed his eyes and savored her touch.

Ethan sighed at the affectionate contact. His control was weak at best, and crumbling by the second.

"Hope," he whispered. A warning for her to stop. A plea that she continue.

She tipped her head and pressed her lips to his once more. Her mouth was soft, coaxing. Intoxicating. Her tongue darted between his lips. Before he had time to think, before he had time to recall where they were and what they were doing, he slid beneath the spell she wove around him.

Tumbled headlong into her kiss.

Ethan groaned and assumed control of the kiss, letting it spin out of control until his arousal became so painful he feared he might pull her down on the bank and ease his torment right there in the blazing

Texas sunlight. Cursing the fact that they weren't upstairs in her room, or in some secluded mountain glade—for then he wouldn't have thought twice about taking what she so blatantly offered—Ethan commanded himself to let her go.

With a bedeviled groan, he took hold of her shoulders and forced her from him. For a split second, she resisted. Then she seemed to come to her senses, too, and backed away from him as if in a trance. Her hand flew to cover her lips. Shock rounded her eyes. It was then that Ethan noticed the shadows beneath her eyes. Before she could turn away, he snagged her wrist and pulled her back to him. He tipped her chin up with the side of his crooked finger and studied her face better in the dying light.

"You're not taking care of yourself again," he accused, frowning.

Her chin lifted away from his hand, her eyes skating sideways. "I am."

"No, you're not," he contradicted. He rested a hand against the side of her face, cupping her cheek with tender concern, bringing her face back into the light. "You've shadows beneath your eyes, Hope." His thumb traced the upper ridge of her cheekbone, and feathered along the bottom edge of her lip as he pinned her with a knowing stare.

"The nightmares are back," he surmised.

Hope gaped up at him, batted at his hand. "They are not."

"They are." The side of his mouth crooked up. "I haven't been sleeping all that well either."

Hope blinked. A becoming blush rose high on her cheeks.

That beguiling hue was more than Ethan—mere mortal man that he was—couldn't resist. Leaning toward her, he smiled velvety smooth temptation. "Maybe I should come to your room tonight. We could—"

He didn't get the chance to finish his statement. A distant voice hailed him as a lone rider came thundering over the barren landscape from the northwest. Instinct pushed Hope behind him. His colt was in his palm and aimed before he recognized the man on the horse. The vaquero didn't stop until he reached their side, splashing through the stream.

The cowboy spared Hope a brief, curious glance as Ethan holstered his weapon, before launching into an explanation in rapid-fire Spanish, motioning urgently toward the Old Mission. He waited as Ethan barked a terse order, then wheeled his mount around and tore off again.

Hope's troubled eyes searched Ethan's face. "What happened?"

A muscle ticked in his jaw as he lowered his resigned gaze to hers. "They found a body."

"A body...you mean another dead steer?"

Ethan heaved a defeated sigh. "No," he denied at last, shaking his head.

Would this never stop?

****

The recovery party rode back to the ranch, somber and silent, trailed by the horse bearing Rodrigo's body. Once they reached the main house, Ethan motioned the other men on and broke away from the group. He rode straight to the stables and dismounted, going through the motions of settling Apollo in for the night, all the while his mind lingered on Hope.

The horse nudged his shoulder, expressing his displeasure over Ethan's inattentiveness. Ethan patted the animal's neck affectionately, promising him a treat come morning. Whether it was the pat or the promise, Ethan couldn't guess, but the horse snorted, mollified, dismissing him.

Ethan plodded to the house, and, once inside,

dragged himself upstairs. He noticed the light beneath Hope's door, broken now and again by her pacing shadow. Standing immobile, he stared at that wedge of light, at the moving shadow. His thoughts circled around one central issue until he acknowledged it, faced it head on, and accepted it. Right or wrong, tonight he needed her. Without pausing to consider what he was about to do, without knocking, he opened the door.

Hope stopped mid-stride and whirled to face him. Relief flowed across her face at the sight of him, making him smile despite his fatigue. Her cheeks were rosy. Her glossy black hair trailed down her back in long, wet strands, soaking the shoulders of her robe, glimmering in the glow from the fireplace and the lamps. She took a step forward, seemed to be considering throwing herself into his arms.

Ethan held up a hand, forestalling her. His gaze darted to the tub in the corner, still full of water...a damned sight more welcome than a cold stream for his tired muscles. The last dregs of her soap bubbles floated on the surface, beckoning him. He'd put in a long day and had the sweat and dust sticking to his skin to prove it. Besides, after seeing Vega's handiwork again, he felt tainted. He wanted to—needed to—wash away that feeling before he could let himself touch her.

"Hold that thought," he ordered gruffly, shutting the door behind him with the back of his booted heel even as his fingers reached first for his gun belt, then the buttons of his shirt.

Hope lifted her brows at his command. A becoming blush stained her cheeks, but she didn't turn her eyes away when he began to undress. Grinning, he shed his clothing as he crossed the room, dropping articles in a haphazard jumble as he went. Hope sat motionless, gawking as he revealed more and more of his sculpted form. Her cheeks were deep scarlet by the time he stood before her without a stitch of clothing.

It took a moment to remember his decision to bathe first and touch later.

He groaned aloud as he submerged himself in the tub, sloshing water over the rim. His eyelids sagged, and his head tipped back to rest on the rim. Jasmine saturated him, easing the ache in his soul as the warm water eased the aches in his abused muscles.

****

Flustered, Hope bolted forward, gathering up his clothing, desperate to divert her own attention lest she make a fool of herself and drool. She folded his dusty clothing and retrieved his boots and gun belt, piling the works on the chair by the window. That done, she crossed the short distance to perch on the side of the bed.

Ethan picked up her bar of soap and began lathering his hair, scrubbing his broad chest and powerful arms. She smiled to herself in impish delight, deciding it would be interesting to hear what the other men might say come tomorrow when they got close enough to notice how pretty he smelled.

Hope cleared the lump of desire from her throat. “Did you find tracks?”

“Nope, didn’t expect I would.” He blew water out of his face as he rinsed the soap from his hair.

“You’re exhausted,” she observed.

“Been a hell of a day…” Ethan sighed, leaning back against the rim of the tub with a yawn and a contented smile.

She debated asking about the body they’d brought back but decided against it. He was clearly worn out. The last thing he probably wanted to do was talk about that mess. Still, she couldn’t help be a bit disconcerted about him sitting there, soaking in her bath. She cast about for some safe bit of conversation.

"I didn't realize what Matt's idea of a 'small party' entailed," she offered. "This is certainly much more elaborate than anything I've ever planned. No wonder Natalia was feeling overwhelmed."

"Yeah, it used to take Ma two full weeks to throw one of these shindigs together, sometimes longer. I was surprised Matt insisted on having it this Saturday, but if he's gonna—" Ethan broke off, his guilty stare snapped to her.

She arched a suspicious brow. "What else is he up to?"

Shaking his head, he replied, "Matt's surprise, you'll have to wait like everybody else."

"But you know what it is?"

Ethan smiled and shrugged, his steady gaze locked on her hands as they twist the belt of her robe. Her question flew from her mind as he suddenly stood up. Water sluiced down over the hard plains of his sculpted body, and Hope feared she might slide right off the side of the bed in a boiling puddle of desire at his feet. She gripped the post of the footboard in a death grip in order to keep herself from doing exactly that as he stepped from the bath and took her damp towel down off the peg to rub the moisture from his virile body.

One luscious muscle at a time.

Her mouth watered.

Corded muscles bunched and rippled beneath smooth, golden skin. His wet hair was the color of raw honey and hung in long, wild strands almost to his shoulders. Her fingers itched with the physical need to touch. Hope dragged in a sharp breath. The sound drew his attention. Ethan glanced up, and his smoldering gaze locked with hers. He straightened, giving her a clear view of the full impact her avid perusal had on his body.

Hope stared, shocked. Excited. Her gaze locked on the rigid length of his arousal. Suddenly he was there, standing before her, drawing her to her feet. His scorching gaze swept over her as he tugged her belt loose. Deft hands slid the robe off her shoulders, dragged it down her arms, letting it fall to the floor where the soft material pooled about her feet. Ethan swept her up into his arms, and carefully lowered her to the bed, stretching out beside her.

His eyes branded her soul.

Hope held her breath as he touched the tip of his finger to the bottom of her chin, and leisurely traced a path down her throat, through the valley between her breasts, and across the plains of her stomach...not stopping until he reached the mound of soft curls covering her womanhood. Every inch of his journey was a study of excruciating pleasure and heady anticipation. Her vision blurred and every thought in her head promptly deserted her when he reached his goal. She let out a gasp as he set about preparing her body for his invasion. He swallowed her moans with kiss after kiss, leaving her floating in a warm haze of passion...mind, body, and soul.

When she began to writhe against him in unspoken demand, Ethan moved to cover her, claiming her once more as his own. He took her with a gentle, yet insistent possessiveness, leaving her trembling and desperate for more. His thrusts were deep and steady as he alternated between drugging kisses and staring deep into her eyes.

When the moment was at last upon her, and the first waves of bliss began to roll through her body, Ethan pressed his lips to her ear and whispered hoarsely, “You’re mine, Hope. You’re all I’ve ever needed.”

She cried out and shattered in his arms, gasping his name as his words drove her even higher, cresting the top pinnacle. Ethan groaned aloud and liquid heat rushed deep inside her core.

It was a long while later before Ethan moved to her side. He left the bed to pad, naked, around the cool room to extinguish the lamps. Hope's appreciative gaze followed his every move. He crawled back onto the bed, pulling the covers up around them. She shivered until his warm body curled protectively around her. His arm slid around her waist, and he drew her pliant body relentlessly to him until her back pressed snug to his front.

She made no protest, he felt so warm and so wonderful she wanted nothing more than to stay like that with him forever. Sleep was immediate, a warm and soothing haven Hope hadn't visited since the last time they'd shared a bed.

****

The next morning, Ethan worked his way through the hearty pile of food on his plate like a lumberjack fresh from the forests. He hadn't realized he'd been so hungry until he'd begun to eat. Across the room, Natalia leaned against the counter and watched him with a knowing smile on her face. She nodded absent dismissal when Xavier excused himself.

Before Ethan could ask for more, she added another full stack of flapjacks and meat to his plate and topped off his coffee Leaning against the counter again, she waited patiently until he finished. Something was brewing in those deep brown eyes of hers, he just hadn't figured out what yet.

"You're remarkably calm after hearing another line shack burned," she commented, her tone bland.

Ethan lifted an eyebrow at her wheedling tone. "What's your point?"

She shrugged, smiling. "I expected a more…heated reaction from you."

"Go on. Get it out of your system," he invited. "Then drop it."

Ethan ran the back of his knuckle up and down the side of his coffee mug, waiting for the criticism that was sure to follow. She'd been chewin' something over from the minute he'd walking into the kitchen. In fact, he'd been expecting it since Natalia had come looking for him early this morning with news of Vega's latest attack, and found him in Hope's bed. Hope had still been sleeping—exhausted from his loving—when he'd slipped from the room this morning. That thought brought a smug smile to his lips that even the prospect of Natalia's criticism couldn't dim.

She cocked her head to the side. "What would you like for me to say?"

"Say whatever's on your mind. Then I don't want to hear anymore about it. And I sure as hell don't want you to be judgin' Hope over it. What happens between her and me is no one else's business." He eyed her, daring her to object.

Natalia's gaze was steady, her expression serious. "It's about damned time..."

His brows shot up in surprise.

"I was wondering how long it would take you to get around to claiming that girl for your own." Natalia sat down in the chair across from him. "I was afraid you were going to be stubborn and let love slip right through your fingers, *mijo*. I knew the minute I met her that she was for you."

Ethan stared at her, baffled. She clearly assumed there was some kind of understanding between he and Hope. He didn't know how to explain to her they'd never even discussed a future. The reality of the situation hit him between the eyes. Hope was a respectable lady. Not some fancy skirt to tangle with when the mood struck.

Hell, she was Matt's daughter.

If anyone else found out about them, her reputation would be in shreds. What the hell had he been thinking?

Then his heart tripped inside his chest. An odd mixture of fear and elation speared through him. Sweet Christ, what if he'd gotten her with child. The very idea snuck up on him, catching him by surprise. He had to admit, the prospect didn't bother him near as much as he assumed it would. A little girl with Hope's hair. A little boy with her eyes. How would Hope feel about a baby?

His baby?

He ran a hand through his hair, and, for the first time since leaving Hope's room that morning, his smile slipped.

Natalia broke into his thoughts, her voice filled with uneasy concern. "Ethan? What have you done?"

His troubled gaze flashed to her face, then darted out the window. The answer was simple, yet he shied away from it. There had to be something else, some other alternative. A proposal had been as good as a death sentence for Christina. It would surely be no different for Hope.

Or would it?

Natalia must have read his thoughts like an open book, for she slapped her hands on the table before him, glaring at him. "I never thought the day would come when I would be forced to say this, Ethan, but I'm sorely disappointed in you. That girl's the marrying kind, not a passing fancy."

She gave him one last disgusted glare, and marched from the room, back stiff with disapproval. Ethan rolled his eyes and dropped his head back on his shoulders, heaving a dark sigh. Why did women have to go and complicate everything? Couldn't a man and a woman share some pleasure, take comfort in one another's arms without those damned words gettin' tossed in the mix? Love... Marriage...

Heaven forbid, was that too damned much to ask?

His answer came in the form of a loud clap of thunder that shook the rafters. The heavens opened up in a swift, violent downpour, and somewhere on the mountain, another bolt of lightning lanced down from the heavens to scorch the ground, lighting up the room.

Ethan snorted, grim now as he contemplated the ceiling. Apparently not when the woman was a respectable lady...and a friend's daughter to boot. Besides, if he were honest with himself, he'd admit what he felt for her was anything but simple and uncomplicated. What he felt for her required—no—*demanded* he stake his claim.

Beautiful, just goddamned beautiful, he groaned, stuck somewhere between the desire to officially claim her for his own, and the urge to hightail it for the hills.

Chapter 22

Ethan's unexpected heart-to-heart with Natalia soured his mood. The morning went to hell in a hand-basket from there on out. To his everlasting irritation—and well beyond any reckoning of his—every man he got close enough to shake a stick at gawked at him as if he'd grown another head. In addition, every hand on the Bar M had taken to twittering like a passel of church ladies at a Sunday social as soon as they thought they were out of his earshot.

Antonio's reaction had been the oddest of all. They'd been discussing plans for the renovations on Matt's stables, when Antonio had stepped closer to help Ethan with a horse that had thrown a shoe. They'd worked, side-by-side, for less than a minute when Antonio's head jerked up and he abruptly stepped back, murder glinting in his deep brown eyes. The younger man's hands fisted at his sides. The vein in his temple throbbed. For a moment, Ethan thought Antonio might take a shot at him. Abruptly, without uttering a word, Antonio spun on his heel and stomped away.

"What the hell?" Ethan stared after him, scowling.

Bewildered, he tramped inside the stables and grabbed up a pitchfork, stabbing it into the nearest clump of hay. The physical labor helped vent some of his frustrations, but every time he tried to reason it out, he just got mad all over again.

Julio's voice broke into his tumultuous thoughts.

"Ain't Matt got somebody to do that?"

Ethan swung a scowl over his shoulder as Julio limped down the center of the stables. "You sure took your sweet time gettin' here, old man." Another clump of hay went flying.

"We've lost line shacks 'fore. Probably lose a few more 'fore it's all said and done, I reckon." Julio propped a negligent shoulder against the door of the stall across the way, twirling a piece of straw between his gnarled fingers. "Xavier said ya took the news well. Said you seemed in a right fit mood 'fore he left. Who pissed in your boot since then?"

Tossing another clump of hay, Ethan grumbled under his breath, "Who hasn't?"

Julio spat a stream of brown juice from the corner of his mouth. Hooking a finger in the side of his cheek, he scooped the wad of tobacco out to toss it onto the hay at his feet before leveling a bored stare at Ethan. "What'd ya call me over fer?"

"So sorry I disturbed you," Ethan snapped. He braced his forearm on the top of the pitchfork, glaring at Julio. "If it's too damned much of an inconvenience to stir yourself when your *boss* calls, maybe you'd be better off drawin' your wages someplace else."

The old cowpoke lifted one sardonic brow, tucking the end of the straw into the corner of his mouth. "D'you call me all the way over here so you'd have somebody to watch yer little snit? Cause I got better things to do. You got somethin' to say, spit it out, boy. I ain't got all goddamned day, and ain't neither of us getting' any younger."

Ethan bristled. *The rotten son of a bitch.* "I ought to fire your insolent ass."

Julio leisurely shifted the piece of straw from one side of his mouth to the other. "Yeah, yeah... We're burnin' daylight, boy. Get on with it."

Nothing like a strong shot of Julio to put you in

your place, Ethan shook his head. "Who started the fire?"

"Same as started the last, I figure."

"Before Rodrigo's body turned up, I was hoping we'd have a bit of a break. I thought for sure he was the traitor when he disappeared so soon after the meeting." Ethan lifted another clump of fresh hay and pitched it into the stall, then leaned the pitchfork against the side of the stall and crossed the aisle to stand beside Julio so they could speak in quieter tones.

Julio's nose twitched. His brow crinkled, and he was silent for a moment. "You don't think he was the one?"

"He's dead, and now there's been another fire," Ethan stated the obvious.

"Well, now. Could be an easy explanation," Julio murmured at length. "Could be he *was* the traitor. Maybe he got nervous, high-tailed it back to Vega. Vega probably decided Rodrigo was no use to him anymore, so he got rid of him. It was pretty dark last night, Ethan, whoever did it could'a slipped away real easy like."

Ethan crossed his arms over his chest and leaned back against the stall door. He weighed Julio's words, conceded that, in all probability what Julio suggested could be true. Still, something nagged at him. It was all too convenient, Rodrigo disappearing, only to turn up dead.

Too damned convenient by half.

"You wanna continue the watch on the others, fine." Julio heaved a sigh riff with blatant exasperation. "Ain't gonna do no good goin' on a witch hunt, I'd say. We got enough to deal with right now. Need to get a move on brandin' the herds. That army unit over to the fort sent in an order for another string of horses, and I hear tell Matt's got a shindig planned. Nope, we surely don't need a witch hunt."

Ethan bit back a nasty retort. He took a long, slow breath and dredged deep for patience he wasn't sure he had. "Post the watch."

Julio shook his head, turning to leave. He hadn't quite made it to the doors when Ethan stopped him. "Did you talk to any of the men before comin' in here?"

Julio glanced over his shoulder and drawled, "A few."

"Did any of them mention what the hell their problem is? They've been shootin' me strange looks all damned morning. Hell, even Antonio got a bee in his ear."

Julio turned to face him with a wide, gap-toothed grin, nudging his hat back on his head. His sun-weathered face lit up with unmistakable glee, and his dark eyes danced.

Hooking his thumbs in his back pockets, the old man rocked back on his heels. "Can't speak fer Antonio, since I ain't seen the boy yet today, but as fer the rest of 'em..." His gape-toothed grin spread like wildfire from ear to ear. "Well, now, I reckon it could have somethin' to do with you smellin' right pretty. Yessiree, like a fistful of fresh picked flowers."

Frowning, Ethan snagged a hank of hair and drew it to his nose. His shoulders sagged as jasmine filled his nostrils. Rolling his eyes to the rafters, he took a deep, tortured breath. Chortling, Julio strolled from the barn while Ethan's vexed curses turned the air blue.

****

Hope tracked Ethan down in the bunkhouse late that afternoon. His raised voice reverberated through the closed door. He was giving someone hell all right, and she was hesitant to interrupt. But Natalia'd sent her on what she'd assured Hope was one more crucial errand, and Hope had had a difficult enough time finding him in the first place. She had enough on her plate to deal with to keep her busy until next Christmas, and standing around, waiting for Ethan to finish blistering some poor cowhand's hide was putting her behind schedule. Hope braced herself and knocked on the door. She choked on a startled gasp as the door flew wide open.

Scowling dark enough to knock the shine right out of the sun, Ethan barked, "What!"

"I…I, ah, I…" Hope stuttered, wide-eyed, searching for her voice. "I need to speak to you."

Ethan spun on his heel and left her to follow at her own peril. Groaning inwardly, she followed him as he stomped back through the bunkhouse to tower over a young vaquero. Mute, Hope stood in the corner, pitying the pale faced cowboy.

Neither man even glanced her way. A vein bulged down the length of Ethan's neck. His face was red as he took the vaquero to task. Said young man cringed, his eyes glued to the floor as if searching for some miniscule crack in the floorboards he might slither through to escape Ethan's wrath. Someday, she was going to have to have to get someone to teach her to speak Spanish. Ethan snapped out one terse word, his voice cracked like thunder in the empty room, and the vaquero jolted.

Hope stepped back as the cowboy scooped up his hat and took off out the door at a dead run, not even slowing to nod in her direction. The door slammed shut in his wake.

Ethan stood motionless, staring at the far wall for long moment. "What do you need to talk to me about?"

Hope cleared her throat and fidgeted with the pleats in her skirt. "Natalia asked me to find you. She wants to borrow the braziers your parents used at their fiestas."

"I'm busy now, but I'll send someone over for them later," he mumbled, heading for the door without glancing her way.

"Sure," she whispered under her breath, suddenly irritated beyond good sense. "Go ahead and disappear, you're very good at that aren't you?"

She didn't even realize she'd spoken aloud until he stopped in his tracks and pivoted to face her, demanding, "What did you say?"

Hope gritted her teeth and tossed her shoulders back, stomping past him. "Oh, never mind. Step aside."

Ethan's hard hand snaked out, snagging the inside of her elbow, forcing her to face him. "What did you say?"

Lips compressed, Hope glared at him. Her temper got the better of her. "I said your manners leave much to be desired."

"No, that wasn't what you said," he reminded her. His eyes narrowed. "You said I'm good at disappearing."

"If you heard what I said, then why did you ask?" she huffed.

"Because I'd like to know what you meant by it…and by the shot at my manners."

His attitude rubbed her raw and, before she stopped to consider her words, she let them issue forth, heated and caustic. "It means that after you came to me again last night, you could have at least had the decency of sticking around long enough this morning to… You promised me that… Oh, dear Lord…" Her voice trailed away, and her eyes widened in mortification at what he'd goaded her into revealing.

Ethan's scowl slowly shifted into a sensual, albeit smug grin. Suddenly desperate to get away, she jerked her arm, but could not free herself from his unrelenting grasp. Heat stained her cheeks. She groaned at her own stupidity. Shaking his head, Ethan leisurely pulled her resistant form into his warm, inescapable embrace. Her alarmed gaze flew to his face, and her heart leaped at the purposeful light in his eyes. Hope was all too aware they were standing in the middle of a deserted room.

A deserted room *full* of beds.

From the look on Ethan's face, he, too, was acutely aware of their surroundings.

And he had every intention of taking advantage of the situation.

Dear Lord in heaven...

He tipped his head until his lips skimmed hers tauntingly. "I believe you meant to remind me of a certain promise I made."

The heat pouring from his deep blue stare was hotter than a Texas blaze. She felt the burn all the way to the very core of her being. Her lids lowered in anticipation of the sensual onslaught that was sure to come.

An unexpected blast of air slapped her hot face when Ethan swiftly stepped back. Her eyes flew open in surprise, and she wobbled on her feet. Ethan steadied her even as he glared at the intruder. Patch was four steps into the room before he stopped, and Hope had regained her equilibrium.

"Oh, hey Ethan...didn't realize y'all was in here. Ma'am..." Patch ducked his head, tipping his hat in Hope's direction. "Antonio told me I'm with y'all for the round up. Let me grab my gear, and I'll get out of your way."

It took him a moment to gather his things. A long moment in which neither Hope nor Ethan moved a muscle. She couldn't tear herself free of the snare of Ethan's blistering stare.

Patch's one-eyed stare bounced between the two of them as he strode across the room, as if just now aware of the tension crackling in the air. "Excuse me," he muttered as he stepped around Ethan.

As he passed close to Ethan, Patch faltered for half a step and loudly sniffed the air. Patch's one visible eye widened in surprise and darted to Hope, then back to Ethan. Heat burst in her cheeks. A knowing smile, wide as the Pecos was long, settled on his face. Hope began searching for the same elusive crack in the floor the young cowboy who'd been receiving Ethan's wrath earlier had.

Scowling, Ethan growled at Patch, "What the hell are you grinning at?"

Patch pressed his lips into a tight line, bowed his head, and ducked from the room. His hoot of laughter broke free before the door closed behind him.

Hope scolded, "That was rude."

"He was the one interrupting." Ethan's gaze slid to the nearest bunk, skidded back to her. A wry grin twisted his lips. It didn't take a mind reader to interpret the look he shot her.

A change of subject seemed in order. "What was he talking about? What round up?"

"Enrique came across a small herd of horses up on the ridge. I'm taking some of the men up to catch 'em. The Circle K got an order from the fort for another string," he explained, tucking a stray lock of hair behind her ear. The gesture was so gentle, so intimate, her breath caught in her throat. "We probably won't make it back till tomorrow night, Saturday morning if we run into any trouble."

"Trouble?" she demanded, frowning.

Ethan smoothed the rough pad of his thumb along the crease between her brows. "Don't worry, sweetheart. The only trouble we're likely to see is a thrown horseshoe."

She didn't want to think about Vega...or the countless other mishaps that could be waiting out there for him. There'd be time enough for worrying once the sun went down, and she was alone in her bed tonight. "You won't miss the party, will you?"

"I'll be back in plenty of time." He grinned, devil-may-care, adding, "And I'll be expecting you to save me a dance."

"I will," she promised. "What was Patch smiling about that made you so touchy?"

Ethan's expression turned disgruntled so swiftly, she almost laughed aloud. Was that a blush on his cheeks?

He nudged her chin up with the curve of his knuckles and brushed a light kiss across her lips. Turning away, he headed out the door, calling wryly over his shoulder, "Soap."

A spare moment after Ethan cleared the threshold, her delighted laughter burst free.

Chapter 23

The traitor pulled away from the Circle K the next morning before the sun broke over the eastern horizon, unable to mask his irritation as he bounced along on the wagon seat. A vaquero's ass was meant to be kissin' saddle leather, not pickin' up splinters on some damned wagon seat runnin' woman's errands. But he sure as hell couldn't say anything about it, not without giving away more than he wanted revealed. Hell, at least he'd have a plausible excuse to make his contacts. No one would raise an eyebrow at any of his stops.

The first place he stopped was the mercantile where he left a list of supplies Matt's whore claimed she needed. He then made his way down the boardwalk. Ducking inside the bank, he nodded to the teller as he approached the counter. His eyes drifted to Masters as he sat at a desk in a small room off the lobby.

The middle-aged teller addressed him in polite, businesslike tone. "What can I do for you today, sir?"

"Need to make a withdrawal."

The sound of his voice drew Daniel Masters' eyes.

Before the teller could respond, Masters stepped from the back room. "I'll help him, Josiah. Why don't you take a break? I heard Mirabella baked a fresh batch of pies this morning. Why don't you run on down and pick one up for me. Grab yourself one while you're there, put it on my tab."

The teller lifted his brows and blinked, clearly

flabbergasted. Masters cleared his throat and lifted a pointed brow. The teller quickly nodded, taking his leave without another word. The traitor stepped forward, leaning his elbows on the counter, waiting for the door to close on the teller's heels before speaking.

A short while later, the traitor swaggered inside the dim interior of the Busted Wheel. As he strolled to the bar, his eyes roamed around the vacant room. Two men—clearly coasting on a bender from the night before—occupied a table in the corner. One slouched precariously low in his chair, the other leaned hard on the tabletop, as if the scarred surface was all that stood between him and the indignity of landing face first on the floor. The only other inhabitant of the bar, besides the barkeep, was a tall, lean man with a boyish, handsome face, nursing a bottle of tequila.

Leaning his forearms on the bar, near but not too close to the lanky man, he addressed the barkeep. "Matt needs a couple cases of whiskey. Might as well throw in a case of whatever else you got back there. Put it on his tab."

"Heard tell Lewis was havin' some kind 'a to-do. What's the celebration for?"

He stared the barkeep down, deadpan. "Wagon's out front."

When it became apparent he wasn't going to get anything else out of the vaquero, the barkeep mumbled something under his breath and made his way to the back room. As soon as the door swung shut behind him, the traitor glanced over his shoulder at the two inebriated patrons. He met Pretty-Boy's sidelong stare in the tarnished mirror behind the bar.

"Full moon Saturday night," he remarked casually.

"Sure is," Pretty-Boy responded, tossing back a

shot, grimacing.

"Huntin' moon." He shifted, braced himself against the bar and crossed his ankles. "Raidin' moon, rustlers call it. Sure would be downright *unfortunate* if Matt's fiesta got disrupted," he drawled.

Pretty-Boy didn't comment. His expression didn't alter, but his steady gaze held the traitor's pointed stare in the mirror, and a faint crease appeared in his cheek. It was then that the traitor noticed the fresh, jagged scar running down Pretty-Boy's far temple, ending on his upper cheek.

"Looks like you tangled with one hell of a wildcat. Who won?"

Pretty-Boy's pale eyes flashed fire, and his nostrils flared. His tone promised severe and painful retribution as he traced a thumb down the mark. "Bitch got lucky, but she'll pay."

The barkeep nudged his way through the door, three crates stacked in his beefy hands. The traitor nodded once to Pretty-Boy, and led the barkeep to the wagon.

****

Saturday dawned, sunny and warm. The braziers were set up nonetheless, spread throughout the yard, interspersed with the numerous tables set up for dining and around the area cordoned off for dancing that evening.

The ranch was all but empty. Most of the men had gone with Ethan, or had headed off to get a jump on the branding. A sparse few hands had stayed back to help with setting up for the party, butchering and roasting the steer. Even now, as Natalia, Hope, and Antonio set to tying decorative bows and ribbons about the yard, the tantalizing aroma of roasting beef tickled their appetites.

Hope held the tail end of a long length of ribbon for Antonio as he stood atop a ladder and stretched to drape it across the trellis on the edge of the makeshift dance floor. The distant sound of thundering hooves drew her attention. Glancing to the west, shielding her eyes, Hope spied a group of riders approaching the ranch at a dead gallop. She glanced up to Antonio with lifted brows.

He, too, shielded his eyes from the afternoon glare, and studied the group. His tanned brow furrowed. Hope worried when Antonio stiffened, his hand dropping to his gun. She was about to ask him if he recognized the group, but he visibly relaxed, answering her unspoken question.

When he turned his eyes to her, his smile was strangely tight. "Ethan's back."

She closed her eyes and breathed the first easy breath she'd had since she'd watched Ethan ride away yesterday. She'd been worried when he hadn't come back last night, and even more worried still when he failed to make an appearance this morning.

"I assumed they'd be bringing horses back with them."

"They should be." Antonio's gaze traveled back to the approaching riders. The lines around his mouth tightened again. "They must have run into trouble." Antonio finished stringing the ribbon and climbed down the ladder. "Go inside and let Natalia know they're back—without the herd. Tell her it looks like someone's hurt."

Hope's startled gaze flew back to the approaching men. How had Antonio known someone was injured? From this distance, she couldn't even tell who was who. Nodding, frowning, she hurried inside, all the while wishing she could go and greet Ethan herself. By the time she and Natalia stepped out onto the veranda, the riders had dismounted. She caught a glimpse of Ethan's backside as he disappeared inside the shadows of the stables, deep in conversation with Antonio. Hope took a step forward, but halted when Natalia's restraining hand landed on her forearm.

"He'll come to the house when he's finished, let them discuss whatever it is they need to without any interruptions," Natalia cautioned.

She stared at the stables, frustrated.

Natalia gave her a little nudge. "Come inside and give me a hand with the cooking while I see to Enrique's arm."

Hope wandered out to the shade of the veranda over an hour later, sinking onto one of the rocking chairs, heaving a tired sigh. She was hot and tired. And worried. Over an hour had passed since she'd heard Ethan and Antonio tromp through the hallway on their way to Matt's study, and still he hadn't come to her yet.

She didn't know how long she'd sat like that—rocking and staring out at the mountains in the distance—but, suddenly, she felt his presence beside her. She pushed to her feet. The questions filling her mind died on her lips as soon as she caught sight of the angry red groove on the side of his forehead. Her heart dropped to her stomach. Her mouth fell open, but she couldn't force words passed the solid lump of fear in her throat. Her eyes raced over the rest of him, searching for further injury.

He looked like he'd rolled in the dust, taking most of it with him when he got up. Dried blood stained his collar and the sleeve of his shirt. It crusted his hair to the side of his head. Aside from the mark on his forehead, however, he didn't appear to have sustained any other injury. By the looks of the salve covering his wound, Natalia had already tended it.

"Oh, Ethan—"

She caught her lip between her teeth and lifted her hand to touch the side of Ethan's forehead near his wound, letting her fingertips trail over his cheek.

Suddenly realizing what she'd done, Hope dropped her hand to her side. Heat surged up her neck to stain her cheeks.

"It's not as bad as it looks, sweetheart." He captured her wrist, drawing her hand back, cupping it against his cheek. Turning his face into her palm, he nuzzled, pressed a kiss to the tender inside of her wrist, and drew a deep breath. He lifted his other hand to grasp the back of her neck. His gaze locked on her lips, searing her unambiguous hunger.

"I missed you," he whispered hoarsely.

Then, tightening the hand on her neck, he drew her forward until their lips met, sealed. The kiss was lightning fast, and just as electric. Her free hand flew to brace against his shirtfront, bunching the flannel in a surprised fist. Her pulses skittered, and her world tipped on its side. As abruptly as he'd initiated the kiss, Ethan drew back. With a blinding smile reeking of smug male satisfaction, Ethan stepped around her and strutted to the bunkhouse. Dazed, Hope stood motionless, gaping at his back.

Her face went up in flames as the small group of ranch hands near the corral set to whistling and cheering their approval.

****

Ethan stood between Antonio and Matt, doing his best not to laugh aloud as Matt shifted from foot to foot and back again, staring at the door of the main house like a startled possum, unable to decide whether it should run for cover, or curl up and play dead and hope for the best. The men had gathered on or near the veranda...Ethan and Julio, Matt and Antonio, Patch, and several others. They were all dressed to the nines in clean denims and crisp, vibrant shirts. All except Matt, who wore a somber black suit that, considering the way he kept tugging at the neck and cuffs, appeared a size too small.

All conversation ceased when the two women

stepped out into the late afternoon sunshine. The men turned as one, gawking like schoolboys with their first crush. Ethan stood motionless, transfixed. Ethan couldn't tear his gaze from Hope. She floored him with a simple, almost shy smile, and he forgot to breathe. Beside him, Antonio sucked in a sharp breath, took a half step forward. Ethan was rooted to the spot, unable to move. Unable to speak.

He'd never, *never* seen anyone so beautiful in all his life.

She'd chosen a dusky rose, formal gown with an open, off-the-shoulder neckline trimmed with ivory lace. Her bare throat and shoulders glistened in the light, rose petal soft and delectable. Her gown had a form-fitting bodice that enhanced her tiny waist, pushing the upper swell of her breasts into tantalizing view. Her sweeping skirts served to draw more attention to her slim waist, and when she moved, the satin toes of her slippers peeped beneath the ruffle. Ethan suffered a confusing mix of emotion. Part of him wanted to sweep her off her feet and kiss her senseless. Part of him wanted to throw the nearest horse blanket over her and demand to know what she was thinking, showing off her…her charms…like that for all the rest of the men to see.

Small diamond teardrops winked from her dainty earlobes, and long, ivory gloves hung from one hand. The other hand smoothed down over her skirts. An artful cascade of blue-black curls piled on the top of her head, studded with multiple decorative pins. The slender ivory column of her neck, the delicate curve of shoulder begged to be nibbled on.

His mouth watered.

Offering her his arm, Antonio leaped forward, blocking Ethan's view.

Ethan ground his teeth as Antonio drew her down the steps and into the crowd gathering near the barbeque. Disgruntled and scowling, Ethan trailed haplessly in their wake, wishing to God he'd pounded the younger man straight into the ground when he'd had the chance. He nodded acknowledgement right and left as he stalked after them, unwilling to stop long enough to talk to anyone, unwilling to take the chance that she might slip out of his sight. Jealousy chewed him raw as Antonio, ever solicitous and grinning like a baked possum, escorted Hope around the yard.

Ethan had just made up his mind up he'd taken all he could—and was about to knock Antonio on his ass after all—when a hand caught Ethan's elbow, halting his progress. Ethan spun around with a snarl on his lips, prepared to tear the owner of that hand limb from limb.

Leaning close to Ethan, apparently oblivious of his eminent demise, Matt whispered, "Is he here yet?"

"I haven't seen him," Ethan snapped. He craned his neck, but his target had disappeared into the crowd near the dance floor. Damn it all to hell.

Matt fidgeted, tugging at a cuff. "You're sure he said he'd be here? What if somethin' came up, what if he…"

"Relax." Heaving a resigned sigh as Hope and Antonio moved on to the next group of merrymakers, he turned his surly attention to Matt. "He assured me—given this momentous occasion—nothing short of the Second Coming would prevent him from being here. His words, not mine."

Matt exhaled an unsteady breath, running a finger around the inside of his collar. "Do we have enough men with the herd? Did you leave enough men at your place? Hell and damnation, it's hotter'n blue blazes out here."

"It's covered. Julio left a few minutes ago to check on things. Stop looking for trouble." His eyes narrowed as Antonio slipped a casual hand onto the small of Hope's back. Focused on that offending hand, Ethan suggested, "You know…if you're that worried about it, why don't you send Antonio out to keep an eye on things?"

"He's supposed to—" Matt began, but cut himself off as the latest arrival steered toward the stables. "There he is. Grab him quick before Natalia corners him. I'll start roundin' everyone up."

Grumbling, Ethan set off through the crowd as Matt's voice boomed over the din, calling everyone to attention near the veranda.

"Friends and neighbors…" Matt waved his arms, motioning everyone closer. "I'm sure you've all been wonderin' why I decided to throw this fiesta."

The crowd murmured, milling near the bottom of the veranda. From the corner of his eye, Ethan saw Matt beckon Natalia to his side. Blushing, she stepped forward and Matt draped his arm around her shoulders.

"Well, I've invited you here to celebrate with us. I've finally come to my senses and asked this good woman to be my wife…and she's accepted." Matt paused, waiting for the applause and raucous cheering to die away before continuing.

While Matt waited, he nodded to Ethan. Ethan slipped up behind Hope. He took her firmly by the elbow and drew her away from Antonio's side. Hope lifted a curious brow, but went along, offering Antonio a puzzled shrug. With single-minded purpose, Ethan pushed his way through the crowd, snagging the wafer-thin man clad head to toe in black with one hand, pulling Hope along in the other. Matt waited until Ethan and his charges were on the bottom step before turning to Natalia.

"I've got a surprise for you." Matt beamed down at her, happy as a pup with two tails. "Father Bernard, if you please."

The slim priest nodded and stepped forward, smiling. As he ascended the steps, the priest's best Sunday voice rose above the crowd, loud enough to reverberate in the back rows. "I understand there is to be a wedding this evening."

Natalia gasped. Her startled gaze flew to Matt. His eyes rested on her, expectant and anxious. With a soggy smile, without taking her eyes off Matt's face, she spoke up, loud and clear. "You heard right, Father Bernard."

Grinning, feeling easier now that Hope was at his side where she was supposed to be, Ethan led her up the steps.

Chapter 24

Beneath a bower of flowers and ribbons, before God and all their guests, Father Bernard united Matt and Natalia in marriage. Hope, the tearful maid of honor, held a small bunch of hastily plucked wildflowers—Natalia's wedding bouquet. Ethan stood in as Matt's best man. Hope thought he must be the most handsome man there.

At Matt's insistence, the ceremony was short and to the point, over almost before it began. When Matt swept his bride up into a bone-crushing embrace for a heated kiss, cheers rose across the yard in deafening proportions.

Hope couldn't tear her eyes from Ethan.

Later that evening, several of the hands broke out their instruments. Matt and Natalia led the first steps of an elegant waltz. Hope stood near Antonio at the edge of the crowd as the happy couple revolved around the center of the crowd. Her inexplicably shy gaze followed Ethan as he approached. His stare was determined, intent upon her. Ethan wordlessly held his hand out to her. Warmth seeped through her veins before he even touched her.

Jolts of awareness shot through her upon contact. His long, strong fingers closed over hers, warm and firm, leaving her no chance of escape. Pulling her into his arms—much closer than socially appropriate—Ethan settled his possessive hand on her lower back. He held her close, refusing to permit the slightest reprieve for her swirling emotions. All the while, Ethan's gaze held her captive. She drifted on the music, oblivious to all but him.

Ethan tilted his head until his cheek brushed hers. His scent surrounded her. She shuddered in his arms. His heat enveloped her, holding her enthralled, and she ached for more. His breath was ragged against her ear, seducing her. His hips brushed against her, the bulge of his arousal unmistakable even through the layers of her skirts. Her knees went weak. Then his thigh nudged between hers. The hand at her waist slipped a little lower, caressed. Her fingers convulsed on his muscled shoulders, her breathing tripped and stuttered.

Her hand trembled in his. Her breath quickened in short little bursts against the side of his throat. His lips curled against her temple, but his smug pleasure at her telling responses didn't bother her. The crowd around them melted away. The hours until he could sneak into her room later stretched long before her.

The dance ended all too soon. Her face was aflame. Her heart raced, and she wanted to kiss him more than she wanted her next breath. It didn't matter who saw them. As if privy to her thoughts, Ethan's stare lowered to her mouth. His head angled.

Seconds before their lips connected, Antonio shouldered Ethan out of the way, claiming her hand for the next dance. Her eyes widened in surprise, but she adjusted, moving woodenly into Antonio's outstretched arms. While Antonio was much more conscious of the space decorum permitted, he still held Hope much too close for her comfort.

He wasn't Ethan.

They shared a comment or two about the success of Matt's party, laughing as a bull of a man stumbled onto the dance floor near them, twirling...a bottle cradled in his arms like the finest of lovers. Matt claimed Hope's hand for the next set. One after another, men began crowding around her, pressing in on her in anticipation of a dance, or even a hint of a smile.

One man in particular stood out. She didn't recognize the newcomer, but then she didn't know a vast majority of those here anyway. The man's presence was commanding and several of the men who'd been vying for her attention shuffled out of his way without the slightest argument. The newcomer reached out, bold as brass, confidently drawing her hand to his lips. Charmed, she couldn't help but smile. She couldn't quite put her thumb on it, but there was just something in his quicksilver eyes...

The owner of those bright gray eyes towered head and shoulders over her. His shoulders were broad, his face handsome in a rugged, angular way. Hair, like dark rich sable, curled over his collar in crisp, glossy waves. His grin was charismatic, but the way he carried himself made her instinctively cautious. He reminded her of one of those dangerous, exotic big cats she'd seen caged in the traveling carnival shows.

"Hello, ma'am..." He doffed his hat, bowing over her hand. "Allow me to introduce myself—Garrett McCabe, late of the U.S. Marshals, at your service." His unusual eyes flickered over her with blatant appreciation before returning to her face. "I'm new to the area, just bought the Hendon place south of Johnston."

"I'm Hope Lewis. It's a pleasure to meet you, Mr. McCabe."

Hope darted a quick glance to Ethan, who suddenly appeared at her side from nowhere, his hands balled into tight fists at his sides. His jaw tightened, and he appeared to be clenching his teeth so hard she half expected them to shatter at any moment.

"No, Ma'am. The pleasures all mine...believe me," McCabe parried with a wide, sexy grin. "I hope you won't mind my crashing your party, but Mrs. Weston down at the mercantile assured me this was the best way to meet all my neighbors."

"Of course, you're always welcome, Mr. McCabe. We'd have sent an invitation around for you if we'd known you'd taken up residence there."

"That's all right, ma'am, the Hendon place was a fairly recent purchase." Garrett McCabe stepped closer, still holding her hand.

Odd, she'd forgotten he'd even taken it in the first place, or that he'd failed to relinquish it. Somehow, despite the dangerous aura, his presence was somehow...soothing.

"I hadn't realized I'd find such a rare flower in the middle of nowhere." He smiled with gallant flare, adding, "If I had, I would've found my way to Johnston much, much sooner. And please, call me Garrett."

"It would have been a waste of your time, McCabe," Ethan growled, low and menacing, settling his arm around her waist in a deliberate show of unmistakable possessiveness.

Garrett acknowledged Ethan at last. He lifted a challenging brow as he raised Hope's left hand into the light and considered her bare fingers with rapt interest. "Beg pardon. Didn't see a ring. I assumed the lady wasn't spoken for."

"I'm not." Hope turned a severe frown in Ethan's direction. Why was he behaving like this?

Her denial widened Garrett's grin, and deepened Ethan's scowl. His arm squeezed her waist. Garrett's fingers tightened on her hand. She had the sudden, unnerving sensation of being the prize two warring titans had decided to lay claim to.

She didn't appreciate the feeling one bit.

So help her, if they started pulling at her like a tug-rope, she'd slap them both silly.

"Well, then..." Garrett smiled tauntingly at Ethan before bending his warm silvery gaze to Hope. "Would you do me the honor of this dance?"

Before she could respond, Ethan lunged forward, looking as if his temper had been stretched to the breaking point. She breathed a small sigh of relief when Matt dropped a hand on his shoulder. Beaming, seemingly oblivious of the brewing confrontation, Matt addressed Ethan.

"Do you have it?"

Garrett McCabe took advantage of Ethan's distraction, and drew her onto the dance floor. He was a superb dancer, and utterly charming. Now, if she could just figure out why Antonio suddenly looked as if he'd like to wring someone's neck, the night would be just about perfect.

****

Ethan scowled at Matt, mad enough to chew a rattler to bits. He reached into his pocket and withdrew a folded handkerchief. Thrusting it at Matt, he turned back to search for Hope. She'd all but disappeared behind the wall of dancers as McCabe led her through the steps. Aggravated, Ethan's gaze flicked over Antonio, who stood on the other side of the clearing. He, too, glared his displeasure at this new threat. Squaring his shoulders, thirsty for blood, Ethan stepped forward, intent on explaining to McCabe—in no uncertain terms—that Hope damned well *was* spoken for.

By God, she belonged to *him*.

Natalia stepped out of the crowd and took firm possession of his arm. Ethan blinked down at her. Growling, he swallowed the harsh oath scorching his tongue.

"Dance with me," Natalia ordered, darting a nervous peek over her shoulder.

Ethan glanced longingly at Hope but allowed Natalia to tug him into the first steps of the next set. Natalia peered anxiously over his shoulder, then ducked down, clearly hiding.

"What are you doing?"

"Cal Levine has been trying to 'kiss the bride'. He's had a few too many shots of God-knows-what, and I'm afraid he won't settle for just one kiss," Natalia mumbled against his shirt. A moment passed in silence, and she began to relax in his arms, commenting conversationally, "Hope has drawn quite a crowd. I see Mr. McCabe managed to wrangle a dance."

Ethan stiffened at the reminder. His gaze swerved to the cluster of men who'd dogged Hope for the better part of the evening. There were so many he couldn't find her now.

"You know, Ethan. A woman wants to feel needed."

The comment drew his puzzled attention. "What's that supposed to mean?"

"It means you close yourself off, just like your father used to do." Natalia stared at him with shrewd eyes. "You've been hiding behind Christina's memory, like a shield for your emotions. You've forgotten there is joy in living. Life is about love and happiness, not just the pain."

"Aren't you just full of advice tonight?" Frustrated, he glared over her head and scoured the crowd. Where the hell was Hope?

"You're running out of time, Ethan. She's not going to wait around much longer for you to come to your senses." Then Natalia knocked the ground out from beneath his feet. "Antonio intends to ask her to marry him, did you know that?"

He missed a step, clipping her toes. "What?"

Wincing, hobbling, Natalia used his shoulders to steady herself. "He told me this morning he is going to ask her for her hand. How long do you think she's going to wait for you to make up your mind before she moves on? Don't think for a minute there aren't a dozen men out here tonight who wouldn't happily leap to attention if she so much as crooked a finger in their direction...no matter what might have passed between the two of you."

Oh, he knew it all right.

And it tied him up in knots.

He caught a fleeting glimpse of McCabe, but Hope was nowhere in sight. Neither was Antonio. His heart skipped a beat. He was barely aware of the couples bumping into them when he stopped pretending to dance.

He craned his neck, his throat constricted. "Where the hell is she?"

"She left with Antonio a few minutes ago. It looked like they were headed to the stream."

"Son of a bitch!" Ethan exploded.

Distracted, he neatly handed Natalia over to a leering Cal Levine, and darted through the dancers in hot pursuit.

Ethan shoved his way through the crowd at the edge of the dance floor, ignoring the greetings aimed his way. He had to get to her before she accepted Antonio's proposal. He managed to break free from the crush, covering the rest of the yard at a flat sprint. He'd just rounded the corner of the house when he drew up short, the wind knocked from his lungs, the beat knocked from his heart.

Antonio and Hope stood by the stream beneath the lone, squat tree, facing each other, holding hands. Hope smiled up at Antonio, nodding her head. That vision seared itself into Ethan's mind and he realized—with a feeling something akin to drowning—that he was too late.

Wanting to howl with rage—longing to draw his gun and shoot Antonio between the eyes—Ethan fisted his hands at his sides and lurched forward, a denial scalding the back of his throat. Hope went up on tiptoe to kiss Antonio, wrapping her arms around his neck, hugging him.

Ethan dropped his head in defeat.

Wheeling around, he dragged himself back to the house.

Without conscious thought, Ethan found his way to Matt's den and reached inside the tall cabinet in the corner, drawing forth a bottle of whiskey. Not bothering with a shot glass, he lifted the bottle to his lips and took one long draw after another, willing the liquid fire to chase the memory of Hope in Antonio's arms from his mind.

Too late. The unmerciful refrain kept circling through his mind.

Too damned late...

Unfortunately, the whiskey wasn't working. He narrowly resisted the urge to throw the bottle against the wall in frustration. Instead, he carried it with him across the room to sit in one of the wing chairs flanking the cold fireplace. Stretching his long legs out, he settled back against the cushion, and stared at the cold hearth, more alone than he'd ever been in his entire life. The ache in his chest threatened to swallow him whole.

He tipped the bottle again, praying for oblivion.

****

Hope followed Antonio from the crowded dance floor, grateful for the reprieve from her over-eager admirers. From the corner of her eye, she'd seen Natalia draw Ethan out for a dance, and so she wasn't worried about him stomping after them as he'd seemed wont to do tonight.

She couldn't understand what his problem was. Ever since she'd stepped out onto the veranda earlier this evening, he'd been prickly, scowling at anyone who got near her. Well, scowling at the men at least, the women he seemed to pay no heed to at all. And their dance earlier had left her floundering. Good heavens above, she'd almost kissed him right there in the middle of all Matt's guests.

What had she been thinking?

In silence, she and Antonio walked side-by-side until they came to the tree beside the stream, the sounds of revelry fading behind them with each step. The fresh scent and quiet shushing of the rushing water lulled her senses. Somewhere in the distance, a mournful hoot echoed in the shadows. Farther off, a plaintive yipping marked a coyote's call to its pack. Insects chirped and hissed, and the gentle breeze rustled through sparse clumps of tall grasses nearby.

Antonio leaned close, tilting his head. "Are you enjoying yourself?"

"Very much." She nodded, drawing the scent of the night in deep, savoring it.

"I'm glad." He stopped by the tree, faced her, and drew both her hands into his. "I've been waiting to speak to you all day." Antonio paused. His face reddened. His mouth opened, closed, opened again. He blinked at her, and blurted, "It looks like everything went off without a hitch. Natalia sure was surprised."

Hope smiled enthusiastically, nodding agreement. Maybe she was only imagining it, but she was nearly certain he'd meant to say something else. "I wish there was a way to let Matt and Natalia get away from the ranch—even if only for a short time. They deserve to have a little time alone."

"Maybe there is." Antonio was silent for a moment, his eyes thoughtful. "Do you suppose we could get Matt to take Natalia into Johnston for a day or two? Or maybe over to Murphy's Hollow. He's good enough now to ride, isn't he? Patch and Xavier are more than capable of finishing the branding, and

Ethan and I can take care of the rest. I know Matt'll be worried about leaving you here alone, but I'd be more than willing to stay back with you—until Matt returned, of course."

"That's a wonderful idea," she exclaimed, tickled with the idea. Matt and Natalia would be so surprised.

She stretched up on tiptoe, pecked an affectionate kiss on Antonio's cheek, and gave him a quick squeeze. Antonio's arms crept around her, and he dipped his head. Caught up in her excitement, she stepped back and patted his cheek, her mind already formulating plans.

"I'll sneak inside and pack a bag for them. You go corner Matt, fill him in. I'm sure he'll go along with it. I'll be back out in a flash." She hesitated, chewing her lip. "On second thought, you'd better give me a few extra minutes. It might take a little bit to find everything. I'll meet you at the stables."

Her mind caught up in her chore, Hope hurried off to the house in an animated swirl of silks. Smiling in anticipation of Natalia's surprise, Hope hurried past Matt's den, but the clink of glass on wood caught her attention. She frowned. Her steps faltered. Slipping back to the doorway, she peered through the shadows. She was about to give up and go on her way, when the flicker of movement near the fireplace caught her attention. She squinted, and finally recognized Ethan in the shadows. Puzzled, she stepped inside the room. Why would Ethan be in here in the dark—alone?

"Ethan?" Even though her voice was hushed, the sound of it cracked through the darkness.

His head shot up and around, but he didn't get up, didn't respond.

She stopped beside his chair. Concerned, she searched his face. His disposition didn't seem to have improved much. An eerie sense of isolation blanketed the room. There were hundreds of guests outside, but here inside the den, it felt as if they were the only two people for miles and miles.

"Ethan, what are you doing in here?"

Ethan lifted the half-empty bottle and swirled the amber contents in the silvery moonlight pooling through the window, as if that should be sufficient explanation. His voice was thick with whiskey and emotion. "What's it look like, darlin'? I'm celebratin'. Hell's bells, ever-body's gettin' hitched. What's not to celebrate?"

She frowned down at him, confused. For one seemingly so bent on celebrating, he looked as if he'd just come from a funeral. "Why aren't you outside with the others?"

"Guess I got sick of watchin' all those men droolin' over you." His scowling gaze raked down the length of her. "Where the hell d'you get that get-up anyway?"

"Get-up? You mean my dress?" She blinked at him, completely lost now. "What's wrong with it?"

"It's just... It's... Damned indecent is what it is," he snarled, leering at the swell of her cleavage. "You're all but fallin' out the top, might as well come down wearin' nothing but that goddamned robe of yours. Sure don't leave much to the imagination. Then again, that was probably the whole idea, wasn't it?"

Baffled, she shook her head and frowned. What the devil was wrong with him? Could he be any more contrary? He certainly hadn't complained earlier when she'd stepped out onto the veranda beside Natalia. He'd done his own fair share of ogling.

"Oh, come on. Don't act so offended," he sneered, swigging a long mouthful from the bottle. He swiped a sleeve across his damp lips. "You got what you wanted, after all. No man out there is able to resist those," he pointed a finger at her chest, "*charms* of yours. You sure got Antonio right where you want him, don'tcha?"

Stunned by his crass criticism, Hope couldn't find her voice. He was accusing her of...of, well...she wasn't sure exactly what he had going on inside that thick skull, but whatever it was, it involved Antonio, her *friend*, and it didn't appear to be at all flattering—to either of them.

"For your information, there is nothing wrong with my dress." She stifled the urge to take hold of the bodice in both fists and hoist it up in self-defense. "Furthermore, I refuse to accept blame for anyone's behavior but my own. I can't help it if those men chose to behave like blithering simpletons, not anymore than I can help it if you chose to act like a...like a...a raving lunatic right now." Then her gaze fell to the bottle in his hand, and she planted her fist on her hips in righteous indignation, amending, "And a drunk, raving lunatic, at that." She crossed her arms over her heaving chest. "And what was that comment supposed to mean about my having Antonio right where I want him?"

Glowering like a bear prodded too soon from hibernation, Ethan pushed to his feet. His voice went soft and dangerous as he edged closer. "I suppose he likes the dress?"

"As a matter of fact, he does," she snapped, lifting her chin. "*He* told me I look beautiful."

"And does he like what's under the dress?" Ethan's accusations blindsided her, so wild and baseless she could only sputter in response. "I'm surprised you'd be willing to settle for the hired help. Then again, now you've got your inheritance, you can afford to marry beneath you. Or are you stringing him along, amusing yourself until some bigger fish comes swimmin' along? Maybe McCabe's caught your eye now?"

"How dare you?" Tears sprang to her eyes, but

she dashed them away with a shaking hand. "Marriage has never even come up between Antonio and myself. Antonio is an honorable man, he's kind and thoughtful, and in no way beneath me. And I don't even know Mr. McCabe. Why are you being so cruel?" She drew back a step, wounded to the quick. Just because she'd been stupid enough to...to let him... That didn't mean she'd let anyone else in her bed.

"Even if you have so little respect for me, how can you speak like that about Antonio? I thought you were friends. He wouldn't have ever suggested that we... How could you even think that I would have...that we could have...?" Hope sputtered in indignation, mortified. Her face burned.

She stomped away from him, stomped back. Her chin elevated in defiance. "I'm not marrying anyone, but at least Antonio doesn't seem the type of man to bed a girl and then run away. I couldn't say the same for Mr. McCabe, seeing as how I've only just met the man, but somehow he doesn't seem the type either. I would think you of all people should be able to recognize the difference—being so adept at it yourself."

Her harsh accusation seemed to draw him up short. "What the hell is *that* supposed to mean?"

"You know exactly what I'm talking about," she hissed. Oh, how she wanted to throw something at his dense head. "And what happens between Antonio and me is none of your damn business."

"You're wasting your time with him." Ethan's voice slipped back into soft and dangerous territory again, and he took that final step, towering over her. "There's no passion between you two, and you damned well know it."

"There is," she countered with false bravado, but her voice sounded hallow and unconvincing to her own ears. Desperate to put as much distance between them as possible, she tried to step back again, but Matt's desk blocked her retreat. "I told you, what happens between Antonio and me doesn't concern you."

Hope twisted, slipping to the side, but Ethan grabbed her by the elbow, yanking her back. She stumbled, falling against his chest. Her hands flew up to wedge between them. Ethan's arms closed around her, trapping her. His head lowered until his face hovered inches from hers, his expression fierce.

"Does he fill you with passion like I can?"

She struggled in his arms, wary and panicked. His hold tightened, fitting her against him.

"Do you tremble at his touch?" Ethan's demand was hard, unyielding. "Do you melt in his arms like you do when you're in mine?"

Dropping his mouth to hers, Ethan cut off her desperate retort. His arms crushed her, caging her to him with the strength of tempered steel. The desk bit into her backside as he pressed against her. One hand fisted in her hair, holding her head still beneath his punishing kiss.

Ethan launched a complete, all-encompassing campaign, using his entire body to effect her capitulation. His lips, so hot and insistent, moved over hers with firm purpose, ravishing, ravaging until she began to melt against him. As soon as her struggles began to ebb, his tongue plunged inside her mouth, sweeping against hers in an erotic tangle. Again and again.

His solid, muscular chest pressed against her sensitive breasts, heightening her awareness of his sheer strength. His hard thigh pushed between hers in intimate demand. His free hand slid down to boldly cup her bottom, grinding her against his rigid arousal.

She clung helpless to him, yielding to his sensual assault. Ethan overwhelmed her, using her own desire like a weapon against her. She was unprepared for the sheer determination in his kisses, for the fierce abandon with which he caressed her body. He laid siege to her defenses, and they crumbled, slow but sure. When at last Ethan tore his lips from hers, she was shaken to the core, set adrift by the sudden loss of his kiss. Ethan leered down at her. His hazy, passion-drugged gaze probed hers.

Ethan's eyes glowed like cobalt embers in the darkened room. His voice was husky and raw. "No one will ever be able to do this to you, sweetheart. No one but me."

Pain knifed through her at his arrogant comment. The realization of her own weakness for him, of her body's betrayal, devastated her. The egotistical smile on his face pushed her over the edge. She shoved at his chest with all her might, taking him by surprise. Anger glistened inside her, cold and brutal. For half a second she stared at him, just stared, flexing her hands in frustrated fists against his chest. Thoughts...partial sentences...scathing and furious, flickered through her irrational mind one after the next, faster than the previous one could be completed, but none escaped her numb lips.

She slapped him.

Ethan's head snapped to the side with the force of it, and he blinked, releasing her as he staggered back a half step. He faced her, slowly, blinked again. Her angry handprint darkened his cheek, glowing proof of her fury.

"Stop it! Just stop it! I can't take anymore of this," she sobbed, flirting with hysteria. "You make love to me as though you can't survive without me, but then you leave me the next morning—every time—as if I mean nothing to you. You kiss me until I can't think straight, you torment me with caresses, then you throw my responses back in my face.

"You're jealous of Antonio, but you won't admit you even have any feelings for me at all. I can't do this anymore! Do you hear me, Ethan? Antonio isn't the one standing between us. You are. You and your memories of Christina. And I won't settle for less than—"

Ethan didn't let her finish. He yanked her back into his arms with a violent oath, sealing his lips over hers with enough force to bruise, effectively silencing her. His lips moved over hers, punishing her a second time. His hands caged her shoulders, preventing her escape.

She pushed against his chest and tried to turn her head away, but he wouldn't allow it. He pressed his body against hers again, his movements rough, desperate. She flailed against him, but Ethan ignored her struggles.

Her anguished sob—the salt of her tears on his lips—must have finally caught his attention, gaining her release. He ripped his mouth from hers and stared down at her once more, shock glowed in his eyes. Ethan dropped his hands to his sides, and he backpedaled. The back of his hand covered his lips. His face leeched of all color.

"Oh God, what have I done?" he murmured hoarsely.

Ethan's face crumpled. His eyes filled with remorse and grief. His hands reached for her, only to fist and drop to his sides once more. How he hated himself for what he'd done; she could see it in his eyes. She lifted trembling fingers to her bruised, swollen lips. Shaking her head, she backed away from him. She didn't know this man before her.

This wasn't her Ethan.

Ethan muttered a ripe curse, spun about, and stalked from the room. Tears welled, spilling down her cheeks as she sagged against Matt's desk. What had just happened? Why was he acting this way?

Chapter 25

Ethan slammed his way out of the house, shouldering none-too-gently through the crowd. His mind had seized on the picture of Hope's anguished face. He'd done a bang up job screwing things up but good. He wasn't fit company for anyone, and he knew it. He had to get away from here, away from every human in a fifty-mile radius. His mind was absorbed with the need to go off alone somewhere to lick his wounds, and so he didn't notice Matt and Antonio until he damned near tripped over them.

Matt took one look at his face and, nipping at his heels, called out, "What happened?"

Ethan's gaze shot to Antonio for a split second, then back to Matt. He couldn't deal with this right now, not when he was so close to the edge.

"Nothing," he grumbled, storming through the stable's open doorway and down the wide aisle. He could hear Antonio speak to Matt in hushed tones, but he kept on walking, didn't even miss a step when the sound of Hope's name pricked his conscience.

Glancing over his shoulder as he opened the door to Apollo's stall, Ethan caught the meaningful glance Antonio shot Matt before the young foreman offered, "I'm going to go see what's keeping Hope."

Matt cleared his throat and nodded. He stepped inside the stall as Ethan swung his saddle up and over Apollo's back. Matt thrust his hands deep in his back pockets, kicking at a small clump of fresh hay. "Party's not over yet."

"It is for me," Ethan shot back without turning

from his task.

"Ethan—"

"Don't…just don't." Dear Lord, he *so* did not need this. Then again, maybe he ought to tell Matt the truth. Tell Matt all about how well he'd been taking care of his daughter. Then maybe—if he was really, *really* lucky—Matt would put a slug between his eyes, make him forget all about the gaping, bleeding hole where his heart used to be. Instead, he heaved a weary sigh and muttered, "I need some time."

Matt narrowed his eyes for a minute, obviously debating whether to push. "You shouldn't go off alone, not in this shape. You haven't been this worked up since…well, since… You ought to—"

"I ought to what, Matt? Stay here? Stay where I can—" Ethan exploded, stopping short, biting his tongue before he blurted out that if he stayed he'd just cause Hope more pain. He'd go to her. He wouldn't be able to stop himself. "No, Matt. I'm headin' up to the ridge for a while. Just…just back off."

Ethan led Apollo from of the stall and through the stable doors. Vaulting onto the saddle, he tore off before Matt could argue.

He didn't make it more than three or four miles when something odd caught his eye. The herd was more than a mile away. There shouldn't be anyone out here. Then other things began to prick at his awareness.

All around him, the night was unnaturally still. The insects crouched, silent and wary. The wind held its breath. By the bright light of the full moon, the silhouette of a stationary horse, an odd mound huddled on its back, stood dark against the shadowed landscape. The closer Ethan got, the more unsettled Apollo became. His own palm itched for the comfort of his gun. Tense, ready to spring, he drew alongside the familiar horse, and froze as comprehension dawned.

****

"Hope?"

Like a puppet whose strings were rudely jerked, she turned away from the cold fireplace at the sound of her name. It took a moment for her glassy eyes to focus on the man in the doorway. Taking half a step forward, she faltered when the toe of her boot clinked against Ethan's discarded bottle.

The glass scrapped along the floor, tottered, and righted itself on its thick bottom. Her eyes felt puffy, her lashes were spiky with tears. It didn't take a mirror for her to know her eyes were red-rimmed, or that the end of her nose was pink. That happened whenever she cried. A strange hollowness filled her chest.

Antonio's large, warm hands settled on her shoulders. His expression was fierce. "Ethan did this, didn't he?"

Her chin dropped at the mention of Ethan's name, and she tried to turn away, but Antonio wouldn't let her. He tugged her back, tilting her chin up with a gentle fingertip until their eyes met.

"Tell me what happened," Antonio demanded, a man prepared to slay whatever dragon tormented her...even if that dragon wore the face of a friend.

Hope searched Antonio's handsome face. Oh, why couldn't she have fallen in love with him? His gorgeous eyes were dark, velvety brown—nearly black with concern. His jaw was smooth and strong. His shoulders were broad, his arms muscular, his skin deeply tanned and unmarred by life. His hair was sleek and dark as midnight, smooth as silk, reaching well passed his shoulders, begging for a woman's hungry, eager fingers.

He smelled of soap and horses, so like Ethan—yet so very different. His hands held her with restrained strength, gentle but firm. Her gaze dropped to Antonio's lips, full and sensual, and Ethan's words came back to her, unbidden.

'No one will ever be able to do this to you, sweetheart. No one but me...' She tried to force the words from her mind, but couldn't. They rang in her head like a cadence. *'Do you melt in his arms like you do when you're in mine?'* Hope's gaze met Antonio's with deliberate determination.

"Kiss me."

He jolted, blinked. "What?"

"Kiss me, Antonio," she demanded.

Antonio stared down at her with a puzzled frown. She raised her hands to his cheeks and stretched up on tiptoe, fitting her mouth to his, sliding her body closer. Antonio stood motionless for a heartbeat. Then he gently gathered her closer, pressing her soft curves against his hard angles. His lips softened on hers, moving slowly at first, tentative...testing. Then he became bolder, tracing the rim of her lips with his tongue, parting them, deepening the kiss. His long hair slid over her bare shoulder, like the sumptuous stroke of silk. One large, splayed hand slid up to the middle of her back, the other lingered at her waist. Possessive...yet undemanding.

The sensations assailing Hope were warm and, without a doubt, pleasant. But somehow lacking all the same. Antonio's kisses didn't steal her breath, didn't make her knees weak. He didn't make her tremble—or melt—not the way Ethan could. Hope couldn't ignore the disappointment, the embarrassment. Ethan had been right, and she was a fool.

A weak, pathetic fool.

****

Hope pulled away, and Antonio immediately released her, sensing something was wrong.

Confusion, worry, and the cold touch of disillusionment wrapped around him. Hope couldn't hide the brief flicker of disappointment in her beautiful, green eyes. In that moment, he realized what she'd been doing, and his heart ached.

She'd been trying to prove something to herself.

And she'd failed.

Antonio took several steps away from her, shaken. Regret and sadness washed over him. But he wasn't angry, and that surprised him. Why hadn't *he* felt more? His heart may ache, may bear bruises. But it was not shattered. How could he have had such a tepid reaction given the woman he'd intended to ask to marry him had just used him in such a way—or that his kiss had clearly left her unmoved?

He'd expected to feel something—anger, rejection, fury even. Instead, the unnerving impression of emptiness filled him. No, he couldn't have been so wrong, couldn't have mistaken his feelings for her…or hers for him…so badly. He closed the distance between them once more and searched her face. The answer was there in her eyes, unmistakable for anyone who cared to look.

Just as Natalia predicted it would be.

Why had he fought so hard against acknowledging it for himself?

"You love him." The words left a bitter taste in his mouth. What an idiot he'd been.

"No!" Hope shook her head, but the truth lay heavy in her voice, and his pride suffered another bruise.

"He doesn't deserve you, you know," Antonio grumbled, smiling with bittersweet understanding. It wasn't her fault he'd been such a fool.

"Antonio, oh dear heavens, what have I done? I'm so sorry. I shouldn't have… I had no right to…" Hope covered her mouth with a trembling hand. Tears welled in her eyes, overflowed.

"Don't cry, Hope." Antonio gently tracked a wet trail down her cheek with the tip of a long finger. "And don't apologize. You can't help how you feel, even if Ethan is an ass sometimes," he assured her, smiling to soften his words. "Much as I hate to say it, he'll come around. Give him a little time." Then, clearing his throat, he added, "Now, then. I believe we have a bag to pack, Matt is waiting for us by the stables."

Hope smiled tremulously up at him. As they cleared the doorway, he slung a friendly arm over her shoulders. She drew a deep breath and glanced sideways at him, offering him a watery smile. Her green eyes were bright, and sincere.

"Whoever she is, she's going to be a very, *very* lucky girl, Antonio."

Smirking, he met her eyes, and chuckled. "I know."

****

Speaking in soothing tones, Ethan reached out with a shaking hand and gathered the skittish mare's reins. Once he had her secured, he reached out once more and grasped the man's shoulder with a shaking hand, pulling him back from the horse's neck. Dragging in a lungful of air, his face twisted in grief as the body shifted to lie against the horse's back, revealing the dead vaquero's face.

"Damn it!" Ethan flinched, snapping his eyes closed.

It didn't help. He could still see that familiar face, frozen in shock. The wide, gruesome gash stretching across the neck from ear to ear mocked him with his failure. The vaquero's one good eye locked on him in an accusatory death stare, the other covered with a black, dusty patch. Forcing his eyes open, Ethan peered more closely at the vaquero, swiftly cataloging the details.

Patch's gun was still in its holster, the strap still

fastened. Blood soaked the front of his chest, splattered over the horse's neck. His body was still astride his horse, stiffening already with death and cold night air. Those facts told Ethan all he needed to know. For Patch's killer to have gotten so close—for Patch to have not even drawn a weapon in self-defense, or fallen from the horse during a struggle, meant Patch had known...and trusted...his killer.

The traitor was still among them.

Ethan got down from his own horse to maneuver Patch's body with gentle hands so it hung face down over the saddle and wouldn't fall off. He remounted and took the mare's reins in his hands. Urging Apollo into a trot, he led the mare with her sorrowful burden back to the Bar M.

Ethan's heart lodged in his throat, choking him with his grief.

****

Hope skirted the dance floor on her way to the stables, Antonio at her side, when Daniel Masters stepped into her path.

"Miss Lewis, I was beginning to despair of finding you without your entourage of admirers. At the risk of drawing their attention, might I request the pleasure of this dance?" His eyes swept over her in a leering, far too intimate way.

She did her best to quell the shiver of revulsion crawling down her spine. Edging a little closer to Antonio, she smiled as politely as she could manage and murmured, "Thank you, but no. Antonio and I are on an errand for Matt." She gave Antonio's arm a little squeeze, silently urging him onward.

"I'm sure the hired hand can manage the chore," Masters replied, stepping into their path once more as he reached for her arm. "I'm sure a pretty little thing like you'd rather be dancing and socializing instead of making sure the help is doing his job."

Antonio's arm tensed beneath her hand, but

before he could react, she yanked her elbow from Masters's grasp. Anger burned her cheeks. With chilly disdain, she glared down her nose at Masters, no small feat considering he towered over her by a solid foot. "Antonio is no 'hired help' as you so rudely put it, *Mr*. Masters. He is the highly capable and respected foreman of the Bar M—the very ranch of which you are currently a guest—and I will thank you to remember that fact, *sir*! Do not take it upon yourself to presume my preferences, for I have absolutely no wish to spend even one minute 'dancing and socializing' with the likes of you." She shook an angry finger in his face for good measure. "I prefer to spend my time with gentlemen." Lifting her chin, she beamed up at her friend. "Antonio, if you please..."

Antonio burst out laughing, and offered her his arm once again. She promptly set off to find Matt in the stables, all but dragging the mirthful Antonio behind her, leaving a furious Masters sputtering in her wake. She found Matt pacing inside double doors of the stables, a small box wrapped in a handkerchief in his hands. As soon as Hope and Antonio stepped inside the building, he strode over to take the bag Antonio held up for him.

Matt and Antonio exchanged a glance, and Matt gave the slightest shake of his head when Antonio glanced to Apollo's empty stall. Hope glanced away. She couldn't deal with anything to do with Ethan right now, even if it was obvious Matt was worried sick about him.

"Are you sure the two of you will be all right here?" Matt shifted the bag in his hand, set it down beside the small carriage she'd ridden in with Antonio the day they'd gone for a picnic together. "The men are stretched thin right now, and I don't want you takin' any chances. We can stay, there's no need for us to—"

"We'll be fine," Hope assured him. She couldn't help but smile, he reminded her so much of James just then. "I have Antonio to look after me, and I promise not to get into any trouble."

Taking Hope by the elbow, Matt drew her to the side of the stables. As he did so, he held his hand out to her. A small box wrapped in brown paper rested on his palm. "I had this commissioned just after you arrived. I just got it a little while ago, I was going to wait, but now just seems like the right time." Matt smiled bashfully as he waited for her to open his surprise.

Puzzled, she smiled and accepted the tiny bundle. Her gaze darted to Matt as she pulled the folds open and peered at the small box. Tipping the box on its side, she poured the contents onto her palm. An oval brooch tumbled out into her hand. The face of the brooch was a delicate ivory inlay...a Grecian carving of a woman's profile. Smiling with delight, she held it up to the light and examined the beautiful piece. It was then that she noticed a small catch on the side. Hope's curious gaze flickered to Matt.

"Open it." Matt shot her a nervous look, running his finger around the collar of his shirt.

She slipped her nail in the catch, and the faceplate swung open on a tiny hinge. A miniature portrait of her parents—Serena and Jacob—smiled back at her. Without saying a word, for truly the ability was beyond her at just that moment, she threw herself into Matt's arms, clinging to him as she wept against his chest.

Matt was immediately contrite. "I'm sorry, darlin'. I didn't mean to upset you. I just thought that you might like..." he trailed off on a miserable groan. "I'm an idiot. I shouldn't have—"

"No, no... I love it," Hope sobbed. "Thank you so much."

"You like it?"

"I do." Hope pulled away from him so she could offer a reassuring smile. "It's beautiful. I don't know how to thank you."

Matt was blushing by that time. The sound of approaching horses drew his attention to the back door of the stable as Hope pinned the precious gift to the bodice of her dress. Matt and Antonio both hurried across the stables to the closed doors, throwing them wide open. Tense, they peered out into the darkness behind the stables, Antonio's hand rested on his gun. Matt cursed, patting at his gunless hip as Hope hurried forward, curious.

Then both men stopped reaching for a weapon, only to burn her ears with inventive curses as Ethan came into view. He dismounted, reaching around to lead the second horse forward. A body bounced over the saddle, face down, and the night Matt had been shot came rushing back to her, filling her with dread.

"It's Patch," Ethan announced before anyone could draw breath. Then, without ceremony, he informed them. "His throat's been slit."

****

Hope gasped, and Ethan could have kicked himself for his tactless announcement. He turned to her just in time to see her face bleed free of all color. He lurched forward, intent on drawing her to him—as much to find solace in her embrace as to provide comfort to her—but he drew up short.

He didn't have any right to offer her comfort.

He didn't have any right seeking comfort from her.

He watched, torn with jealousy, as Antonio slid a comforting arm around her waist for a moment, lending her his strength. Hope turned grateful eyes to her protector and nodded at length. Antonio released her and stepped carefully around Apollo, catching the mare's reins in his hand. He wordlessly led the horse into the stables while Ethan stayed behind to speak to Matt.

Ethan was conscious of Hope's presence, aware that what he'd said had upset her terribly. What he was about to say would probably be just as bad, but he was too concerned with her safety to send her away.

"I found him out on the range barely a mile from the herd. He was still in the saddle. His gun's still in the holster." His gaze drilled into Matt's eyes, willing him to understand the implications.

Hope demanded, "What are you saying?"

Matt turned to her. A worried frown creased his brow when he replied, "It means he didn't put up a fight, he trusted whoever it was that killed him. It means there's still a traitor in the outfit. Whether or not Rodrigo was one, there's still another one—maybe more."

Antonio stepped back into the doorway. The grim lines on his face confirmed he'd heard. "I laid Patch out in the back stall."

"It's just a gut feeling, but I think Vega's—" Ethan started to voice his warning, but his name—shouted from the yard, followed by the words every cattle rancher dreaded more than anything else—cut him short.

"Ethan, Matt—*Stampede*!"

All hell broke loose.

Chapter 26

With a hot ball of apprehension burning in his gut, Ethan rushed to the yard with Antonio hot on his heels. Matt and Hope trailed close behind. All around the yard, men and women scrambled about, yelling and shrieking as if the herd were bearing down upon them right then and there. Ethan drew his colt, aimed it into the air, and fired. Stunned silence fell over the suddenly frozen crowd.

"We need more men." Xavier shouted, red-faced and panting. "Herd's headed south to the canyon."

Xavier didn't wait for a response or orders, but wheeled his mount around and disappeared into the night in a cloud of dust, while every vaquero in the yard sprang into action. Ethan sprinted back through the stables to retrieve Apollo. Antonio and Matt ran inside a moment later, arguing heatedly. It only took Ethan half a second to understand the cause of the debate, and he leaped to Antonio's defense. Together they had their hands full convincing Matt to stay behind, but in the end, by combining their efforts with Hope and Natalia, Matt didn't stand a chance.

Ethan and Antonio caught up with Xavier before they reached the herd. He shouted over the sound of pounding hooves, "Where's Julio?"

"Said he was gonna to check in with the others," Xavier shouted back. "When the herd took off, it looked like he was headin' to the southeast, tryin' to angle around 'em, maybe divert 'em. I didn't see him after that."

Ethan's stomach dropped to his boots. That long ago, stormy night he'd lost his father came back to him, and he worried about Julio…the ever-present thorn in his side and the next closest thing he had to a father besides Matt. While it was true Julio was only in his late forties and had decades of experience with the herd under his belt, Ethan figured he was too old to be trying to stop a stampede. Besides, there was a traitor out there—a traitor working hand in glove with a murderous renegade—waiting to spring their trap.

In the distance, the bright moonlight faded behind the thick, billowing dust cloud. A low rumble shook the ground, and the heavens trembled with the ever-growing thunder of hooves. Ethan gritted his teeth, focusing his determination. Lifting the bandana at his throat to cover his mouth and nose, he urged Apollo on.

****

Pablo arrived as Matt stood beside Father Bernard's buggy, absently thanking him for performing the service. Man and horse puffed hard. "Señor Matt, *Ayúdame*! Where's Señor Ethan?"

"He's not here. The herd stampeded, he's out with the men. What's wrong?" Matt grabbed hold of the lathered mare's reins as she danced sideways. His heart lurched when he realized the mess covering the stable hand's face and clothes was soot and ash.

Hell and damnation, not again…

"Señor Ethan's horses…the string we broke for the army has been set loose, and the stable," he broke off, shaking his head. "Señor Matt—the new stable—she is gone, burned to the ground."

Matt cursed with furious enthusiasm, setting the priest's cheeks aflame. Without a backward glance, he took off at a dead run, leaving Natalia behind to make his apologies. On the way to the stable, he spotted two of the men who'd stayed back at the ranch on his orders. He yelled at them to follow, and went straight to Vixen's stall. Ignoring the bite of pain in his chest and shoulder, he threw a saddle on his mount's back, gritting his teeth as he worked on the cinch.

He led Vixen from her stall, and met a curious Garrett McCabe. "What's going on? Can I help?"

Hope and Natalia rushed inside the stables a moment later.

"Manuel, stay here," Matt shouted over his shoulder. "The stables at the Circle K just burned, and the horses are loose. Billy, Robbie, McCabe—saddle up."

The men leaped into action.

"Matt," Natalia interjected, wringing her hands. "You can't—"

He stilled her protests with a swift kiss. "I have to go, darlin'."

Turning to Hope, he patted her cheek and smiled. "Help Natalia get everyone sent home. We'll be back soon."

In moments, the four men left the ranch, heading due north.

****

Hope swung about, wide-eyed, to stare at the approaching riders in morbid shock. Straggling partygoers scattered before the marauders like leaves in a good, stiff wind. The waif of a stable boy, Roberto, stood between her and the veranda, staring open-mouthed at an approaching horse and rider. The horse wasn't slowing. The rider smiled. Time slowed to a snail's trudging pace.

Instinct hurtled her at Roberto. She knocked the boy down, catching him up in her arms, rolling with him. The sharp edge of a step lanced pain through her shoulder blade, stopping her mid-roll. In a thrice, she was back on her feet, tugging the stunned boy up behind her. She pushed and pulled him up onto the veranda, thrusting him into Natalia's arms. Manuel vaulted onto the veranda behind her, shoving all three of them inside the house. They fell into the hallway, and Manuel kicked the door shut behind him.

She whirled around, frantic. "Natalia, where are Matt's guns?"

"The den—"

Natalia raced down the hallway, the others falling in behind her. She pulled a small Derringer from the top drawer of Matt's desk and pushed it at Hope, cautioning that it was loaded. Hope handed the pocket-sized pistol to Roberto, directing him to point it at the floor. Natalia turned to the tall cabinet and flung the doors open wide. She pulled a scattergun and two old peacemakers from the storage case, fumbling one of the horse pistols in her haste. When Natalia handed one of the guns to Hope, her hands shook so bad Hope worried Natalia might shoot someone by accident.

She could only pray it would be one of Vega's men.

Natalia frowned, her eyes darting to Hope. "Do you know how to use these?"

"Yes, Uncle James showed me—" Somewhere outside, a sharp scream pierced the night, went abruptly silent. Hope's stomach flopped over. "We'll be trapped in here soon. We have to get out of here now, away from the ranch. We need to hide."

With every step, her skirts dragged at her legs, slowing her down. Turning away from Manuel, she lifted the outer skirt and stripped away several layers of petticoats. Her fingers trembled making the process take several moments longer than it should have, and she cursed beneath her breath.

"If we can get to the horses, we might be able to make it to the Circle K," Natalia suggested, clutching a gun to her chest. She shot a quick explanation to Manuel, and he nodded agreement. It was a long shot, but it was the only chance they had. Staying inside, waiting for the raiders to come in, was a death sentence...a long and painful one.

"We'll sneak out the front. Hopefully they haven't surrounded the house yet." Hope scurried to the window and peered out at the back yard. "They're coming. We have to go, now!"

Huddled together, they scurried down the hall to the front door. Manuel peered out into the night. He gave a curt nod, and stepped out into the silvery moonlight, drawing Roberto and Natalia out behind him. Hope followed close behind. She'd no more than cleared the doorway, when the bang of the rear door crashed through the house. Shutting the door behind her with a soft click, she hurried the others along.

The quartet pressed close against the house, crouching in the shadows until they came to the end of the adobe wall. Manuel peeked around the corner of the main house, then motioned them on. Ever vigilant, they crept forward, scuttling through the maze of overturned tables and chairs and across the empty dance floor. Then they came to the point of no return.

There was a fifty-foot stretch with no shadows—no cover of any kind—between the dance area and the stables. Manuel took Hope's hand and pulled her forward. She peered around the edge of the building. Loud crashes and angry mutterings drifted from the open windows of the main house. Three lifeless bodies sprawled in the dirt a short distance from the veranda.

Escape no longer mattered to those poor souls.

Manuel urged Hope forward. Averting her eyes from the dead, she plucked up her courage and dashed across the clearing, half expecting a bullet to pierce her back at any moment. By the time she'd reached the shadows of the stable, her heart was slamming against her ribs with enough force to crack them, and her head swam in dizzy fear. She ducked inside the stable doorway, could have cried with relief to find it deserted. Turning back, she waved to Manuel. Natalia scurried forth, and then Roberto. Manuel arrived a spare moment later.

He hurried to saddle the only three horses remaining in the stable—Phoenix, a mare Hope had once fed a carrot to; Crossfire, a spirited gelding she'd learned the hard way to steer clear of; and the ever-reliable Daisy. Manuel helped Natalia to mount Phoenix and settled Roberto behind her. Then he turned to assist Hope onto Daisy's saddle. Daisy's ears twitched as angry voices neared the stable doors. Manuel checked the rear doors, and frantically motioned Natalia and Hope onward. They crouched low over the horse's necks, and pushed their mounts into a gallop through the rear doors.

Manuel, mounted on Crossfire, had just cleared the doors when the first shot shattered the night. Hope glanced over her shoulder and breathed a sigh of relief when Manuel and Crossfire pounded after her in a dead gallop. Her relief was short-lived, though, when another shot rang out, and Manuel toppled from the saddle. The horse sprinted on without a backward glance, leaving its rider laying face down in his dust. Hope sawed on her reins, wheeling Daisy around. Natalia slowed Phoenix.

"No! Go on!" Hope waved them away. "We'll be right behind you!"

A glimmer of relief shot through her when Natalia complied.

Why wasn't Manuel getting up? She drew rein alongside him and tumbled to the ground beside him, struggling with her skirts. Kneeling beside the fallen man, she pleaded and tugged with all her might to pull him up. She succeeded only in turning him over, rolling him onto her lap, but got no farther.

"Manuel, please...*por favor*...you have to help me get you up. They're coming. Please..."

Manuel's feeble moan filled her with panic. His eyes fluttered and closed. Blood gushed from the gaping wound in his back, soaking her gown.

The sound of pounding hooves grew louder.

True terror shot through her veins.

****

Ethan and his companions managed to get the herd stopped just at the rim of the gorge, though only God knew how. The animals were beyond nervous. It would take next to nothing to send them fleeing once more. He made his way forward to join Antonio and Xavier, murmuring soothingly to the beeves he passed. Pulling the bandana off his face, Ethan scanned the surrounding area, his eyes squinting, trying to pierce the dense dust clinging persistently to the air. Like all the rest of the men, dust and sweat covered him from head to toe.

"Did anyone find Julio?"

The old cowpoke was an icon around both ranches. He'd been on the Circle K since before Ethan's father had died. The outfit just wouldn't be the same without him. For Ethan to lose Julio like that—the same way his father had died—it was unimaginable. If it hadn't been for Ethan's quick thinking and daring actions earlier, Antonio would have met the same fate this evening as well. Antonio shook his head, pulling his bandana off as well. Dust coated the upper portion of his face, clinging to his long, dark lashes, rolling from him in waves with every movement.

"I'm sorry," Antonio offered.

Unable to stand the sympathy he saw in his friend's eyes, Ethan turned away to scan the herd once more, half expecting Julio to come riding through the herd, chewin' his ass for wasting his time when there were more important things to be done than sitting around gossiping like a bunch of women. From the corner of his eye, he saw Xavier lean forward, rest his forearm on the pommel.

The vaquero wiped muddied sweat from his brow and sighed. "Gonna be a long night keepin' 'em calm."

The thudding hooves of the approaching horse had them all holding their collective breath. Inexplicable dread settled in Ethan's chest, sank deep in his bones, when he identified Pablo.

"Señor Ethan..." The mass of nervous cattle shifted behind him, lowing anxiously, but Ethan's sole focus was on Pablo's sweat-streaked, soot-covered face. "The new stable burned. The horses...they are loose. Señor Matt went to the Circle K with a few men to round them up. He sent me to fetch you."

Reeling from the latest blow, something niggled at his mind. Ethan clarified with growing dread, "Matt left the Bar M?"

"Si," Pablo nodded. "He and Señor McCabe, Billy and Robbie... We recovered a dozen or more so far."

Ethan's troubled gaze flew to Antonio as he scrambled to place all the men. He didn't like the figures that were adding up. Antonio must have been running the same tally too, because he turned sharp, dark eyes on the slim vaquero and demanded, "Who'd he leave at the Bar M?"

"Manuel."

Ethan exploded. "He only left one man to look after Hope?"

The herd shifted. The lowing increased. At that moment, Ethan wouldn't have given a tinker's damn if the entire herd swam across the Rio Grande and set up camp on President Gonzalez' front step. His horrified gaze shot to Antonio again. The two men kicked their mounts into motion, racing for the Bar M. The fire and the loosing of the horses came too close on the heels of the stampede for the sake of coincidence.

This had Vega written all over it, and it sent tremors of icy terror racing down Ethan's spine.

Chapter 27

The thunder of horse's hooves snapped her head up. A cloud passed over the moon, casting the surrounding landscape in shadows. Fear paralyzed her. She knelt on the ground, exposed, cradling Manuel's head in her lap. Her hand shook when she pointed the barrel of Matt's huge horse pistol square at the approaching rider's chest.

The cloud cover broke, and the rider smiled down at her in the pale moonlight.

"Hope, it's me." Daniel Masters' voice drifted to her, low and soothing, as he dismounted. He held his hands up and faced her, empty palms turned outward. "You can put the gun down. Is Manuel dead?"

Relief rushed through her so swiftly that, for a moment, she was actually light-headed. Bowing her head, Hope closed her eyes and forced air in and out of her lungs. Hands shaking, Hope lowered the gun to the ground, turning her attention to the wounded man on her lap.

Her hand hovered over Manuel's cheek. "I, I don't know. He was breathing a moment ago, but I can't get him to wake up."

Masters eased forward and knelt beside her. His gaze scanned Manuel, though he made no move to touch the injured man in her arms. Why wasn't he helping? Didn't he understand they had to hurry? Vega's men could be on them at any moment.

Hope struggled to her feet, pulling desperately at Manuel's limp arms. Her chest heaved with her exertions. Blood pounded in her ears. "Help me, Daniel. We have to get him on the horse and get out of here before Vega's men find us."

Masters pushed to his feet, but he made no effort to lend his aid. An odd thumping sound finally snagged her attention. Glancing over, she squinted through the darkness at the odd shape he held in his hand. The cloud cover passed once again, and Hope caught the glint of moonlight on aged steel.

He'd picked up the gun she'd dropped, she realized gratefully. At least one of them was thinking clearly. How horrible would it have been to be caught out here, unarmed, should Vega's men catch up to them. Hope turned her focus back to Manuel's motionless form, and frustration swelled once more.

"Help me, Daniel," she demanded. But as she glanced up at him, she froze, suddenly uneasy. Why did he continue to stand there, thumping the barrel of the pistol against his thigh?

A smug smile spread slowly across his face, sending a bone-deep chill racing through her body.

"So it's 'Daniel' again, is it? Oh, Hope," he drawled, shaking his head. "You never should have chosen Kincaid over me. I guess in a way I could understand Christina's decision, stupid though it may have been. But I'm very surprised by your lack of judgment."

He stepped forward, and she scrambled away. He shook his head, tsking his disappointment. "I really would've thought someone like you would've been more selective in your choices. I assumed you'd require a man with more breeding, more sophistication than some cowhand. I could've given you so much. But now the chance is lost to you, just like it was lost to her."

"Lost to whom? To Christina?" Confusion had settled around her like a veil. But with every venomous word he spewed, understanding slowly began to peep through, like sunlight punching holes in a blinding fog.

Denial fought for the upper hand, but she was just too practical, had too much Lewis in her to sit back and let circumstances walk all over her without putting up a fight. How long would it take for Natalia to get to the Circle K? How long would it be before Natalia sent someone to look for her?

Too long, a tiny voice in the back of her mind whispered.

It broke her heart to do so, but she slowly straightened, letting Manuel slide to the ground. She had to go for help. She'd be no good to Manuel if she waited for Masters to shoot her, or drag her back to the ranch...and Vega's men. She slowly edged closer to Daisy, gathering her skirts in her shaking, bloodstained hands. Her gaze flickered over Manuel, but she couldn't help him now. She just prayed she wouldn't be too late to help him later...provided she could get away from Masters, of course.

Masters seemed content to ramble, and so she let him gloat. "She was such a beautiful girl—and so talented—but she was stupid, wasting herself on the likes of Kincaid. Vega was kind enough to enlighten her." He grinned at his own sick jest. "I wonder, will you beg me as she did? Will you offer yourself to me if I keep you safe from Vega?"

She'd rather die trying to get away.

Whirling around, Hope made a wild dash for Daisy. Before she made three steps, a shot rang out in the silence. Fresh blood splattered on the ground near her feat.

The spiritless beast fell to the ground, silent and still. Masters' maniacal chuckle sent gooseflesh racing over her skin. Bright burst of agonizing pain exploded throughout her skull, then inky darkness swept her away.

****

Pain knifed through her skull. Angry voices pierced her ears. Hope squinched open her eyes with slow caution, careful to stifle the groan swelling in her throat. The area rug beneath her cheek blurred then sharpened. The pattern was familiar. She was on the floor in Matt's den. A pair of expensive, polished boots paced in and out of view, boots that had never seen a hard day's work.

"You were supposed to wait for me the last time, but you didn't. You let your men have at her first. You let them get carried away. The bitch was dead before I could even get a taste. I'll be damned if that's going to happen again. I want my share of this one. I'm not staying behind. Not again!"

A guttural voice replied in Spanish. The response must not have agreed with Masters. Red-faced, he stopped pacing a short distance away and turned to glower at the man behind her.

"The hell with that," Masters shouted. A vein bulged on the side of his neck. "You want Kincaid, fine. But I'm gonna get mine first."

Frantic now, she watched in growing horror as his hands went to his belt buckle, loosening it. The voice of gravel barked once again, a harsh, unmistakable warning.

Masters snarled. Why he didn't quit while he was still alive, Hope couldn't fathom. The unmistakable threat in that low, rusty voice sent chills down her spine. Masters must be insane to continue this argument. "Why the hell do we have to leave? Let's just finish this now!"

Masters' eyes flare wide for a split second as the lethal click of a gun echoed in the room. Lying on the floor as she was, she could still see the color drain from his face.

His hands flew up in a placating gesture. "Wait! You need me. The money—"

A bullet cut his words short, penetrating between his eyes. Masters hung motionless in the air for a split second. Then he toppled to the floor beside her.

Hope stared in mute horror.

A hand fisted abruptly in her hair, jerking her to her feet. Tears sprang to her eyes, but she blinked them away, refusing to let this monster have the satisfaction of seeing her grovel. She almost went back on her vow when she came face-to-face with the notorious renegade. To her credit, the only concession she made was a slight widening of the eyes. Everything about him screamed absolute brutality.

Vega grunted when she didn't cower in fear. His eyes narrowed, calculating and assessing, then he grinned. That grin hit her like a February blizzard, freezing her heart in her chest. He grunted and shoved her to the door, following close behind. She tripped out onto the veranda, and staggered in shock. The yard swam before her dizzy eyes, and bitter bile rose in her throat.

Manuel's lifeless body twisted at the end of a noose tied to a beam protruding from the side of the house. Blood and dust covered him from head to boots. His clothes were shredded, his hair matted to his skull with dried blood. Gravel and clumps of bloodied dirt clung to him.

The sound of cruel laughter hit her like a slap in the face. She spun about and came face-to-face with her would-be abductor from the mountains, the one with the pretty face. Although she now noted—with no small amount of satisfaction—his face wasn't quite so pretty any more. A long, hideous scar ran down his temple and over his cheek, right where she'd aimed her rock.

Vega shoved her toward Pretty-Boy and walked away. Pretty-Boy's eyes danced with wicked anticipation. As he took rough possession of her, he drew his long blade from its sheath and caressed the tip of it just below her right ear. With wicked, slow intent, he drew the point down her jaw. A trail of white-hot fire followed his blade, then the warm trickle of blood dribbled down her neck.

As the blade reached her chin, his lips pressed close to her ear. "You will pay for this scar, *puta*."

Something snapped inside her. She sneered, "All I did was make your face the same as your soul—hideous."

Fury ignited in Pretty-Boy eyes. The tip of his knife press harder into her flesh and blood trickled down her throat. She welcomed it, preferring a quick and relatively painless death over what she knew Vega had planned for her.

However, Vega refused to be denied his victory. His barked order stayed Pretty-Boy's hand, or at least his knife. Pretty-Boy stepped back. Without warning, his arm snaked out and he backhanded her hard enough to knock her to the ground. Pain exploded in her cheek, and she reeled for a moment. The sting in her palms and knees came a moment later.

The metallic taste of blood filled her mouth, and she pressed her tongue to the shredded skin on the inside of her cheek. Darkness swirled at the edges of her vision, waiting to consume her. Before she could gather her wits, he grabbed her by the hair and dragged her to his horse. Tossing her up onto the saddle, Pretty-Boy leaped up behind her, holding her in a punishing grip. Hope fought to remain lucid as long as she could, but the darkness triumphed, and she slumped forward, slipping away to a place where Pretty-Boy's vicious taunts could not follow.

****

Ethan took one look at the carnage Vega left behind, letting his eyes linger on Manuel. Then he spotted the unmistakable tracks leading away from the ranch. He regretted leaving Manuel like that, but he couldn't spare the time to cut him down. He had to get to Hope. He wouldn't stop until he found her. And if she was dead...well, he figured Antonio could just bury them together, for he honestly didn't want to go on. He'd been afraid of betraying Christina's memory if he gave his heart to Hope. Now he realized, just as Hope didn't have to choose between Jacob and Matt, he didn't have to choose between Christina and Hope.

Christina was his past, Hope was his present—his future.

He was in love with Hope.

He'd caused her such pain. Guilt clawed at him. Her tears stained his soul. He pushed it all aside, swearing he'd make it up to her. He just prayed he wouldn't be too late. She was all that mattered now, and he vowed he'd tell her that, just as soon as he found her. No man was going to stand in his way—not Vega, his enemy. Not Antonio, his friend. He would fight, he resolved.

For Hope, he would fight Satan himself.

****

A sharp stinging sensation lanced across her cheek, drawing Hope up from the depths of oblivion. As she hung there in that precious limbo—not completely conscious, yet awake enough to feel pain—Pretty-Boy struck her again, cursing her to perdition. She struggled, but he pulled her across the encampment, undaunted, stopping only to smack her one more time. A tall, thick timber stuck up out of the ground, an iron loop nailed near the top of the post. Pretty-Boy bound her wrists together, yanking the restraints tight, then tethered them to the rusted ring high above her head before joining Vega beside the fire.

Her shoulders burned, and her hands were fast

going numb. Her knees threatened to buckle. A movement at the edge of the clearing caught Hope's eyes. A lone rider flickered in the shadows, his face peeped in and out of the moonlight. She knew that face. Rescue was at hand, for Ethan trusted this man.

But the man dismounted and swaggered through the middle of camp, straight to Vega's side unimpeded. What was he doing? Hope gaped, incredulous.

Oh, dear God, no...

Vega greeted the man with a clap on the shoulder, and the two squatted by the fire, conversing in low tones. When they finished, the traitor ambled toward her, a grim smile on his lips. It took all her self-restraint not to spit in his face.

"Won't be much longer now, I expect."

"How could you?" She railed, straining against her bonds. What she wouldn't give to be able to sink her claws into his eyes. "Ethan trusted you!"

"Ethan's too trustin', always has been. Gettin' rid of him'll be almost as easy as it was to get rid of his father."

Hope's eyes flared, and his smirk grew.

"That's right, missy. *I* finished off the old man. Did such a good job at coverin' my tracks no one was the wiser. The knife slid in, nice and easy like, right between his ribs. He never saw it comin'. Stampedin' cattle took care of the rest. It was too easy—almost took the fun out of it."

Her skin crawled just to be near him. "You killed Patch, too, didn't you?"

Julio snorted disdainfully. "Another damn pushover."

None of this made any sense to her. "How could you betray Ethan and Matt like this?"

"Don't ya know, missy. It's all about the land," he sneered, spitting on the ground at her feet. "It's always about land. But tonight it ends. Ethan'll come for ya, and he'll die. With any luck, Antonio'll be with him. Save me the trouble of goin' after him later. After that, it's just a matter of catchin' Matt at the right time. Damned near got him once already. Next time, I'll take care of him myself. *I* won't miss."

"Why have you dragged this out for so long? Why not just finish it, like you did with Ethan's father?"

"Ain't you just the curious one?" Julio smiled at her as if she amused him. "I found I enjoy watchin' the sufferin'. Ethan's father showed me that, it was over way too fast with him…no enjoyment. I've had me a downright good time this last few years watchin' Ethan suffer, Matt too.

"The land's rich, the herd's established now. It'll be a simple matter to combine the ranches. All the grunt work's done," he sneered. "The profit'll be large, the effort minimal. And I like the location—what can I say?" He tossed a careless shrug.

Hope wrenched at her restraints. "Those ranches belong to Ethan and Matt. They aren't yours, they never will be…"

"Oh, but they will," Julio assured her. "After all, who'd be a better choice than me to step in once Ethan and Matt meet their maker? It's a natural choice, considering the fact the only other person with a legal right to the place will be dead." He stared pointedly at her. "I'm in the perfect position."

"You're forgetting Natalia. If we die, she gets the ranch."

His grin turned lascivious. "Wouldn't mind marryin' me a rich wida'."

"You've been on his payroll all this time? You've deliberately tortured them for enjoyment—until you're boss got bored?" Hope jerked at the rope tethering her, snarling, "You're vile!"

Julio just shook his head. The very essence of

evil lurked in his eyes. ‘I see you still don’t understand. I ain’t on anybody’s payroll. Vega ain’t my boss…he’s my brother. Didn’t expect that, did ya?” He cackled aloud when her eyes widened in shock. “My little brother’s good with the muscle end of things. Oh, he’s good at plannin’, too. He can be very…creative. Ya don’t honestly think I’d trust anyone but myself to work inside the outfit for so long, did ya? Besides, where better for me to be than in the front row to watch ’em squirm?”

Hope stared at Julio, stunned. He’d been the mastermind behind it all. And he’d been living right beneath Ethan’s nose all this time.

“Now, much as I know the men enjoy the screamin’, we can’t have you yellin’ warning to Ethan when he gets here.” Julio drew a bandana from his pocket. He secured the gag, satisfied she couldn’t manage more than garbled, unintelligible sounds. And she made plenty of those, cursing him with every despicable word she could think of, and inventing a few of her own.

“There now, I best head out. Wouldn’t do for Ethan to find me here. Don’t wanna spoil the surprise.”

Too many emotions boiled inside her for Hope to define any of them. Terror. Hatred. Outrage. Frustration. She jerked at her bonds until blood trickled from her wrists. Tears burned her eyes, but she’d be damned if she’d let them fall. She wouldn’t give them the satisfaction.

Closing her eyes, Hope prayed for all she was worth.

If not for rescue, then for the courage to face her fate with dignity.

Chapter 28

Thoughts of Hope rolled through Ethan's mind as he and Antonio picked their way through the rocky terrain. The moonlight was both blessing and curse this night, illuminating their path but providing them no protection, casting them into sharp relief against the stark countryside. Neither of them spoke, too tense and apprehensive about what they were going to find.

They both saw the rider at the same moment. Both men palmed their guns in anticipation. As soon as Ethan recognized Julio, he lowered his weapon and motioned for Antonio to do the same. Antonio narrowed his eyes, slow to follow Ethan's order. Ignoring Antonio's hesitation, Ethan breathed a sigh of relief, surprised and thankful to see his foreman alive.

Julio searched the moonlit landscape behind Ethan. "Where are the others? We gotta hurry. They're just over the ridge—ain't got much time."

"You know where Vega's men are?" Ethan glanced over at his friend's sharp tone. Antonio may have lowered his weapon, but his finger was still on the trigger. The hammer still cocked. His expression was fierce…and suspicious. What the hell was wrong with him?

"I rode back to the ranch for help with the stampede. I must'a just missed ya." Julio shifted in the saddle, eyeing Antonio. "I saw 'em—Vega and his men. They were just leaving the ranch. They got Hope. I followed 'em up here. Ya got more men with ya?"

"It's just us." Ethan stared at the trail ahead of them, grim.

Julio wheeled his horse around on the narrow path, calling over his shoulder, "Come on then."

Antonio pushed his mount forward and grabbed Ethan's arm. "Something's not right, Ethan," he warned beneath his breath.

"She's up there with that bastard! We have to go, now, before it's too late."

Antonio hesitated, nodded. "Just be careful, something's going on here."

His brows pinched together. "This is Julio, for Christ sake. Come on!"

"Watch your back, Ethan," Antonio insisted, but he let go of Ethan's arm.

Shooting his friend a reproving look, Ethan urged Apollo up the trail. The trio came to the end of the track a few moments later. The three of them dismounted, looping their mounts' reins over the lower limbs of a scrub oak, and crept through the dark tangle of trees, weapons drawn and at the ready.

As they neared the edge of the clearing, Ethan got his first good look at Hope. His stomach dropped to his toes.

Hope's dress was torn and drenched with the blood. Fresh blood smeared her cheek and chin. Her hair straggled down her back, and the shadow of a bruise had begun to form high on her cheek. When she turned her head toward the campfire, the fine crimson line running along the underside of her jaw was exposed. Blood crusted in drying rivulets down her throat. They'd gagged her and tied her to the post like a side of beef.

Ethan saw red.

He tensed and stepped forward, preparing to charge to her side to cut her loose. Antonio's restraining hand on his forearm brought sanity. Frustrated, Ethan nodded, waiting for the right moment. A tall, lean, scarred man approached her with his knife drawn. Ethan clenched his teeth so hard his jaw ached.

****

Wary, Hope eyed Pretty-Boy as he drew that damned knife of his again, but she refused to cry, wouldn't so much as whimper. He held the blade up so moonlight glinted on the lethal edge. His smile was depraved. His eyes glittered. He swaggered closer, so close his putrid breath brushed her cheek before he slithered behind her, drawing the edge of the knife down her neck and over the curve of her tattered bodice. He leaned around her side, his lips hovering near her throbbing cheek.

"You pray Kincaid comes, don't you? You think he can save you?"

Pretty-Boy stepped sideways, circling his arms around her to switch his knife from one hand to the other. He let his free hand trail down the side of her breast. The knife's honed edge scraped across the bared skin above the bloodied material like a lover's caress.

Pretty-Boy boasted, "The gringo can't save you. When he comes, it will be the end for you, and for him—a very long, very painful end."

Hope fought back the tears. She closed her eyes, forcing herself not to react. She tried to focus on the memory of Ethan's embrace, and on Antonio's warm smile. The remembrance of Matt's laughter. The fact that Natalia had gotten away. None of it worked, Pretty-Boy's cruel words filtered through, and they left her cold and trembling. But it was the sudden realization that she'd never know Ethan's touch again, never be able to tell him what was in her heart—and not Pretty-Boy's cruel words—that finally freed a lone tear to slip down her cheek.

Pretty-Boy purred into her ear, "When Kincaid comes, *El Jefe* ain't gonna kill either of you—at least not right away. He's going to make Kincaid watch when we..."

Hope's eyes scrunched shut, and she bit back the gasp of terror as his words sank into her, one vicious thrust after the next. Filled with despair, she prayed—prayed Ethan would *not* come. She didn't want him to see—to be forced to watch—what these brutal beasts planned for her. She prayed something would happen, and she'd die quickly, spared the atrocities Pretty-Boy promised her.

She couldn't stifle the sob that slipped by, cringing when Pretty-Boy crowed with wicked glee. She opened her eyes and forced herself to count the men. Eight including Vega—nine once Julio came back. Hopelessness swept over her in waves.

Oh, dear God, please let me die quickly.

Could she provoke Pretty-boy enough? Could she goad him into killing her outright...before the horrors began?

Panicked swam up her throat when Vega rose from his place by the fire and swaggered toward her. She went light-headed, her heart shuddered, and her breathing quickened until she was in danger of hyperventilating. Had her time come already? Was it to begin now?

Oh, please, not yet...she wasn't ready to die.

****

Ethan watched, narrow-eyed, as Pretty-Boy circled her, tormenting her with vicious words Ethan could only guess at and that lethal knife. His hand convulsed on his gun, and he shook with rage. She didn't make a sound, but stark terror showed plainly on her face. Even from this distance, he could see it. It was killing him, but he forced himself not to react, knowing if he lost his control, she'd be the first to die.

Then motion in the periphery of his vision snared his attention. Vega—it had to be. Only one man could look like that. He lifted his gun and cocked it, his eyes narrowed on his target. Antonio, too raised his gun, but his eyes were not on the clearing. Antonio tensed beside him when Julio reached out and grasped Ethan's forearm, restraining him.

"Wait," he whispered, "if you start shootin' now, they'll kill her. She ain't got any protection."

Ethan nodded. He lowered his gun, but his finger ached to squeeze the trigger. Antonio leaned close and whispered in his other ear.

"Send Julio around to the south. Tell him to come in when he gets the signal."

Ethan glanced questioningly at Antonio for a moment, then he turned and whispered to Julio. The older man didn't like this unexpected change of plans. For a few heated seconds he argued with Ethan. Nevertheless, in the end he complied, skulking away.

Antonio leaned close to Ethan and began elaborating on his plan. Once he finished, he sat back on his heels and waited. Ethan stared at him in astonishment. Antonio had obviously begun to doubt Julio's loyalties.

His doubt gave Ethan pause.

Antonio's plan could work. Or...they'd all end up dead. Ethan nodded. It was the only option at this point. They both shifted, crouched low, and sidled to the north, closer to the post.

Closer to Hope.

****

Hope cringed as Vega spoke to Pretty-Boy. When he finished, Vega turned away—not even sparing so much as a glance in her direction—and swaggered across the clearing to disappear inside the mouth of the cave. Her breath rushed out, only to lodge in her throat when Pretty-Boy stepped around to face her.

"Vega says once we have Kincaid, I'll be first." He traced the scar on the side of his face with the tip of his knife, and he sneered. "Payback for what you have done. He says I cannot kill you until the others have finished with you." His eyes roamed down over her frame and back up to her face. His voice held vindictive promise. "I will enjoy your screams. Will you beg when I carve out your heart?"

He sauntered a few yards off, crossed his arms over his chest, and leaned back against a large boulder to bide his time. His eyes gleamed with sadistic anticipation. Terror pushed bile up the back of her throat until she gagged.

Hope's blurry gaze shifted to the fire on the other side of the camp. Vega's men huddled close to draw warmth. Her skin prickled from the chilly mountain air, but the minor discomfort was beyond her now. She stared long and hard at the flames, fighting not to let the terror take over, trying to ignore the lecherous looks aimed her way.

A sudden explosion of gunfire tore through the night. Before her startled eyes, three of the men beside the fire toppled over before they even had a chance to draw their guns. The rest dove for cover. Two more fell in rapid succession as Hope felt the rope tying her to the post come loose. Her heart soared in sheer relief, only to plummet again when she realized Pretty-Boy, and not Ethan, held her. He hauled her in front of him with rough hands, using her as a shield, dragging her back with him as he slid along the boulder. His knife drew another trickle of blood at her throat, and she scrambled to keep up. If she tripped over her own feet now, she risked of cutting her own throat, literally.

Elation and fear battled inside her. Ethan had come for her. Hope scanned the darkness, praying for some indication of what he wanted her to do. Underbrush at the edge of the camp shifted, drawing her eyes. Julio. Her heart raced, and she cried out a garbled, unintelligible warning.

One of Vega's men, the last one still alive aside from Pretty-Boy, made a mad dash for the safety of the cave. A bullet in the chest dropped him mid-stride.

Hope took advantage of Pretty-Boy's distraction, wiggling her hands around in front of her, desperate to regain feeling. Her wrists remained tied, but she managed to finagle some room in her bonds. Clumsy from the painful return of blood flow, she forced her aching hands to her face, her tingling fingers pried at the gag. She had to warn Ethan before it was too late. The sting of Pretty-Boy's knife pressing against her throat stilled her movements.

"Come out here where I can see you, gringo." Pretty-Boy snarled like a rabid, cornered animal, applying pressure to the knife as he spoke. Hope winced, crying out before she could stop herself. "Unless you're *trying* to get her throat slit."

Ethan stepped out into the open. The barrel of his gun leveled at Pretty-Boy's forehead.

"Put the gun down, Kincaid, or her blood will be on your hands." The knife pressed deeper, and blood did indeed flow. "Get the rest of your men out here where I can see them. I know you're not alone."

Hope flinched, but she managed to keep the sounds of pain and fright trapped in her throat. Ethan's eyes narrow, his knuckles turned white as he gripped the gun before lowering it to the ground. The muscle in his jaw ticked. Antonio stepped out into the open a short distance from Ethan, his gun trained on the cave.

At nearly the same moment, Julio stepped out too. His gun pointed at Pretty-Boy. Hope's eyes flared, and narrowed as she glared at Julio. Ignoring the sting of bloodthirsty steel biting into her skin, she shook her head from side to side, then nodded from Ethan to Julio, mumbling beneath the gag.

Ethan's brow wrinkled. Antonio noticed, as well. He kept his gun leveled on the cave, but his eyes were now riveted to Julio. Julio glowered. In her peripheral vision, she caught Pretty-Boy's slight nod in Julio's direction.

In that moment, Ethan knew the awful truth. Hope saw it in his eyes—the anguish, the betrayal, the fury. Julio must have seen it as well. The barrel of his gun swung to Ethan, and Hope screamed against the vile cloth stuffed in her mouth. Ethan shifted, but he wasn't fast enough.

A torrent of gunfire echoed in the clearing once more. Julio's aim went askew when Antonio's bullet ripped into his side. Ethan dove and rolled, coming up gracefully with cocked gun in hand, blood blossoming on his shoulder. Hope thought surely her heart would stop dead in her chest. Ethan's bullet was much more accurate, finding its way to the center of Julio's black heart.

With no time to savor justice, Ethan glanced over his shoulder as a shot exploded from the cave. Antonio dropped, face down, in the dust and lay motionless. Grief seared its way through Hope, but Ethan was still in motion, and her fear for him was greater. She watched as his head whipped around as Pretty-Boy shifted, lowering the knife in order to draw his gun. As soon as the knife cleared Hope's throat, she lunged to the side and Ethan fired, catching Pretty-Boy by surprise. Her captor released her to clutch at his chest, his gun dropped unheeded to the ground, discharging harmlessly into the shadows beyond the encampment. Crimson blossomed beneath his fingers, spreading across his shirt.

Pretty-Boy sank to the ground as Hope

scrabbled out of the way on hands and knees. He reached for her, his outstretched hand covered in his life's blood. A small red bubble formed at the corner of his mouth. He spoke, the sound little more than an incoherent gurgle. Then he, too, toppled over sideways, a look of stunned disbelief frozen on his once handsome visage.

Ethan ran forward, scooping Hope up in his arms. He carried her around the boulder and gently set her down. His fingers trembled as he struggled to untie the knot in the bandana. Frustrated, he drew his knife and made short work of the gag, as well as the ropes binding her wrists. She gasped as blood surged, unrestricted, into her stiff digits.

Sheathing his knife, his hand snaked around to grip the back of her neck. He pressed his lips to hers in a fierce kiss. So sweet, and so fleeting. As he broke the kiss, he shoved one of his guns into her hands.

"Stay here," he barked before claiming one last, fleeting kiss. His hand rose to cup her cheek, his thumb smoothed across her lower lip, moist from his kiss. Then he rose and stalked around the far side of the boulder, his second gun already palmed.

Hope crawled on hands and knees to peer around the side of the rock. Antonio lay prone on the hard-packed dirt, and her throat squeezed tight, tears ran unheeded down her cheeks. Then his hand moved, fingers stretching to bring his gun closer. His eyes opened, his alert gaze darting around the clearing. Ethan edged his way around the side of the cave, just out of sight of the entrance. A dark shadow loomed closer to the mouth of the cave. If she yelled warning, would she distract Ethan? Would she hinder Antonio from reacting in time?

A thick arm extended into her line of sight. The dark barrel of a gun tilted down at Antonio's back. Hope didn't think—she just reacted. Lifting the barrel of Ethan's gun, praying she wouldn't hit Ethan or Antonio by accident, she squeezed the trigger. The recoil vibrated through her throbbing wrists.

The shot went wide, but it ricocheted off the inside of the cave, forcing Vega to draw back. Ethan darted a surprised glance at Hope and hurried forward, intent on providing Antonio cover fire so he could roll safely away. At Ethan's nod, Hope lifted her gun again and aimed for the mouth of the cave. She squeezed off two more rounds, vowing to herself that when this was all over, she'd force Ethan to give her proper shooting lessons.

Under the barrage of gunfire, Antonio rolled through the dirt until he was out of range. Ethan helped him to his feet, bracing him when he swayed. Hope tried to keep her gaze trained on the mouth of the cave and the shadows within, but she couldn't help glance at Antonio. She sucked in a sharp breath at all the blood covering his shirt.

Antonio pressed his fist hard against his shoulder, his face fixed in a grimace of pain. The two men conversed briefly. Hope would have given her eyeteeth to be able to hear what they were saying. So absorbed was she that she very nearly missed the subtle shift in the shadows at the mouth of the cave.

Firing off another warning round just in time, she gained Ethan and Antonio's attention once more. When they blinked at her, she waved the gun toward the mouth of the cave in annoyance. They ought to be paying better attention to matters at hand rather than having a little tête-a-tête in the middle of a bloodbath.

Keeping a wary eye on the cave, the two men edged back to the boulder until they were beside her as she guarded the cave's entrance. Ethan rested his palm against the rough stone, his gun cocked and ready to fire. Antonio sagged against the boulder.

Reassured Ethan was in charge of the situation, at least as far as Vega was concerned, Hope crawled over to Antonio's side. She grasped the hem of her skirt and pulled the soiled fabric aside, tearing a wide strip from her petticoat. Rolling it into a thick pad, she pressed the material against his wound, ignoring the flinch he struggled to hide.

"You know, getting shot is becoming a nasty habit with you, Antonio. You really should consider a less painful way to get a girl's attention," she scolded. Worry drew her brows tightly together and compressed her lips.

Antonio's grin was a bit lopsided, his breathing labored. "Ah, but it's so very effective."

Ethan's gaze remained riveted on the cave, his tone determined as he broke into their banter. "Can you ride?"

Antonio gritted his teeth. "I'll manage."

"Get Hope to the Circle K, find Matt—" Ethan began, but Hope cut him off mid-sentence.

"What about you?"

Ethan flicked a glance in her direction, before turning back to the cave. His tone was flat, obsession simmered in his eyes. "I'm not leaving until Vega's dead."

Hope protested, "I'm not going anywhere without you."

She looked to Antonio for back up, but he was clearly torn. It was obvious he agreed with Ethan, wanted to get her as far away from Vega as possible. But he, too, wanted to see this thing finished, and he didn't want to leave Ethan here to do it alone.

Hope could have screamed her frustration with the two of them.

"I'm not leaving, not without you. Antonio's wounded. He's too weak to force me to go anywhere with him. What if he falls from his horse, I'll never be able to get him back on it on my own." The memory of Manuel left a lump in her throat before she could suppress the vivid, hideous images of his tattered body suspended beside Matt's door.

"Hope," Ethan warned, turning aggrieved eyes on her, but again she interrupted.

"What if he passes out? I'll get us lost out there in the dark, Ethan. What if—"

"Enough!" Ethan barked, turning to face her fully. "I'm not leaving until Vega's dead. I'm not going to let him slip away again and have to live with the threat of him hanging over our heads any longer."

"And I'm not leaving without you!"

"God, woman, I love you more than life itself...but right now, if I had the time, I'd turn you over my knee for being so damned stubborn."

"Good luck with that," she snapped back, too furious for his declaration to fully sink in.

Then, without warning, some hundred yards to their right the underbrush moved. Swearing, Ethan spun on his heel, sprinting toward the rustling brush. Hope stared after him, confused, until she saw Vega straighten and step out from behind the thicket.

In that second, his words finally hit her. "*God, woman, I love you more than life itself...*"

Hope rocked back on her heels. Stunned.

Antonio glanced at the cave, turned his head, winced. "A hidden escape route—that sneaky bastard."

Ethan loved her. Her vision blurred as she tried valiantly to zero in on the combatants, her heart lodged in her throat.

Vega faced Ethan, his deadly knife drawn and ready. He spread and planted his feet, holding his arms poised to face a charge. Hope couldn't believe her eyes when Ethan drew his own knife rather than just shooting Vega outright. Her eyes widened in horror as the two men circled in an ever-tightening vortex, a grisly dance of death. She wanted to scream.

"You'll distract him," Antonio warned, as if reading her mind. He drew his own gun closer, readying it with less than steady hands. Oh God, did he have such little confidence in Ethan's chances for survival?

Hope chewed her lip, clutching Ethan's gun close, wondering if she shot in that direction, which of them she'd hit. Somewhere in the back of her thoughts, it occurred to her it would serve Ethan right if she winged him by accident. He deserved it for pulling such a stupid stunt and scaring her half out of her mind. Nonetheless, she remained motionless...and silent, watching in horrified fascination as Ethan dodged and lunged, Vega swiped and retreated, and moonlight glinted portentously off lethal steel.

****

Ethan jabbed and feinted, slicing at the bastard who'd made his life a living hell...well, one of them at least. He wouldn't let himself think about the other one right now. He couldn't afford to lose his concentration. Sweat broke out on Vega's brow and upper lip. Blood flowered here and there upon his filthy shirt.

Vega was big, but Ethan was much more agile, driven by vengeance—for Christina and for Hope. He slipped below Vega's thrusts, gliding below Vega's defenses to inflict wound after wound. Part of him took savage pleasure in inflicting as much pain as possible. Visions of Christina's brutalized and lifeless body filled his mind—and the sight of Hope tied to that post, helpless and terrified, panic in her eyes. The memory distracted him, allowing Vega to get in a lucky swipe. Searing pain ripped through Ethan's focus as Vega scored a vicious gash to his bicep.

Ethan swore at the bite of metal against his flesh, swore again when he missed with his next thrust. Then he recalled Hope was there, watching, and he couldn't stand the game any longer. He just wanted it over, wanted Hope safe once and for all.

Vega deflected Ethan's thrust and struck with lightning swiftness belying his size, drawing a long burning slash down Ethan's back. The bite of Vega's blade centered Ethan's focus where it should have been—on the fight at hand, not the woman watching. As Vega's knife came away, saturated with his blood, her sharp cry tore at him. Ethan resisted the urge to look her way. To take his eyes off this opponent was akin to suicide.

Instead, he dove beneath an outstretched arm and plunged his knife hard into Vega's side, high up under the armpit. Steel skidded against bone, grating as it withdrew. Vega panted, gasping aloud as he staggered to the side, clutching at his chest.

The bandit gripped his knife, slick with blood, in a white-knuckled grip, while his strength flowed from his body through the dozens of cuts and slashes. That last thrust had hit something vital and Ethan knew it. Vega bellowed his rage and charged Ethan, swinging madly. At the last moment, Ethan dodged to the side and brought the knife up into Vega's stomach. With Vega's momentum propelling him forward, Ethan's knife not only penetrated Vega's soft belly, but sliced its way across its width as well.

Vega cried out in shock, stumbling to his knees, grasping his spilling innards in his desperate hands before collapsing in a heap in the middle of an ever-widening pool of glistening, crimson. Ethan stood over him, staring down at his fallen foe, waiting for the relief, waited for the elation of victory to sweep down upon him.

It didn't come.

Confused, Ethan turned to Hope. He dropped the knife, drawing a deep, deep breath as he wiped the blood from his hands onto his pants. Hope staggered to her feet and stumbled to Ethan's side, tears coursing down her cheeks.

She catapulted into his arms, sobbing and babbling inaudibly. Ethan wrapped her in a fierce embrace, sweeping her up and burying his face in the side of her neck. Hope was in his arms, and she was safe. Only then did the relief and the elation—the overwhelming feeling of freedom—come over him. He swirled her round and round. When at last he set her down upon her own feet, his hands lifted to cup her cheeks. He searched her eyes with a determination and an intensity that he couldn't express any other way.

Hope opened her mouth to speak, but he headed her off with a swift kiss. "Remember when I told you that you have enough room in your heart for both Jacob and for Matt?"

Hope nodded. Her brow wrinkled, and she bit the side of her lower lip.

"I loved Christina. I loved her...but she's my past. *You* are my future, Hope. I need you, sweetheart. To be whole again, I need you. I don't want to go back to half a life. I want it all, and I want it with you." He pushed a curl behind her ear and dropped his forehead to hers. "I can't fight what I feel for you anymore, I won't. I don't want to. I'm tired of chasin' my tail, woman. You're the most stubborn, passionate, infuriating female I've ever met. I love you, Hope Lewis—and you are *mine*."

Hope stared up at him. Tears spilled down her cheeks. She wasn't speaking. Why wasn't she speaking? A thousand emotions raged through him. Was he too late in confessing his feelings? Had he ruined his chance to win her heart? Could he ever repair the damage he'd done to her trust? Dear God, he couldn't live without her. What if she couldn't forgive him? What if she...

No. No, he refused to give in to the fear. He would win her back. He *would*. Whatever it took, he would make her love him...somehow.

"I love you too, Ethan...I love you so much." Her response nearly brought him to his knees. Relief, hope, joy overwhelmed him. She loved him. After all that had happened, she loved him.

Ethan's heart did summersaults inside his chest. The radiance of her smile stole his breath. But he wasn't content, not just yet. Not by a long shot.

"Marry me," Ethan demanded. "Fight with me. Love me. Make babies with me, and never leave me." Then, remembering her vow to make her own choices, he amended, "Please?"

He expected her to lunge at him, to kiss him, and babble again. At the very least, he expected a teary smile. Instead, a serious and thoughtful expression shadowed her face. She waited one uncomfortable heartbeat, then two, before she responded at last.

"On one condition..."

Ethan blinked. A cold knot formed in the pit of his stomach. He'd pushed her too far, demanded too much too quickly. Worry made speech difficult. "What?" He'd gladly promise the moon and stars, anything at all, if she'd swear never to leave him.

She smiled up at him through the shimmer of tears. "I will marry you...only if you promise I won't wake up alone—*ever again*."

Relief soared inside him. He whooped one loud burst of laughter, tightening his hold on her once more. His lips swooped down to claim hers with such force he bowed her back over the band of his arms. He didn't stop until she melted against him, until her heart pounded in time with his, and his body throbbed with want of her. Only then did he let her surface, let her recall they weren't alone.

Antonio pushed a little higher against the boulder where she'd left him. Deathly pale, he shook his head at Ethan and smiled wryly. "You suppose, if it's not too much trouble, you could dump me off on Natalia's doorstep before you go ridin' off into the sunset?"

Epilogue

Hope lay curled against Ethan's side, warm and sinuous, her head cradled against his shoulder, her fingers tangled with his over his pounding heart. A dreamy smile softened her features. Masculine contentment slid languidly through his veins. All around the room, a wild tangle of clothing littered the floor, hung from the backs of chairs, and spilled off dressers. Stockings and garters. Boots and trousers. Ethan's suit and Hope's wedding gown.

"Thank you, again," Hope murmured.

His fingers traced lazy circles around her knuckles. "You're very welcome," he rumbled, then thought to add, "For what, by the way?"

"For Thea, of course," Hope giggled, referring to the beautiful chestnut mare Ethan had given her as a wedding gift.

"Are you happy with her?" He pulled her tighter against him, reveling in the sensation of his thoroughly satiated wife snuggled up in his arms. The long slice from Vega's blade down his back—too shallow for stitches—smarted with the motion, but it was a twinge of satisfaction. He'd closed that chapter in his life. He had eyes only for the future now.

And his future snuggled in the circle of his arms, rubbing her cold foot against his calf.

Her smile, as she tilted her face up to him, was moonbeam bright. "She's absolutely perfect."

"Hmm." He dropped a kiss to the tip of her nose. "You seemed a little distracted earlier. You're not regretting gettin' married already, are you?"

Hope twisted around to look down into his eyes, her gaze direct and penetrating, fierce with unmistakable conviction. "Never. I love you, Ethan."

Her words comforted him, and, as it did every time she told him she loved him, his heart melted, just a little. Still, he couldn't help but wonder about the moment just before the ceremony when she'd frowned. "Then why did you look so upset before the wedding? It wasn't Matt was it? I know it meant a lot to him that you asked him to walk you down the aisle."

She shook her head. "No. We've grown close these last few weeks while Natalia planned the wedding, and I'm happy about that. But..." Skating the tip of her finger over his chest, she lowered her eyes. "I'm just not ready to call him father, not yet. I know he doesn't expect me to, but I also know it would mean the world to him if I did. I just don't know if I'll ever be able to—"

"It's all right," Ethan reassured her, sliding his hand up and down her arm. "Matt understands. He doesn't want anything more from you than you're willing to give. He loves you, sweetheart. You have to do what you feel is best. If it wasn't Matt, then what was it?"

"You'll think me silly, but I was thinking about my friend, Emma, just then. I'd always imagined she'd be there, standing up with me when I got married. I miss her."

Ethan reached up to brush a stray curl behind her ear. "I could send for her, if you like. She could come to stay with us for a while if it would make you happy."

Hope's eyes lit up. He felt the warmth of that smile, all the way to his heart.

Abruptly, her look turned calculating. "You could send Antonio to collect her."

Ethan grinned as understanding dawned. "I

would do anything for you, my love. Don't you know that by now?"

Hope leaned down and nibbled kisses across his cheek, then his chin, then his lips. His stomach rumbled, and she leaned back.

"You're hungry," she accused. "You should have eaten at the reception. You didn't touch your plate. Matt was put out that there was so much food left over."

"That's *his* wife's fault. I swear that woman cooks enough for two armies every time something like this comes up." Ethan's voice dropped a silky octave. "Besides, at the time, my—appetite—was leanin' elsewhere."

His eyes bore into hers. His hands grew bold in their caresses. Hope's grin was mischievous as she reached across his chest to pluck a shiny red apple from a basket on the nightstand. Ethan drew a sharp breath as her breasts slid across his bare chest.

She held the fruit up to him, a sinful twinkle in her eye. "Might I tempt this appetite of yours, husband?"

His hungry stare devoured her as she leaned above him in all her naked splendor. Warmth swelled inside him—primitive possessiveness, wrenching desire, and a love that healed his soul. His lips curled in a shameless grin as he took the apple from her hand, wrapped an arm around her, and flipped her over, pinning her beneath him.

"My dearest wife, you tempt me beyond compare," he growled. "You truly do."

Tossing the apple over his shoulder, he claimed her lips in a kiss that stole her breath and demanded nothing less than complete surrender.

A word about the author...

Always a voracious reader, Brenda Huber closed the cover on a book by one of her favorite authors and said to herself...*I can do this!* Brenda enjoys writing both Historical and Paranormal Romance. She lives in Iowa with her husband and two children.

www.ingramcontent.com/pod-product-compliance
Lightning Source LLC
Chambersburg PA
CBHW070158260626
47160CB00002B/383
9781601547859